THE FLAMES OF DRAGONS

Book Three of the Dragoon Saga

Josh VanBrakle

 Arboreal Press

Arboreal Press
Sidney, NY 13838
www.arborealpress.com

Library of Congress Preassigned Control Number: 2016905642
ISBN-13: 978-0-9891957-4-4
First Edition: 2016
Dragon image copyright Kuma/Fotolia.com

Find out more about the author and upcoming books by following Josh VanBrakle on Twitter @joshvanbrakle or by visiting www.joshvanbrakle.com.

ACKNOWLEDGMENTS

Well, folks, this is it. When I started thinking about these characters in high school, I had no idea that twelve years later I would have a trilogy published following their adventures. There are so many people who helped me along the way, and I want to do what I can to thank them.

First, I want to thank Emily Reinert, the Creative Writing teacher at Hershey High School. Her class led me to create Iren Saitosan, Rondel, and the continent of Raa. I also want to thank the remarkable people at Indian Echo Caverns who taught me to open up and tell stories. They even inspired one of the locations in the *Dragoon Saga*.

Next on my list is someone I can't thank enough, but I am determined to keep trying. Shannon Delany, author of the YA series *13 to Life* and *Weather Witch*, you have my eternal gratitude. It was your workshops that inspired me after a decade away from writing to come back and become a professional author.

I want to thank all those who reviewed drafts of this book: Jenny Lay, Tom Foulkrod, and my wife and copy-editor Christine. Your willingness to dig into my drafts and make them better is much appreciated.

As with the other books in the *Dragoon Saga*, I offer major kudos to Heather Hilson. Once again you have shown your skills with a fantastic cover design.

Finally, this book is dedicated to my father. He was the first and best storyteller I ever met, and it's my greatest regret that he never had the chance to read my books while he was alive. Dad, I'm sending a copy of this series to Heaven for you. I'm sure they have an awesome library.

TABLE OF CONTENTS

CHAPTER ONE
Shogun

Hana Akiyama wiped her hands on her pink kimono, the one decorated with white cherry blossoms. It was her favorite. It found her body's curves better than any of the other flowing garments. Whenever she faced a nervous situation, she preferred this kimono.

There was no reason to be nervous. Hana repeated that to herself. She had succeeded this time. Her hand drifted to her right hip where the ten-foot katana sat. Despite its length, the blade's curvature and the way it hung in her kimono's sash kept it from scraping the floor.

It still looked ridiculous though. The weapon clearly hadn't been designed for her—or anyone else of normal stature. Lord Melwar had forged this weapon for a twelve-foot-tall Oni.

An Oni who was dead.

Hana glanced up and down the corridor. No servants were in the hallway with her. Lord Melwar had ordered them away from this part of the castle. If any of them so much as brushed against the sword by accident, the whole building could go up in flames.

Hana couldn't turn around with the giant weapon, so she couldn't pace. It wouldn't have helped anyway. Even the masterwork paintings of animals on the walls, so lifelike they might leap out at any moment, could do nothing to lift her mood.

After fifteen minutes a single word issued from the other side of the sliding rice paper door in front of her: "Enter."

Hana shivered at the calm, even voice. It relieved and terrified her at the same time. She opened the door and walked inside.

Two steps into the room, Hana dropped to the straw mats covering the floor. She prostrated herself. The posture was awkward enough on its own, but it was nearly impossible with the Karyozaki on her hip.

She made it work. Tonight was her best chance to regain Lord Melwar's good graces after the debacle with Iren Saitosan. She wouldn't risk that chance over something as minor as bowing courtesy.

As the minutes passed, though, Hana found her brow knitting against her will. Lord Melwar had sent her on this mission. He wanted the Karyozaki, the Fire Dragon Sword, so badly. Why was he dallying?

It was to prove he was in charge. There could be no other reason. He would show her that even with her Stone Dragon Knight abilities, she was nothing to him. Nothing at all.

Just as Hana's back started to cramp from her splayed position, Lord Melwar said, "Rise."

Hana climbed to her feet. She stepped forward and placed the Karyozaki on the mats between her and Lord Melwar. She then retreated, standing as close to the door as she could without seeming rude.

Lord Melwar watched her with those brown eyes that missed nothing. He sat on a wooden throne adorned with carvings of serpentine dragons. There was no other furniture. Candles on sconces gave the space an ethereal glow. The shadows they cast over Lord Melwar's face seemed deeper than those in other parts of the room.

"It took you three days longer than expected," Lord Melwar said.

Hana gulped. She had hoped to hear the Maantec lord praise her success. Instead, the coldness of his tone cut through her.

"I apologize, Lord Melwar," she said, her voice barely controlled. "The Yokai aren't reliable guides. But once they got me to the Kodamas' village, I had an easy time of it. Most of the scum knew the Forest Dragon Knight had hidden the Karyozaki, but they didn't know where. Fortunately, their blacksmith helped her. Unfortunately, he was reluctant to tell me where they put it."

She paused and forced herself to smile. It was what Lord Melwar would want to see. "I persuaded him."

Lord Melwar mirrored her expression. "How many tried to stop you from taking it?"

That one smile from Lord Melwar was all Hana needed to relax. She shrugged. "I lost count after thirty-seven."

The Maantec lord stepped off his throne and walked to the massive katana. "Both the Karyozaki and Toryokiri are back where they belong," he said, "with the Maantecs. Soon the rest will join them."

Hana ticked off the list of Ryokaiten—the eight Dragon Weapons—in her head. Iren Saitosan had the Holy Dragon Sword, Rondel Thara the Storm Dragon Dagger, and that Kodaman bitch the Forest Dragon Bow. Hana herself had the Stone Dragon Hammer, and she had already recovered the Fire and Ice Dragons' weapons for Lord Melwar. That left just two unaccounted for: those belonging to Ariok, the Sky Dragon, and Mizuchi, the Water Dragon.

Though if she were honest, there was really only one. Hana knew who had the Auryozaki, the Sky Dragon Sword, but she hadn't been able to tell Lord Melwar.

It was critical information. If he knew she was keeping it from him, he would punish her.

But she couldn't tell him. She knew what his order would be. He would send her to kill the Sky Dragon Knight.

He would send her to kill Balear.

Hana had to keep that from happening. "Lord Melwar," she ventured, "if you're deciding how best I may serve you, please let me hunt down the Forest Dragon Knight and retrieve her bow. I won't lose to her again."

Lord Melwar stroked his chin a moment, as though considering. But his lack of immediate response made it clear what his answer would be.

"No," he said. "That one will have to wait, as will Rondel's and Iren's weapons. Right now those three are busy with each other. I do not want that to change. Were they to unite against me, my plan could still unravel."

So that was it. Hana knew her part in Lord Melwar's latest plan: hunt down the Ryokaiten and return them to her master. If Lord Melwar had elected to ignore Iren, Rondel, and Minawë, that meant only Balear and the Water Dragon Knight remained. What would she do if she had to go after Balear?

She would kill him. There was no other choice. If she didn't, she would die.

Lord Melwar thought another moment. "The next Ryokaiten you must find belongs to the Water Dragon, Mizuchi."

Hana couldn't help it. She loosed a sigh of relief.

The right side of Lord Melwar's mouth crinkled upward. "My order pleases you?" he asked. His tone mocked her.

Hana panicked. If she said the wrong thing, he could easily catch on. Her head spun, but she forced herself to maintain an air of composure. She tossed back her long black hair. "I could slay the Forest Dragon Knight easily. By sending me after the Water Dragon Knight, you've given me a real challenge. I appreciate the opportunity."

The Maantec lord shrugged. "Well, I am glad it worked out."

Hana didn't believe him. Lord Melwar couldn't care less about her feelings.

"Based on my information," Lord Melwar continued, "the Water Dragon Knight lives in the Tacumsah Archipelago, so you will not be able to travel underground to reach him. You will have to take a ship, but a vessel from here bears too much risk of a storm at sea. Go underground north to Kataile in Lodia and depart from there."

"The Tacumsah Archipelago has hundreds of islands," Hana pointed out. "How will I find the Water Dragon's Ryokaiten? What does it look like?"

Lord Melwar laughed. The sound made Hana shudder. "What does it look like?" he repeated. "The Zuryokaiten can look like anything. It could also be anywhere; I was not able to get any more precise information than that it was in the archipelago. That is why it is the next one I am sending you after. We have some time now, so it is the perfect opportunity for a search. Besides, I need it for the next stage of my plan."

Hana furrowed her brow. "And what stage is that?"

The Maantec lord knelt and picked up the Karyozaki. Hana tensed. Lord Melwar wasn't a Dragon Knight. Feng would test him now. Lord Melwar would either become the Fire Dragon Knight or die.

Hana knew which outcome she wanted.

But the sword didn't test him. He just stood there holding it. It was impossible.

The shadows in the room seemed to deepen. "The next stage," Lord Melwar said, "is the same as it would have been had Iren Saitosan become the emperor. We restore the Maantecs."

Hana was already off balance from the Karyozaki not testing Lord Melwar. Now she was utterly thrown. "How?" she asked. "Can we really do that without an emperor?"

It was a rude question. It implied that she doubted Lord Melwar's abilities. Hana winced, preparing for the rebuke.

None came. Lord Melwar was in a good mood after all. "Until recently I believed we could not," he admitted. "Now my mind has changed. You see, there is no longer a rightful emperor. Iren Saito is dead, and his son has rejected the throne. The line of emperors has ended. As such, the highest noble of our people must rise and lead them. We will not have an emperor. We will have a shogun."

The man half-smiled. "We will have me."

CHAPTER TWO
Katsu

Goro poked his head out the door of his two-room farmhouse. He scanned the garden and terraced rice paddies. "Katsu!" he called. "Hey, Katsu!"

He waited a minute, but no one came. Goro rolled his eyes. Typical.

"Where is that man?" Goro grumbled. He slipped on a pair of sandals and stepped outside. "Katsu! Dinner!"

Maybe the stranger had packed up and left. It wouldn't surprise Goro. Katsu had shown up three weeks ago out of nowhere with torn clothes and a thin body. Despite Goro's misgivings, Chiyo had taken pity on the man and offered him a meal and even one of Goro's old homespun kimonos. Since then Katsu had become an unofficial farm-hand, doing chores in exchange for food.

Goro wandered the farm calling Katsu's name. The place wasn't that big; Katsu should have no trouble picking up Goro's rolling bass.

The farmer was about to give up when he heard a low *chunk*. It came from the other side of the tool shed. Goro walked the hundred feet to the building, and there he found Katsu.

The mysterious new helper was standing in front of a chopping block with a two-foot log on top of it. He raised a short-hafted axe in his left hand, and then with a smooth motion, he brought the tool down on the log.

Chunk. The wood split down the middle and fell to either side of the block. Without pause, Katsu picked up another log and repeated the motion.

Chunk.

Goro had to admit he was impressed. He'd tasked Katsu with splitting firewood just this morning, and already the piles on either side of the farmhand towered taller than Goro was. It usually took Goro weeks to split this much.

"Katsu," Goro said between cuts, "that's enough for today. Let's have some dinner."

Katsu appeared not to hear him. The man's eyes were distant. He didn't even seem to notice the logs he grabbed.

That concerned Goro. All the productivity on Raa would be meaningless if the man overswung and cut off his leg by not paying attention.

Chunk.

Goro had to put a stop to this. He grabbed Katsu by the shoulder. "Hey, Katsu!"

It was like he'd snapped the man out of a deep sleep. Katsu shivered, and he blinked several times. He set down his axe and looked up at Goro. For a moment he didn't seem to recognize the farmer. Then he shook his head. "Oh, Goro, sorry about that," he said. "I got in a rhythm and lost track of time."

Katsu's voice was soft. Goro liked that. A good person was quiet and humble, not like the prudes down in Hiabi so stuck up in their class system. "Come on," Goro said. "Chiyo's made dinner. We'll both hear about it if it gets cold."

Katsu wiped off his kimono. "All right, just let me take the axe back to the shed."

They returned the tool together and then headed to the house. When they entered, Chiyo smiled at both of them. Like any Maantec she still looked young, but she had the plump hips, sturdy build, and gentle expression of a wizened farm woman.

She would make a good mother, Goro knew, if only they could afford to have kids. Scrabbling in Shikari's rocks wasn't a great way to make a living.

Goro and Katsu sat on the floor beside each other. Chiyo brought each of them a six-inch-high wooden tray with a pair of chopsticks, a cup of sake, and a wooden bowl filled with rice, edamame, and daikon radishes tossed with soy sauce. She then retrieved her own tray and joined them.

While the trio ate, Goro said, "I'm amazed you cut all that wood in one day, Katsu. Did you just forget about lunch and breaks or what?"

The farmhand shrugged. "I didn't have anything better to do. Besides, I want to help out."

Goro shook his head and whistled. "Even at the end of the day you were splitting those logs one-handed on the first cut. I could never do that. Aren't you tired?"

"Not really. I guess I'm used to it." Katsu popped a slice of radish into his mouth.

"With that much wood, we'll have no trouble keeping the house warm all winter," Goro said.

"It won't season like that though," Katsu replied. "Tomorrow I'll stack and cover it so it dries well."

"You don't need to push yourself so hard, dear," Chiyo said. "We're very happy with you."

Katsu swallowed a large bite of rice. "No, I prefer it this way. You helped me when I had nowhere to go. It's the only honorable thing to do."

The farmhand set down his bowl. It was empty. Goro's eyebrows rose a fraction. He'd barely eaten a quarter of his.

"I should rest," Katsu said. "Tomorrow will be a long day. Thank you for the meal." He bowed so his head touched the floor, then stood and walked to the door.

"Wait!" Chiyo said. "You don't have to run off every evening. You're among friends. Stay a while and share some stories."

"I'm sorry," Katsu said. The man's eyes drifted to his right as he added, "I don't have any stories to share. I'd be a boring guest. I'll see you tomorrow."

Then he was gone.

Chiyo sighed. "He's a hard worker, but I wish he'd open up a little. He seems sad."

Goro wasn't so sure. "I hope we didn't make a mistake taking him in."

"How can you say that?" Chiyo put her hands on her hips. Goro tensed; he was in for it now.

"That man has done more on this farm in three weeks than you and I normally handle in three months," Chiyo said. "He's peaceful, humble, and hardworking, and Juusa blessed us the day he came here."

"But why did he come here?" Goro insisted. "He says he's a wanderer. Well, why is he wandering? People don't do that for no reason. He's hiding something. Maybe he's planning to rob us."

"Goro, if he wanted to rob us, he would have done it by now. We don't have anything worth three weeks of farm labor to steal."

"Maybe he's here to hide. Maybe he's on the run from some noble in Hiabi. It wouldn't be the first time a criminal tried to disappear in these mountains."

Chiyo glared at her husband. "You always think the worst, don't you? Look, that man's doing great things for this farm. With his help, the gardens and rice paddies are planted ahead of schedule. The wood's cut. He even fixed up the shed. If he sticks around, we'll have our best harvest in two hundred years. We might even be able to sell some of it. Wouldn't that be nice? We might finally have enough money to add a nursery."

There it was. Goro sighed. He couldn't argue with Chiyo about that. "All right," he said, "I'm sorry. He can stay. I'll ask no more questions."

All that night, though, Goro wondered about the farmhand. Maybe the man was a blessing, but there was still something off about him. Goro would keep his promise to Chiyo, but he'd find his answers somehow. This farm was all he had. He wouldn't let anyone threaten it.

প্র

The man who called himself Katsu left the farmhouse at a brisk walk. He was already late, and he knew his partner would be waiting for him.

Tracing one of the few dry paths through the terraced rice paddies, Katsu climbed into the hills above the farm. The fresh growth of early summer was evident even as twilight fell over the land.

It made Katsu think of Lodia, his birthplace far to the north. It was on the other side of the continent, and the seasons were reversed there. It would be winter there now, the snow cold yet soft on the land. Katsu wondered whether he'd ever see it again. He had his doubts.

The paddies gave way to a scraggly pine forest, but still Katsu hiked.

Half an hour after leaving Goro and Chiyo's farmhouse, he reached his destination: a small cavern concealed from view by a boulder as tall as he was. Channeling magic into his limbs, he pushed the rock aside without effort and entered the cave.

Once inside, Katsu groped in the darkness a moment before he found the object of his search. A white katana lay on the ground, hidden behind a stone. Katsu picked it up and slid its sheath through his belt, a feeling of completeness settling on him. He felt naked without this sword.

Katsu knelt on the cold rock of the cavern floor. He closed his eyes, even though it made no difference to his vision. The sun had set by now, and the blackness of the cave was absolute. All the same, it helped him focus.

He drew his katana and held it in his lap. From deeper in the cave came the sound of dripping water. It had a steady pace, and Katsu found his breathing keeping time with it. He was ready to meet his partner. With a final exhalation, he opened his eyes.

The cave around him had vanished. He stood on a seashore. A full moon hung in the east and cast its glow across the water. The waves lapped against the beach at the same speed that the cavern drips had fallen.

Katsu took a deep breath of the salty air and shivered. He loved this scent, and he missed it in the mountains. If only this place were real.

A few feet in front of him sat his partner, Divinion. The massive white serpentine dragon was coiled around himself, his scales glowing with inner light. Blue hairs ran down the length of his spine, and even in rest his wings seemed to stretch to the heavens. His legs were tucked up beneath him, but Katsu knew that they each carried talons that made his katana dull by comparison.

The dragon did not turn around. He must have noticed Katsu's arrival though, because he growled, "You're late."

"I'm still not used to them calling me 'Katsu.' Goro had to come looking for me."

The dragon uncurled and stretched his body. His square head rose thirty feet in the air, one blue whisker undulating off either side of his muzzle. The sky blue of his eyes pierced Katsu's heart and froze him in place. "When you must conceal who you are from those who care about you, it's time to rethink your position in life," the dragon said. "Wouldn't you agree, Iren Saitosan?"

Iren shivered at his real name. He'd gone by "Katsu" ever since he'd arrived on Goro's farm. He couldn't tell them his actual name, not given who it connected him to.

"Telling them who and what I am would put them in danger," Iren said. "I'm looking out for their safety."

"Your mere presence jeopardizes their safety, whether they know the truth or not. Melwar and Hana might still be hunting you. You can't harm the farmers by revealing your identity. But then, perhaps you have another reason?"

Iren threw himself back on the beach, face up. He grabbed a handful of sand and let it slip through his fingers. It was amazing how real it felt considering this seaside only existed in his mind. It was a construct that allowed him to meet with the Holy Dragon, who was otherwise imprisoned inside the katana Iren held.

Divinion stood over him. The dragon's eyes were unrelenting.

Iren sighed. There was no point in hiding something from Divinion. The dragon knew everything about Iren; he just wanted to see if Iren would have the courage to admit the truth. "I want them to think of me as a farmer," he said. "That's all. It's been on my mind ever since I arrived here. If Mother and Father had lived, I think I could have been happy on their farm with them, never knowing about magic or dragons. No offense, but I never wanted to be the Holy Dragon Knight. I never wanted to get swept into a thousand-year-old vendetta." He loosed a long breath and murmured, "I never wanted to hate someone."

"So don't," Divinion said. "There's no reason for you to. Don't let the past destroy you. Let it become the load that makes you stronger."

"I wish it were that easy, but I can't let it go. The past has made me who I am." He stood. "Rondel killed my parents, and I will avenge them. Now train me."

Divinion's lips curled back, revealing rows of teeth longer than Iren was tall. "If that's what you want." He stepped back and changed shape. He shrank, and his scales melted into wrinkled skin and brown linen clothes. At his waist a belt appeared, and on that belt hung a dagger.

The most important change, though, was to his eyes. They shifted from blue to green, and within them sparks danced.

Iren raised his left hand, and his katana, the Muryozaki, appeared in it. He faced the apparition of Rondel that Divinion had become. "Let's begin."

They started slowly, dancing to a melody only they could hear as each sought to find the other's weaknesses. Iren knew Divinion could sense his every move, but that was the point. It meant that, at least when fighting Iren, the Holy Dragon had the same instantaneous reflexes as the old Maantec. It made Divinion the perfect sparring partner.

After two minutes, Divinion accelerated. Iren's body could match the dragon's pace, but his eyes couldn't. The apparition of Rondel became a blur, and its dagger struck home. It stabbed Iren in the gut and forced itself up into his lungs.

Had the fight been real, Iren would have died. Just like he would have died every night since he and Divinion had started this routine three weeks ago. He was no closer to figuring out a way to kill Rondel than he'd been the night he'd left her and Minawë behind.

As the battle was only in his head, all Iren felt was a punch to his stomach to let him know the dagger had hit him. He and Divinion separated, and the dragon resumed his former shape.

The pair said nothing for a long time. They stared together over the churning waves of Iren's mind.

It was Iren who broke the silence. "I can't defeat her, can I?"

Divinion shook his head. "Not as you are now."

"What should I do?"

"Reconcile with her. She is not your enemy."

Iren scowled. "She murdered my parents. I can't forgive that."

"Then Melwar has already won."

"Melwar?" Iren asked. "What does he have to do with this?"

"Are you that blind?" The dragon rounded on him. "Do you think his ambitions are over just because you decided not to be his puppet emperor? He will move forward with or without you. Together you and Rondel could stop him. Instead, you're wasting your time trying to kill each other."

"In that case, what about you?" Iren demanded. "If you feel so strongly that I shouldn't fight Rondel, why help me train to defeat her?"

The anger in Divinion's face fell away, and a deep sadness replaced it. "Because I don't want you to die," he said. "You are the only hope for this world. If Rondel kills you, there won't be another like you. Melwar will conquer Raa."

Iren dropped his eyes. "You don't have to say it like that. There would be other Holy Dragon Knights."

"Not like you. You are Iren Saito's son and the last of his clan. You became the Dragoon. You have magic beyond what most Maantecs can imagine. Even if by some miracle I found another like you, I could never train that person to match Melwar in time to stop him. So yes, I disagree with your pursuit of revenge. I think it's foolish and short-sighted and puts the world at risk. But if my aid means you'll survive and ultimately refocus on Melwar, then I will bury my misgivings and help you. The sooner you put your revenge to rest, the better for Raa."

The dragon snarled deep in his throat. "We're wasting time. Our training method isn't working. I will give some thought to what we should do next. Until tomorrow."

He flicked his wings to their widest shape. With a single flap he was airborne.

Floating in midair, Divinion fixed his piercing gaze on Iren one last time. Iren met the dragon's eyes a moment, but then he could look upon the god no longer.

Divinion flapped his wings again and flew high into the sky. As he vanished into the night, he called out the words he told Iren at the end of all their sessions. They echoed out of the past:

"Commit to what's most important."

Iren knew what Divinion wanted him to answer, but the Holy Dragon didn't understand. He didn't know what it was like to have those he trusted most betray him. He couldn't comprehend how it felt to know that his teacher had killed his mother and father, that his allies had manipulated him, and that his best friend had chosen his parents' murderer over him.

The seaside vanished, and Iren was back in the cave. The Muryozaki still rested in his lap. Iren sheathed it, then felt along the cavern floor until he found the straw padding he used for a bed.

"What's most important?" he asked the cave, the same question he asked it every night.

Just like every other night, as he fell asleep, Iren told himself he knew the answer.

Revenge.

CHAPTER THREE
Twilight Meeting

They should have come back by now.

Prince Narunë stared out from the southern border of Aokigahara Rainforest. He wiped the sweat from his face, not that the action did any lasting good. More just dripped in his eyes.

But he needed them clear. He couldn't afford to miss even the smallest sign.

A month had passed since Minawë and Rondel had left the forest and entered enemy territory. Shikari wasn't that big. With the speeds those two could travel, they should have needed only a couple days to cross it and reach Hiabi. At most, they should have been gone a week.

They should have come back by now.

Narunë studied Shikari's cracked, karst topography, his position putting him inches away from death. The tip of his nose almost broke the final band of leaves between the rainforest and the bleak land beyond. If he took even a single step forward, he would leave the forest. In that moment, the curse Iren Saito had cast on Narunë's people would claim his life.

He had no choice. He had to be this close in order to see anything. Aokigahara had dense plants at every level. In most places visibility was only a few feet.

At least Shikari wasn't like that. As long as Narunë could see past the rainforest's boundary, he could observe miles of territory. Shikari was desolate, a sharp land of craggy peaks, deep crevasses, and scrubby plants. A trio of people approaching would be visible for miles.

That made it all the more frustrating that no such trio had yet appeared.

They should have come back by now.

Narunë had long pictured their reunion in his mind. They would run up to him, and his niece would hug him the way she had when they'd parted.

There were other Kodamas along the border watching for Minawë and her friends, but Narunë hoped he saw them first. He wanted to meet this Maantec boy Minawë had traveled across a continent to find.

Today would be the day they returned. He was sure of it. Nothing had happened to them. Rondel Thara was the most powerful Maantec in a thousand years, and Minawë was stronger still. She didn't know it, but she'd already surpassed her father Otunë.

As the day wore on though, Minawë and Rondel didn't appear. When Shikari darkened with sunset, Narunë gave up his vigil for the day. He stalked deeper into the rainforest and rejoined his companions to set up camp.

The group looked as wild as the forest. Their green hair matched the jungle's leaves, and their leather clothes matched its bark. Tattoos of rainforest animals adorned every exposed inch of skin. None wore swords, but each carried a bow on his back and a machete at his hip.

They were Narunë's finest scouts. He'd hand-picked them to accompany Minawë and Rondel to Shikari, and they'd all sworn they wouldn't leave until the journeying pair returned.

For the first week they'd been excited. They'd told fanciful stories and placed bets as to what might be happening in Shikari.

That enthusiasm had vanished in recent days. Now, as Narunë and his squad passed around supper bowls, there was no conversation. The Kodamas ate in brooding silence. Narunë could guess what they were thinking. Oath or no oath, how much longer were they going to stay out here, waiting for people who might be dead?

Narunë was halfway through his stew when a rustling behind him made him pause. He tensed, immediately on alert. Things in the jungle didn't make noise without reason, not if they enjoyed living. The air was still and heavy. Not a trace of wind passed through the forest floor that could have made the sound.

The Kodaman prince glanced around at his companions. They were all as focused as he was. Narunë stood and faced the sound, but he could see nothing. Between the dense brush, the darkness of evening, and the campfire that had ruined his night vision, he was blind.

Fortunately, there was more than one way to see in the forest, at least for Narunë. He placed his palm against a nearby tree and connected his magic to it, feeling the forest around him through its roots.

He only needed to touch the tree's smooth bark a few seconds before he figured out what had made the sound. He laughed aloud, a bellowing cry that made him wink his right eye when he did it.

"Minawë!" he shouted. "Rondel! You're back! We're over here!"

A rustling of leaves followed, and then a high-pitched female voice whined, "Make me sit in a cave for a month, then drag me back to the forest after dark. Honestly, children these days have no respect for their parents at all. I'm going to trip over a root and break my neck."

Narunë laughed again. That voice could only belong to Rondel. Better still, her complaining meant she was in a good mood.

But as Rondel emerged into the circle of firelight, Narunë's laughter died. The silver-haired Maantec glared at the Kodaman prince with cold eyes that sparked with Lightning Sight.

Behind Rondel came Minawë. When Narunë saw his niece's face, any lingering joy he might have felt at their reunion fled. Her emerald eyes bore just as frosty an expression as Rondel's. Even though a month had passed since she'd seen her uncle, she didn't say a word to him. She kept her gaze fixed on Rondel.

Rondel walked up to Narunë. With her diminutive frame, the crone had to bend her neck back to look him in the face. "It's been a long time," she said. Her voice was friendly, but the blue sparks leaping across her irises told Narunë the tone was false. "I'm sure a lot's happened to you since we left. Walk with me, and let's swap stories. Minawë, we'll be right back. Why don't you stay here and warm yourself? It looks like they're just sitting down to eat. You must be starving. I'm sure they'll share with you."

Narunë caught the hint. "That's a good idea, Minawë. We'll catch up when Rondel and I return. Boys, make sure my niece is well fed. She is your queen after all. Give her your utmost care and attention." He stressed the last word.

Minawë cocked an eyebrow, but she shrugged and sat down in the fire ring. She refilled Narunë's own bowl and ate like it was the first food she'd seen in days.

Rondel gestured to her left. Narunë let her guide him away from camp.

They'd walked in silence about ten minutes before Rondel said, "This should be far enough."

"Did she follow us?"

Rondel's Lightning Sight flashed. "I don't see anyone else, and all the animals within earshot are native."

Narunë nodded. "So what happened? A month is far too long to spend in Shikari."

"It was necessary," Rondel said. "The mission went as expected."

Narunë pressed his thumb and index finger into the bridge of his nose. "I'd dared to hope that it wouldn't," he admitted. "Minawë believed so much in that young man. I wanted to think he would come back with you."

"Melwar has twisted Iren beyond recognition. He's become a demon obsessed with revenge."

"Did you kill him?"

Rondel's wrinkled fists clenched. "I had him in my grasp, but Minawë intervened and saved his life. He escaped."

"So what will you do now?"

"Isn't it obvious? I'll carry out Okthora's Law. Evil must be annihilated. If Iren isn't slain, he'll corrupt Divinion and throw all of Raa into chaos. I'm going back to Shikari to find him. Iren Saitosan must die, just like his father."

Narunë folded his muscular arms. "How does Minawë feel about that?"

Rondel sat on a fallen log. She shook her head. "I'm sure you know. I originally recruited her to deal with the Stone Dragon Knight. That was before I knew what Melwar had planned for Iren. Had I known that, I never would have brought her along."

"She cares for him."

"Not that the boy deserves it. After Minawë went to the trouble of saving him, the fool turned his back on her. He up and left, saying he would kill her if she interfered in his revenge."

"Is that why you were so late in returning?"

Rondel nodded. "Minawë thought Iren would change his mind. She thought he was just speaking out of anger, and that he'd come to his senses. We waited for a month, but he never showed."

"Why come back at all then? Had you waited, he might have returned, and even if he didn't, you would already be in Shikari. The trail will have gone cold by now. How will you find him again?"

Rondel looked up at him. There was an expression on her face he'd never seen from her. It was pleading. "There's something I need you to do for me."

Narunë pressed his fingers into his nose again. "Why do I get the feeling whatever it is will be unpleasant?"

Rondel grinned. "Oh, it's not that bad. It's—"

She cut off. Her smile disappeared. Her eyes swiveled across the jungle.

"You did better than I expected," Rondel said. "Black cat on a black night. That was smart."

A low vibration came from the forest. Narunë tensed. He knew that sound.

Then he saw them. A pair of yellow eyes gleamed through the brush.

The jaguar stalked up to them, teeth bared. It snarled, but it didn't pounce. Instead, it reared up on its hind legs. As it did, those legs changed shape, lengthening and melting into brown leather with green embroidered leaves. The yellow eyes morphed into emerald ones, and the hair on the cat's head changed to the same color.

Minawë stood before her mother and uncle. Though she was now a Kodama instead of a cat, she looked as close to lunging as she had before the change.

"Don't think you can wander off," Minawë growled. "Either of you."

Narunë held up both hands. "Hold on, don't lump me in with a troublemaker like Rondel!"

Minawë wasn't in a joking mood. Her eyes fixed on her uncle. "You knew she wanted to escape. That's why you told your men to keep such a close eye on me."

Narunë gave his most innocent smile. "You're their queen. There are a lot of dangerous things in this jungle. I wanted them to protect you."

"Don't lie to me. This jungle won't hurt me. If you want to protect me, then don't let Rondel out of your sight."

"Why not?"

"Because I won't let her escape. Iren's beyond my reach, but Rondel isn't. If they want to kill each other, eventually they'll have to meet. I plan to be there when they do."

Narunë frowned, his mouth a thin line. So that was the game.

"Let's head back to camp," he said, "and don't worry about Rondel. I'll make sure she comes back to Sorengaral with us."

Rondel flashed him an aggravated expression. She opened her mouth, surely to spit some nasty comment, but Narunë stopped her with a look.

Minawë eyed the two elders for a moment. At last she nodded curtly. "Fine," she said. "I'll walk behind you two on the way back to make sure you don't try anything."

Narunë shrugged and motioned for Rondel to take the lead. After a few steps though, he came level with her. Without turning his head he murmured, low enough that Minawë couldn't hear, "Give me until Sorengaral. She's my niece. I can convince her to stay there. Then you can disappear without her following you."

Rondel kept her body position unchanged as she replied, "I'm counting on you. I saw how Minawë reacted when Iren turned from her. She had an opportunity to stop him, and she let it slip away. I can't risk her interfering."

"Why?" Narunë asked. "Are you afraid Iren will attack her?"

"No," Rondel whispered, "I'm afraid I will."

CHAPTER FOUR
The Female Mayor

"There it is," Dirio said from the head of the column of villagers, "Kataile."

Balear crested the small rise so he could stand beside Veliaf's mayor. It was a strange title, considering that thanks to Balear, Veliaf no longer existed.

"It's beautiful," Dirio breathed.

Balear frowned. From here he couldn't even see the city itself. Kataile was built into the side of a white limestone plateau that jutted out from the Eregos Mountains' northeast corner. The plateau curled around into a crescent-shaped barrier that surrounded the city and shielded it from view. From this angle, all Balear could see was the out-side of the cliff and the ocean east of it.

But Dirio's eyes were wide with hope, so Balear nodded. They had come so far, and they couldn't go back. They could do nothing but hope.

The only way in or out of the city was along the beach that separated the cliff from the sea. Balear and Dirio headed down the hill toward it, the villagers following behind.

Despite his lack of a view, Balear couldn't help but feel a small share of the balding fifty-year-old mayor's excitement. Here was a place, perhaps alone in Lodia, untouched by the civil war. With Kataile's natural protection, no other city's army could invade it. In addition, the city's port gave it access to the sea for food and trade with the Tacumsah Archipelago.

As Balear crossed onto the sand, though, his optimism fell. A drift-wood barricade blocked off the beach, and armed guards stood behind it. Dirio motioned for his people to stand back. He and Balear approached the guards alone.

The men behind the barricade looked confident, but Balear could tell it was an act. Either that, or they were such complete novices that they really believed this shoddy pile of wood could protect them. It was barely four feet high and wasn't even nailed together. Balear figured he could breach it with one swing of the Auryozaki strapped to his back. For that matter, he could probably crush the blockade just by setting the massive sword on top of the wood.

Not that there was a need to break it. The barricade extended to the cliff wall, but with the ocean's changing waves, it couldn't block passage on that side. As long as you didn't mind getting your feet wet, you could just walk around it.

The barricade's guards were no more formidable. There were six of them, each armed with a fishing spear. Only two had any armor, and that was boiled leather. Just one had a sword, and even with it sheathed, Balear could tell it was useless. The handle had too much decoration. It was a weapon designed for parades, not combat. Balear doubted it was even sharp.

From back on the hill, Balear had thought Kataile impregnable. But if this paltry blockade was any indication, the city might be relying on reputation alone to secure itself.

"Welcome to Kataile!" one of the guards called to the newcomers. "We wish you a pleasant and peaceful stay!"

Balear cocked an eyebrow. Those weren't the words a sentinel said to strangers during a civil war. The man's tone was even less soldierly. What kind of guards were these?

Then again, it made sense. Kataile thrived on tourism, with visitors coming from all over Lodia to swim in the ocean and enjoy the views atop the plateau. These guards knew nothing of war. All they knew was how to welcome people.

In a way Balear found it refreshing. In another it terrified him.

Dirio took the unusual greeting in stride. "Thank you," he said with a broad smile. "I'm certain we all wish for our stay to be pleasant and peaceful. My name is Dirio Cyneric, and I'm the mayor of Veliaf. I've come to treat with Lady Elyssa Orianna. Might I speak with her?"

Whatever response the guards had been expecting, that wasn't it. They huddled and conversed among themselves.

At length the man with the parade sword turned to Dirio and Balear. "We're used to guests here, but not this many. I'm sorry, but you'll have to turn back."

Dirio frowned. "We've come a long way. We've traveled through deep snow and chilling cold. Many of our women and children are starving and on the verge of frostbite. Surely the famed hospitality of Kataile is not so poor as this?"

The guard stiffened and spun back to his men. The conversation this time was more heated. Balear half-smiled. Dirio was mayor for a reason.

"We apologize for any rudeness," the guard said. "Please come with me. We must ask that the rest of our new guests wait outside until we decide how best to accommodate you."

"That will do," Dirio replied. "Of course as mayor, I'll need an honor guard." He gestured to Balear. "This is General Balear Platarch of the Castle Guard. He's here to ensure my safe passage."

When Dirio said Balear's name, the guards blanched, and Balear winced. Everyone in the country knew him. Unfortunately, they knew him as the traitor who had tipped off the Kodamas to King Angustion's invasion. In so doing, he'd allowed them time to prepare for and defeat the king. For many Lodians, Balear was the reason the country was in this civil war in the first place.

"We have orders to bring General Platarch to the mayor immediately, should he come," the guard said. He walked around the barricade and up to Balear. "Sir, I'll carry that sword for you."

Balear grinned despite himself. "No you won't, but please feel free to try."

He grasped the weapon with his lone hand. It no longer felt strange to have only one arm, even though it was his left one.

The Sky Dragon Sword came off its specially designed harness on

Balear's back without trouble. The weapon was huge; the blade portion alone was seven feet long, six inches thick, and a foot wide at the base. In Balear's hand, though, it weighed no more than a grain of sand.

Not so long ago Balear would have declared the weapon and its bizarre powers "devil magic." He knew better now. Then again, considering the monster sealed inside it, perhaps that description was accurate after all.

Balear set the Auryozaki on the beach and stepped back. The guard knelt, grasped the weapon with both hands, and tugged.

It didn't move. The Katailan yanked with all his might, veins popping on his forehead. The sword refused to budge. Two more guards came to help, but even three of them together couldn't lift it. Though weightless to Balear, the Auryozaki maintained its original, mammoth weight to anyone else who touched it.

"I have no intention of using it," Balear said. "For the sake of all your dignities, please permit me to carry it. It shouldn't block up your city's otherwise fine entrance."

Even these amateurs knew enough not to be happy letting an armed stranger see the mayor, but they knew they had no choice. Considering that stranger could swing the heavy weapon as daintily as a dagger, there was nothing they could do to stop him. The guard with the parade sword nodded, and Balear returned the blade to its harness.

That harness was a miracle of craftsmanship, and like so much else in his life, Balear had Dirio to thank for it. Rather than use a sheath or loops that would make drawing the sword impractical for a one-armed man, the harness had a magnetic strip between the shoulders that held the weightless blade in place.

"I'll take you both to the mayor," the guard with the parade sword said. He gestured for his men to step aside. Dirio and Balear waited for an ocean wave to retreat, then walked around the barricade with him.

The guard led Dirio and Balear past the cliff wall, and at last Balear could gaze upon Kataile itself. It had been worth the wait. He'd traveled through most of Lodia during his time with the Castle Guard, but he'd never had occasion to visit Kataile. He regretted it now. The city rose in a sweeping arc up the cliff face, the whitewashed buildings almost invisible against the limestone.

In the lowest level of town sat the docks. Balear could see from the beach that the ocean curved inward to form a round, deep-water bay where even large ships could dock. Several masts rose above the buildings surrounding the pier. Most flew Lodian colors, but two sported Tacumsahen flags.

The guard took them into the city and up a long staircase. Balear looked on either side as the buildings rose in levels around him. Those closest to the water were small and simple. The higher they climbed, the bigger and more intricate the structures became.

As much as the architecture itself, Kataile's cleanliness impressed Balear. Most cities were grimy and smelly, but Kataile gleamed like someone had scrubbed the place down just this morning.

Balear paused on a landing to catch his breath and examine the view. They were three quarters up the cliff face now, and the sight across the ocean astounded him. Even the view from Haldessa Castle hadn't been this grand. This place was perfect, an island of untouched peace and beauty. Standing here, it was like the war didn't even exist.

The people gave that impression too. Even though it was the middle of winter, they all looked well fed. Children ran in the streets, shouting and playing as they surely did every day. Merchants and shoppers wandered around the markets of the lower levels.

Dirio and Balear's escort motioned for them to continue, and they resumed their hike up the cliff. Dirio wiped his brow as they ascended, and despite his military training Balear could feel himself tiring as well. He wondered how often the people up here descended to the docks, and how often those below rose to the upper levels. He doubted it happened much.

The guard with them stopped at last before the tallest building at the city's highest level. This structure was the only one in Kataile to reach above the plateau, though several staircases led up to the cliff top.

Balear once more turned his head to face the ocean. From here he could see all of Kataile laid out below him. With a wary eye, he looked up at the building the guard had led them to. It had windows on every exposed side. Nothing happened in this city without someone up here seeing it. Balear wasn't sure how he felt about that.

When the guard opened the building's door, Balear had to duck to get the Auryozaki through the opening. Once inside though, he had plenty of space. The ceilings were ten feet high, and all the doorways were wide, curved arches that allowed several people to walk through them at once.

Like the building's exterior, the inside walls were white. Murals, tapestries, and sculptures lined them to break up the otherwise blinding appearance.

Dirio and Balear's escort led them to a flight of steps. Together they climbed to the building's third and highest floor.

"Wait here," the guard said when the trio reached a pair of carved wooden doors enclosing an arch even wider than the ones they'd passed through on the first floor. "I'll inform Lady Orianna of your arrival."

The man tapped on one of the doors. A moment later it opened inward, and he entered. The door boomed shut behind him.

Balear looked at Dirio. "I never want to see another step in my life," he said. "This place is exhausting."

"But secure," Dirio replied, "and that's why we're here. By the way, please keep disparaging comments like that to yourself when we meet the mayor."

Balear flinched. Kataile was a tourist town after all. He wouldn't win friends by speaking ill of it. "So," he said, hoping to change the subject, "have you ever met Lady Orianna?"

"Until two years ago, I was an underling at a mine in a backwater village on the northern frontier. I didn't get out much."

"I feared so," Balear said. "I've never met her either. But I do know that Lady Orianna has been Kataile's mayor since before I joined the Castle Guard. She's also Lodia's only female mayor."

Dirio pursed his lips. "This could be interesting."

The wooden door opened again. The man with the parade sword appeared and motioned for them to come in.

Balear walked into the room and suppressed a gasp. The space rivaled the glory of Haldessa Castle before its destruction. A plush seafoam green carpet with an intricate wave pattern covered the floor; Balear had seen its equal only in the late King Azuluu's throne room.

Four clay pots dotted each of the room's corners. Balear wasn't familiar with the style, but judging from the pair of soldiers stationed by each one, he guessed they must hold tremendous value.

Most impressive, though, was the entire wall devoted to a mural of Kataile at dawn. Far from the blinding white Balear had anticipated, the painting showed a glittering mix of yellows, reds, and oranges as the early-morning light reflected off the limestone cliff and cityscape.

The painting was so realistic Balear at first mistook the wall for a gigantic window. Then he saw the prominent "Feidl" signature in the painting's lower right. He shivered.

At the room's far end, on a throne of silver and cushions, sat the woman who must be Elyssa Orianna. She was older, perhaps of an age with Dirio. Her clothes matched the room's opulence: a fine dress of cerulean silk with sapphire earrings and a matching headpiece. She kept her hair short, in contrast to most noblewomen in Lodia, and only the faintest streaks of gray had begun to show through the auburn.

Balear and Dirio's escort crossed the room to stand at his mayor's side. He gripped his sword's hilt in case his charges decided to get any stupid ideas.

Elyssa paid the man no mind. She locked her eyes first on Dirio, then on Balear.

Balear swallowed when her gaze settled on him. Her eyes were keen, and Balear felt naked under their look. The Katailan mayor examined every inch of him, in particular his empty right shoulder and enormous sword.

Elyssa leaned back in her throne and steepled her hands. For a long time she said nothing. Balear glanced at Dirio, but the Veliafan mayor was silent.

Balear was about to speak when Elyssa said, "You're shorter than I expected, based on your wanted poster."

The single sentence ruined Balear's concentration. Of all the things he'd expected her to say, that wasn't even close to being on the list. "Excuse me?" he asked.

"Are you truly Balear Platarch, the man who betrayed our country and caused the deaths of thousands, including King Angustion?"

Balear was too off balance to guard his tongue. "No, I'm not," he spat. "The man you describe does not exist. My name is indeed Balear Platarch, but I never betrayed our country. Nor have I caused the deaths of thousands. Those actions belong to King Angustion. He took our proud nation and turned it into a paranoid death trap. Thanks to his insanity, we wasted the lives of our finest young men in an unnecessary assault on a peace-loving people. King Angustion killed himself and all those who died with him the day he let magic take control of him."

All the guards in the room drew their swords. Evidently people didn't speak to the mayor this way.

Balear didn't care. He was tired of being called a traitor. He would tell them the truth whether they liked it or not. His hand rose to the Auryozaki's hilt. "If you attack me," he warned, "don't expect to walk away. I didn't come here to fight, but I will defend myself and Dirio. Our mission is too critical for me not to."

None of the guards backed down. Balear loosened his sword from the magnet that held it. He hoped it wouldn't come to a fight. The room was large, but it wasn't large enough. He couldn't attack the soldiers on the other side of Dirio without hitting the man, and the ones on Balear's side were so close that a strike on them would plow through the wall too. That wouldn't slow the Auryozaki, but Balear wasn't sure the building could take it.

A laugh rang out, sharp and piercing. Balear's eyes shifted to Elyssa. The mayor had her head thrown back as she cackled. "You're just like him!" she said through tears. "You're just like Balio."

Balear tensed at his father's name. The man had been Balear's role model his whole life, even though Balio had died at sea when Balear was just a toddler.

"You knew my father?" Balear asked.

"You could say that," Elyssa replied. She had a hungry expression that Balear didn't like. "Maybe I'll tell you a few stories about him some-time, but not now. The important thing is that you're here, and that you brought his sword. That's good. I was afraid it had disappeared after he died."

Balear scoffed. "Things might have been better for us all had it sunk to the bottom of the ocean with him."

"Not likely," Elyssa said. Her disturbing look got even worse. "That sword is what both Kataile and Lodia need right now. Don't you think so, Sky Dragon Knight?"

Balear's heart skipped. Elyssa couldn't know about the Dragon Knights unless . . .

"Lady Orianna, are you—"

She held up a hand to stop him. "Perhaps we'd best speak alone. Everyone, please wait outside. This man is no threat to me."

The guards all looked as shocked as Balear, but they reluctantly sheathed their weapons and obeyed. Dirio gave Balear an apologetic look, and then he too exited the chamber.

When they were alone, Elyssa said, "I'm not a Left, if that's what you were going to ask. That would have been a rude question, by the way."

Balear winced, recalling a similar situation between Iren and Rondel a long time ago. He hadn't reacted well back then. "That's why you wanted to speak in private," he said. "It was to avoid me embarrassing you by accusing you of being a Left in public."

Elyssa shrugged. "No one here would have taken your question seriously. All the same, I haven't led this city for twenty-five years by being reckless."

"But if you aren't a Left, how do you know about the Dragon Knights?"

"That one's easy," she said. "Your father told me about them. He was the Sky Dragon Knight. It's how he was able to earn such a reputation as a guard on ships. He used magic to overwhelm his enemies. And the ships he protected never lost course, because he could change the winds so they were always favorable. That's what he told me anyway."

"You two were close?"

The mayor smiled mysteriously. "You're just full of rude questions, aren't you?"

Balear scowled. He didn't like this talk of his family. Besides, it wasn't relevant to his reason for coming here. "I'm not here to pry," he said. "I'm here as a bodyguard. That's all."

Elyssa nodded. "Yes, for the mayor who just stepped outside. You and his people seek asylum, all four hundred of you."

"How did you know Dirio was a mayor? Or that we brought four hundred people?"

"My guards do tell me things, you know. More important, we see everything from atop the plateau. We've known you were coming since dawn."

Balear furrowed his brow. He'd just met this woman, but he could already see the cunning in her. He put his sword away and said, "You're right. We'd like sanctuary from the cold and the civil war."

"Four hundred mouths are a lot to feed," Elyssa replied. "My observers didn't see many weapons or suits of armor in your retinue."

"The Veliafans are hard workers. They'll earn their keep."

"Veliaf?" Elyssa seemed genuinely confused. "The stone-mining town? I figured they'd be one of the last to fall."

Balear looked at the seafoam rug. "It's been leveled."

For the first time Elyssa lost her composure. She leapt to her feet. "Leveled? How? Did Terkou attack it?"

"No," Balear said. He forced himself to meet her panicked gaze. "I did. Rather, the Sky Dragon that lives inside this sword did. He used my body as a conduit."

Elyssa's eyes went wide. "Now I see," she said, her voice quivering. "That's your plan here, isn't it? Leave the villagers outside while you come in alone. You release this dragon and level the city. Who are you working for?"

Balear held up his lone hand in a pleading gesture. "Wait, it was an accident! Veliaf was attacked by Fubuki, monsters out of the frozen land of Charda. I fought to stop them, and my magic went out of control. I agreed to help the Veliafans find a new home, but I also swore that I'd never use magic again."

"I see," Elyssa replied, her voice reined back in. Her ability to rebalance herself was something not to underestimate. "In that case, I can't let you or Veliaf's former residents into Kataile."

Balear flared. "Why not?"

"Because Kataile is a business town, and the costs outweigh the benefits. You bring more people we have to feed, clothe, and house, yet you offer no soldiers in return."

Elyssa smirked and sidled up to Balear. She was at least thirty years his senior, but the flirtatious look in her eyes still set him on edge. "You might tip the balance though," she whispered in his ear. "I saw a little of what Balio could do. Having someone like that on our side would make all the difference in this war. If you joined my army, we could win with your magic."

Balear jumped back from her like she was a venomous snake. "No!" he shouted. "You don't understand. I wiped out a town. There's nothing left of Veliaf; it's shattered into pieces no larger than my hand. If you bring me into your army as a Dragon Knight, Kataile is as likely to be destroyed as the enemy."

He took a deep breath. An idea had just come to him. "If it's a question of cost and benefit, perhaps I can still change your calculation," he said. "I can't use magic, but I was an officer in the Castle Guard. I'm the only one left. I saw your guards on the way in, and let me tell you, you're in trouble. They aren't soldiers. They're cowards who hid from King Angustion's draft order. They don't know how to fight, and they know even less about how to defend a city. If Terkou or anyone else attacks, I don't care that you have this cliff at your back. They'll overrun you."

Elyssa folded her arms. "A cold assessment," she said, but then she added, "and unfortunately, I must admit it's one I've made too."

"Yet done nothing about," Balear replied. "I can change that. I'll turn your guards into a military force to be proud of, one that can defend this city if it's attacked. I won't use magic, but to be honest, teaching your men will do more for Kataile than having a Dragon Knight ever could."

"I suppose in exchange, you want food and lodging for the people of Veliaf?"

Balear nodded. "Yes, but I have one more condition. I want the man who came with me today, Dirio Cyneric, to still be considered a mayor responsible for his people and equal in rank to yourself."

Elyssa offered her hand. "It's a deal."

Balear took the mayor's right hand in his left. "I'll let Dirio know, and then we'll start moving his villagers in. They'll find ways to help out soon enough."

He headed for the door, but Elyssa called to him. Balear looked back at her. She had a wry smile on her face. "By the way," she asked, "I understand why you want sanctuary for the Veliafans, but why would Dirio's title matter to you?"

Balear mimicked her expression. "Because only a mayor is eligible for the throne."

Elyssa scoffed. "You think the leader of a demolished mining town could rule this country? He doesn't have a chance on Raa."

Balear shrugged. He didn't bother to answer before he left the room.

CHAPTER FIVE
New Training

Iren stood alone on the beach inside his mind. The waves churned, reflecting his impatience. He'd been waiting for twenty minutes now.

At last a light appeared down the beach. Iren shifted to face it and saw Divinion walking toward him. The dragon could fly and be here in a second, but instead he ambled along like he had all the time on Raa.

Iren ran to him. "What kept you?" he demanded.

Divinion cocked his head sideways. "This is the same time we meet every night. Why are you so early?"

Iren seethed at the dragon's nonchalant manner. "You told me yesterday that you would think of a way to improve our training. Did you come up with anything?"

"I am a god, after all. I may have thought of something."

"Then what is it? Stop dragging this out!"

Divinion loosed a low huffing sound that Iren guessed was laughter. "Deep down you're still the same impetuous boy I met in Veliaf," the dragon said. "If more of that child remains besides your rashness, there may yet be hope for this world."

Iren scowled, not sure if he was supposed to take that as a compliment.

The dragon brushed off Iren's sour expression. "Anyway, I did come up with an idea. The problem you confront in fighting Rondel isn't her speed. It's your inability to process it. Your body can move as fast as Rondel's does, but your mind can't keep up. That's why Rondel uses Lightning Sight. It enhances not only her eyes' ability to see detail, but her brain's ability to interpret that detail."

"What does that have to do with our new training model?"

"It occurred to me that while Rondel relies on Lightning Sight in combat, there have been times when she has moved quickly without using it. That suggests that it's possible to train your mind to interpret what your eyes see as quickly as you move. It would take more work than using a spell like Lightning Sight, but it might be doable."

Iren thought for a moment. "You could be right. When my father fought Rondel the night she murdered him, he kept up with her movements, at least for a while. He used magic to enhance his night vision, but he didn't have any spells that could speed up his brain. He must have trained himself to view objects moving at high speeds."

"And if he could do it," Divinion finished, "then perhaps you can too."

"That's how you figured out what our training model should be. You realized my father had gone through similar practice. I'll just copy what he did."

"Indeed, though you may not like what I propose."

"If it helps me defeat Rondel, I'm up for anything."

Divinion's whiskers twitched. "All right, but I did warn you."

The dragon blinked his enormous blue eyes, and the seaside image in Iren's mind vanished. Iren and Divinion now stood in a dense forest. It looked a little like Ziorsecth, but the trees weren't as large or evenly spaced. Rocks and decaying logs littered the ground, and the terrain was heavily pitted where old trees had fallen and uprooted themselves. Divinion's sinuous body curled away into the woods farther than Iren could see.

"Where are we?" Iren asked.

"In one of the primeval forests of Teneb, the continent my brethren sank ten thousand years ago," Divinion replied. "This place no longer exists, but an image of it will serve our purposes."

Iren eyed the forest doubtfully. "What do you want me to do?"

"It's simple. You need to practice seeing things that move quickly. Rather than move objects around, we'll move you around. Your task is to run through this forest at top speed. You will not slow down no matter what. Avoid touching anything except the forest floor."

Iren put both hands on his hips and blew out a long breath. He'd run through Ziorsecth Forest back when Rondel had trained him, but that forest had enormous trees and a fairly open understory. This forest was so dense there were spots a person couldn't squeeze between the undergrowth. Moreover, the few relatively open areas had such irregular terrain that Iren doubted he could climb over them at a crawl. He was supposed to run through this place at his full speed, so fast his body blurred?

"No stalling," Divinion said. "Get going, and don't hold back."

There was no getting out of it. Divinion would know if Iren didn't give it everything he could. Settling into a crouch, he worked out a path and took off.

Trees flashed past him, hazes of brown and green. He knew the first fifty feet from examining it beforehand, and he effortlessly avoided the rocks and logs in his path.

That ease lasted less than a second as he reached the end of what he'd been able to see from his starting point. A fallen log appeared out of nowhere. Iren tried to jump over it, but he was a fraction too late. His ankle caught it, and he sprawled forward. Unwilling to give up, he managed a forward roll and regained his feet.

But even as Iren stood, a brown wall loomed in front of him. He crashed into it face-first and fell onto his back. Blood poured from his nose in a torrent.

The forest vanished, and Iren awoke in the cavern with a gasp. Instinctively he reached up and touched his face. It was unharmed. The blow hadn't been real; it had just been in his mind.

Even though he wasn't injured, Iren still needed five minutes before he could calm his pulse enough to focus again. He took a series of deep breaths and returned at last to his mental seaside.

Divinion was waiting. "How do you feel?" the dragon asked.

"Shaken," Iren admitted. "What happened?"

"You ran into a tree."

"Thanks. I mean, why did it kick me out of my meditation? That's never happened before, even when you pretended to be Rondel."

"When we fought on this beach, the terrain was all the same. You didn't have to concentrate to maintain it. But the forest's continuity is critical to your training. It can't be uniform, so it requires more focus to keep it going. Apparently, it's too much to balance it, your high speed, and pain at the same time."

"Grand. So how am I supposed to train?"

A dangerous glint appeared in the dragon's eyes. "Well . . ."

Realization dawned. "Hold on," Iren said. "You can't be serious."

"To be fair, I did say you weren't going to like my idea."

"Yeah, but what you're suggesting is crazy. It doesn't matter if I hurt myself in here. If I slam into a tree in the real world like I did just now though, I'll have more than a broken nose. I don't even want to think about all the internal injuries I'll have when I break all my ribs."

"Good thing you have the Muryozaki to heal you."

Iren gulped. Rondel had trained him in a similar manner two years ago. She'd used lightning magic against him and relied on his katana's healing power to keep him fit. Granted, that training had toughened him in a short time, but all the cuts, bruises, and broken bones made it something Iren had no desire to repeat.

"Of course," Divinion continued, "if you'd rather give up on fighting Rondel, I would understand."

Iren's expression turned to ice. "I won't," he said. "If this is what I need to defeat Rondel, then I'll do it. There's a forest outside this cave. I'll turn it into my training ground."

Divinion sighed. "I had to try. So be it. Our meditation sessions won't help you with this training, so we'll stop them for now. When you can run through the forest outside at full speed without hitting anything, come see me again for the next step."

Iren blinked twice. "The next step? What do you mean? This isn't enough to beat Rondel?"

"Not even close. All this will do is let you follow her movements. She's still an exceptional fighter. Even if you match her speed, you'll have a long way to go to surpass her. Don't worry about that for now though. It's better if you focus on what's right in front of you. If you knew the next step, it would only depress you."

"What's that supposed to mean?"

"It means this is the easy part. The hard part is yet to come."

Iren groaned.

"Don't give me that. This is what you said you wanted. Oh, and before I forget, I have one piece of advice for you. When your father underwent this training, he did it not for minutes or hours, but for days on end. He would move at full speed until he collapsed, and then he would sleep. When he awoke, he would accelerate himself again. He followed that pattern over and over, never slowing down for weeks. By doing that, his eyes and mind adjusted and began to think moving at that speed was normal. That's what this training requires."

"I can't train that way on the farm. Goro and Chiyo might see me."

"True, but when you're alone, you should do everything as quickly as you can. The more time you spend at high speed, the faster your mind will adjust."

Iren nodded. "All right, I guess I'll see you in a few days."

Divinion laughed.

❧

Goro's eyes snapped open. He'd run this farm for more than two hundred years. He knew every sound it made, so when it made an unexpected one, he caught it immediately.

He pulled himself out of bed and dressed himself. It was well after sunset. No one should be about this late at night, especially not in the uphill forest.

Yet that was where the sound had come from. He was certain of it. It was the only place nearby where trees could fall.

Chiyo looked at her husband, bleary-eyed. "Goro? What's the matter?"

Another crash came from the forest. That made four now. One he might understand; trees did die and fall down on their own. But not this many so close together. It was a windless night, and there had been no heavy rains that could have weakened the soil. There was only one explanation. Someone was cutting down trees.

At best, it was one of the neighboring farmers being stupid and trying to catch up on his firewood. At worst, it meant someone was stealing their timber.

Goro cursed. The forest up there was the source of firewood and building materials for all the local farms. They shared it and cared for it, and there was always enough for everyone. If someone was sneaking away wood to sell, though, it would be easy for them to overcut the forest and hurt all the farmers. Goro couldn't allow that.

Chiyo had a worried expression. "What's going on?" she asked.

Goro realized he hadn't answered her the first time she'd spoken. He gave her his most reassuring smile, trusting in the dark to hide its falseness. "I forgot to lock the tool shed," he lied. "It's probably fine, but it'll keep me up all night unless I take care of it. I won't be long. Go back to sleep."

His wife didn't look convinced, but she seemed too tired to argue. She rolled over, murmured, "Be careful," and started snoring again.

Goro walked to the door and grabbed the lantern. He didn't have any real weapons, but a good farm implement could serve in a pinch. He ran to the shed, unlocked it, and pulled out a pair of kamas, one-handed sickles used for harvesting rice. He kept one in his dominant left hand and put the other in his belt behind his back. Holding the lantern in his right hand, he set out across the farm toward the forest.

As he passed into the trees, Goro heard more crashes. Now that he was closer, he realized the sounds were different from when a tree hit the ground. These sounded more like something heavy hitting the trees.

Goro followed the crashes deeper into the woods, wondering what could make so much racket. None of the wild animals would cause such noise. Someone had to be up here.

At last Goro caught the sound he'd really been listening for: a person speaking. Right after one of the impacts, he heard from somewhere not far ahead of him, "Ow! Damn!"

The farmer edged forward and raised his lantern and kama. "Who's there?" he shouted. "Come out! What are you doing out here?"

The woods went silent. Goro peered into the darkness. At the edge of the lantern's light, he caught a glint from a pair of eyes. Goro stepped forward, and for a second the lantern shone on a man with tan hair and blue eyes wearing a dirt-stained kimono.

"Katsu?" Goro asked. Relief and shock poured into his voice with equal measure. "What on Raa are you doing out here?"

The man didn't answer. He didn't even move. Goro watched him another moment, and then, without warning, Katsu vanished as though he'd never been there at all.

"Katsu?" Goro called. "Katsu! Where are you?"

There was no response. Goro waited fifteen minutes, but the man, if he had been there at all, made no further sound.

Goro hiked back to the farm. The entire way, he warred with himself. Had that really been Katsu? It didn't seem possible, yet the person he'd seen had looked just like the farmhand.

Whoever it had been, it was all the more reason to figure out who— or what—Katsu was, and to figure it out soon. Because if Katsu could hit trees with that much force and walk away, then he wasn't just some wanderer. He was something else. Something dangerous.

CHAPTER SIX
Lyubo

Minawë stared into the flames of the Kodamas' campfire. She longed to lose herself in them, but she couldn't escape. She kept hearing that terrible conversation over and over.

"So you'll choose revenge?" she'd asked. "I told you before that revenge can't make you happy. It can't make anyone happy."

"You think I care about happiness?" Iren had shot back. "My happiness vanished eighteen years ago when Rondel took away my parents."

"I tried to stop you today. What if I do that again?"

Iren had paused for only a second. Then he'd said the words that had shattered her, "I don't know if you'll believe me or not, but I do still care for you. That's why I'm walking away tonight. I could have killed Rondel while she was helpless. I held back on your account. But I will fight her again; that's a promise. If you get in my way when that day comes, I'll kill you as well."

Minawë hugged herself. Iren had changed so much. Just two years ago he'd been an immature teenager who hadn't even realized the mess he'd landed himself in. But even though Minawë had mocked him, he'd risked his life to save her. He'd become the Dragoon to protect her and everyone else in Ziorsecth Forest. He'd been a hero.

Not anymore. What Iren was now Minawë didn't know, but "hero" wasn't it.

There was a shuffling across from her. Minawë looked up to see Uncle Narunë take a seat on a rock.

"You've barely said a word since you returned last night," he said. "I miss hearing your voice."

Frustration flashed across Minawë's face. "You had plenty to talk about with Mother," she spat.

Minawë's eyes flicked across camp to where the old Maantec lay. She wondered if the woman was really asleep, or if she was just waiting for Minawë to drift off so she could abandon her.

Narunë sighed. "I'm sorry. Frankly, though, I understand where Rondel's coming from. She doesn't want to hurt you any more than you already have been."

"I know that," Minawë said, "but what would hurt me more is knowing that one of them killed the other and that I did nothing to stop it."

For a moment Narunë said nothing. He took a few deep breaths as though steeling himself. At length he said, "You don't have to be loyal to him, you know. He turned his back on you."

Minawë flared. "What makes you think you know anything about it?"

Narunë didn't rise to her anger. Instead he smiled, and when he did his eyes glittered in the firelight. "Even though I've only known you a few months, I think of you as the daughter I never had," he said. "I want to protect you, just as I'm sure my brother would have wanted to protect you. Whatever I say, no matter how hard it is for you to hear, it's for that end."

He stood. "Minawë, I have a request to make of you. When we get back to Sorengaral, I'd like you to stay with me for a while."

"I'm going where Rondel goes," Minawë replied. "There's no point in discussing it."

"You can't be a slave to Rondel or Iren," Narunë said. "You're not just any Kodama. You're our queen. We need a strong leader. Don't run away from that responsibility."

Minawë scowled. "I'll consider it," she said in a tone that made it clear she would do no such thing. "Until tomorrow, Uncle."

Narunë bade her good night and headed off to sleep. Minawë stayed up, watching the flames. She knew she should sleep too, but too many thoughts were knocking around her head.

"You'll go blind if you don't blink," a male voice said from the other side of the fire ring.

Minawë raised her head. A young-looking Kodaman man stood six feet away. Minawë hadn't noticed him until now. He was one of the members of their party, one of the scouts if she recalled.

"May I join you?" he asked.

Minawë shrugged and gestured to the stone her uncle had vacated.

The Kodama sat. He wore the same wild outfit as the rest of them, and in the firelight he looked frightening. He'd scrubbed the brown paint from his face, but he couldn't hide the black jaguar tattoos on each arm.

"I'm Lyubo," he said. He put his right hand in front of his chest and raised his first two fingers in the Kodaman friendship sign.

Minawë returned the gesture. "Minawë," she replied. "You know, it's funny. You and I traveled all the way from Sorengaral to Shikari, and this is the first time we've talked."

Lyubo looked into the fire. "About that. In truth, I've wanted to talk with you since before we left Sorengaral. I could never bring myself to do it. Queens tend not to be approachable."

"I'm no high and mighty ruler," Minawë said. "I'd have thought you'd gather that much from seeing my uncle in action."

Lyubo laughed. "He's not exactly the picture of formality, is he? Still, I didn't know what to expect from you. You're so strong and determined. I was afraid."

Minawë looked at the man with respect. It took a lot for someone to admit what he'd just shared. He must have been thinking about this meeting for a long time. "I'm glad you changed your mind," Minawë said. "I haven't had the chance to get to know many Kodamas on my journey."

She paused. There was something familiar about Lyubo, something deeper than just his being another travel companion. "Have we met before?" Minawë asked. "I mean, before we set off for Shikari?"

Lyubo gulped. "Well, that's the other reason I was afraid to talk to you. Remember the Kodamas who ambushed you when you first came to Aokigahara? I was part of that team. I was the one who bound your hands."

Minawë shuddered. Those weren't memories she enjoyed. It had turned out all right once they'd reached Sorengaral, but for a while she'd wondered whether her own kin would murder her.

"I worried you would hate me for what I did to you," Lyubo said.

"You didn't know we weren't a threat back then," Minawë replied. "I can't hate you for doing your job. If anything, I should thank you for taking such good care of this forest. It's all any of you have. It needs to be protected."

Minawë shook a second time. She hadn't meant to say that, but now that she had, she knew it was true. This forest did need protection. Her uncle's request came back to her.

Lyubo met her gaze. "I'm afraid I have to apologize again. I overheard a little of what you and Lord Narunë were saying. That's not an easy choice, to decide between your people and the man you love."

Minawë didn't answer. The man she loved . . . was it really that? Did she love Iren? Maybe a year ago she had, but now? How could she love what he had become?

Lyubo stood. "I'm beat. I'm a little nocturnal, but this is too much even for me." He made as if to leave the fire ring, then paused. "Say, Minawë, there isn't much I can do for you. I can't stop Rondel or this Iren guy. I'm no Dragon Knight, and I don't even have a lot of magic. But I won't pressure you like Lord Narunë. If you need to vent, I'll listen."

He smiled, and his genuine warmth surprised Minawë. No one had looked at her that way in a long time.

She blushed. "I might take you up on that," she said.

"Until then," Lyubo replied. He disappeared into the night.

For a long time after, Minawë sat up next to the fire. Conversations swirled in her head. What was she supposed to do?

The answer wouldn't come.

CHAPTER SEVEN
Ronin

Chiyo placed the bowl of rice porridge in front of Katsu and went to retrieve her own. By the time she came back, Katsu's breakfast was gone.

The farm woman blinked. "That was fast."

Katsu wiped his face and grinned. "It was delicious, Chiyo. Thank you."

Sitting at Katsu's left, Goro looked up from his porridge. His eyebrows dropped. Chiyo tried to stop him with a glare, but the man either couldn't see her or chose to ignore her. "What happened to you last night?" he asked Katsu.

"Oh, you mean this?" The farmhand tugged at his kimono. Mud stains covered it. "I fell."

Goro's eyebrows lowered even farther. If he wasn't careful they'd drop right off his face. "You fell." His tone betrayed his disbelief. "What, off a cliff?"

"Something like that. It was dark last night. I had a little trouble finding where I usually sleep."

"That's why you should sleep here," Chiyo interjected, her bright smile aimed as much at her husband as at Katsu. "We only have the one futon, but we have a spare blanket or two. They would serve just as well. You could sleep here in the kitchen."

Katsu shook his head. "I've imposed on you enough as it is. I'll be more careful tonight."

Chiyo sighed. She'd made the same invitation to Katsu twice a week ever since he'd arrived, but he always refused her.

Still, it didn't keep her from asking. Katsu was so gentle. It pained her to see him suffering.

"Well, just watch yourself out there," Goro snarled. He could be so dense. "I hear there's all sorts of crazy things in the forest at night. Ghosts, demons, and others of a more ordinary sort. Timber thieves maybe." Her husband locked eyes with Katsu as he said those last three words.

Katsu started to raise an eyebrow, seemed to think better of it, and then shrugged. "I'll be on the lookout," he said. "One thing's for sure: I won't let anyone steal your timber."

Chiyo smiled at that, but Goro's frown didn't lessen. What was wrong with him? Couldn't he see Katsu was trying to help? Men just didn't understand people.

Katsu rose from his seat. "I should go weed the rice paddies. Goro, are the kamas in the shed in case I need them?"

Goro started. "Of course they are!" he said, louder than was warranted. "Why wouldn't they be?"

"No reason. I just wanted to be sure. See you at dinner." Katsu left the house.

"I wish he'd stick around sometimes," Chiyo said. "He doesn't always need to think about work."

"He sticks around too much," Goro growled. "He could have picked any farm to bother. Why'd he go and choose ours?"

"Goro!" Chiyo cried. Her husband met her glaring eyes and instinctively shrank back. "You promised."

"Promised what?"

"You promised no more questions."

"I know what I promised. But you didn't see what I saw last night. It was him, Chiyo. He was the one out there knocking down the trees. That's why he's all banged up. I don't know what he's doing out there, but it isn't normal. He isn't normal."

"We've been over this. He's a blessing. So what if he's a little odd?"

"Aha!" Goro cried. "So you do think he's odd."

Chiyo reddened. "That isn't what I meant. I meant he's in pain. Something happened to him, something terrible. I can tell. He needs us, Goro, and we need him."

"Do we?"

"If we want a nursery someday, then yes."

That line always stopped Goro. He wanted a family as much as she did. Mentioning that desire was the ultimate way to win any fight between them.

Except today. "If we want a nursery, we need safety as much as money," Goro countered. "That man isn't safe to have around. Think about it. He works harder and faster than the two of us combined, yet he's never tired. He can spend all day chopping wood one-handed like it's nothing. Normal folk aren't like that. There's only one answer, Chiyo. He's highborn."

Chiyo kept her mouth shut. She'd guessed Katsu's status the moment he'd arrived on their farm. It wasn't just the man's strength. The way he spoke, how he carried himself, and his eyes—especially his eyes, blue as the summer sky—all shouted that he was of noble birth.

She had never told Goro. He held a deep resentment toward the upper classes.

Goro took advantage of Chiyo's silence to continue his tirade. "If he's highborn and came all the way out here, it's obvious what happened. He's on the run. He's an outlaw. He's a ronin." Goro spat the last word.

Chiyo put her hand to her mouth. It had of course occurred to her, but she had never accepted that it could be true.

"That's why we have to get rid of him," Goro said. "If he's a ronin, how long do you think Lord Melwar will let him wander free? Men will come looking for him. If they find out we've helped him, we'll be as guilty as he is. They'll kill us, Chiyo. I won't let that happen. I promised your father I'd protect you until my dying breath. I won't let anyone hurt you."

Chiyo bowed to Goro so her head touched the floor. "You honor me beyond words."

When Chiyo rose, Goro was wide-eyed. They were always informal with each other. Such a display almost never happened between them.

"That man has known more pain in his life than either of us can imagine," Chiyo said. "I don't want to add any more on top of that. If you say he has to leave, then let's tell him together, gently."

Her husband bowed back to her. "Thank you, Chiyo. It's for our own safety, and for the safety of our child yet to come."

Chiyo wanted to believe him. As she stood and cleared the dishes, though, she wondered what the ronin Katsu would do when they told him.

CHAPTER EIGHT
Rookie and Veteran

Balear and Dirio stood in Kataile's third level, midway up the cliff face. This area sloped more gradually than other parts of the city, so it sported one of Kataile's few large, open courtyards. A white stone fountain burbled in the center, and around it gathered the officers of the city's militia. Balear had summoned them here so he could learn more about them and how best to turn them into soldiers.

The results were discouraging. A portly middle-aged man leaned against the fountain while guzzling a tankard of ale. Next to him, a sixteen-year-old picked his nose and stared at the clouds. Rounding out the set, a white-bearded man twenty years older than Dirio lay on the stone, snoring.

"This is what I'm supposed to train?" Balear murmured.

Dirio shrugged. "At least they came."

"Not quite," Balear replied. "According to Elyssa, Kataile's forces number one thousand. They're divided into ten companies of one hundred soldiers each, and each company is divided into ten squads of ten."

"How mathematical."

"With Elyssa in charge, I'm not surprised. Anyway, my point is that there should be one hundred and ten people here—the hundred squad leaders plus the ten company leaders."

Dirio frowned. At best forty men had come. "Oh."

"Yeah," Balear replied. "Oh."

"To be fair, they only had a day's notice," Dirio said. "Maybe some of them had other assignments."

"They were told this meeting took first priority." Balear blew out a long breath. "We have an enormous task ahead if we can't even get half our officers to show up for practice."

Dirio gestured at the men. "So inspire them. Most of these guys either didn't qualify for Amroth's draft order, or they outright ignored it. I doubt any of them were at the Battle of Ziorsecth. They don't understand war."

"How am I supposed to make them understand war? They've lived in a luxurious tourist town all their lives."

Dirio smirked. He pointed to the gigantic sword on Balear's back. "That could make for a good demonstration."

Balear's eyes narrowed. "I'm not going to use magic."

"You don't have to. You just need to teach them about war. Show them what it's like. You've been there after all."

Balear subconsciously reached over and touched the empty socket of his right shoulder. "Yeah," he said, "I have. All right, I'll give it a try."

He stepped forward. A few of the soldiers focused on him, but most were engaged in side conversations and ignored the one-armed man. Balear cleared his throat. "Good afternoon!"

A few half-hearted "Good afternoon's" came back.

Balear scowled. "That won't do. I said, 'Good afternoon!'" He shouted the words.

"Good afternoon!" The reply was a little stronger this time.

"Better," Balear said, "but I'm in charge of this city's defense now. You'll address me as 'sir.' One more time: good afternoon!"

"Good afternoon, sir!"

Balear eyed the teenager with his finger up his nostril. The boy hadn't answered with the others. "You there," Balear said, "what's your name?"

The boy jumped at Balear's sharp tone. He hid his finger behind his back as though he could avoid Balear noticing what he'd been doing. "Pi. . .Pito," he stammered.

"Pito, sir," Balear growled. He stalked up to the boy and glowered at him. Balear had a solid six inches on the kid, and the gigantic sword on his back made him that much more imposing.

The kid gulped. "Pito, sir."

"That's better. Have you ever been in a fight, Pito?"

"Yes, sir. I'm the best brawler among the teens. That's why they made me a squad leader."

Balear's eyebrow twitched. If this whelp was the best fist-fighter among those his age, Kataile was in big trouble.

He kept that sentiment to himself for the moment. "Good to know, Pito," he said. "Now then, have you ever been in a war?"

The boy shook his head. "No, sir."

Balear took three steps back and removed the Auryozaki from its harness. He leveled the enormous sword at the boy. Its tip was less than a foot from the kid's face. "Well," the general said, "you're about to be."

Pito's eyes bulged so much Balear wondered if they would pop out of their sockets. "Sir, you . . . you can't be serious."

"You have a sword," Balear said. He gestured with his head to the short sword on the boy's hip. "You say you're the best brawler. Prove it. I'll give you the same test someone named Ariok once gave me: live."

Balear swung the Sky Dragon Sword in an overhead strike.

Pito barely managed to jump sideways in time to avoid the blow. The Auryozaki slammed into the fountain behind him, throwing a shower of stone and water across the courtyard.

Screams filled the space as the officers closest to Balear panicked and fled. No one had told them their new general was insane.

Despite the chaos, a few of the more distant officers stood their ground. They drew their weapons and surrounded Balear. "No one attacks a man of Kataile!" one shouted.

"Outsider!" another screamed. "Traitor!"

"We won't accept you!" yelled a third.

Balear leveled his sword at each in turn. "That's fine," he spat. "You don't have to follow me if you don't want to. To be honest, I'm not thrilled about being here. I'm even less thrilled to instruct a bunch of draft dodgers. So I'll make you a deal. If any of you want my job, you can have it. There's just one condition. You have to beat me first."

Four of them tried. Balear didn't want to kill them, so even striking them with the Auryozaki's flat wasn't an option. He returned the weapon to its harness and faced them bare-handed.

The first three went down with a single punch to each of their solar plexuses. The fourth managed to swing his weapon, a halberd, once before Balear got inside his guard and dropped him with an elbow to the jaw.

Balear thought that would end it, but then a fifth man stepped forward. Unlike the other officers who had challenged him, this man's expression wasn't one of anger or resentment. It was cold and detached.

The new challenger raised an old, rusty sword. Then, without a word, without a shout, without the slightest sign that he was about to move, he thrust at Balear's chest.

The man's speed and ferocity caught Balear off guard. He dodged sideways, but the man tracked him. This fifth fighter must have held back intentionally, observing Balear's fighting style against the other contenders.

With Balear on the defensive, the challenger pressed his advantage. Slashes aimed for Balear's elbow and wrist as well as more vital areas. He barely avoided each attack.

Balear grimaced. There was no choice. He reached back and pulled out the Auryozaki.

The challenger hesitated an instant, but then he regained his composure. He charged, and Balear guessed the man's strategy. He would get close to Balear and take advantage of the Auryozaki's apparent mass.

It would have been a good plan were it not for the Sky Dragon Sword's magical weightlessness. Balear whipped his sword around as quickly as a dagger and blocked his opponent's thrust. A flick of his wrist sent the rusty sword flying.

Balear expected the man to surrender after that, but instead, his opponent kept running and slammed into him. The man shoved his forearm under Balear's jaw and forced him to the ground.

Before Balear could recover, the officer leapt on top of him. The man pinned Balear's arm with one hand and pummeled his face with the other.

Through the rain of blows, Balear knew he'd made a mistake. He'd assumed everyone here was a novice. This man was a veteran.

Even so, he wasn't a match for Balear. The man's punches had little force behind them. They should have knocked Balear out by now, but instead he just had a bloody nose and lip.

Balear pushed back against the hand holding his arm to the stone. Spitting blood into his opponent's eyes, he twisted the Auryozaki so its pommel drove up into the officer's stomach.

The man fell to his knees. He gasped for breath as he wiped his face. Balear stood, spat more blood, and leveled the tip of his sword at the man's throat.

Despite his obvious discomfort, the defeated veteran stared defiantly at Balear. His pale green eyes dared the general to finish the battle.

Instead of killing the man, Balear smiled and put away his sword. He couldn't see his own face, but he guessed it must look horrible. He could feel blood running down his chin, and one eye was swollen shut. "You were at the Battle of Ziorsecth," he said.

"How did you know?" the man on the ground wheezed.

"Your expression. The way you fought. Everything about you screamed that you had experience. But I wasn't certain until I disarmed you. Someone with training but who had never been in a battle would have given up. They would have assumed the match was over, that it wasn't a fight to the death. You kept on going. You knew that if you didn't, I would kill you. Isn't that right?"

"I didn't know," the man admitted, "but I wasn't about to guess wrong."

Balear laughed. It made a raspy sound in his throat. "What's your name?"

"Riac," the man said, "and don't tell me to call you 'sir.'"

Balear held out his hand. "Riac, how would you like to be my second-in-command? You know these men. You know war. You can prepare them for what to expect when another city's army comes calling."

Riac didn't answer right away. He grasped Balear's hand and pulled himself to his feet. He was a grizzled man, with a chiseled jaw and a scar on his left cheek. His sandy brown hair had flecks of gray. Balear hadn't realized the man was that much older than he was.

The veteran stared a long time into Balear's unswollen eye. What he looked for Balear didn't know, but the general held firm, unwilling to falter in front of his men.

After what felt like hours, Riac nodded. "Sure, no problem. Sir."

Balear smiled. One down, nine-hundred and ninety-nine to go.

Then he snapped his fingers. "Oh, Pito!" he said. He looked around. "Where's Pito? I'd like to put him in your company, Riac. He could learn a lot from someone like you."

One of the officers standing nearby shuffled his feet. "Um, sir? Pito left."

"Left?" Balear asked. "Where'd he go?"

The soldier stared at his boots. "Well, I'm not certain, but I got a whiff of him as he ran past me. I think . . . um, sir, I think he went to change his pants."

CHAPTER NINE
Gentle Heart

The paddy blurred as Iren dashed across it. With both hands he ripped at the weeds growing between the rice plants.

At this speed, telling the difference between what to pull and what to leave was almost impossible. But that was the point. He had to learn to pick out subtle differences even at high speeds.

Iren doubted his father had ever trained this way. In fact, he doubted pulling weeds had ever been part of any Dragon Knight's training.

Still, it seemed to be working. When he'd started this morning, he couldn't even tell where the weeds were. Now, as the sun set, he was getting the hang of it. He still occasionally grabbed a rice plant, or tripped and fell in the muck, but those mistakes came less and less often.

When dusk fell, Iren gave up for the day. Exhausted from running flat-out since morning, he left the paddy at a leisurely pace. He stopped at the well to draw some water and wash off the mud that caked him.

With his clothes and skin visible again, he headed for Goro and Chiyo's home. His stomach grumbled at the thought of dinner. Even though Chiyo had only the most basic ingredients, her cooking was excellent. The meals were earthy and informal, like the woman who made them.

As Iren neared the tiny farmhouse, though, Goro and Chiyo were outside in front of the door. Goro had his jaw set like he was about to enter battle, and Chiyo wrung her hands as though she feared he wouldn't come back from the fight.

At first Iren worried the two of them had seen him racing around, but he dismissed the possibility. The rice paddies were at a higher elevation than the house, so the angle was wrong to see a person working in them.

Iren put a hand behind his head and smiled nervously. "I hope I'm not late for dinner again. I wanted to finish the weeding before I came down."

Chiyo's eyes widened. "You pulled all the weeds in one day?"

"I guess so," Iren said. "Is that unusual?"

Goro's scowl deepened. "Not at all," he spat. "It's perfectly normal for a ronin."

Iren rocked back on his heels. He knew the word "ronin" from his education in Maantec culture from Hana. It wasn't a title that garnered respect. A ronin was a highborn warrior who had lost his lord's favor. Usually they picked up odd jobs as mercenaries, but occasionally they stooped to banditry.

"So I'm right," Goro said. "Why don't you tell us what you're really doing here? You're no wandering farmhand; I'm certain of that. I know that was you running around the forest last night."

Iren sighed. Where to even begin? Lying wouldn't help, and he doubted he could pull it off anyway. At the same time, though, he didn't want them to find out that he was Iren Saito's son, or about Divinion.

Maybe a partial truth would work. "I did come from Hiabi," he said, "but I wasn't sworn to service by anyone there. I'm originally from Lodia, far to the north. I came to Hiabi for training, but it wasn't what I expected. I couldn't return to Lodia, so I started wandering Shikari."

It was all true, though it left out a lot of important details. It seemed to work for Chiyo, but Goro remained unmoved. "A highborn up and leaves Hiabi, and nobody there gives a damn?" he asked. "I don't buy it. Lord Melwar doesn't seem the type to let someone like you leave without a plan to get you back. He'll send men after you. Wouldn't you agree?"

Iren frowned. He had no idea what Melwar would do. It had been more than a month since the showdown outside Hiabi, and Iren had seen nothing of the Maantec lord or his servants since. Surely if Melwar or Hana wanted to find him, they would have done so by now.

Still, he had no choice but to agree with Goro. Melwar had put months of effort into Iren's training. Iren thought it unlikely the noble would forget about him. "I don't know of anyone pursuing me," he said, "but that doesn't mean they aren't. It's a possibility."

"And that's why you're hiding here," Goro finished for him. "You want to avoid Lord Melwar's patrols."

"Not at all. I just needed a way to keep fed while I continued my training."

"What are you training for that's so important?"

Iren paused. If he said much more, everything was going to come spilling out. "My parents were murdered," he told them. "I want to become strong enough to avenge them."

Chiyo's left hand went to her mouth. She wrapped her other arm around Goro's. "Please, Goro, stop this."

"We agreed, Chiyo," Goro retorted. "It has to be done. Katsu, you can't stay here. You've put this farm in danger. If Lord Melwar's men find out we're harboring a ronin, they'll kill us. You have to leave."

Iren felt like the man had punched him in the face. He'd only worked here a month, and already they were tossing him out.

"I understand," he said at last. "I won't endanger you further. I'll leave immediately." He turned and walked away.

&#x03;

This was wrong. Everything about this was wrong. Chiyo watched Katsu get smaller and smaller. Why had she agreed to this?

"It's for the best," Goro said. "Come on inside. Let's have dinner."

"All right," she replied, but then a thought came to her. "Goro, you head on in. I didn't say goodbye to him. I want to do that. Will you let me?"

Goro folded his arms, but he said, "Be careful."

"I will."

Her husband went inside. The moment the door shut, Chiyo ran to catch up with Katsu.

"Katsu, wait!" she called.

The man hesitated a moment, then stopped and faced her. "Chiyo?" he asked. "What's the matter?"

Chiyo bowed to him. "I wanted to thank you," she said. "Goro might not see it, but you've done a lot for us. I'm glad you stayed here as long as you did."

Katsu briefly inclined his head. "You're welcome. Farewell."

"No, wait!"

Chiyo's heart raced. What was she doing? She and Goro had agreed.

"You told us you were training to avenge your parents," she said. "Why did you come all the way here to do that? What about Lodia? Couldn't you train there?"

Katsu looked at the sky. It had darkened into night. A half moon shone through a thin veil of clouds.

"Lodia hates me because I'm a Maantec, a 'Left,'" he said. "All humans are right-handed, so a left-handed Maantec sticks out. There was no place for me but Shikari. Yet even here . . ."

Chiyo's lips turned down even as her eyes softened. She had been right about this man all along. She had let Goro's suspicions get to her, but now she would make things right. "Katsu," she said, "may I see your hands?"

The man's brow furrowed at her request, but he held out his hands. Chiyo took them in hers. A month of farm work had calloused them, yet beneath that was a softness, an innocence wounded but not destroyed.

"You're a good person," Chiyo said.

"If you knew me, you wouldn't say that."

"It's because I know you that I can say it. You say you want to avenge your parents, but I feel in your hands something different. That isn't the reason you've come this far. You have a gentle heart. It doesn't want to fight."

Katsu yanked away his hands like Chiyo had stabbed them. His eyes were huge.

"What is it?" Chiyo asked. "Did I say something wrong?"

Katsu held taut for several seconds before he gradually relaxed. "I'm sorry," he said. "Long ago, someone I cared about a lot said something similar to me. I never thought I'd hear those words again, especially not here in Shikari."

Chiyo made up her mind. "Katsu, please stay. We need you. Goro and I have a hard time keeping the farm going. We struggle every year just to feed ourselves and pay our tribute to Hiabi. Thanks to your help, we could have our best harvest in centuries."

"What about Goro?" Katsu asked. "What about Melwar?"

Chiyo winced, as much from the mention of Lord Melwar's name as her husband's. The lack of honorific showed how Katsu thought about the noble. He considered Lord Melwar an equal. He really was a ronin, someone of incredible status and power.

She wouldn't hesitate though. What she'd told him was true. They did need his help. But more important, Chiyo sensed, in a way she couldn't express, that Katsu needed their help too.

"Let me handle Goro," she said. "I was weak this morning, but not anymore. I'll make sure he understands. It's best if you don't come for dinner tonight, but be around for breakfast tomorrow. I'll straighten it out by then."

Katsu was motionless a moment. Then he stepped back. He bowed so low his eyes faced the ground.

Chiyo blushed. "A highborn shouldn't bow to a farmer's wife."

The man straightened. "I'm a ronin," he said, like it was as basic an admission as saying he was male. "I'll bow to anyone who earns my respect."

Chiyo smiled. She had made the right choice. There was something broken inside this man. Maybe together, they could fix it.

CHAPTER TEN
Leverage

Elyssa Orianna, mayor of Kataile, sat on her padded silver throne doing something she almost never did: tap her foot.

The nerve of that man! He was late. He was just like his father.

A loud, echoing knock came at the door. Elyssa knew it must be him. Any of her guards or couriers would have given a tentative strike. This person had no such reluctance. He walked his course straight ahead, without shame.

"Come in," Elyssa said, forcing down her emotions. No matter who he might look or act like, Balear was Balear.

The one-armed man entered the chamber. Elyssa motioned for her guards to exit.

The last time she'd asked them for privacy with Balear, they'd looked on the edge of defiance. Today none of them hesitated.

"Shut the door," Elyssa commanded when she and Balear were alone. She had to be in charge of him. Balear understood order, discipline, and rank. Elyssa needed to establish where each of them sat in relation to the other.

Balear did as instructed. That was a good start.

"I've heard a curious rumor," Elyssa said. She leaned back in her throne. "I understand you broke the fountain on the third level."

The former general shrugged. If he had any regrets about his action, he kept them hidden. That was like Balio too. "The Auryozaki isn't a delicate weapon," he said, as though that were all the explanation warranted.

"I trust you intend to pay for the damage."

The corners of Balear's mouth tightened. "Not at all," he replied.

Of course he didn't. There was no way a wandering traitor could replace a broken fountain. This just meant Elyssa could get more work out of him in retribution. He had walked right into her trap. She put a hand to her chest in mock surprise. "What?" she asked. "Are you suggesting the town should bear the cost for your irresponsible actions?"

The general's face grew stern. "No," he said, "I'm saying it should be left as it is."

His seriousness took Elyssa aback. "But it cannot stay that way," she countered. "We're a tourist town. We survive by being clean and beautiful."

Balear's expression did not relent. "All the more reason to leave it. It'll be a good reminder. Far worse destruction will befall Kataile if another city attacks. If your people are so angered by that small blemish, then it should encourage them not to let any more happen."

Elyssa's eyebrow twitched. She had no response to that.

"If that's all, Lady Orianna," Balear said, "I'm missing a training session."

Elyssa chewed her lip. Balear was like Balio in several ways, but this sternness was different. Balio was always relaxed. He was the rare man who could cross lines, equally comfortable wining and dining with Kataile's elite as he was belting out bawdy tunes in a portside tavern.

Balear wasn't that man. If people listened to him, it was through the sheer force of his presence. He could do what no man—not even Balio—had ever done to Elyssa.

He could intimidate her.

Those indomitable blue eyes were still on her. She couldn't bear them, but neither could she let him have the advantage. There was only one way to take back the initiative.

She smiled. "Actually, there is one more thing," she said. "I thought you might want to hear more about how I knew Balio."

That got his attention. Balear's shoulders slackened. His eyes lost their fire.

Elyssa kept up her warm expression, but inside her grin was more devious. Every man had a weakness she could exploit. For some it was money. For others it was sex. For Balear it was knowledge of his father.

"Tell me," Balear said.

"I trust you know your father served as a bodyguard aboard Lodian ships. Even though Ceere was closer to his home, Kataile was his port of choice. Do you know why?"

Balear shook his head. Elyssa forced herself not to smirk. "It was because of me. If he boarded in Kataile, he would get to see me."

The soldier's lone hand clenched. "Are you telling me my father had an affair?"

The challenge in his voice made Elyssa flinch. "Nothing like that," she stammered, off balance again despite herself. "We were friends. Much to my disappointment, that's all we ever were."

Balear's hand relaxed. "I should get back to the men. Farewell."

Elyssa frowned. So even knowledge of his father wasn't an effective tool.

It was time to up the stakes. She hadn't wanted to use this weapon so soon, but it might be the only way to rein in Balear before he swept control of her city out from under her.

"One moment, Balear," Elyssa said. "Your father and I might only have been friends, but I was closest to him among all the learned class in Kataile. The last time I saw him alive, he asked me for a favor. You see, your father never learned to read or write. That day, he wanted me to record his thoughts on a scroll, a scroll that was to be read only by his son."

Balear went limp. His arm trembled. "I was a toddler when my father left. Why would he leave a scroll for me?"

"When you read it, you'll understand."

"Where is it?" Balear asked. He seemed to choke on the words. "Is it here?"

She had him. "I wouldn't risk it being left in the open," Elyssa said. "I keep it under lock and key. I'll tell you what. I plan on visiting you tomorrow during your training session. I want to observe it. If I like what I see, perhaps I'll show you the scroll."

Balear cocked an eyebrow. "And if you don't like what you see?"

Elyssa gave him her most mysterious smile, one honed over two decades of politics. "Then I'll show it to everyone."

CHAPTER ELEVEN
Hana!

The next day Balear returned to the square on Kataile's third level. Ahead of him the fountain was still smashed, but aside from that, everything about this place felt different from two days ago. All one hundred and ten officers had shown up and given Balear their utmost attention, even Pito.

Their path forward was simple. Balear, Riac, and Dirio couldn't teach a thousand men by themselves, so instead they would teach the teachers. The trio would work with the officers to hone their skills with various weapons and formations. The officers in turn would instruct their squads and companies.

All around Balear the officers drilled, sweat heavy on their brows and uniforms even though the afternoon was cold. They were breathing hard, yet no one showed any sign of backing off in his efforts.

No one, that was, except Balear himself. His thoughts kept returning to what Elyssa had said. His father had left a message just for him? The way Elyssa had described it, it must have been written after Dad had left Tropos for good.

What had he written, and why would Elyssa threaten Balear with its public release? Balio Platarch was one of Lodia's heroes, especially in Kataile. Countless merchants lived and prospered today only because he had saved them from pirates. What in that scroll could be so damning that it would override that legacy?

Balear shook away the question. He needed to focus. Whatever the scroll said, the message would be meaningless if Kataile fell.

Balear scanned the officers, looking for someone who needed help. As he did, he spied Riac. The veteran circled among the men, correcting errors and offering words of encouragement.

Balear smiled to himself. He'd had a stroke of luck in finding that one. Riac was more motivated than any of them, and he could speak to the Katailans with a familiarity that Balear could never have.

As he continued to look over the assembly, Balear's smile shifted into a grimace. Out of the corner of his eye he noticed an auburn-haired woman walking down the steps from the fourth level to the square. Even before he saw her face, he could tell by her precise walk who she was.

"Lady Orianna," he said when she arrived, "I'm glad you could make it. Welcome to our training session. It's going well."

"Indeed," the mayor replied. She looked over the men. "I can't tell if you've inspired their loyalty, or if they're just curious what stunt you might pull next."

"As long as they train with everything they have, I don't really care about their reasons."

The pair watched the officers in silence for some time. At length Elyssa murmured, "Now that you have them motivated, what comes next? You can't win this war with a few drills."

Balear hesitated. The image of a scroll flashed before his eyes. Elyssa had him at her mercy. He had to keep her happy.

But more important, he had to protect Lodia. He couldn't do that by lying to Elyssa, so he said, "You can't win this war."

The mayor reacted as well as Balear had expected. She whipped to face him, her eyes sharper than the Auryozaki. "What?" she snapped.

Balear forced himself to stay calm. Elyssa might not like it, but she would respond to logic, and Balear had reasoned it through after his first day with Kataile's officers. "No matter how much your soldiers train, they're only a thousand men," he said. "With a force that small you can't conquer even one city, let alone all of them. Also, if you sent your forces on a campaign, you would leave Kataile defenseless. Another city could sweep in and conquer you."

"Then what do you want me to do, oh great general? Sit here and wait for them to come to us?"

The corners of Balear's mouth rose. "That's exactly what I propose."

"How is cowering here supposed to win us the war?"

Balear shook his head. "I just told you, you can't win the war. If you want to sit on Lodia's throne someday, your only chance lies in a peaceful solution. You need to convince the other mayors to hold the Succession Council."

"That seems far-fetched, considering I don't have any communication with them."

"True, but if I'm right, that won't matter. For now, we need to—"

Balear cut off. It couldn't have been.

"Balear?" Elyssa said. "Balear!" She waved her hand in front of his face.

He ignored her, his attention on a group of civilians rushing along the square's periphery. They were headed down to the docks. A merchant ship was leaving for Tacumsah this afternoon, and the last longboats out to it were due to depart soon. The people rushing were probably last-minute boarders.

And in the middle of that group had been a young woman with sleek black hair.

Balear had only seen her face for a second, but that had been enough. That face haunted his dreams.

It belonged to Hana.

The memories flooded back. Hana. The woman who had rescued Balear and Iren in Orcsthia, the woman who had hidden her Stone Dragon Knight powers at the cost of Balear's arm, the woman who had cried over him minutes before abandoning him for his best friend, was here in Kataile.

Balear barely noticed Elyssa's hard gaze on him. The soldiers kept practicing, but he no longer paid them any mind either. All his focus was on the Maantec hiding in plain sight among the crowd.

He had to talk to her. He stepped toward the throng.

"Where are you going?" Elyssa snapped. "We're not finished here."

Balear looked at the mayor, then back at the group of merchants. In that brief moment, Hana had disappeared.

Had he really seen her? Maybe it was an illusion, a trick of his imagination. There were so many questions he wanted to ask her. He could have just seen someone who looked like her.

He couldn't take that chance. If the woman Balear had seen was Hana, then she must be headed for that ship to Tacumsah. She could be on it in moments. The merchants had already left the square and started down the stairs toward the docks. They traveled at a run now, racing to avoid missing their ride. There was no time to delay.

"I have to go," he said.

Elyssa surely made some remark, but Balear didn't hear her. He was already racing to catch up with the merchants.

Balear chased them down Kataile's steep steps into the port district. The tang of fresh fish assaulted his nostrils. Short, wooden shacks dotted the area seemingly at random, turning the whole port into a maze.

The crowds were dense here. Balear couldn't even pick out the merchants anymore, let alone one person among them.

He wouldn't give up. "Hana!" he shouted. If she heard him call her name, maybe she would turn her head in response. "Hana!"

His shout had the opposite effect. Balear already stood out thanks to his missing arm and the seven-foot-long sword on his back. Half the people in earshot turned to regard him.

It didn't stop him. He charged through the crowd, parting it like a ship through water. "Hana!" he cried as he ran. "It's Balear! Hana, wait!"

A whistle sounded from the bay. Balear cursed. It was a ship's call, signaling to other vessels that it was leaving port. Balear reached the docks just in time to see two longboats rowing hard toward a caravel two hundred feet out.

"Hana!" he cried one last time, though he knew it was futile. The people on the longboats couldn't hear him over the water, and they were too far away for Balear to identify anyone.

All the same, he waited at the dock until the longboats reached the ship. Then, as it turned toward open ocean, Balear trudged his way back to the square.

Elyssa was waiting for him where he'd left her. Her foot clicked against the stone as she tapped it repeatedly.

"What on Raa were you thinking?" she demanded.

The one-armed general looked over his shoulder toward the ocean. The ship was a dot from this distance. "Nothing," he finally said. "A ghost from the past. I was imagining things. Let's get back to work. What were we discussing again?"

ଔ

Hana Akiyama stood at the *Sparkling Dawn*'s stern as the caravel left the Bay of Kataile. Her hands gripped the rail so hard she left divots in the wood.

Balear had been right there, shouting her name. It had taken every shred of willpower she possessed not to turn around.

She couldn't let herself see him. When she returned to Shogun Melwar's side, he would ask her if she had seen the Sky Dragon Knight in her journey. This way she could tell him the truth. No, she hadn't.

CHAPTER TWELVE
The Things Trees Know

Minawë and Lyubo had tracked their quarry since dawn. They had yet to lay eyes on it, but Lyubo insisted they were getting close.

"These tracks couldn't have been made more than an hour ago," he said, gesturing at the spots in the mud. "They're close together too, which means he's moving slowly. We'll catch him before we have to get back to the group."

Minawë hoped so. Everyone was counting on them.

She wiped her brow. Midafternoon in the rainforest was a poor time to be active. The humidity clung to her skin, and her leather outfit gripped her in all sorts of uncomfortable ways.

"Hold up," Lyubo said. "Let's take a break."

"And let him get farther ahead of us?"

"He isn't on the run. Besides, determination's no good if it gets you killed. You'll dehydrate tracking all day. You need to drink up."

Minawë lifted her water skin, but Lyubo put out a hand. "That's for emergencies," he said. "Here in the wild, you rely on the forest as much as you can. Check these out."

He walked to a nearby tangle of vines each as thick as Minawë's forearm. "These will be our water supply," he said.

Minawë cocked an eyebrow.

"Watch." Lyubo pulled out his machete and hacked off a three-foot section of vine. He raised one end, and a few drops came out the bottom. He let them fall on his hand.

"They're clear," he said, "and they don't burn. This one's good to drink." Lyubo tilted back his head and raised the vine above it. Minawë thought he'd only get a little, but water gushed from the vine like it was a giant cup.

Lyubo wiped his mouth. "Now you try," he said. He handed her his machete.

Minawë cut off a chunk and raised it above her head. Before she could tilt it though, Lyubo grabbed the vine. "Test it first," he said.

She shrugged and lowered the plant. She did as he had and let a small amount pour onto her hand. It was milky white and stung her skin.

"Some of the vines are poisonous," Lyubo said. "There's no way to know which ones unless you test them. If you'd drunk that, it probably wouldn't have killed you, but you wouldn't have had a comfortable night either."

Minawë dropped the vine and tried another one. This time the liquid ran clear. She looked to Lyubo, and he nodded. She raised the vine above her head and drank. The water was warm but refreshing.

"All right," Lyubo said when Minawë had drained the last drops, "let's get after our quarry again. He won't escape this time."

They traveled another hour before Minawë felt a tingle from the plants around her. She reached a hand out and touched one of the trees. Her eyes closed. A few hundred feet out, something large shuffled through the forest. It was bigger than any Kodama by at least a hundred pounds.

She gulped. "He's close," she whispered. "He isn't aware of us yet, but he's facing our direction. He'll see us before we get in range."

Lyubo's gaze drifted to where Minawë's hand touched the tree. He examined the spot for a few seconds before saying, "In that case, let's get up in the canopy."

He swung his arm around a low-hanging branch and leapt up. Using the multi-layered forest, he climbed higher and higher like a monkey.

Minawë frowned. She didn't think she could manage the complex maneuvers Lyubo had just done. Fortunately, she knew a better way. Pulling out the Chloryoblaka, she transformed into a sparrow and fluttered up to meet her fellow Kodama.

Lyubo folded his arms. "That's cheating."

Minawë returned to her Kodaman form, ran a hand through her long green hair, and winked. "Not for me."

"We'll work on your climbing tomorrow," Lyubo pressed. "You may not always be able to rely on Dendryl's magic."

Minawë doubted that would be the case. Still, the idea of learning to leap among the trees like Lyubo got her excited, so she kept her feelings to herself.

Lyubo looked ahead of them down to the jungle floor. "You were right," he said. "There he is."

Minawë followed his gaze. Sure enough, she saw a shifting brown mass two hundred feet in front of them. "I can't get a solid view through all the brush," she said.

"That's no problem," Lyubo replied. "We'll go from tree to tree until we get a clear shot."

He took off, moving with a practiced precision that made Minawë jealous. She changed back into a sparrow. Cheating or not, she wasn't about to let her poor climbing spook their opponent.

A hundred feet from the target, Lyubo stopped. Minawë transformed again. She could see it clearly now.

"So that's a tapir?" she whispered.

Lyubo nodded but said nothing.

It was a weird animal, to be sure. It walked on four legs like most of the forest creatures Minawë had grown up with, but it was shorter and stockier than them.

It was heavier too. Only Ziorsecth's bears could match it in weight.

The animal's strangest feature, though, was its snout. Instead of a short nose, it had a long trunk that extended past its mouth. The tapir was using that trunk to grasp low-hanging branches and strip them of leaves.

"I have a shot," Lyubo murmured.

Minawë eyed up the scout. He had his bow out and an arrow nocked. Lyubo was a skilled marksman, and Minawë had no doubt he would hit the tapir at this range.

Yet something made her reach out and touch his bow. He looked at her quizzically, and in answer she pulled out the Chloryoblaka. He smiled and put his own bow away.

Minawë sized up her target. To Lyubo the tapir was food for the traveling Kodamas. To Minawë he was something more. She had connected with plants and animals in the past. She heard their voices in her sleep, and at times even when she was awake. Lyubo could hit the tapir, but his single arrow wouldn't bring down a beast this large. The Chloryoblaka had more power in it than Lyubo's short bow. If they were going to kill this animal, Minawë would do it quickly and cleanly.

After a long wait, Minawë exhaled. Her fingers released.

She felt a brief stab of pain as the tapir died and its voice ended. "Thank you," she said, "and I'm sorry."

Lyubo was already climbing down the tree. Minawë transformed into a sparrow and flew to the tapir's body before changing back.

"That was a great shot," Lyubo said. "I don't know if I could have done that."

"Let's just get it dressed and head back," she replied. She appreciated his praise, but it wasn't something she wanted to be praised for.

Lyubo took the hint and got to work in silence. Minawë helped. She had felled the tapir; the least she could do was be respectful of it. At first Lyubo tried to keep her away, but he soon gave up.

The meat was a lot even for both of them to carry, but Minawë refused to let any of it go to waste. Lyubo packaged it in two skins he'd brought with him in his pack, and he handed one to Minawë. Dinner for the group secured, they started back toward the others.

Minawë led the way. In spite of the wrapped meat weighing her down, she walked without hesitation.

"I'm impressed," Lyubo said from behind her. "This path should put us on a direct line back to the others. But how did you know exactly where they are? That takes complex estimates of how far both we and they have gone today as well as precise knowledge of directions. It's a challenge even for me, and I've scouted in Aokigahara for centuries."

"The forest tells me," Minawë said. "The trees know what's moving among them. They have to so they can protect themselves from threats. If you can hear their voices, they'll tell you what's around."

"Can they tell the difference between a Kodama and a Yokai?"

"It's not that they have names for them, but you can get a good idea from what they do know. I sensed the tapir because it was big, heavy, and alone. I can sense the group because of the number of people and the way they're walking."

Lyubo paused. "That's how Lord Narunë knew you and Rondel were approaching our camp."

"The trees' roots likely felt the vibrations of two animals moving toward him, both on two feet. He figured it had to be us."

"That would be an amazing skill for a tracker to have," Lyubo said.

"You can't do it?" Minawë asked. "I thought since Uncle could do it, lots of Kodamas could."

Lyubo shook his head. "You two are part of the Kodaman royal family. I don't know of anyone in Sorengaral who tracks by listening to the trees."

Minawë smiled. "It's not that hard once you can hear the trees' voices. Why don't I teach you? We're at most an hour from the others, and we have plenty of daylight left."

"Why not?" Lyubo said. He set down his pack and the meat he'd been carrying. "My arms could use a rest anyway."

Minawë put her load next to Lyubo's and walked to the largest nearby tree. "This one will do well," she said. "She's old, so she'll have a lot of stories."

Lyubo didn't look convinced. Minawë placed her left palm against the tree's bark. "Like this," she said.

Her fellow Kodama mimicked her. "What am I supposed to hear?" he asked.

Minawë shut her eyes. "It isn't what you'll hear," she said. "It's what you'll feel. Trees aren't like Kodamas or tapirs. They live slow, steady lives. Their voices are vibrations, hums in the forest."

There was a pause, then, "I don't hear anything. Or feel anything. It just feels like bark."

Minawë already had the thrum of the tree's voice echoing through her mind. How could she help Lyubo experience it? Uncle Narunë could connect with the trees even though he wasn't a Dragon Knight, so surely Lyubo could do it too.

An idea came to her. "I couldn't hear the voices for most of my life either," she said. "I had to be the Forest Dragon Knight before I became sensitive enough to connect with them." She pulled the Chloryoblaka from her back and held it out with her right hand. "Grab onto this," she said. "Keep your other hand on the tree. Maybe you'll hear the tree through me and Dendryl."

Minawë let herself sink deeper into the tree's soft rhythm. The old woman indeed had lots to tell. She told of fires old and new, of rains that flooded, of countless animals that had wandered past. But she did not know what to make of the pair touching her, nor of the circle the three of them made.

The circle . . .

Minawë's eyes snapped open. She looked to her right. She hadn't noticed before because she'd been connected with the tree, but now it was obvious. When she'd told Lyubo to hold the Chloryoblaka, he'd misunderstood.

He'd grabbed her hand instead.

"I never realized trees could share so much with us," Lyubo said. "You've opened a new world for me."

Minawë said nothing. Lyubo opened his eyes and looked at her. "What's wrong?" he asked.

She pulled away. Her heart smacked against her chest. "It. . .it's nothing. It's getting late. We'd better hurry, or Uncle will worry about us."

They gathered their supplies and the meat from the tapir. Within a few minutes they set off.

Their journey back to the others took another hour. The whole time, Minawë kept silent.

It wasn't because Lyubo had upset her. It was because he hadn't.

CHAPTER THIRTEEN
Mizuchi

When Hana Akiyama arrived at Awakimundi, the largest of the Tacumsah Islands, she had never been more grateful. She'd spent most of the three-week voyage in her cabin trying not to vomit. She'd failed miserably.

More unsettling than her seasickness had been the loss of her dragon's magic. At almost six feet long the Stone Dragon Hammer wasn't a subtle weapon. There was no way she could have had it aboard without everyone on the ship knowing. Instead she'd let it follow her belowground as it always did. Out in the ocean, though, the distance between them had been miles.

Even had she been able to bring it on the ship, the hammer's power would have been useless. There'd been nothing but water all the way to the horizon in every direction.

Hana rushed off the gangplank and jogged down the wooden pier until she reached the shore. When her feet struck the sand, she laughed aloud. She didn't care who saw her. She took off her shoes and rubbed her bare toes in the beach. The Stone Dragon Hammer met her, the tip of its long handle pressing against the bottom of her heel.

The moment Hana felt her dragon's magic, she used it to harden her skin into her invisible layer of armor. The lack of that armor had been the most disquieting part of the journey. Alone on a ship of primitive, low-class thugs, anyone could have attacked her. More than once she'd felt a crewman's eyes on her. She would have held her own had it come to a fight, but she hated the idea of those filthy humans touching her bare skin.

With her armor in place and magic restored, Hana at last felt comfortable enough to take in her surroundings. The Tacumsah Archipelago was famous throughout Raa for its surpassing beauty, and Hana could see how it had earned that reputation. Awakimundi was lush with palm trees and forests that reminded Hana of Aokigahara, though less dense and therefore more inviting. The white-sand beach around her was flat, and the island sloped up gradually to its peak in the center.

Oval-shaped wooden huts dotted the island's perimeter. Most were here around the dock, but a few were scattered about in rough villages of perhaps thirty or forty inhabitants.

None of the homes looked like anything special. They didn't even have walls; they were just simple pole structures. Roughly constructed, they used a mishmash of logs, driftwood, and broken planks. Thatched palm fronds formed their domed roofs.

The huts looked even more pathetic compared with the island's most dominating feature. Atop the mountain at its center sat a castle that matched Haldessa's before its fall. The stone structure was the tallest point on the island, and its eight turrets aligned with the four cardinal directions and their midpoints.

That castle was the place to start. With that vantage point, Hana would be able to see every part of the island.

Yet even as she started walking, Hana felt doubt gnaw at her. She had no idea where the Water Dragon Knight might be, or even who he or she was. The Tacumsah Archipelago had more than a hundred islands, and while Awakimundi was the largest, most had at least a few hundred residents. If she had to search them all, she would never find her quarry.

Hana left the beach and headed inland. She initially had to dodge large groups of dark-skinned Tacumsahens working near the docks. After fifteen minutes though, she passed through the rings of huts and found her way to a packed-sand road that led toward the castle.

As she hiked, Hana marveled at the stone structure before her. It had an architecture unlike anything she had seen in either Lodia or Hiabi. In contrast to the sharp angles of Lodian design, or the graceful concave arcs of Hiabi's keep, this castle had a teardrop shape. The southwest-facing portion was wide and bulging, while the part opposite it tapered to a point. The turrets all bore a similar cross section.

"She's a beauty, ya?" a slow, musical voice called from behind Hana. She jumped. She hadn't noticed that she'd stopped walking to gawk at the castle.

Hana turned around. Approaching her was a dark-skinned man of medium build, perhaps twenty years old. He wore simple clothes: a wide-brimmed straw hat, short-sleeved linen shirt and shorts, and straw sandals. In one arm he carried a stick with a cloth satchel tied to the end.

"By de glory of Mizuchi," the man said, "now she's lookin' right at me!"

Hana started. Mizuchi was the Water Dragon. What did this bum know about him? Could he be the Water Dragon Knight?

She doubted it. The man was unarmed, and there was no way he could fit even a weapon as small as Rondel's Liryometa in that satchel. If this guy was the Water Dragon Knight, he didn't have the Zuryokaiten with him.

Still, the man was the best lead Hana had for the moment, so she decided to play along. "Hey," she said, twirling her hair, "were you talking about the castle just now, or me?"

"Well you are both beautiful, ya?" the man answered with a fast, low laugh that came from deep in his chest. He walked up to Hana and offered his free right hand. "I'm Faro."

Hana shook the man's hand reluctantly. It was smooth and supple, not what she expected of a drifter.

"Hana," she replied. "I'm from Lodia."

"Long way for a young lady to come," Faro said. "What brings you to Awakimundi?"

His voice was like the waves on a beach. The words flowed into each other without a care on Raa. Hana could get used to it.

She could also get used to his eyes. They were black, with no difference between the iris and pupil. Others might find them creepy, but Hana wanted to fall into those bottomless pools of night.

She shook her head to clear the thought. She was here on a mission. "The Lodian civil war," she lied. She had practiced this potential conversation numerous times on the ship. "My parents were sheep-herders, and they died early on in the fighting. I scrounged up what money was left in the farm and bought one-way passage here. I figured I'd start my life over."

"Well, you picked a good place to do it. Tacumsah's de safest place in de world dese days. I'm sure you can make a good life here. If you need help findin' your way around, you just ask anyone where old Faro is. I'll help you out."

"That's kind of you," Hana said. She blushed. "I do have one question, if you don't mind. You mentioned 'Mizuchi' when we first met. What's that mean?"

Faro threw back his head and laughed. "Hoo, if you don't even know Mizuchi, you got a lot to learn about Tacumsah. Tell you what. I'm headed to de castle. Why don't you come with me? You can learn about Mizuchi dere."

Hana smiled. "That sounds wonderful."

They walked up the sandy trail together. With each step, the castle's proportions came more and more into focus. Hana had thought it looked huge from the shore, but as they neared it, she realized she had underestimated it. It wasn't as large as Hiabi, but it dwarfed the former Haldessa Castle.

"Who rules that place?" she asked.

Faro smiled. "Dat's de home of Awakimundi's chief, Iokua."

Hana looked over her shoulder at the distant beach. The huts along it were almost invisible now. "It's hard to believe he could command such a place," she said. "There's such disparity of wealth here. You'd think the people would overthrow him."

She turned back around to find Faro staring at her. "You say fancy stuff for a farm girl," he said.

Hana swore inside her head. She was supposed to be playing the ignorant sheepherder. "I guess it's the civil war," she improvised. "I can't get away with only thinking about whether my sheep are fed anymore. I don't want to have traveled all this way just to get caught up in another war."

Faro's solid black eyes bored into her another moment. Then he laughed, reached out, and touched her on the shoulder. "No worries, ya? You're not in Lodia anymore. What happened dere can't happen here."

"Why? Because Iokua has a big army?"

"No, because he rules at de will of de people. A chief who doesn't share isn't chief long." He pointed at the fortress ahead of them. "See dat castle? Iokua lives in it, but he doesn't own it. De people of Awakimundi own it. When de storms come, dat's where dey go. Everyone on de island takes shelter dere."

"The storms?"

Faro nodded. "Dey come every year, always from de southwest. Not every island gets hit every year, but it's hard to go ten without one hittin' you. When dey come, most homes on de beach get destroyed. If people stayed in dem, dey'd die. So dey go to de castle. Every island in Tacumsah has one. De bigger de island, de bigger de castle."

Hana examined the castle more closely. Its teardrop shape no longer seemed random. It was deliberate. If the winds came from the southwest, they would flow around the oddly shaped structure. It could withstand nature's wrath, even when the rest of the island was being torn apart.

She was more surprised by Faro's description of Chief Iokua. He voluntarily opened his home to all the people of his island, even the lowest of the low. No Maantec would do that. Lowborn Maantecs would sully everything. They had to be held in check through power, through magic. Highborn Maantecs and Dragon Knights could wield magic the lower classes couldn't hope to conjure. That kept the people in their place.

Here, though, the leader was one of the people. It made no sense.

But then, Faro must be a low-class citizen, judging by his outfit and miniscule pack. He wouldn't fit in at a Maantec fortress, but here he didn't seem out of place at all.

The pair arrived at the castle entrance. Hana expected a heavy gate with guards, but instead they came to a wide arch with a cascade of orchids adorning either side.

Hana and Faro crossed the threshold without anyone questioning them. Hana swiveled her head in search of soldiers, but she couldn't spot anyone armed. It was unheard of. No city was so well protected that it had no need of guards.

Faro seemed to guess her thoughts. "No one would dream of attacking a Tacumsahen castle. Dey're too important to people's survival. To come here with intent to destroy is de worst crime a man can commit. It's a crime against everyone on Awakimundi."

Hana worked hard not to look at her feet, at the Enryokiri buried just beneath them. If the Water Dragon Knight was in one of these island castles, odds were the fortress wouldn't survive their battle.

"Follow me," Faro said, waving his arm in a wide arc. "I'll show you Mizuchi."

Hana jumped at that. "Please," she replied, "I'm excited to learn more about him."

Faro led Hana through the castle courtyard. Rather than grass or sand, a mix of short trees and five-foot shrubs laden with colorful fruits adorned the area.

Hana had never seen fruits like these before. "What are those?" she asked, as much for her own curiosity as it was to keep with her farm-girl character.

"Oranges," Faro said as he pointed at one tree, "and de ones near de ground are pineapples. Bet you never had dem in Lodia, ya?"

Hana had traveled from one end of Raa to the other, but she'd never heard of a pineapple. The fruit didn't look at all appetizing, what with all those spikes and sword-like leaves sticking out of it.

"In here," Faro called. He opened a wooden door that led to a stone staircase. Hana thought it would head up to enter the castle keep, but instead it led underground. She followed Faro, and together they walked down the steps.

Aside from the stairs, the passage lacked any sign of manmade construction. The walls were curved and smooth, like any natural cavern in Shikari.

"Underground, de storms don't blow," Faro said. "Dis is de safest place on de whole island. Dat's why Mizuchi's here."

Hana's heart fluttered. Why Mizuchi was here! Faro was taking her to the Zuryokaiten!

The steps led farther and farther down. Hana lost track of how many they'd walked. Torches lined the cave walls, so they had plenty of light.

The deeper they went, the wetter it became. The walls glistened with water, and Hana had to watch her step on the slick stairs. The air was much cooler in here than outside, like going from the middle of summer to late fall in a few moments. If anything, it was more humid here than in the tropical climate outside.

At last the steps ended at a door, this one made of blue stone. "Mizuchi's in here," Faro said as he pulled the door open.

Hana couldn't help but rush in first. It wasn't in character, but she couldn't restrain her anticipation. If the Water Dragon's weapon was in this room, she could take it and be on a ship back to Lodia before nightfall.

The room was forty feet across and dome-shaped. Seafoam green tiles coated both the walls and the floor. At the far end was a circular pool of water ten feet in diameter.

Three rows of carved stone pews separated Hana from the pool. A smattering of people sat in them, lost in silent prayer. Candles on sconces lit the room, and they gave everything in it a warm, soothing glow. Hana smiled despite herself.

The room's focal point was a painting that hung suspended above the pool by a pair of metal chains. Mounted in a gold frame, the image depicted a steel-gray sea serpent wreathed by a tidal wave. Flecks of gold accentuated the beast's wingless curves, and golden hairs cascaded down its spine.

Hana walked as close as she could to the painting without falling in the pool. The frame bore a plaque at the bottom: "Mizuchi, the Water Dragon."

She sighed. So that was it. There was no Ryokaiten here after all. It was just a place to worship the Water Dragon himself. Divinion had once possessed a similar shrine in Haldessa Castle, though the Lodians had long since forgotten its purpose.

Hana turned back to face Faro, and she was shocked to see the worshippers had stopped praying. They glared at Faro as though he were a demon. He strode up to Hana. "Dis is Mizuchi," he said. "Is he what you expected?"

"Not exactly," Hana admitted.

Faro knelt before the painting and folded his hands. Hana hadn't expected the carefree bum to be religious. Low-class or not, he impressed her more with each second.

At length Faro unfolded his hands and reached for the bundle at the end of his stick. He untied the knot, and all his possessions were laid bare for Hana to see. There wasn't much: four slices of dried fruit, a leather bladder that Hana guessed held water, and a metal hip flask that likely held something stronger.

The only strange object was a steel rod no longer or wider than Hana's index finger. Before Hana could get a good look at it, Faro snagged it, dipped it in the pool, and closed his eyes.

Hana heard rustling behind her. She craned her head around, instinctively expecting an attack.

Sure enough, one of the worshippers was on his feet, fists clenched. Another man held him back, murmuring in his ear. Hana couldn't tell what the man said, but it was clear this pool was off-limits.

If Faro noticed or cared about the angry worshippers, he didn't signal it. He stayed in his position for more than a minute before he rose and retied his bundle.

Hana looked at the pool and frowned. The water line had changed. It had dropped almost six inches from its previous level.

"Sorry to leave you, Hana," Faro said, "but Iokua expects me. I should amble on up dere."

Hana was taken aback. The island's chief wanted to see this drifter? She couldn't help herself. "You have an appointment with Iokua?"

Faro laughed his rapid laugh. "Oh, I forgot to tell you my full name! Dey call me Faro de Magnificent. I'm de greatest conjurer of de Tacumsah Islands!" He gave her an exaggerated bow. "If you're stickin' around, you should see my show tonight. I perform for de chief dis evening, but afterward I give a special show for de people by de docks. I'll see you dere, ya? It'll be a lovely night to spend time on de beach!" He winked.

Hana's smile was strained. "I just came from down there, but maybe you'll see me. I don't have anywhere else to be right now."

Faro grinned and bowed again. Then he headed back up the stairs.

The moment Faro left, Hana's smile disappeared. When the man had bowed to her the first time, that's when she had seen it. He had thrown his arm out to the side, and in that second, he'd shown Hana the steel rod's face. It had three concentric kanji rings on it.

That rod was the Zuryokaiten. That charming man was the Water Dragon Knight.

And now Hana had to kill him.

CHAPTER FOURTEEN
Battle in the Past

Iren Saitosan crouched in the forest north of Goro and Chiyo's farm. His eyes focused on the array of rocks, trees, and fallen logs before him. He'd run through these woods every evening for three weeks straight. He always started from a different place and ran in a different direction. He didn't want familiarity with the terrain to influence the results.

"One more time," he said through gritted teeth. "Here we go."

He drew the Muryozaki and took off. Trees blazed past him. A boulder sprang into his vision. He almost tripped, but he saw how high the rock was and jumped just enough to clear it. The bottom of his leather boot tapped it ever so slightly, enough to give him a burst of speed.

As he landed, a fallen log threatened to send him spilling into the dirt. Iren put his empty right hand on it and vaulted over the dead tree without losing momentum.

Midway through his flip, he spun in midair so he landed facing to the left of the way he'd originally traveled. He shot off in this new direction. It wasn't good enough only to go in a straight line. Rondel was more than fast; she was precise and flexible too. Iren had to maneuver at least as quickly.

A clump of trees loomed ahead. They were too tightly packed to run between and too wide to run around. A week ago Iren would have slammed into them, but not anymore. He stepped onto one of their trunks, ran up the tree, then sprang off it so he landed pointed in the direction he'd come from. He ran back that way, appreciating the different perspective of the various obstacles.

Iren kept up the weaving, dodging, and sprinting for another hour before he decided it was enough. He returned to his cave and went inside.

This was the third time in as many days he'd run through the forest without so much as catching his foot on a loose stone. It was enough to convince him that it wasn't a fluke. He'd done it. He'd trained his eyes and mind to respond to high speed movement.

His pulse pounding as much from the thrill of success as from the run, Iren needed ten minutes before he could calm himself enough to enter his meditative state. He couldn't wait to tell Divinion the good news.

The Holy Dragon was waiting for him on the beach inside Iren's mind. Iren rushed to him, but Divinion was already smiling. "Well done," the dragon said.

Iren pouted. "You know, I was hoping to surprise you."

Divinion made his huffing laughter. "It's hard to surprise a god who can see all your memories."

"Good point. So do I pass?"

The dragon nodded his enormous square head. "I expected it to take you a month. It helps that you can work at high speed on Goro and Chiyo's farm."

"Now that they know I'm a ronin, there's no point in hiding my abilities from them. Goro still avoids me, but I think Chiyo likes the change. And if nothing else, I get my chores done faster."

"That's good," Divinion replied, "because the next part of your training will demand all the time you can find."

Iren tried not to let his excitement show, but he knew Divinion could sense it anyway. "What do I do next?" he asked.

"I could tell you," the dragon said, "but the best way for you to understand is to see it in a memory. Did you know that the night your parents died wasn't the first time Rondel and Iren Saito fought each other?"

Iren was taken aback. "I thought they loved each other up until the Kodama-Maantec War, and after that my father avoided Rondel. When did they fight?"

"More than twelve hundred years ago, when they were teenagers. It was part of their training to become mages. Before the Kodama-Maantec

War, Maantec nobles gained rank by defeating each other in one-on-one matches."

"Were they Dragon Knights at the time?"

Divinion shook his head. "Rondel hadn't even developed Lightning Sight when this battle took place. You'll have to view the fight from the perspective of your grandfather, Emperor Hideki Saito. But I shouldn't spoil the fun. Shall we?"

"Yes," Iren replied. "Show me the secret to defeating Rondel."

⚘

The world darkened a moment. When it lightened again, Iren sat in a plush box at the highest point of a massive arena. Thousands of Maantecs sat in the bleachers around and beneath him.

At the arena's center was a circular pit three hundred feet wide and thirty feet deep. Hard sand formed the ground, and stacked stone bricks lined the walls.

Emperor Hideki Saito pushed down his nervousness. He had to look confident for the crowd. They had all come for one purpose: to see the emperor's son fight the wonder child, the girl who had bested the prodigy Katashi Melwar: Rondel Thara.

Hideki stared down at Rondel on the arena floor. She was small and wiry even for a girl. Her dark brown hair was tied in a tight bun on top of her head, much like the favored style of her adopted mother, the Storm Dragon Knight Caly Thara.

Rondel's unassuming appearance meant nothing in this bout. For reasons no one could explain, the former farm girl had magic that surpassed the highest nobles. Adding to that natural talent, she had fighting skills and tactical prowess honed by Caly herself.

Despite all that, no one in the crowd called Rondel's name. They cheered only for Iren. They weren't about to root against him when his father was in attendance.

Hideki shifted his attention to his son. Iren didn't seem affected by the crowd. He'd fought in the arena before, so he knew what to expect. He would ignore the crowd and focus on his opponent.

That might be a problem. Hideki knew how his son felt about

Rondel. The boy had always been obstinate, rebelling against the order and hierarchy of the court. Rondel, a walking breach of etiquette, was an irresistible attraction.

A man in a white kimono ran onto the arena floor and positioned himself between the combatants. He called them over and had them stand ten feet apart.

Hideki couldn't hear the man over the crowd, but he'd seen and taken part in enough arena matches over the centuries to know the words by heart. "Don't leave the arena," he saw the proctor's mouth say. "You may not receive outside help. Aside from these restrictions, you may use any method to win. There is no time limit. The first to concede, lose consciousness, or die loses. Do you understand?"

Iren drew his katana and nodded. Across from him, Rondel pointed her dagger at Iren's stomach.

"Begin!" the proctor shouted, and then he had to leap out of the way as Iren shot toward Rondel.

Hideki smiled his approval. There was no point giving Rondel any more time to think than necessary. Strategy was her strength; Iren couldn't give her the space to use it.

Their blades clashed, and sparks cascaded from the impact. The crowd cheered, but neither fighter reacted to the sound.

Rondel launched a flurry of thrusts, so rapid even Hideki had difficulty tracking them all. With her short arm and weapon, Rondel could attack faster than Iren could block with his katana. He withdrew, using a flash of light to distract Rondel and buy him a second's worth of distance. He followed up with three quick beams fired from his right index, middle, and ring fingers.

An ordinary opponent would still be dealing with the second of blindness and have taken all three shots in the torso. Rondel, though, was far from ordinary. Rather than recover while standing still, she had run away even though she couldn't see. The arena had no obstacles, and Rondel was well away from the wall. She could regain her sight without risk.

The pair of fighters were now more than two hundred feet apart. Iren tried another light beam, but Rondel dodged it effortlessly.

Hideki frowned. Iren couldn't win at long range, because Rondel could avoid his spells. Nor could he win at close range, because Rondel's dagger could strike faster than Iren's katana. That left only one conclusion.

Iren couldn't win.

The boy looked up and locked eyes with Hideki. The message was clear. Iren also knew he was outmatched.

Rondel didn't take advantage of her foe's distraction. She must have guessed her victory too, and she was hoping Iren was smart enough to give up.

Hideki shared that hope. "Concede," he mouthed. "Concede."

It was dishonorable, but it was better than risking death. Iren was Hideki's only son and heir.

Iren sheathed his sword and held out his left hand, palm up. Hideki breathed a sigh of relief.

Then his chest tightened. Iren's mouth hadn't moved. He hadn't announced his withdrawal. He was going to continue the fight. But why? He had no spell that could overcome Rondel.

Unless . . .

Hideki leapt to his feet and pointed to his attendant in the back of the box. "Get down to the arena floor. Find the proctor. Tell him to stop the fight."

The attendant sucked air through his teeth. "Exalted Emperor, I don't understand. They've only just begun—"

"No time!" Hideki roared. "Get moving!"

The man nodded frantically and took off. Hideki turned back to the arena. A light appeared in Iren's palm. It grew and grew, brightening until Hideki couldn't look directly at it.

Fool of a child! Hideki could guess why his son was doing this. Iren, Hideki, and Rondel knew the fight's outcome, but the people in the stands didn't. All they'd seen were a few thrusts and a minor light show. Any noble with a year of training could do all that. Iren and Rondel were supposed to be the most talented young mages in a thousand years. The crowd expected a show.

More problematic, they expected Iren to win. He was a Saito, one of the divine imperial lineage. If he gave up without a fight, the Maantecs in the stadium would riot.

But if he released the spell he was preparing, they would die instead.

The light in Iren's palm churned and swirled as it took shape. It grew larger and brighter.

Then came the moment Hideki had dreaded. The light itself caught fire.

A *whoosh* filled the arena as the spell ignited. White flames shot six feet in the air.

Hideki gripped the rail of his box. Where was the attendant? Where was the proctor?

It was too late now. Hideki leapt over the box wall and landed hard on the bleachers in front of him. He charged through the spectators, heedless of the stares they gave him. He had only one thought: to stop this match before anyone got killed.

As Hideki neared the arena wall, Rondel charged across the sand toward Iren. She must have figured out the boy wasn't going to surrender. When she came within fifty feet, she threw out her right hand and shot a lightning bolt at the emperor's son.

It never reached him. The flames curled around Iren and warded off the blow.

Rondel closed to short range. She stabbed with her dagger, but again the flames acted as a shield.

Hideki landed on the arena floor and rushed toward the far end. The proctor had appeared by now too, but he was too far away.

It was for the best. Iren's spell demanded release. The farther away people were from him when it went off, the better.

Iren lunged at Rondel. She backed up, but Iren's speed matched hers. She couldn't get away from him. His palm reached out for her.

Just before Iren's spell brushed Rondel's clothes, a magenta blur flashed into the stadium. Hideki recognized the color as Caly Thara's formal clan kimono. The Storm Dragon Knight grabbed Rondel and fled backward, away from Iren's spell.

Unfortunately, that wouldn't save them. The boy's technique could be contained no longer. It erupted from his hand in a geyser of white flame.

The spell struck Rondel and Caly when they were forty feet away. Both screamed as the attack burned away their clothes and seared their flesh.

Hideki saw the panic on his son's face. He was trying desperately to make the spell stop, but that was impossible. The energy all had to come out. Once cast, there was no reversing it.

Finally Hideki was close enough. He drew the Muryozaki and poured magic into it. White light shot between Iren and Rondel. It formed a shield and deflected his son's technique up.

The two spells clashed for more than ten seconds, but at last Iren's magic was spent. He collapsed, his breath heaving.

Hideki ran to his son. He dropped to the sand alongside him. "Fool," the emperor murmured. "You damn fool."

CHAPTER FIFTEEN
Muryoka

Iren Saitosan snapped out of the memory. He was back on the beach inside his mind. He looked up at Divinion with wide eyes. "What . . ." he panted, "what the hell kind of an attack was that?"

Divinion didn't answer right away. He was looking across the ocean, his gaze fixed on something Iren couldn't see.

Suddenly the dragon reared back his head. He then thrust it forward, opened his mouth, and loosed a torrent of white flame. It shot across the imaginary ocean, boiling it in a second.

When the spell ended, water rushed to fill the space the flames had evaporated. The level of the surf dropped half a foot.

"Whoa," Iren said. It was all he could manage.

"You know the dragons once sank a continent," Divinion said. "Didn't you ever wonder how we did it? The dragons are gods, Iren. Together we contain enough magic to rip this world asunder."

Iren exhaled. "Then the spell my father used mimicked your breath."

"It's called Muryoka: Holy Dragon Fire. The first Holy Dragon Knight declared it forbidden, though plenty since him have defied his order. As you saw, the results aren't pleasant, and your father's was one of the better attempts. Most who use it die; the flames can consume the caster before he ever releases the magic. Even after casting though, a backwash of energy kills the caster if he's too close to the impact site. That nearly happened to your father. He would have died that day, but Hideki was smart enough to redirect Muryoka's energy up and away from the arena. That's the only reason your father, Rondel, and everyone else in that stadium survived. Even with Hideki's intervention, both Rondel and Caly Thara almost perished from their burns. Hideki healed them after the fight."

Iren put his hand on his head. "This is the spell you want me to learn? If I use it against Rondel, I'll wipe out whatever countryside we're fighting in, not to mention myself."

Divinion's penetrating stare locked eyes with him. "Muryoka is the only spell a Holy Dragon Knight has that can defeat Rondel. You said you wanted revenge. How far will you go to get it?"

Iren opened his mouth to respond, then shut it. Chiyo's words to him three weeks ago rang in his head. She believed he was gentle, that he didn't truly want revenge. Minawë had once told him the same thing.

But they were wrong, at least mostly. He would kill Rondel, but he wouldn't do it with this technique. "There must be another way," he said. "My father wasn't able to restrain his Muryoka at all. It was just blind destruction, like the time I lost control in Ziorsecth. If mere power was all I needed, you wouldn't have shown me that memory just now. There must be more to Muryoka than what my father cast."

Divinion smiled. "I was hoping you'd figure that out. Hold on a moment; there's something I want to show you."

The beach scene disappeared into darkness. When the landscape refilled, Iren and Divinion were in a vast mountain range. The peaks stretched beyond the clouds and as far in every direction as Iren could see.

The pair stood at the base of a cliff. Iren looked up, but he couldn't see the top. "Are these the Eregos Mountains?" he asked. "Hana and I stopped in them on our way to Hiabi last year, but I don't remember them being this tall."

"They aren't," Divinion replied. "These mountains no longer exist. Like the primeval forest I showed you, these mountains were part of Teneb. They formed the continent's western edge: the Tacumsah Range."

"Tacumsah . . ." Iren's mouth fell open. "You mean like the island chain?"

"When we sank Teneb, these mountains were too much even for us. Their tops still poke above the waves."

They were impressive for sure, but Iren still furrowed his brow. "What do these mountains have to do with Muryoka?"

Divinion pointed a claw at a mountain perhaps ten miles ahead of them. "Keep your eyes focused that way."

The dragon concentrated a moment. Then he reared his head back. The white flames shot out, crossing the space to the mountain in a flash.

The explosion was blinding, but it made no sound. Then, two seconds later, a concussive force knocked Iren to the ground.

He struggled to his feet. A crater at least the size of the one the Heart of Ziorsecth had made appeared at the impact site.

"That's the Muryoka I used on the ocean," Divinion said. "It's also what your father attempted. But this is the weaker of Muryoka's two forms. As you said, it's power without control. If we harness that energy, we get a different result."

The dragon held out a clawed hand, palm up. White flames appeared, just like they had for Iren Saito.

Only this time, the flames shrank. They started out the length of the dragon's immense claws, but they grew smaller with each second.

"There," the dragon said at last. "It's done."

Iren frowned. "I don't see it anymore."

"It's there. It's the size of a grain of sand."

"And that makes it more powerful?"

"The energy is the same," Divinion corrected. "Both forms use the same amount of magic. The difference is control. This Muryoka focuses all its magic into a single point. And when it's released—"

He reached out and grabbed the cliff next to them. Iren shouted, "No, don't!" but it was too late. White light filled the cliff face.

Iren shielded himself behind Divinion, but he knew it was futile. The blast would ignite and slay them both.

"Open your eyes," Divinion said. "We're both fine."

Iren unclenched himself. "Right," he said, his voice and body shaking, "this place isn't real."

"True, but that's not the reason. Even in the real world, that blast wouldn't have killed us. It transferred all its energy to its target, so there was no backwash. See for yourself."

Iren stepped around Divinion. He dropped to his knees in shock.

The cliff was gone. The whole mountain was gone. Iren could see across miles and miles of empty space.

"H. . .How?" he managed.

"The imperfect Muryoka wastes its energy in a big explosion. The perfect one does not. The target receives it all, and that means complete annihilation. But when the target falls, the Muryoka's energy is expended. Only light leaches out. It can blind, but it can't kill. The perfect Muryoka will destroy anything you desire, and only what you desire."

Iren was still stunned, but he forced himself to say, "I've seen this before. Or at least, something similar. When I became the Dragoon, I used a spell like this to stop Feng."

Divinion tossed his head back and forth. It made his whiskers shake. "Same idea, but a different level of execution. What you used against Feng was simple compared to Muryoka. That time, you squeezed the Dragoon's magic into a ball the size of a cherry. A perfect Muryoka can be no larger than a grain of sand. That's a hundred thousand times smaller."

Iren couldn't grasp the number Divinion described, but he understood the point. Even though he had used a similar technique in the past, a perfect Muryoka was far and away more challenging. It demanded at least as much magic as he had gathered as the Dragoon, and it required a level of control far exceeding what he had managed back then.

"So that's my next task," he murmured. "I need to learn how to focus magic into smaller and smaller spaces."

Divinion nodded. "That's the only way you'll defeat Rondel without killing yourself or anyone else."

"How do I do it?" Iren asked. "Did my father ever figure it out?"

"After that day in the arena, your father never attempted Muryoka again. He feared what might happen, especially after he became the Holy Dragon Knight and truly had my power at his fingertips."

Iren gulped. Even his father had failed to learn Muryoka. The Holy Dragon Knights before him had considered the spell so hazardous they'd declared it forbidden. To defeat Rondel, Iren would have to surpass them all, and the price of failure was death and mass destruction.

He already missed running into trees.

CHAPTER SIXTEEN
Land and Sea

As the sun set over Awakimundi's teardrop castle, Hana returned to the shore alongside the island's port. She removed her shoes and dug her toes into the dry sand. The soothing crunch distracted her from what she knew she had to do tonight.

It wasn't fair. Faro was so gentle. He had no idea about the wars of the past, or the revenge the Maantecs sought. He was fun and carefree. He didn't deserve to die.

Hana shook her head. Faro was nothing. She'd met him on the road just today. He was a nobody, a human unworthy of her time and attention. Once she killed him, she would return to Shogun Melwar in triumph.

And what then? The shogun seemed content to let Iren, Rondel, and the Forest Dragon Knight chase one another. That left only one Ryokaiten unclaimed: Balear's Auryozaki. As soon as Hana returned and handed over Faro's weapon, the shogun would send her to kill Balear.

There was no avoiding it. The alternative was death.

Besides, this was the only way to restore the Maantecs and let them assume their place as Raa's rightful leaders. Once the Maantecs were in charge, Raa would have peace. Faro and Balear were sacrifices to that noble purpose.

Cheering from the wooden huts pulled Hana from her thoughts. She faced the sound, and through the light of fifty torches she saw a crowd of Tacumsahens mobbing a central figure. Everyone was shouting "Faro de Magnificent!" over and over. He might be a heretic in Mizuchi's temple, but out here he was a champion.

The crowd washed over Hana like a wave. As Faro passed her, she forced herself to honor him with a subtle smile. He said nothing in response, but she could tell from his widened grin that he had noticed her.

Hana had expected to be the only light-skinned person in the crowd, but more than a few of the Lodians who had ridden on the ship with her had come out as well. "Faro de Magnificent" must have a reputation among the sea-traders.

The crowd's presence wouldn't make Hana's job any easier. If Faro knew anything about the Water Dragon's abilities, the battle between them would be messy. Anyone nearby was likely to die.

It would be better to take Faro unawares during his show. Hana fingered the smooth pebble she'd picked up during her walk back from the castle. It was the perfect assassination tool. With it Hana could pierce Faro's skull from a distance without anyone knowing she was involved.

Taking the man's Ryokaiten would be no issue either. Mizuchi would test anyone who touched his weapon after Faro died, and there was no way anyone in this crowd could pass. After the first few failed and died, the others would fear to touch the cursed object. Hana could sweep in, take the Ryokaiten, and promise to hurl it into the ocean far from land. She would be a hero.

Having a plan made Hana feel better. She settled in to watch the show. She hoped Faro lived up to his reputation; tonight was going to be his last performance.

Faro separated from the mob and stepped into the surf. Rather, he stepped onto it. He walked across the shifting surface of the waves as easily as if he were still on the beach. The crowd cheered.

The Dragon Knight next raised his arms, and with them two snakes of water rose from the sea. They curled around Faro, slowly at first but speeding up until the man was all but lost in the churning foam.

Then Faro threw his arms out over the crowd. The water snakes shot out and dissipated over the beach. Salty mist rained on the audience.

The dark-skinned Tacumsahen continued his act for another fifteen minutes, performing various tricks with the water. He created three fist-sized water balls and juggled them. He added two more, but these he bounced off his knees, elbows, and head while keeping the original three in the air. He kicked all five balls above the audiences' heads so that they landed on the beach with a solid impact. With the group's attention diverted, Faro created a wave and doused the front row from behind. He cackled his deep, rapid laugh at them.

"And now for my encore!" he shouted at last. He dipped his hand into the sea, and Hana saw the tip of his Ryokaiten sticking out by his thumb. Faro swirled his hand in the ocean once, twice, three times. He spoke an incantation that sounded reverent but that Hana guessed was nonsensical stage acting. Faro then threw up his hand, and with it a cone of water launched into the air. It spiraled upward, forming a tight cylinder. In shape it mirrored Faro's initial tendrils, but this one was as wide as Hana was tall and stood more than a hundred feet high. Whitecaps flecked its length to give it the look of a great sea serpent. Completing the appearance, the apex formed a toothy reptilian mouth.

Hana's eyes glittered. This was the moment she'd waited for. Everyone's attention, Faro's included, was on the huge water creature. Hana released her pebble, floated it above the crowd, and shot it faster than an arrow at Faro's head.

Just before the stone hit him, though, the sea serpent twisted subtly. Its undulating curves snagged the rock and held it fast. Hana struggled to free it, but the water had it. Defeated, she released the stone and let it sink into the ocean.

Faro made no indication that he had noticed the rock. He kept right on with his act. "Behold our guardian, Mizuchi!" he cried as he gestured at the water serpent. "He keeps us safe, but if we're evil, he will punish us. Like dis!" He swung his arm in an arc above the crowd, and the Mizuchi look-alike descended. It crashed into the ocean, and a great wave rushed forward. Hana shielded her eyes just before it broke over the crowd, soaking everyone.

Hana threw back her wet hair and looked around. She expected everyone to be as surprised—and upset—as she was. Instead, they were all laughing. Faro joined in and made an exaggerated shrug. "Well, maybe his punishment would be a little worse," he said. "I am a simple conjurer after all."

Faro bowed and stepped back onto the beach. The wet audience mobbed him, all but one. Hana held back, fists clenched. Now she would have to do this the hard way.

Still, she didn't want the spectators involved if they didn't have to be. She waited as they slapped Faro on the back and congratulated him for his show.

At length the crowd thinned, more from Faro's repeated claims that he must rest than from the audience's tiring of his presence. Half an hour after the show, Hana and Faro were the only two standing on the beach.

The Tacumsahen approached Hana. "You came," he said. "Did you like my show, farm girl?"

He said those last two words with such irony that Hana took a step back. "It was impressive," she admitted.

"Lodians don't care about dragons, but people here remember Mizuchi. They know him. Even so, they don't like Lefts."

Hana's eyes widened in surprise. She'd thought Faro was a human, but he was a Maantec. Everything about him, even his islander accent, was an act. He'd spoken those last few sentences with a deep voice as clear as any noble Maantec in Hiabi.

"Didn't know there were dark-skinned Maantecs, did you?" he asked. "Your bigotry extends even to your own kind."

Hana blinked several times in rapid succession. "What are you talking about?"

"I knew Melwar would send someone eventually. I didn't expect a beautiful woman. It figures."

There was no point in denying it. "How did you know?" Hana asked. "I hide my Ryokaiten."

"It traveled under the sea floor to get here," Faro replied. He pointed down. "I felt it. I knew you were coming before you landed. It wasn't hard to pick you out, the only person on that ship who looked like she didn't belong on the water. Then, when you were so excited by my mention of Mizuchi, I knew for certain what you were and why you'd come."

He paused and loosed a long sigh. "Are you going to kill me?"

She nodded. "It's Shogun Melwar's command."

The Tacumsahen Maantec looked at her with those endless black pools he had for eyes. "You don't have to follow him, you know," he said. "You could be like me. The only bowing I do anymore is for show." He made one of his mock bows for emphasis. "I'm free. I can live in Tacumsah, and nobody cares. I walk across the water from island to island, and instead of fearing my magic, the people love it. Just because I call myself a showman! That's how I live. You can live that way too."

To run away and leave it all behind . . . if only Hana could do that. Shogun Melwar would never allow it.

Memories of her blood pouring out of her filled Hana's mind. She had fought the shogun once. She knew the outcome of doing so again.

"I'm sorry, Faro," she said. "I wish this could have ended differently."

Faro shrugged. "Too bad." He grinned and slid back into his fake accent. "I was hopin' you'd change your mind, ya, and we'd make love under de stars all night long."

Hana flushed. It was time to end this. She sent magic through her feet into the beach. Sand rose up around Faro and engulfed him. Hana then ordered it to contract. It would crush Faro to death.

The sand constricted, and a pool of liquid dripped out the bottom of it. Hana released her spell and stepped forward to claim Faro's Ryokaiten.

They were almost the last steps she took. Even as she knelt, the water at her feet erupted in a torrent. It knocked her to the ground, and while she spluttered amid the sand, Faro reappeared. His hand clutched his Ryokaiten, but the weapon had changed. A tendril of water twelve feet long extended from it.

Faro swung his arm, and the water rushed forward. It struck Hana's hardened skin with a sharp *thwack!*

The blow didn't pierce her armor, but it still stunned Hana. The water had acted like a whip.

"I hope you didn't expect an easy kill," Faro said in his clear voice. "I may be a showman, but I save my best tricks for when it counts."

The water around Faro's Ryokaiten shifted. It changed into a bow. Faro drew back his Ryokaiten handle, and an arrow of water appeared. It shot toward Hana as fast as any normal arrow.

She didn't even flinch as the water struck her. Her hardened skin absorbed the shot without trouble.

Still, the water's force surprised Hana. The Forest Dragon Knight had shot arrows at her outside Hiabi, and they'd just snapped. These liquid arrows pushed against her armor as though trying to drill into it.

Hana rose. She reached out over the water and called to a dozen stones of various sizes from pebbles to fist-sized cobbles. They floated in the air for a moment, and then they launched themselves at Faro.

The Tacumsahen stood still. The rocks struck him and passed through his body without pause. Drops of water flecked the sand, but Faro was unharmed.

A stab of fear ripped through Hana. She'd seen a spell like this before. Shogun Melwar had used it the day he'd nearly killed her.

Hana forced away her panic. Faro wasn't the only one with a strong defense. Unlike Shogun Melwar, Faro had yet to penetrate even Hana's basic hardened skin armor, and she could add extra layers of stone if necessary.

The Tacumsahen charged, and his Ryokaiten changed shape again. This time it formed a gigantic sword as big as Balear's Auryozaki. Faro swung, and the water crashed into Hana. Its force was the strongest the Tacumsahen had yet inflicted, but it was weaker than the Forest Dragon Knight's tree from outside Hiabi. He'd need to do better than that.

Faro leapt back. He seemed to study Hana. She smiled. This outcome happened to most opponents who fought her. Nothing about Hana's appearance suggested that she had armor, yet the enemy's techniques couldn't wound her. The Forest Dragon Knight had grasped the situation quickly enough; Hana wondered if Faro would be as fast.

"I don't want to kill you, Hana," Faro said. "Please leave this island. Go back to Lodia."

Hana blinked twice. So far Faro's attacks had proven useless against her. Why was he acting like the battle was over, and that he'd won?

He must be bluffing. "That's sporting of you," she said, "but you know I can't return in failure to Shogun Melwar."

"Then you'll die on the next blow."

Hana saw red. Faro was just mocking her. He didn't have anything that could breach her armor. She was invincible against all but the shogun. That was why she had no choice but to serve him.

She raised her arms, and a column of sand engulfed Faro. A second later, though, he stepped through it. "There's a lot of space between grains of sand," he said, "plenty for water to pass through."

Faro pointed the Zuryokaiten's tip at Hana. "I'm sorry."

Hana never had time to dodge. The knucklebone-sized ball of water shot out of Faro's weapon with a speed that surpassed even Rondel Thara's attacks. It struck Hana on the tip of her right shoulder and sliced through her hardened skin like it didn't exist.

Hana cried out and gripped the wound with her left hand. She felt light-headed. Since she'd become the Stone Dragon Knight, no one but Shogun Melwar had made her bleed. Who was this man to injure her? A low-class street urchin had no place wielding this much power.

"I should have killed you," Faro said. "If I'd aimed that shot at your head or your heart, you'd be dead now. Put water under enough pressure, and it'll drill through anything, even rock."

Hana gritted her teeth. What was she supposed to do? Faro could kill her any time he wanted with that attack. She would have no warning. One second she would be alive, and the next she would be dead.

Maybe that was for the best. If she died here, Shogun Melwar wouldn't get Faro's Ryokaiten. He needed it for his invasion to succeed. Maybe dying on this beach was the best way to thwart the shogun's plan.

But no. If she died, her master would send someone else. He would keep sending people until one of them succeeded. Perhaps he would even come himself. Faro couldn't defeat the shogun. Whether Hana lived or died, the result would be the same. Shogun Melwar would win.

"What do you say, Hana? Stop this. Don't make me kill you. You're better than that. You're better than Melwar."

Hana shook her head and smiled sadly. "No," she said," I'm not." She looked at Faro. "That's why you have to die."

With all the magic she could summon, Hana raised four stone walls around Faro. She had called them from deep in the ground, far below the beach. They slammed together and formed a cube prison. A fifth slab floated up and formed a ceiling, while another met the bottom to create the floor. Hana joined the six sides together so there weren't any cracks. Faro couldn't change into water and drip his way out of this cell.

He might still be able to cut through it though. Faro had said water could drill through rock.

Hana wouldn't give him the chance. She knelt and pressed her palms into the sand. The prison responded and sank into the ground. Hana let it drop deeper and deeper, as far as she could make it go without losing control of it. It was half a mile below the surface when she decided it had reached the limit of her ability.

She would give Faro a week down there. Hana didn't know how long he could stay in water form, but every second he couldn't, he would be using up the small amount of air in the cube. A week was more than enough. After that she'd haul the cube back up and take the Ryokaiten.

Hana sighed and fell back on the wet sand. It clung to her. She hated it. Despite her exhaustion, she forced herself to her feet. She left the beach to find an inn.

CHAPTER SEVENTEEN
What Makes Her Happy

Minawë brushed her palm against a tree in her path. All afternoon, she'd been getting a feeling of déjà vu. Every patch of Aokigahara was different, yet after five weeks of travel, they also started to feel the same.

At least, that's what Minawë had thought until this afternoon. Now the forest really did feel the same, as though she'd been here before.

Her touch on the tree confirmed it. The voices here were definitely ones she'd heard in the past.

Lyubo descended from the trees. The pair of them had taken on the group's scouting duties. It was a solitary job for the most part, and Minawë found herself waiting for the moments that brought them together.

"Something wrong?" Lyubo asked. "You seem distracted."

"This place feels familiar somehow," Minawë said.

"I would think so. Come into the canopy, and I'll show you. You can't see it from down here."

They leapfrogged up a series of rising limbs until they were halfway up one of the trees. Lyubo pointed to the east. "See it now?"

She did. In the distance the forest ended. A thin, black line cut through it. Nothing lived within the blank space.

Minawë shuddered. "That's where I fought the Oni Fire Dragon Knight, the spot where Mother and I almost died."

"And all of us with you," Lyubo said. "If you hadn't been here, that Oni would have wrapped that dead zone around Sorengaral. He would have trapped us, then burned us to death. You saved us all that day."

Minawë peered through the wide, flat leaves. She could just make out the mound of vines that had crushed and killed the Fire Dragon Knight. She'd been so angry back then. She'd wanted to protect Rondel and the Kodamas, but she'd also wanted revenge for what the Oni had already done.

"The sun's setting," Lyubo said. "It's too bad. With a few more hours, we might have reached Sorengaral today. I'm certain we'll arrive tomorrow, though."

Minawë tried to keep her reaction passive, yet she couldn't help but clutch her hand to her chest. Sorengaral, her people's home in Aokigahara. What would she do when she reached it?

"Let's head back," Lyubo said. "The others will be excited to know how close we are."

They returned and met up with Narunë, Rondel, and the rest of the troop. Rondel argued that they should keep going, but Narunë silenced her with a wave.

"Traveling the forest at night is dangerous," he said. "We do it only in great need. Sorengaral will wait until morning."

Rondel huffed and pouted, but she didn't press the point. She sulked as the rest of them set up camp and collected firewood.

Lyubo sat next to Minawë through dinner. He joked a lot, and Minawë smiled to see him in such good spirits.

She understood his mirth. He was a day from home. Coming home always made you happy. It was the place you belonged.

Without a word, Minawë stood and walked away from the fire. She felt the others' eyes on her, but she paid them no mind. She needed a few minutes alone.

She wouldn't get them. She'd barely wandered from camp when Lyubo called, "Minawë, hold on!"

"I'm sorry, Lyubo," she said. "I know I shouldn't go off by myself after dark."

Lyubo shook his head. "It's all right. I know these woods well, so even if you got lost, I could find you." He gave her a lopsided grin.

Minawë didn't return the expression. "Could you?" she asked. "These woods are familiar to me too, but I feel more lost now than ever."

The male Kodama thought for a moment. "Minawë, I just realized there's a place nearby I know you'll like. Can I show it to you? It might cheer you up."

Minawë shrugged. "Sure. Lead the way."

They hiked through the jungle, heading west from camp. In spite of the almost total darkness, Lyubo walked with confidence. He seemed to know the way by feel as well as by sight.

He stopped at a solid mass of timber. Minawë looked up, but it was like staring at a palisade.

"What is this?" she asked.

"The only way in is up," Lyubo said. "We have to climb."

He set to work on one of the trunks, wrapping his arms and legs around it as best he could. With his Kodaman strength, he slowly made his way up the tree.

Minawë cocked an eyebrow. Lyubo's method worked, but it was embarrassing and difficult. She transformed into a squirrel and shimmied up a neighboring trunk, winking at Lyubo as she passed him.

"Hey, no fair!" Lyubo called.

A hundred feet up, the tree trunks at last narrowed enough that Minawë could slip between two of them. She skittered down the other side and waited for Lyubo to catch up. When he arrived, Minawë returned to her Kodaman form and looked around.

She whistled. They were in a glade in the rainforest, hemmed in by a tight ring of trees. The opening was perhaps seventy feet across, and only a soft undergrowth of ferns filled the space. The canopies of the encircling trees formed a roof over their heads.

"I discovered this place while scouting long ago," Lyubo said. "Ever since, it's been a place I come to for guidance. What do you think?"

Minawë was in awe. "It's beautiful. How did it get here?"

"All the trees in the ring are the same," Lyubo pointed out. "I think there used to be a massive tree here that broke off in a storm and decayed. The trees around us are its children, growing off the remains of its base."

"It must have been immense," Minawë said, "maybe as big as the Heart of Ziorsecth."

Lyubo shrugged. "I wouldn't know. I never saw the Heart before I joined the war."

Minawë looked at him. The Kodama's silver eyes sparkled in the filtered moonlight.

Then Minawë realized they sparkled because they were wet. She reached a hand up and touched his cheek. "Why are you crying?"

Lyubo loosed a breath. "I dashed off to war so young I never understood what we were fighting for. Now I'm trapped here by Saito's curse. I won't ever see the Heart."

"The Heart's gone," Minawë said. "Feng destroyed it."

"It'll regrow eventually, but even if I live another thousand years, I won't see it."

"You will," Minawë promised, though she had no idea how. "I had the curse removed. If it could happen to me, it can happen to you. We'll find a way."

Lyubo smiled. "Thank you, but I'm all right. I've always regretted that I left Ziorsecth so young, but these past few weeks with you, I've let those feelings go. I found something else I want to protect, something real: you."

Minawë blushed. "You told me yourself you can't protect me. You aren't a Dragon Knight."

"That isn't what I mean. I've spent enough time with you to see the pain you're feeling. I can't stop Rondel or fight any wars, but I want to be there for you. I want to give you a place you feel secure, a place you can call home."

Home. Minawë shivered even though the jungle was still warm from the day's heat. When she'd first come to Aokigahara, she'd wondered if it might someday be home to her. Back then she'd dismissed the notion in favor of pursuing Iren, but now . . .

The Oni's scorched path from earlier in the evening came back to her. If she hadn't been here, all the Aokigaharan Kodamas would have died.

Then another image flashed before her eyes. Iren and Rondel battled across the fields outside Hiabi, their blades crashing together. Iren would have died if Minawë hadn't intervened.

Minawë wiped her eyes. She didn't know when she'd started crying, but now she couldn't stop.

"No matter what I choose, people I care about will die," she said. "I can't be everywhere. I'm not all-powerful."

Lyubo hugged her. His grip was firm and warm. She let her head rest against his chest, and his thudding heart slowed her sobs.

"You don't have to be all-powerful," Lyubo said. "You're a Kodama. Let Maantecs deal with Maantec things. If you run all over the world trying to stop them, you'll only exhaust yourself. There are people right here who need you, who want you. We'll never turn our backs on you."

Minawë's eyes whipped up to Lyubo's. It was on a night not so unlike this one that Iren had walked away from her. He didn't want her to interfere. Neither did Rondel. If she kept following the old Maantec, no matter what happened, she would only find more pain.

There was no happiness in pursuing those two. Revenge couldn't make you happy. It couldn't make anyone happy.

But here, here there was something that could make her happy. Minawë studied Lyubo's face, his wild yet gentle eyes.

She raised herself up and kissed him.

CHAPTER EIGHTEEN
Balear's Strategy

Dirio climbed to the top of Kataile's stairs and stepped onto the plateau above the city. Sparse pines dotted the area, but most of the space was open. Even here, a quarter-mile from the outer ledge, Dirio could see all the way to the plateau's border.

He could also see the object of his search. Balear Platarch sat on the plateau's northeast corner with another man. They were pointing in multiple directions and talking intensely.

Dirio walked up to them. "Hey, did you forget about practice?" he asked. "I had to direct the officers myself, and they weren't happy about it."

Balear looked up, and so did the other man. Dirio recognized him as Riac, the veteran Balear had selected as his second-in-command.

"Sorry," Balear said. "This was more important."

"What could be more important than training your soldiers?"

"Figuring out how we're going to use them."

That got Dirio's attention. Up to now, they'd focused on the basics: how to fight with a spear, how to move in formation, and how to order your men so they actually listened. Dirio had never given thought to how that training might be applied in battle. Balear obviously had.

"The question is one of defense," Balear said. "No matter what we do, we don't have the forces to launch an attack. I told Elyssa as much. The best we can do is protect this city."

Dirio sat down and looked over the waves. He'd never seen the ocean until he'd come to Kataile. It really was an impressive view. "I don't see how you can block off entrance to the city," he said. "The tide goes in and out. You can't build a wall on shifting sand and water."

"My thoughts exactly," Riac replied. "Even if we used the largest stones we could move, they wouldn't make a difference. At high tide they'd wash away, and at low tide there would be bare sand exposed."

Balear scratched his chin. Unlike the other two men, he was looking north. Dirio opened his mouth to bring the young general's attention back to the problem of the ocean, but before he could speak, Balear asked, "Do you know what this city can't handle?"

Dirio cocked an eyebrow. "With its current forces? A dozen cats would probably be too much."

Riac glowered, but Balear just shook his head. "Open warfare," he said. "For all our training, we lack the raw materials to make the shields or heavy armor needed in field combat. If another army shows up, we won't be able to repel them before they enter the city."

Dirio frowned. "Right, and that's why we're trying to figure out how to secure the beach. What's going on in that head, Balear?"

Balear stroked his chin. "We don't need to secure the beach. It will do its job just the way it is."

"I don't get it," Dirio said.

"I do," Riac jumped in. "Even without fortifications, the space between the sea and the plateau is narrow. An attacking army will need to bunch up to get through it. Even if they far outnumber us, those numbers won't mean much if they can only field a few men at a time."

Balear nodded. "We'll set up what barricades we can, and then block off the open areas with our best melee squads. The real defense, though, won't come from any of that. It will come from the archers. We'll position them just inside the city and up here on the plateau. They'll shoot over our front line into the oncoming ranks. Our enemies' corpses will become our wall."

Dirio shivered, and not just because the afternoon's winter wind flowed unobstructed across the plateau. "That's pretty heartless."

Balear's eyes were set. "It's war."

Dirio had a flash of memory. He'd seen Balear like this before, after the soldier had first lost his arm. Balear had applied this single-minded determination when he'd trained to fight the Fubuki. "What will you give up this time?" Dirio asked before he realized he was speaking.

"What?" Balear snapped.

It was too late to back out now. "You threw away Veliaf to defeat the Fubuki. What are you tossing aside now?"

"This is the only way," Balear insisted.

"Do I need to fight you again?" Dirio asked. "Do I need to prove to you that you're being hotheaded?"

Balear looked back at him, and despite Dirio's confident statement, he quailed before the soldier's eyes. There was something different about Balear this time, something that made him even fiercer than when he'd challenged the Fubuki. "War is on its way to us, Dirio," Balear said. "We have to be ready."

When the words left Balear's mouth, Dirio knew they were true. He had no idea how Balear knew, but Dirio was certain the soldier was right.

"What do you want us to do?" Riac asked.

"Get straw targets made, as many as possible," Balear ordered. "Find any bowyers and fletchers in the city and get them working double-time. I'm sure you have metalworkers who make fish hooks. Have them make arrowheads instead. As for the soldiers, half of them will switch from short-range weapons to archery practice. Another quarter will keep focused on melee combat to serve in the vanguard. Take only volunteers for that; the melee teams will have the riskiest assignment."

"What about the other quarter?" Dirio asked.

"They'll meet me up here from now on," Balear said. "They're going to build catapults."

"Catapults?"

"If the melee vanguard does its job, the enemy army will get bunched up. They'll have no defense against rocks from the sky."

Dirio whistled. "It's a plan, anyway. I just hope it works."

Balear looked at Riac. "What do you think?"

Riac didn't answer for a long time. He looked down at the city below them. "King Angustion sent five thousand of us against the Kodamas," he said. "He didn't bring cavalry or siege weapons, just a mass of men. He thought that would be enough. Instead, we were slaughtered by the people you went to join. If you say this will work, I'll support you."

"In that case, I say it will work," Balear replied. "We have a few hours of daylight left. Get the word out to the officers that I need to speak with them this evening. No exceptions. We don't have the luxury of wasting time."

As they headed back, Dirio leaned in and murmured to Balear, "This won't solve the broader problem, you know. Defending this city won't end the war."

"On the contrary," Balear said, "this is the only way to end it. You'll see."

Dirio slowed so he walked behind Balear. He smiled. After all this time, Balear was finally acting like the general Amroth had made him.

CHAPTER NINETEEN
Discovery

"Come on!" Minawë called. She tugged on Lyubo's arm. "We'll reach Sorengaral by noon if we hurry. I want to be the first to see it!"

"All right, all right," Lyubo said. "We're the scouts anyway. Show me what you've learned these past few weeks. Lead the way."

The pair of them took off into the jungle, faster than Narunë would normally deem prudent. Yet as he watched them go, he smiled. "I told you I'd convince her to stay."

Next to him, Rondel huffed. "It's not like you did anything. All your conversations with her just upset her. I should be thanking Lyubo for taking advantage of her situation and getting all romantic."

Narunë laughed. "That's not something a mother should say."

"Then how would you describe it?"

"I would say it was my fantastic leadership in picking the right men to accompany us from Sorengaral."

Rondel huffed even louder. "At least she's changed her mind, even if it was thanks to luck."

"That's the spirit!" Narunë bellowed his laugh again, his right eye winking.

Within a few seconds, though, his laughter fell aside. He looked seriously at Rondel. "So when will you be leaving?" he asked.

"You made me promise to see you all to Sorengaral. If I left now, Minawë might still follow me. I'll wait for you to settle in. Then I'll slip away some evening."

"It's too bad," Narunë said. "There aren't many people I can talk to like this. It's lonely."

"You're surrounded by Kodamas who love and admire you. You're getting a niece that a year ago you didn't know you had. What's lonely about that?"

"The niece I'm excited about. As for the rest, you know the answer. You were an emperor's wife. It's a lonely spot at the top."

Rondel winked. "Maybe when Iren's dead, I'll come back and visit."

Narunë looked Rondel up and down. He wondered if she really meant that. He hoped she did.

They walked and talked together another hour. Narunë's pulse quickened with each step. After three months away, he would finally see his home again. He couldn't wait.

In a way, he found his longing strange. Three months was nothing compared with his fifteen-hundred-year life, but he had grown attached to the collection of tree homes that marked the core of Kodaman civilization in Aokigahara. They had started out as warriors, but over a thousand years, they had changed into something more: a people.

A shout from the branches above and ahead of him pulled Narunë from his thoughts. "Lord Narunë!" the voice called.

Narunë recognized the caller as Lyubo. That was odd. It was too soon for even him and Minawë to have reached Sorengaral. "What news?" Narunë shouted back.

Lyubo landed beside the Kodaman prince. Minawë was next to him. Narunë blanched when he saw his niece's expression. She looked in shock.

Then another female Kodama dropped from the trees. Narunë blinked. It was Eritas, one of the scouts he'd left at Sorengaral. "Lord Narunë!" she said. "I'm glad you're all right! We've feared the worst."

Narunë brushed aside the concern with a wave of his hand. "We were delayed waiting for a slowpoke old Maantec," he said with a wry glance at Rondel, "but we're fine."

Eritas wasn't amused. "Were you attacked?"

"Attacked? The Yokai are on the run. They wouldn't have dared to threaten us."

"No, Lord Narunë, not by Yokai, by Maantecs."

"Maantecs? The only Maantec in Aokigahara is this useless crone." He jabbed a finger at Rondel. She scowled and put her back to him.

"Uncle, you don't understand," Minawë said. "Something's happened."

Narunë was tired of these games. "Someone spit it out, then," he ordered, his face hard.

Eritas gulped, but she managed to say, "It's Sorengaral. The Maantecs attacked it!"

Narunë's heart caught in his throat. The Maantecs had never dared to invade Aokigahara. The rainforest terrified them; they called it "Suicide Forest."

Rondel abandoned her fake insulted pose. She stormed over to the group, sparks in her eyes. "How far are we from the city?" she asked.

Eritas opened her mouth, but Narunë got there first. "A few hours at most. Eritas, lead the way. I must see it for myself!"

The group set off at a jog, the fastest they could manage in Aokigahara's tangle. Rondel ran ahead of them, using her enhanced speed to clear a path through the brush.

Every fifteen minutes or so, a new Kodama appeared and joined their group. Each took up a position around the periphery to guard the troop.

No, Narunë realized, not the troop. They were guarding him and Minawë.

Sweat pooled in Narunë's eyes, and try as he might, he couldn't clear the stinging salt. Whatever had happened must have been serious to make his sentries act this way. They all knew Narunë's battle prowess, and they'd all heard about Minawë killing the Fire Dragon Knight. Whoever these Maantecs were, they were powerful enough that the Kodamas feared their leaders might not be enough to handle them.

Two hours after Eritas met them, Narunë and the others reached Sorengaral. To most, the city would have seemed like just another patch of jungle. Apart from a few clearings between trees, the rainforest here was as dense as anything they'd traveled through on their way from Shikari. Even looking up, it was hard to spot the wooden houses nestled in the canopy and sheltered by huge, waxy leaves.

That was how it should have looked. Instead, as Narunë entered the city, he doubled over in horror. Dozens of trees lay uprooted, their houses shattered against the ground. Narunë hadn't seen this much light on the forest floor since they'd moved in a thousand years ago. Great mounds of rock and soil jutted up. To Narunë's eye, they looked like the crags of Shikari, only in miniature.

Then there were the Kodamas. Narunë's people were always watchful, but today they seemed especially vigilant. Even before Narunë could identify himself, he counted twenty arrows trained on him. When he called out the all-clear, a horde of his brethren descended upon him and started talking at once.

Narunë held up a hand, and everyone fell silent. He looked through the crowd and found Kenwë, the Kodama he'd left in charge when he'd escorted Rondel and Minawë to Shikari. He gestured for the man to step forward. "Tell me what happened. Leave nothing out."

Kenwë wrung his hands. "Two months ago, this woman rose up from the ground. She demanded that we hand over the Karyozaki. When we refused, she lifted the earth around several of the trees and knocked them over."

Next to Narunë, Rondel clenched her fists. Minawë did the same. She growled through her teeth, "Hana."

Narunë looked at his niece. "You know who did this?"

Rondel answered, "The Stone Dragon Knight, a Maantec named Hana Akiyama. We fought her in Shikari, but she was too strong. We couldn't kill her."

Narunë knew he shouldn't, but he couldn't avoid looking at his niece for her reaction. The woman stared at the ground, her arms limp. Narunë could guess what passed through her mind.

But now wasn't the time to call out Minawë for blaming herself, not when a hundred of her subjects were within earshot. There would be time for that discussion later, in private.

More important at the moment was the Karyozaki. "Where is Palentos?" he asked.

Now it was everyone else's turn to look at their feet. Narunë frowned. The blacksmith Palentos was the only person besides Minawë who had known where she'd hidden the Fire Dragon Sword.

Kenwë spoke without raising his head, "We tried to fight the Maantec, but our weapons were useless. Even our best plant magic couldn't break her armor. She butchered our people. I thought no one knew where the Karyozaki was, and I feared she would slay us all. But then Palentos offered to take her to the sword if she left the village."

Rondel's eyes narrowed. "And she agreed?"

"Yes. Once she had the Karyozaki, she sank into the ground and left. But before she did, she . . . well . . ."

"Speak up!" Narunë roared. "What happened? Where's Palentos?"

Kenwë sighed. "Palentos tried to stop her. I guess he figured that while she was distracted with the Karyozaki, he could attack her. But his attempt to breach her armor was no better than any of ours. When the Maantec saw what he was doing, she raised a . . ." he paused and cleared his throat, "a metal pole from the ground and speared him through the stomach."

Kenwë's nostrils flared. "She intentionally didn't kill him," he growled. "She avoided vital organs and instead let him die slowly from blood loss. She's a monster."

Narunë couldn't believe it. If only he'd been here, maybe he could have done something.

Then again, even Minawë couldn't defeat this Maantec, and she was the Forest Dragon Knight. Had Narunë been here, he would have been killed too, and the Maantecs would still have the Karyozaki.

What were they going to do? Hana could return at any time. They couldn't stay here.

No, it was worse than that. Not only couldn't they stay here, they couldn't stay anywhere. The only way Hana could have known Sorengaral's location was if the Yokai had told her. The beasts must be acting as spies for the Maantecs. If the Kodamas stayed in any place more than a month, the Yokai could potentially carry that information back to the Maantecs. Then Hana would return.

"Stand firm, Narunë," Rondel said in that low, terse voice that refused argument. "Your people need not cower in fear. You have a queen now. You have a Forest Dragon Knight. Minawë fought Hana to a draw on the bare fields outside Hiabi. Here in Aokigahara, she would crush Hana effortlessly. You have nothing to fear now that she has chosen to stay with her people."

Narunë raised his head. The old Maantec was right. He threw his arms up and addressed his people, "So a Maantec damaged our home. What of it? We'll rebuild. We'll become stronger. The Maantecs think they can strike us with impunity, but we'll show them they're wrong. If this Hana is so foolish as to attack a second time, she won't survive it. We have Queen Minawë, the Forest Dragon Knight, to protect us! And she won't fight alone. I'll join her. We'll all join her. We'll show Hana and the Maantecs and any other damn fools who mess with us that the might of King Otunë lives on in his kin!"

Everyone cheered. Kodamas came up to Narunë and slapped him on the back, praising him and his leadership.

Narunë was glad for their reaction, but he was more interested in how his niece had taken the speech. He searched the press of Kodamas for her face. He probably should have checked with her before declaring her their savior.

His eyes swept the crowd twice before his shoulders slumped. His fellow Kodamas kept up their celebrations, but he didn't hear them.

"What's the matter?" Rondel asked. Then her eyes widened. Lightning Sight flared, and she swiveled her head around.

"Seriously?" she demanded. "I wish Iren hadn't rubbed off so much on that girl."

Minawë was gone.

CHAPTER TWENTY
The Allure of Revenge

Lyubo tore through Aokigahara, his senses alert. It was the toughest tracking job of his life. Minawë could be anywhere. More problematic, she could be any animal. That capybara grazing on the river grasses. An ant crawling out of that acacia tree. One of the spider monkeys in the family group above him.

But Minawë wouldn't be any of those. She didn't want to hide. She wanted to run. Lyubo knew which animal he would choose if he wanted to do that.

That's why he slowed when he saw the flash of black. Few jaguars had that black pattern to begin with. Fewer still would be running flat-out through the jungle in the midafternoon heat.

And none would have missed the hunter from above who descended upon it.

Lyubo landed hard on the black jaguar. It was a soft enough landing not to break bones, but it should have stunned the creature. Lyubo took advantage of the beast's surprise to pin its head down. The claws were damaging enough, but those canines could tear out his throat or pierce his skull with a single bite.

The jaguar struggled with an unreal strength. That, more than any other sign, convinced Lyubo. "Minawë!" he called. "Get a hold of yourself! It's Lyubo! I want to talk!"

The animal still struggled, but it reduced its thrashing. It spoke with a female voice, "Get off me!"

"Are you going to run away if I do?"

There was a moment of hesitation, and then, "Fine. No." The jaguar stopped fighting.

Lyubo slowly released pressure. The jaguar stayed where it was. When Lyubo had gained his feet and stepped back, the big cat stood. It reared back so its front feet left the ground. It stood of a height with Lyubo. The fur melted into skin and leather clothing.

"What do you want?" Minawë asked, her Kodaman form restored.

Lyubo held both hands before him, palms out. "I told you already. I just want to talk."

"Don't expect me to listen. I'm going to Shikari. I'm going to kill Hana."

"I thought you'd decided to stay and help your fellow Kodamas. I thought you'd decided to forget the Maantecs."

"That was before I saw Sorengaral," Minawë said. "I can't forget them now. I can't forget her. She's taken away everything important to me."

"Can you even win against her?" Lyubo asked. "You fought her in Shikari before, and it ended in a draw."

"That won't happen again. Iren and Mother's fight distracted me back then. This time, Hana will get my full attention." Her eyes flashed, and she bared her teeth. "And when my jaws close around her throat, she'll finally know what it feels like to be prey."

Lyubo stepped back. Minawë might look like a Kodama, but part of that jaguar was still in her. If he didn't play this carefully, she might yet attack him.

Before he could speak, though, he saw Minawë's eyes focus on something over his shoulder. He turned just in time to see two people break through the undergrowth toward them.

He breathed a sigh of relief. He might not be able to stop Minawë alone, but with Lord Narunë and Rondel here, surely they could convince her to stay.

Rondel spoke first. "Where do you think you're going, Minawë?" she asked. She spoke casually, as though curious which fruit trees Minawë was off to pick from.

Minawë didn't relax. "Don't try to stop me, Mother. I know you'd rather I stay here, but I'm going back to Shikari. I'll kill Hana for what she's done."

Rondel cocked an eyebrow. "What has she done?"

Lyubo didn't understand why the old woman was so nonchalant. Minawë was on the edge, and Rondel's unfeeling attitude would only push the queen further. What did this Maantec hope to accomplish?

"What has she done?" Minawë roared. "She destroyed Sorengaral! She killed dozens of Kodamas!"

"True," Rondel admitted, "yet your anger is misdirected. Why did she do those things? Have you stopped to ask yourself that question?"

"What are you talking about?"

"You're angry at the wrong person," Rondel said. "Getting angry at Hana is like getting angry at my rondel. She's just a weapon. Melwar is the one wielding her."

Minawë had already started to rebuke her mother, but she stopped short. Lyubo was caught equally off guard. Was it possible Hana wasn't responsible for her actions?

No, it wasn't, and Minawë came to the same conclusion. "Even if Melwar ordered her," she spat, "Hana could have refused. Besides, what about Palentos? She impaled him and left him to die!"

"Because he tried to stab her in the back."

"She was stealing the Karyozaki!"

"On Melwar's orders."

Minawë threw up her hands. "Why are you protecting her? Did you forget that she almost killed you? Or that she gave an Oni the Karyozaki so he could exterminate my people? Oh, and let's not forget how she manipulated Iren so she could kidnap him, take him to Melwar, and turn him against his friends!"

"Again, all on Melwar's command," Rondel said. "You're missing the point. Evil must be annihilated. I agree with your desire for justice. What concerns me is that you're succumbing to the allure of revenge."

Rondel may as well have punched Minawë. The queen reeled. Her eyes dropped to the forest floor.

Lord Narunë spoke for the first time, "There's a teaching among the Kodamas. Revenge can't make you happy. If you fail, you'll either die or suffer for the rest of your life. If you succeed, you'll be left with nothing, a void in your soul that you can't fill."

"I know that," Minawë said. "Mother—Aletas—told it to me."

"And she was right to caution you," Rondel replied. "Look at Iren. He let his desire for revenge consume him. Don't let it do the same to you."

The old woman paused. When she spoke again, her voice was quiet, as though she were speaking to herself, "Otherwise you might make a decision you'll regret. You might kill the wrong person."

Lyubo frowned. What did that mean? It must be significant, judging by the look of realization on Minawë's face.

But that comprehension didn't translate into a change of opinion. Minawë's expression hardened. "Hana's a mass-murderer," she said. "Even if she acted under Melwar's orders, that doesn't make her innocent."

"Doesn't it?" Rondel asked. "Melwar has a way of manipulating people. It's been his greatest weapon ever since we were children. I'm not convinced Hana is evil. She's no hero, but she isn't a villain either."

Rondel sounded so certain, but Lyubo had his doubts. "What makes you think that?" he asked.

The old Maantec's baleful stare made Lyubo wish he'd kept his mouth shut. "The attack on Sorengaral," she answered. "The more I think about it, the more convinced I am that Hana never wanted to go there, and that once she was there, that she didn't want to hurt anyone."

This time even Lord Narunë scoffed. "I find that hard to believe."

Rondel's harsh look passed to the Kodaman prince. Lyubo loosed a breath to have her eyes off him. "Consider Kenwë's description of what happened," Rondel said. "Hana arrived and demanded the Karyozaki. When your people refused, she knocked over trees. It was a mighty stunt that showed her power, but in truth it was harmless. Only after the Kodamas attacked her did she fight back, and as soon as she had the Karyozaki, she left. Do you get it? Her goal was to obtain the Karyozaki. That must have been what Melwar ordered her to do."

Rondel's eyes fell on each of the Kodamas. "I know this is hard for you all to accept, but consider the alternative. Had Hana wanted to wipe out the Aokigaharan Kodamas, this was her opportunity. They were gathered in one place. She knew the only one who could stop her—you, Minawë—was miles away. They were helpless."

This was the chance Lyubo had been looking for. He jumped in on the old woman, "That's why we need you here, Minawë. Hana could come back at any time and kill us all, but if you're here, you can protect us. We need you." He braced himself and gave her his most caring smile. "I need you."

Minawë's hands trembled. She seemed unable to meet Lyubo's gaze. "Do you . . . really mean that?" she asked.

"Of course I do."

Rondel cocked an eyebrow. "Do you? Or are you saying that because Narunë told you to?"

Lyubo stiffened. "What?"

Lord Narunë looked just as panicked. "Rondel?" he asked. "What do you mean? What are you accusing me of?"

Sparks filled Rondel's eyes. "Manipulating my daughter's emotions."

"That's preposterous!"

"Is it? I asked you to convince her to stay in Sorengaral, but you knew you couldn't persuade her. The only way to make her stay was to give her someone to take Iren off her mind. So you ordered Lyubo to befriend and woo her."

Lyubo flashed a look between Lord Narunë and Rondel. What was the old Maantec doing? Convincing Minawë to stay had been her idea from the start! Why was she giving him up just when he had succeeded?

Minawë met Lord Narunë's eyes. "Is it true, Uncle?"

Lord Narunë could lie and manipulate with the best of them, even Rondel. Lyubo knew the man would work his way out of this.

Only he didn't. He lowered his eyes. "Your mother's right," he said. "I asked Lyubo to make you want to stay in Sorengaral."

Then his expression hardened. "And I did it because your mother asked me to. So tell me, Rondel, what are you playing at? Just a few minutes ago you were saying the Kodamas were safe because Minawë was staying here."

"I spoke too quickly back at the village," Rondel replied. "After thinking about it, I realized Minawë can't stay here."

"But she must!" Lyubo cried. "If Hana comes back and Minawë isn't here—"

"That won't happen," Rondel interrupted. "I'm certain Melwar's determined that we could have reached Sorengaral by now. He knows Hana can't defeat Minawë here, and he won't send her into a fight he knows she'll lose, not when the risk is him losing the Enryokiri. It's his best weapon against me."

Minawë loosed a long breath. "That's what convinced you Melwar is controlling Hana. Hana knew she had one chance, and only one chance, to kill the Aokigaharan Kodamas. Yet she didn't take advantage of it. Melwar ordered her to get the Karyozaki, but he must not have mentioned the Kodamas. She followed his order, but she didn't go beyond it."

Rondel nodded. "Melwar didn't leave out the Kodamas by accident. He knows you're a threat. He hoped you would see the devastation and stay in Aokigahara to protect your people. I don't know what he's planning, but he wants you here when it happens. That's reason enough for me not to."

Lord Narunë frowned. "So what will you two do now?"

Minawë looked at him with eyes that reminded Lyubo of the jaguar's. "Nothing's changed," she said. "I'm going back to Shikari. If Melwar's controlling Hana, then I'm going after him."

"And I'm going too," Rondel added. "It's past time I introduced Melwar to Okthora's Law."

"You're five weeks from Shikari," Lord Narunë pointed out. "Whatever you hope to do, can you reach Melwar in time?"

"You don't need to escort us this time," Rondel said. "Now that I've made the journey a couple times, I have a better sense of where to go. Minawë, change into a fly. You can ride in one of my pockets while I run through the forest with my speed enhanced. It won't be as fast as if we were on an open plain, but I think we can cut that five-week delay in half, if not more."

Minawë considered a moment, then smiled. "I have a better idea. Going through the jungle twice doesn't make you an expert. There's a lot here that can tangle up the unwary. Even Lightning Sight isn't enough. You need more than one sense."

"Oh? What's your plan, then?"

The queen changed back into the black jaguar, but the fury was gone from its eyes. Instead, they looked excited.

Rondel cocked an eyebrow. "You really think you can keep pace with me in that form?"

Minawë tilted her head sideways and flashed a cat-grin.

"Minawë!" Lyubo had to try one last time. "I never lied to you. I really do care about you. I have ever since I first met you. I love you."

The jaguar regarded him. "When Iren turned his back on me, I didn't understand why," Minawë said. "I think now I do, at least a little. I'm sorry."

Then she was gone, off through the jungle. Rondel gave her a five-second head start, and then the old Maantec ran off as well.

Lyubo watched them go. "I failed you, Lord Narunë."

The prince shook his head. "You did no such thing. I failed by not understanding Minawë. She's like her mother; she won't be caged. Even if she didn't feel betrayed, she still would have left."

"Will she come back?" Lyubo asked.

"Maybe," Lord Narunë said, "but then again, maybe not. If she does, I don't think you'll have another chance with her."

"You knew how I felt about her. That's why you asked me to approach her. I never could have worked up the courage without your blessing."

"For that I am truly sorry. I turned her against you."

Lyubo wiped his eyes. He would not cry in front of his prince. "No, I'm glad I got to spend even a few weeks with her. She's something special."

Lord Narunë sighed. "That she is. Come on. Let's head back to Sorengaral. They'll need our help to rebuild. Rondel and Minawë have their mission. It's time we returned to ours."

ↃБ

Minawë raced through the forest on four padded feet. Rondel dashed alongside her, cutting through branches and vines with her dagger.

The Kodaman queen hadn't felt this way in months. For a time she'd believed her place was between Rondel and Iren. Then she'd believed it was in Sorengaral with Lyubo.

Now she realized those were mere distractions. Melwar had played them all for fools. He wanted to keep Iren, Rondel, and Minawë busy with fear and revenge so he could achieve his true goal, whatever that was.

But Minawë was onto him now. He wouldn't get away.

Even so, it made her wonder. Iren was likely still in Shikari. Mother had said she would fight Melwar, but she hadn't abandoned her desire to kill Iren either. Shikari was a small nation. What would she and Minawë do if they met Iren along the way?

Minawë's thoughts drifted back to Lyubo. He had manipulated her, as had her uncle and mother. She had no doubt that Lyubo's feelings were genuine, but she couldn't get his betrayal out of her head.

That was how Iren must have felt about Minawë and Rondel. Minawë could see how those feelings could make him want to leave everyone behind.

Now that she understood that, she also had her answer. What would she do if she ran into Iren? The same thing she'd planned to do since leaving Ziorsecth more than a year ago.

She would save him.

CHAPTER TWENTY-ONE
Unexpected Visitors

A cold southern wind pummeled Iren atop a bare mountain several miles from Goro and Chiyo's farm. It cut through his increasingly threadbare kimono and threatened to send him into shivers, but he resisted. He couldn't let anything distract him, not if Muryoka was going to succeed.

Despite its bleak conditions, the mountain peak was the only place Iren felt comfortable practicing the spell. The summit was a five-mile hike from the nearest farm. It was also above the treeline, so there weren't even animals or plants to worry about killing. If the worst happened, at least Iren would be the only casualty.

Iren held out his left hand, palm up. His right hand gripped the Muryozaki. It was strange, holding the weapon in his off hand like that. But he had better control with his left arm, and control was the problem. He had enough magic to cast Muryoka, if only he could harness it.

His palm glowed. The brightness increased for ten seconds. Then, with a *whoosh*, it caught alight.

It was progress. The first two weeks after Divinion had shown him Muryoka, Iren hadn't even been able to get the fire started. That required making the magic clash with itself to raise its temperature.

Unfortunately, making the flame was the easy part. Once it lit, Iren had to force it to take an unnaturally dense form as a ball in his hand.

That step was where his father had failed. The burning magic wanted to do anything but condense, and Iren Saito had lacked the control necessary to make it do otherwise.

After a month of trying, his son was finding that he had the same problem.

The worst part was that Iren couldn't hold the spell indefinitely. The flame burned through magic at an astonishing rate. From his attempts so far, Iren had determined that he had only twenty seconds before the spell consumed all his magic, and that was under ideal conditions. In a battle, where he would be using magic throughout the fight, he would have even less time.

That was why his father had released Muryoka early. If he hadn't, the spell would have begun drawing on his biological magic, possibly killing him.

Iren tamped down all those thoughts as he condensed the white flame in his hand. Today's was a good attempt. The fire had started out taller than he was, but Iren shrank it to the length of his arm.

His energy sagged; he couldn't last any longer. Abandoning hope of success today, Iren thrust out his hand. The white flame shot forth, burning the air in front of him. The peak was the tallest around, so there was nothing Muryoka could bounce off of and kill him with backwash.

All the same, Iren never escaped Muryoka unscathed. The failed spell left his hand and lower arm charred with heavy burns. Even the Muryozaki needed a few minutes to repair the magic-induced damage.

Iren dropped to his knees, spent. He fought a wave of nausea. He could only try the attack once per day. It used up all his magic to cast it.

While he rested, he looked down at Goro and Chiyo's farm. He could see the pair of them—specks from here—working in the garden together. It made him smile. They were perfect for each other.

He was about to stand and head back when he happened to glance down the overgrown dirt track that led to the farm. Goro and Chiyo rarely traveled, and visitors were even rarer. Aside from the annual tribute collector, Iren had been the first in more than a decade.

That was why Iren's breath quickened when he spotted two dots moving toward the farm.

As with Goro and Chiyo, Iren couldn't make out the newcomers' details at this distance. They were moving quickly though, too quickly for them to be on foot.

Iren frowned. Almost no one around here owned a horse. The few farmers who did had low-quality draft animals suited only to plowing fields. No farmer ever rode his horse. Only high-ranking samurai and nobles did that.

Nobles.

Damn.

Iren scrambled down the mountainside as quickly as he dared. It wasn't a sheer cliff, but a misplaced foot could still end with him dropping a hundred feet in places. Even for a Maantec, falls like that could kill.

At last he hit more sloping terrain and took off. He didn't have magic, but his Maantec strength and training gave him a speed far greater than most. He rushed through the miles of forest between the mountain and the farm, hoping he could make it in time. The newcomers had looked perhaps twenty minutes from the farm when Iren had seen them. If he hurried, he might just beat them.

He approached the farm from the direction opposite that of the strangers and hid behind the tool shed. He wanted to know who they were—and why they were here—before he revealed himself.

When the pair came into view, Iren knew he'd made the right choice in coming back. Both strangers wore full steel lamellar armor and rode on horseback. They each carried two swords, one a full-length katana and the other a shorter wakizashi.

Iren grimaced. As if it weren't blatantly obvious whom these two served, one of the men bore an enormous flag twice his height. Emblazoned on the plum-colored fabric was the insignia of a mountain, the Melwar clan's crest.

At least Iren didn't have to worry about the samurai spotting him behind the shed. With steel helmets wrapped around their skulls, their peripheral vision would be nonexistent. They wouldn't see him unless they turned to look straight at him.

The samurai stopped in front of Goro and Chiyo's house. "Come out!" the one with the flag roared. "By order of His Excellency, Shogun Melwar!"

Iren's brow furrowed. Shogun? He knew the word from his Maantec culture training with Hana. It signified a general, a military leader who outranked even the highest nobility. But Melwar hadn't used that title during Iren's time in Hiabi. In fact, from what little Maantec history Iren knew, there hadn't been a shogun in more than five thousand years. There hadn't needed to be. The emperor ruled the Maantecs.

Goro and Chiyo came around the side of the house. The moment Goro saw who had arrived, he jumped and started shaking. The farming couple prostrated themselves on the ground.

"To what do we owe the honor of receiving Shogun Melwar's samurai?" Goro asked from the dirt.

"Shogun Melwar has ordered a draft of Maantec males," the flag-bearer said. "Every family must supply a man as part of their tribute to His Excellence."

Iren released a breath he hadn't realized he'd been holding. When he'd first seen the samurai, he'd thought they might be looking for him. But what was this about a draft? What was Melwar planning?

"With all due respect, my lord, I am the only man in this family," Goro said. "We have no children. Some of the harvest has come in, but we're nowhere near finished. If I leave, my wife will starve."

Iren couldn't see the samurai's expressions from this angle, but neither seemed moved. "We must all make sacrifices for the restoration of the Maantec people," the empty-handed samurai said.

"But—"

"Enough!" the other samurai roared. "Or would you prefer us to run down your wife to save her the trouble of starving?"

Iren clenched his fists and teeth. Across the way, Goro did the same.

"Now on your feet, peasant," the samurai with the flag ordered. "We'll lead you to the camp with the other conscripts."

Goro slowly rose. Chiyo climbed up alongside him. "Please, Goro, don't go," she begged. She wrapped her arms around her husband.

"Hey!" the flag-bearer shouted. "I didn't tell you to get up. Get back on the ground." He charged his horse forward and kicked Chiyo in the face. She sprawled in the dirt.

Goro didn't react. "It's all right," he said, the hate in his voice so poorly contained even Iren picked up on it. "We don't have a choice. No one else is here."

As he spoke that last sentence, Goro tilted his head ever so slightly, just enough that one eye faced the tool shed. That eye locked with the one of Iren's that peeked around the building's wall.

Goro knew Iren was there. He'd known all along. Why hadn't he said something? If Iren went with the samurai, then Goro could stay. Why was the man lying to them?

"What will I do?" Chiyo cried.

"Pray hard," Goro told her. "Maybe an angel will come to help you."

Iren felt tears on his cheeks. Chiyo often told him how much more productive the farm was with him around to help. By keeping Iren from the samurai, Goro was ensuring his wife's survival.

"No angels around here, peasant," the flagless samurai laughed. "The only one you should pray to is Shogun Melwar!"

Goro bowed. "I'll keep that in mind. Thank you for telling me."

"Goro," Chiyo said from the ground. "Please don't. Please don't do this."

The flagless samurai dismounted. "I never said you could speak. You're a disobedient little bitch, aren't you? We can't allow such a lack of respect among Shogun Melwar's people."

The samurai drew his katana. "It's for the best," he said. "You'll starve once your husband leaves anyway."

Goro's control snapped. "No!" he shouted. He ran at the samurai, but the soldier thrust his gauntleted hand at Goro's face. Blood spurted from Goro's nose as metal fist and katana crossguard smashed into it. He dropped to the ground beside his wife.

"So easily overcome," the flag-bearer said. "These peasants will be useless in the war with Lodia."

Iren stifled a curse. So that's what the draft was for. Melwar was raising an army to attack Lodia!

"They'd only slow us down and take up rations," the dismounted samurai replied. "A drain on the army. Better to end them both now." He raised his katana over Goro's prone form.

This had gone far enough. Iren stepped out from behind the shed. "Stop," he said. "You will not touch these kind people again."

Both samurai turned to regard him. Iren could only see their eyes through their helmets, but he saw the disdain in them. He expected it.

With his ratty clothes worn from training and chores, he looked even lower class than Goro and Chiyo.

Then the samurai's expressions changed to shock and fury. Their eyes settled on Iren's waist.

"You!" the flag-bearer said. "It's punishable by death for anyone other than a samurai to carry a katana. Where did you get that weapon?"

Iren drew the Muryozaki. "If you want it, come and take it. Dole out your justice."

"No," Goro wheezed through his blood-stained face. "Run away."

"Shut your mouth!" the dismounted samurai yelled.

Iren didn't give the man a chance to do anything else. He charged. The dismounted man noticed and ran at him as well. When they were only a few feet apart, the samurai swung his katana at Iren's head.

With an easy motion, Iren ducked the blow. The samurai's bulky armor slowed him and left him open. Worse, it wouldn't protect him from the Muryozaki's dragonscale blade. Iren slashed.

His sword barely paused as it sliced through the steel and bit into the flesh beneath. The samurai fell and did not rise.

Iren marched forward. "Now talk," he spat at the mounted flag-bearer. "What's this about a war with Lodia? What's Melwar planning?"

The samurai's eyes trembled inside his helmet. He careened his horse around and galloped away.

If Iren hadn't exhausted his magic on Muryoka, he might have chased after him. He might have fired a beam of white light and shot the horse out from under him. But he'd only recovered a sliver of magic in the time since he'd left the mountain, and he needed it for a more important purpose. He rushed to where Goro and Chiyo lay.

Iren put a hand on each of the two farmers and let his scraps of energy flow into them. Their cuts stitched together.

Goro raised his head and felt his repaired nose. "Katsu, how did you do all that?" he asked.

"With this," Iren said. He held up the Muryozaki. "I suppose there's no point in hiding anymore. You were right to distrust me, Goro. I lied to you. My name isn't Katsu. It's Iren Saitosan. I'm the Holy Dragon Knight."

The farmer's mouth fell open. "Iren . . . Saito . . ."

Goro dropped back to the dirt. "Forgive me, my emperor, for not showing you the proper respect!"

Iren rolled his eyes. "That isn't necessary. I know how much you dislike the class structure. On your feet. You too, Chiyo."

They both stood. Chiyo looked at Iren with admiration. "I knew there was more to you than what you let on," she said, "but I never would have guessed you were the emperor."

"I'm not," Iren said. "Iren Saito's dead. I'm his child."

"That makes you the emperor, son," Goro said, "whether you acknowledge it or not."

Iren didn't miss the way Goro had spoken to him. He'd called Iren "son." In the three months Iren had stayed here, Goro had never used that word to describe him. In fact, it was the first time in his life Iren could remember anyone calling him that. The sound of it choked him up.

"Goro, don't push the man," Chiyo interjected.

"I'm sorry I didn't tell you," Iren said. "To be honest, it felt good to be thought of as nothing more than a farmhand."

"So that was you that night in the forest," Goro replied. "I knew it."

Iren nodded.

"What will you do now?" Chiyo asked. "You're welcome to stay here and continue your training. We'll welcome you with open arms, won't we Goro?"

Goro looked at his wife, then at Iren. It took him a few seconds to respond, but then he said, "Of course. You're the best thing ever to happen to this farm. If you hadn't come along, those samurai would have killed us. You'll always have a home here, if you want it."

Iren took a step back. A home. He'd had one of those once, in Ziorsecth Forest with Minawë. It seemed like a lifetime ago. How he longed for one! And here were these farmers offering one up to him freely, not because he was the emperor, but because they felt it was the right thing to do.

But Iren shook his head. "I'm sorry. After what happened today, I can't stay here anymore. I wanted to escape the world and focus on revenge, but outside this farm, Raa still moves. I won't let Melwar bring war to Lodia or any other land. It's my responsibility as the Holy Dragon Knight, and," he paused to steel himself, "as the Maantec emperor."

Goro put a hand on Iren's shoulder. "An emperor needs subjects, son. He needs people who can support him. Let me come with you."

Iren smiled and returned the gesture. "Thanks, but where I'm going, I'll be better off alone. You should stay here with Chiyo. You two will have a splendid harvest this year. Use it to grow this farm and this family."

He walked away from them. He briefly considered taking the slain samurai's horse, but then he reconsidered. He wouldn't need it once his magic recovered. "Goro!" he called over his shoulder. "This is a good horse. He's yours now."

The farmer's mouth dropped open a second time. "That's a samurai's horse, the finest-bred animals in Shikari. He's worth gold."

"Should be useful for building that nursery, then," Iren said. "See you!"

Iren dropped into a run and left the farm following the hoofprints of the retreating samurai. With luck, he would catch up to the man and wring out a few answers. If not, Iren already had a good idea what his next destination should be.

Hiabi.

CHAPTER TWENTY-TWO
The Melwar Clan's Genius

Hana prostrated herself in Shogun Melwar's chamber. In front of her lay the Zuryokaiten. The small metal pipe looked pathetic compared with the other Ryokaiten Hana had seen, but she knew firsthand how dangerous it was.

The shogun stepped forward and picked up the weapon. Like before, when he'd touched the Karyozaki, the weapon didn't respond to him.

It made no sense. Shogun Melwar wasn't a Dragon Knight. Why didn't the weapon test him?

"Rise, Hana," her master said, "you have done well."

Hana stood and felt relief at the pleased expression on Shogun Melwar's face. She had feared her delay while waiting for Faro to die underground might have angered him. Instead, his eyes glittered with excitement. She had never seen him this energetic.

"Only one Ryokaiten remains unaccounted for," the shogun said, "the Auryozaki."

All Hana's comfort vanished. She forced herself not to swallow. She had prepared for this.

"I do not suppose you saw any sign of it on your journey, did you?" her master asked.

She couldn't lie, but she could tell partial truths. "I did not, Shogun."

"None at all? Not even a rumor as to its location?"

She'd heard plenty about the Auryozaki's location from Iren Saitosan and Balear, but she didn't need to tell Shogun Melwar that.

He'd asked about her most recent journey, not ones in the past. "No, Shogun. The Lodians know little of dragons."

Melwar's eyes examined every inch of her. She felt naked under that look.

"We could go after Rondel," Hana offered. "If it's a matter of overcoming the storms at sea, Okthora would be the dragon to find."

The shogun's mouth became a thin line. "As I recall, you had that opportunity once and failed."

This time Hana couldn't resist gulping. "I defeated her before. I can do it again."

"I doubt it. Besides, you know we cannot afford to have Rondel focused on us. For now, we will make do with what we have. Mizuchi is enough to get us what we need."

"As you say, Shogun," Hana replied.

In truth, though, she doubted him. Mizuchi was powerful, but could a new Water Dragon Knight really get them through the storms alive?

The corners of Shogun Melwar's mouth rose. His eyes warmed in a way that would have been reassuring had anyone else made the expression. "Relax, Hana," he said. "In truth I appreciate your efforts. In fact, I would like to reward you for your success."

Hana rocked back. Shogun Melwar didn't bestow favors upon his servants. You did what you were told because he was in charge, and because the punishment for disobedience was unpleasant.

The Maantec leader's smile widened. "It is a small thing, and yet, it is the rarest gift I could bestow. I want to tell you a story."

Curiosity replaced surprise. What was he planning?

Shogun Melwar sat in his high-backed chair at the room's far end. "Until now this tale has been limited to members of my clan," he said. "It is passed down among the family's main line with the strictest confidence that no one outside the clan may learn it."

He paused and smiled. "So, Hana, it is with great pleasure that I induct you into the Melwar clan. You are no longer Hana Akiyama. From now on you shall be Hana Melwar. As shogun and head of the clan, it is my right to grant you this status."

Hana was spellbound. The Akiyama clan had some minor nobility to it, but it was nothing compared with the Melwar clan. Before the Kodama-Maantec War, the Melwar clan had been the strongest of all the Maantec families save the royal Saito household.

"I am the last of my clan," Shogun Melwar said. "We are about to embark on a great mission, one I have spent a thousand years contemplating. I take no risks in anything. When you live forever, why rush and chance a mistake? Still, war thinks little of plans. I do not anticipate anything happening to me, but if something did, someone must know. There is no one else suitable."

He paused again to clear his throat. "Hana, how many dragons are there?"

Hana's brow furrowed. So far the shogun's story wasn't much of a story. It was an honor to be named one of his family, but practically speaking, it meant little. Her Dragon Knight status conferred as high a rank, and it wasn't like she had married him.

She didn't want to question him though, so she answered, "There are eight, Shogun."

The Maantec leader smiled. "Ah, in that you would be wrong. There are nine."

Hana blinked twice. She couldn't stop herself. "Every Maantec child knows the tale of how Juusa the Creator built the world and left eight dragons to keep its balance of nature intact."

"And that tale is true, but it is incomplete. Juusa did create eight dragons, but in his haste to preserve the world's balance, he almost destroyed it. He created Divinion, the Holy Dragon, to oversee all that was good in this world: light, healing, and kindness. But what are these things without their opposites? For balance to occur, another dragon was needed. So in secret, Plutanis the Destroyer created a ninth dragon: Shadeen, the Darkness Dragon."

Hana was shocked. She had never heard of Shadeen.

"No one knew Shadeen existed," Shogun Melwar continued. "He disguised himself as a man and worked to disrupt the dragons' unity. It was Shadeen who provoked the other eight dragons into warring with one another and ultimately sinking Teneb ten thousand years ago."

Shogun Melwar gestured at Hana. "You know what happened next," he said. "The Maantecs and Kodamas feared the dragons would destroy Raa as well. To stop that, a hundred mages from each race combined their magic and cast the spell to seal the dragons into gems. But when the spell finished, there were nine gems, not eight."

"No one noticed that an extra gem had appeared out of nowhere?" Hana asked.

"Remember your history. The spell the mages cast consumed their biological magic and killed them. No one was around to see the results of their handiwork. It was only later that one of my ancestors happened to be the first person to arrive at the site of the spell. He had been instructed to locate the gems and turn them over to the emperor. But the emperor only expected eight gems, and that is how many he received. The ninth my ancestor kept for himself."

Hana's curiosity about Shogun Melwar's supposed gift had disappeared. The man was rambling like an old fool. What was the point to all this?

Something in her boredom must have shown on her face, because the shogun gave one of his subtle smiles. "You wonder what this has to do with you. That is fair. But you must know the beginning in order to understand the end. For instance, did you know that it was a Melwar who first proposed the Ryokaiten? He wanted to know more about this mysterious ninth gem. He convinced the emperor of the idea, and a team of mages went to work. When the mages finished, the Melwar clan used what they had learned and made their own Ryokaiten for Shadeen. It was only then that the clan discovered Shadeen and learned his history. We have sworn ourselves to him ever since. We keep his secret, and in exchange, the strongest Melwar clan member becomes the Darkness Dragon Knight."

The shogun held out his left hand. Black smoke appeared from nowhere and curled around it. The smoke condensed in his palm, and a katana appeared there. The weapon seemed as insubstantial as the smoke that had created it, but Hana remembered it from a sparring bout between Shogun Melwar and Iren last year. It was both solid and not at the same time. It would pass through an enemy's blade and then slice that enemy in half.

"Everyone believes I am not a Dragon Knight, but I am," the shogun declared. "I am the Darkness Dragon Knight."

Hana couldn't help but tremble. She knew Shogun Melwar was powerful, but the man had held back his true strength all this time, more than a thousand years, to keep Shadeen's existence secret.

That begged a question. "Forgive me for asking," Hana said, "but why reveal Shadeen now? You aren't the type to do anything without purpose."

"I needed you to know so you would understand what I have to show you next. This strength is the true key to our victory. Hana, have you guessed why I sent you looking for Ryokaiten these past few months?"

"I assumed you wanted to create Dragon Knights to aid us."

Shogun Melwar shook his head. "For a thousand years I have used others to achieve the long task of restoring Maantecs to glory. I believed the best I could do was direct the plan from the shadows. Now I see that was foolish. I put my faith in Iren Saito and his son to serve as our figureheads, but they abandoned their people. I expected the Fubuki to conquer Lodia, but they lost. I relied on Azar to kill the Aokigaharan Kodamas, but he was slain. The time to watch has passed. It is time the Maantecs had a leader they can depend on, a shogun with power so immense no one would dare resist him."

"What does that have to do with the Ryokaiten?" Hana asked. "How are they useful to you if you won't give them to others? You're already a Dragon Knight."

The excited glitter returned to Shogun Melwar's eyes. "That is the real secret I wanted to share today. You needed to know Shadeen's past in order to understand it. Now, let me show you why we will triumph where even Iren Saito failed."

He stood and removed both his shirts so that he stood bare-chested before Hana. She gasped; both the Burning Ruby and Frozen Pearl were embedded in Shogun Melwar's torso. A pair of kanji rings were tattooed around each of them.

"Do you understand?" he asked. "This is the power of a shogun. This is the Melwar clan's genius. We who proposed the Ryokaiten have now perfected the design."

He pointed to the two rings encircling the Burning Ruby. "The Ryokaiten have three rings. The first lets you use the dragon's power. The second lets the dragon test would-be Dragon Knights. The third prevents the dragon's will from escaping except when you draw on its magic. It was the second ring that was the problem. It gave the dragons a choice in who could use their magic, and it prevented a person from wielding more than one dragon at a time. I removed it, so now both Feng and Yukionna have no choice but to accept me as their master."

Hana dropped to her knees. With three dragons at his command, Shogun Melwar was invincible.

Then Hana panicked. It wasn't three dragons. It was four. She had brought him Mizuchi's Ryokaiten. The Aqua Sapphire now belonged to Shogun Melwar.

And if he had four dragons, why stop there? He could kill Hana at any time and take the Rock Topaz. Then he would have a majority. Even if every remaining Dragon Knight assaulted him at once, he would still have them outnumbered.

Shogun Melwar must have read her fear. "Worry not, Hana Melwar. Your Ryokaiten is safe. Even with all this power, I am but one person. I can only be in one place at a time. I will need another leader to help me win this war."

Hana thought back on the people she'd killed, the destruction she'd unleashed in the name of Maantec restoration. A few years ago she would have enjoyed it. Now it appalled her. She'd become a monster, just like her master.

But maybe it was worth it. There was conflict in Raa because it lacked a strong ruler. Once Shogun Melwar was in charge, there would be peace. No one would dare oppose him after they saw the dragons' gems embedded in his flesh.

There was only one response Hana could make: "How may I serve?"

CHAPTER TWENTY-THREE
Preparations

Balear stood alone on Kataile's plateau. The catapult crews had left for the day, gone back to their families for dinner and rest.

Not Balear. He'd spent the day supervising construction, so he hadn't had time for his own practice.

It had been worth it, though, to see the progress. Most of the catapults were built, and the crews had begun hauling stones from the plateau over to them. Balear helped where he could, inspiring them to greater effort. If their general could keep going with only one arm, surely they could do the same with two.

Balear wandered to the plateau's edge and looked north. How soon would the enemy come? Spring had arrived, and the inland cities' winter stores would be all but exhausted. If the war continued, they would starve.

But the war wouldn't continue. Balear had worked through the scenarios. He knew the one he'd settled on would play itself out.

They would come soon. They wouldn't risk giving Kataile any more time than necessary.

Balear turned from the edge and looked through the deepening gloom. He confirmed that he had the place to himself, and then he drew the Auryozaki.

He tried a few practice swings, slowly to get the momentum down. There was plenty of room up here. In fact, it was the only place in the city Balear felt comfortable using the gigantic sword after he'd wrecked that fountain.

Balear slashed the weapon in all directions, working through the motions of past battles. The wind whistled off each attack.

It wasn't magic. Balear kept telling himself that. It was just that the weapon was so large, yet so light, that he could swing it fast enough to push away the air.

Yet with each strike, he wondered: when the enemy came, could he raise this sword against them? Could he keep his oath?

Visions of Veliaf danced in his mind. He would keep it. The Sky Dragon would never see daylight as long as Balear lived.

The other cities would come, and Balear would face them as he was. One way or the other, Lodia's civil war would end here in Kataile.

He would be ready.

CB

From a window on the top floor of Kataile's city hall, Elyssa Orianna watched Balear practice. She ran a hand through her graying auburn hair.

Try as she might, she couldn't take her eyes off the young general. He was amazing. He started before everyone else and finished after everyone else. She had never seen anyone so motivated. Even Balio hadn't been this strong.

Her right hand gripped Balio's scroll, the one he had dictated to her twenty years ago. Every night since Balear had started the catapult construction, Elyssa had come to this window to watch him practice. Every night she brought the scroll, and every night she thought about going out onto that plateau and giving it to him.

She'd promised Balio. She owed it to him.

But no. The time wasn't right yet. Elyssa couldn't afford for Balear to be distracted. Later, when her city was saved and she made queen, there would be time. She would give him the scroll and apologize for using him.

Until then, he would have to be her pawn.

CHAPTER TWENTY-FOUR
Maantec Armada

Iren Saitosan tracked the fleeing samurai back to a massive camp. Fifty samurai kept watch over five hundred conscripts from the surrounding farms.

Their draft effort must have finished, because a day after Iren arrived, they broke camp and set off in the direction of Hiabi. Iren had no trouble following them. By day the samurai drove the men hard, but each night they stopped and rested. Iren kept clear while they marched, using the time to search for food in the wilds of Shikari. In the evenings he followed the samurai's trail at high speed and caught up.

He had no fear that he might lose them. The force made no effort to disguise its passing, and the man at the head of the column kept the banner of Shogun Melwar aloft at all times.

Iren didn't worry about someone noticing him either. The samurai positioned themselves not to defend the conscripts but to guard against them escaping. The notion that someone might stalk them must never have entered the samurai's minds.

After a week of travel, Iren entered lands he recognized. The conscripts had almost reached Hiabi. Once there, maybe Iren would get some answers about this war Melwar had planned. With luck, he'd find a way to stop it too.

Iren topped a craggy hill coated in scrub and beheld Hiabi splayed out below him. Even though he'd spent several months in the city, its appearance still astounded him. It surpassed any Lodian city in size, and its castle keep made Haldessa's look like a farmhouse. The sweeping, concave roofs of ceramic tiles guided the eye up.

Not only was the city beautiful, it was also a cunningly devised fortress. Its stone perimeter wall was a hundred feet tall and twenty feet thick. Even if a force somehow breached it, Hiabi's narrow, twisting streets would quickly split up and disorient the attackers. All the while, the defenders could take them out with arrows, rocks, and burning pitch.

Today though, it was neither Hiabi's strength nor its splendor that most drew Iren's attention. That prize went to the twelve enormous ships stationed in a semicircle off the city's coast. Four hundred feet long, they dwarfed the largest ships Iren had ever seen set anchor in the Bay of Ceere. Each had four decks and half a dozen masts. Wooden beams stretched in rows across the square sails that were as tall and wide as the ships themselves.

Atop each ship's tallest mast flew a purple banner with the symbol of a mountain. Iren shuddered as he realized what those ships were: an invasion fleet.

The rumors from the samurai at Goro and Chiyo's farm were true. The Maantecs were going to war.

ଓଃ

A few hours past dawn, Rondel and Minawë lay prone on a hill northeast of Hiabi. They stared in wonder at the ships below them.

"I never thought he would do something like this," Rondel whispered.

"What are those things?" Minawë asked.

Rondel furrowed her brow, but then she remembered that Minawë had grown up in a forest. She'd never seen a ship before. "They're called junks," Rondel said, "and don't think they're worthless because of their name. Those ships are the largest Raa has ever seen. Each carries a thousand men, and they'll be well armed with everything from clubs to katanas to fire-arrows. See how the sails have wooden bars going across them? The sailors can change their configuration in any number of ways to grab the wind. Even without a breeze, there are spots to extend oars to row the ships. Junks are big, fast, and designed to carry a lot of men into combat."

Minawë gulped. "So that's Melwar's plan. He's going to invade another country, but he doesn't want to risk sending his army through Aokigahara."

"It's still too big a risk for him," Rondel said. "There are only twelve junks. Assuming they're full, that's more than ten thousand Maantecs. That would be more than enough to conquer Lodia or Tacumsah, but even junks can't survive the ocean storms between here and those countries."

Rondel activated Lightning Sight and examined the junks. Melwar was too careful not to realize they couldn't make the journey. He must have another plan.

Maybe he didn't intend to go up the eastern coast. The western ocean didn't get storms like the eastern one did.

But that wouldn't improve his situation. The only landing sites along that route would be in Serona or Charda. Those wastelands would wipe out his army as easily as a storm.

There had to be a clue somewhere. Melwar had waited a thousand years for this war. He wouldn't gamble his plan on the vagaries of weather.

Even at this distance, Lightning Sight made every detail of the junks clear. Still, Rondel saw nothing that suggested they were any different from junks she'd sailed on during the Kodama-Maantec War. Whatever Melwar's plan was, the ships themselves weren't part of it.

Then Rondel caught sight of Melwar himself. He stood on the middle deck of the junk at the fleet's center.

Rondel took an involuntary sharp breath. Melwar was in full formal dress, his plum-colored kimono flowing around him. Hana stood at his side, looking tense.

"What do you see?" Minawë asked.

"Hana and Melwar are talking. Let me focus; I might be able to read their lips."

She watched them for several seconds. Then she said, "Melwar's saying that preparations are complete. They'll be leaving within the hour. They're going to take the ships north along the coast, but far enough out to sea that they won't risk running aground." She paused. "Hana wants to know her orders. Melwar says they'll land in Ceere.

Hana will captain the *Torment*, while Melwar will command the *Shadeen*."

"*Torment* sounds like Melwar's style, but what does *Shadeen* mean?"

"I have no idea," Rondel admitted. "I've never heard the word before, and I was raised by the best Maantec teacher in history."

The old Maantec frowned. "Something else is odd," she said. "Hana belongs to the Akiyama clan, but Melwar keeps calling her by his name: Hana Melwar."

"He married her?"

"It's possible, but I doubt it," Rondel said. "It's more likely that he adopted her into his family as a sign of status. Heads of clans have that privilege. Still, it's a softhearted move for him."

"Maybe you were right back in Aokigahara, and Hana isn't convinced she wants to help Melwar," Minawë said. "If Melwar suspected that Hana doubted his cause, then bringing her into his family might be a way of securing her loyalty."

Rondel smiled. "For someone unfamiliar with clan politics, you figured that out quickly. That's my guess too."

She kept watching them, and then she gasped. "So that's it!"

"What's it?" Minawë asked.

"Hana was as in the dark as we were about how they were going to avoid the storms. They aren't going to avoid them. Melwar plans to sail through them. He has the Aqua Sapphire, and he'll use its magic to steady the seas so the ships can keep moving. It's clever. I didn't know Melwar was the Water Dragon Knight."

She paused a moment, then smirked. "If Melwar's the Water Dragon Knight, that should make our fight against him easier. My lightning magic will have an advantage over him."

"In that case we should head down there," Minawë said. "If Melwar can calm the sea, then our only chance to stop him is here in Hiabi. Once the Maantecs leave port, they'll be too far away for us to damage their ships."

Rondel nodded. "Let me see if I can find an unguarded route down. If we get in close, I can distract Melwar and Hana while you manipulate the kelp to grab the junks and rip them apart."

"Kelp?" Minawë asked.

"It's an aquatic plant. In shape it looks like the vines you're fond of using."

Minawë whistled. "I didn't know there were plants underwater."

"Minawë, there are a host of creatures great and small in that ocean. For someone who lived in a forest all her life, most are beyond your imagining. In my younger days, I remember seeing beasts larger than those ships; whales, I believe the Tacumsahens called them."

"Whoa," Minawë said. "I hope I see one someday."

"With your abilities, perhaps you'll be one someday," Rondel said with a wink.

The old Maantec turned her attention back to the distance between their hill and Hiabi. Melwar didn't expect an attack. He would have a few guards stationed just because he was careful, but they would be stretched thin. There had to be a clear path to the water's edge.

As she searched, she noticed a figure on the hill next to theirs. It was sneaking through the scrub toward the city. Rondel focused on the creature and realized it was a man.

Rondel's eyes narrowed. Recruits would be in companies led by samurai. Even if there were lone volunteers, they wouldn't sneak around. They would walk boldly and announce their intention to join Melwar's cause.

Rondel examined the sneaking man more closely, and that's when her heart suddenly skipped. Lightning Sight had caught a flash of white amid the green bushes and brown kimono. A final look at the man's face told Rondel everything she needed to know.

It was Iren Saitosan.

What was he doing here? From the way he was moving, it was clear he knew about Melwar's plan. Was he here to stop Melwar like Rondel and Minawë were, or did he intend to join the Maantecs?

Neither choice would surprise Rondel. If Iren thought helping Melwar would get him closer to revenge, he would ally with the noble in a second.

Rondel had to know the answer. Lasting long enough against Hana and Melwar to let Minawë cripple the junks would be difficult as it was.

If Iren joined the fray too, Minawë's mission would become impossible. Even if Iren intended to stop Melwar, once he saw Rondel under attack, he would take advantage and target her. Rondel's only chance was to reach Iren before he entered Hiabi.

That just left the matter of what to do with Minawë. If Minawë saw Iren, she'd forget the junks and intervene. Rondel couldn't allow that.

Then an idea came to her, a way to distract Hana and Melwar, let Minawë complete her mission, and fulfill Okthora's Law all at the same time. Rondel smiled. If she and Minawë lived through today, this was going to be fun.

CHAPTER TWENTY-FIVE
The Promised Hour

Iren Saitosan crept along the ground down the hill to Hiabi. He couldn't let anyone spot him until he got to the beach. Once there, he could use light beams to blow holes in those ships. They were huge, but they weren't numerous. If he sank even half of them, it would cripple Melwar's force. It might even convince the self-proclaimed shogun to give up his war.

A rustle in the bushes to Iren's left made him pause. He hadn't noticed any patrols on this hill, but that didn't mean they weren't here. He stared in the direction the noise had come from, alert for any movement.

Nothing happened. It must have been an animal or the breeze blowing the stiff plants against one another. He resumed his crawl.

"I could have killed you just now, if I'd wanted to."

Iren froze. He knew that voice. It haunted his dreams.

He stood and revealed his presence on the hill. "Rondel," he spat the name like a curse. "How did you find me?"

Rondel was five feet away, the brush up to her waist. That was good; with Rondel's shorter height, the plants would slow her more than they would Iren.

The old Maantec pointed to a hill east of them, perhaps a mile distant. "I was observing the same situation you were, though I'm sure in more detail." She gestured with her thumb at her eyes. They sparked with Lightning Sight.

"Then you know about the war?" Iren asked.

"From Melwar's own lips. They're going to Ceere."

"No they aren't. I'm going to stop them."

Rondel half-smiled. "Are you now? Here I thought you might be going to join them."

"Don't lump me in with Melwar. Once I finish with you, I'm going down there to sink those ships."

"Once you finish with me? As I remember our last meeting, you were the one lying helpless on the ground."

Iren unsheathed his sword. "I'm different now. You won't win this time."

Rondel drew her dagger. "Well, do your best."

She was goading him. That was Rondel's style. She didn't make the first move.

Still, Iren was surprised. He'd been off guard when Rondel had snuck up on him. Why hadn't she taken advantage and slain him then? Even if Rondel was confident of victory, she wouldn't risk even the smallest chance of losing if it wasn't necessary.

She must have some other purpose. "If I'd wanted to," she had said. Did that mean she didn't want to kill him?

That was impossible. Were it not for Minawë, Rondel would have murdered him the last time they'd fought. There was no way the old woman's attitude had changed. She considered Iren evil like his father.

Which meant she did want to kill him, just not at that moment. Why? What was she planning?

"Whatever you're thinking of using, make it flashy," Rondel said. "Let's give the people of Hiabi a good show."

Iren smirked. If she wanted flashy, there was always Muryoka. Here on this hill, there wouldn't be much to destroy even if the technique wasn't perfect.

But a flawed Muryoka would at best kill Iren along with Rondel. Worse, a poorly aimed shot could end up in the heart of Hiabi. Iren wanted to stop Melwar, not obliterate a city.

"I'm in a hurry," Rondel said. "If you won't start, I will."

She held out her right hand and grasped one of the bushes next to her. Sparks jumped between her fingers.

Iren's brow furrowed. What was the point of that?

Then he realized what the hag had done. The dry tinder burst into flames, and the dense scrub spread that fire. In seconds an inferno engulfed them both.

Iren took off through the choking haze of heat and smoke, trusting in the Muryozaki's healing power to recover from any burns. He couldn't see Rondel, which must have been her intention all along. Lightning Sight would likely still detect him.

He cursed as he ran. Even though it benefited Rondel, Iren didn't understand her strategy. Melwar's ships were only a few miles away. Hiabi was even closer. Every Maantec down there would see the burning spectacle, and Melwar and Hana might recognize it for what it was: a battle between Dragon Knights.

A glint of reflected firelight was all the warning Iren received. Rondel leapt in, her dagger thrusting at his head.

Six months ago the blow would have brained him. Today, his training at Goro and Chiyo's farm saved his life. Iren saw the blade coming and blocked.

Rondel's eyes widened momentarily, but they quickly returned to normal. The old hag followed up with a series of frantic slashes that forced Iren to retreat.

Iren was shocked. The flames, starting the fight, this wild assault . . . none of them were Rondel's style. She preferred a defensive fight. Lightning Sight and her fast speed gave her an instantaneous reaction time. It was to her advantage to wait until her opponent committed to an attack before she struck. She would end a fight quickly if the opportunity presented itself, but she was more apt to study an opponent and figure out a weakness to exploit.

In this battle, though, she fought like something possessed. Instead of taking her time and working out a strategy, she cut and thrust with reckless abandon. Iren had no idea what drove her, but he no longer had time to think. It was simply block or be gutted.

Rondel pushed Iren farther up the hill. The sea breeze carried the fire with them, so no matter how far Iren went, flaming bushes still surrounded him. He wanted to kill Rondel, to take revenge for his parents, but he couldn't get in any attacks. The old hag was pushing herself harder than he'd ever seen.

Sweat poured off Iren. The fires threatened to overwhelm him, and still Rondel pressed her assault.

In desperation Iren cast a shield of light around himself. Rondel struck it twice, but then she stopped. A similar, larger shield had protected both Iren and Rondel from Feng's attacks two years ago. Rondel wasn't going to breach this one.

Still, Iren knew it would only give him a few seconds to catch his breath. He would need them all to figure out how he was going to live through this mess.

ℝ

Minawë flew in low, her seagull form angling around the junks to get a closer look at them. They had thick hulls, likely several feet of solid wood.

Crushing those, even with the vine-like kelp Rondel had described, would be next to impossible. Minawë would have to manipulate the kelp from the shore, and the farther she was from the plants she controlled, the more magic she needed to use.

Maybe she didn't need to sink them all. Each one she damaged was one fewer Melwar could wield against Lodia. If Minawë sank enough, Melwar wouldn't risk an invasion.

Minawë banked and headed for the beach to find an out-of-the-way spot to attack the junks. As she did, she caught sight of Rondel's diversion. The old woman had set the hill north of the city on fire. No doubt such an inferno so close to Hiabi would draw the Maantecs' attention. Minawë just hoped Rondel wasn't anywhere near the blaze.

ℝ

Hana Melwar stood at the railing of the junk *Shadeen*. Next to her, her new namesake watched the flames rising from the hill north of Hiabi.

"A spyglass," the shogun ordered. A few seconds later a sailor ran up to him and handed one over.

"It's late in the year for a fire," Hana said.

"It is," Shogun Melwar replied, "which is why I guess that this one is unnatural. It spreads too quickly."

He looked through the spyglass. "I am correct. There you are, Rondel."

"Rondel Thara?" Hana asked. "What's she doing here?"

The shogun smiled. "Fighting Iren Saitosan, and setting the hill alight as she goes. Each stab of her rondel is only to distract Iren so he will not notice. As she runs, she creates sparks in her right hand that ignite the brush."

"Why would she do that?"

Shogun Melwar lowered his spyglass. "Perhaps she wishes to remove the scrub. It is tall enough to hinder her, but not tall enough to slow Iren. Still, it seems like a poor long-term strategy. Iren can heal himself if the flames burn him, but Rondel cannot."

He stroked his chin a moment. "Okthora's Law," he said at last. "Rondel is as obsessed with carrying it out as Iren is with avenging his parents' murders. She has abandoned rational thought in her desire to kill him."

Hana watched the blaze grow to engulf the hill. "Should I go over there? With all that going on, I could kill them both before they realize I'm there."

The shogun raised his spyglass again. He watched the combatants for more than a minute before he said, "You will remain here. We have a schedule to keep. No matter who survives their fight, they will be in no condition to follow us to Lodia."

Hana nodded and turned away, but as she did, a thought struck her. When Rondel had last traveled to Hiabi, the Forest Dragon Knight had come with her. Could she be nearby as well?

No, she couldn't. That Kodama had risked her life to stop Iren and Rondel's fight. She would never let those two battle this way. Rondel must have made her return to Aokigahara.

It was too bad. Hana had looked forward to a rematch.

CHAPTER TWENTY-SIX
Out of Options

Iren eyed Rondel through the solid light of his shield. Inches outside the barrier, the old woman paced like an animal. She was breathing hard, and she had burns all over her body.

For all that she was still dangerous, perhaps even more than usual. Something about this fight was different for her.

It wasn't the chance to kill him that drove her. Against Iren's father, Rondel had been as cold and emotionless as in any fight Iren had seen her undertake. There had to be another reason driving this savage behavior.

Then again, the reason didn't really matter. What mattered was that by fighting this way, Rondel had sacrificed her biggest advantage: her strategic mind. Her aggression had overpowered Iren at first, but now that he saw it, maybe he could turn it to his advantage.

Iren raised the Muryozaki at the same time that he lowered his shield. Rondel leapt on him at once, slashing high at his head. Iren side-stepped the blow and attacked for the first time in their battle. He aimed a low cut at Rondel's right hip.

The old hag almost died then. She was so focused on her strike that she had overextended herself. She couldn't block in time. At the last second, though, she spun on her heel, came in close to Iren, and thrust her dagger at his right shoulder.

The wicked dodge and counter caught Iren flat-footed. Jolting pain shot through him as Rondel's blade pierced his arm. He leapt back, retreating from Rondel to give the Muryozaki time to heal him.

But Rondel wasn't going to give the sword the chance. She dashed forward and lunged low at Iren's knees. He blocked, and even though his right arm was still injured, he used his apparent disability to take Rondel by surprise. He channeled magic into his right finger and fired at her head.

The blow connected, and Rondel stumbled backward. It wasn't enough to finish her, but at least it proved Iren could hit her. More important, while she recovered, the Muryozaki could finish healing him.

The brushfire had shifted farther up the hill, so the flames and smoke were now beyond the two foes. Iren was glad for the change. At last he could see Rondel clearly.

She attacked again, fifteen strikes in less than three seconds. Iren blocked every one. He took off downhill. Rondel chased him, and soon the pair exchanged blows at a pace so fast anyone watching from the city must have seen nothing but two blurs flashing across the hillside.

How long they battled that way, Iren didn't know. Unfortunately, the fight was progressing just as Divinion had said it would. Iren's speed training allowed him to keep pace with Rondel, but that was the best he could manage. It wasn't enough to win.

He only had one chance. He hated to risk it, but the longer this fight dragged on, the more likely Rondel would kill him. Even if she didn't, more time also allowed for Melwar or Hana to interfere.

Iren stopped and raised his shield again. Rondel paused outside the barrier. She didn't try to attack it this time.

"Am I doing better than you expected?" Iren asked.

Rondel scowled. "You've kept up well," she admitted.

"It's about time you respected me."

To Iren's surprise, the old woman closed her eyes, shook her head, and smiled sadly. "I've respected you from the moment you healed Dirio in Veliaf," she said. "If you ever lost that respect, it's because you let Melwar wrench you away from the kind person you used to be. For what it's worth, I'm sorry we ended up this way. Killing you isn't something I wanted to do."

"That's good," Iren said, "because you aren't going to kill me." He switched the Muryozaki to his right hand and held out his left one, palm up. "Let me show you why."

☙

Minawë crouched behind a piece of driftwood on the beach. With her long leather cap obscuring her green hair, she would be all but invisible to the anchored ships.

In her right hand Minawë clutched the Forest Dragon Bow. Its energy flowed through her, and she sent that power into the sand and out into the water. As Rondel had claimed, there were plants out there, though they felt unlike any Minawë had interacted with. Their speech had a long rhythm to it, a flow like the waves that came and went.

Strange as the kelp were, Minawë could understand them well enough. She told them the mission she had for them, and they knew they could handle it.

Minawë focused her attention on the most distant ship. With luck everyone would be watching Rondel's diversion. They wouldn't be looking back over the water.

Guided by Minawë's magic, the kelp beneath her target ship grew. Their stems lengthened and thickened until they rose from the sea. They attached to the ship, lashing themselves to any imperfections they could find in the wood.

Minawë let the kelp build. She had probably gathered enough to sink the junk, but she didn't want to risk attacking too soon. She didn't want the Maantecs to realize what was happening until it was too late to stop.

At last she was ready. Minawë poured the full might of her magic into the kelp, and it erupted up the junk's sides. It climbed onto the masts and rigging and ripped them all down. The ship was crippled.

But that wasn't good enough. The junks could be repaired. The only way to ensure they didn't travel to Lodia was to sink them.

That proved a harder task. The ship's thick hull resisted compression, and the kelp lacked sharp edges or thorns to cut with.

Even so, Minawë wouldn't give up. This was their only chance to stop Melwar before he set off for war. She was the only one who could do this.

Sweat poured off her, but finally the kelp broke through the hull. A sickening *crunch* reached Minawë over the surf. She gulped. It wasn't just that the sound would alert the Maantecs to what she was doing. It was also the realization that she'd just cast a thousand men into the sea.

She released her spell on the kelp; the vessel was doomed now. Minawë could see it sinking, see the dots leaping off it as the crew tried to save themselves. Most would swim to shore and live, but any soldiers in armor would sink along with their ship.

Minawë put both hands on the beach and panted. She hadn't expected destroying one ship to be so draining. She had no idea how she was going to take down eleven more.

There was no time to worry about it. The Maantecs on the remaining ships were running about the decks. They knew they were under attack now.

Let them worry. Maybe it would make them second-guess launching a war that would inflict the same fear.

ᴄᴈ

Today should have been Shogun Katashi Melwar's moment of glory. Instead he had to listen to the sound he abhorred most: chaos.

His soldiers ran about the *Shadeen*'s deck, pointing and shouting. Even as the *Mountain Wind* finished sinking, new tangles of kelp wrapped themselves around the *Abyss*.

Melwar took it in without emotion. This had been Rondel's plan all along. Melwar had thought she had attacked Iren to satisfy Okthora's Law, but Iren had just been a fortunate means to create a diversion.

That left Melwar two choices. He could stay and root out the Forest Dragon Knight, or he could order his fleet to withdraw prematurely. Most of the soldiers were already on board, but some of the supplies still had to be loaded.

He scanned the beach with his spyglass, but he could not spot the Kodama. There were piles of driftwood she could hide behind, and numerous dunes as well.

"Shogun?" Hana asked. "What are your orders?"

Melwar frowned. If he left now, the Forest Dragon Knight would have time to claim at least two more ships before they rowed out of her reach. If he stayed and searched for her though, she would have time to destroy even more.

That made the difference. The supplies they already had should last until Lodia. More to the point, even if he found and killed Iren, Rondel, and the Forest Dragon Knight, those victories would be meaningless if he lost his fleet.

"Retreat," Melwar commanded. "Pull the fleet away from the kelp beds. Get us into deep water and moving north. We head for Lodia."

He could tell Hana wanted to question him. She wanted to stay and butcher the Kodama who had proven herself so dangerous.

In the end Hana's loyalty won out. She ran to the ship's helmsman and gave the command to withdraw. The helmsman changed course, and the sailor in the crow's nest signaled with flags for the other ships to do the same.

As they retreated, Melwar put his spyglass back on Rondel. She had been so strong and beautiful once. It was hard to look at her now, at this frail remnant the loss of her biological magic had made her. Iren fought more or less evenly with her. Had he seen her in her prime, the boy never would have challenged her.

But then, Iren himself was a remnant, a half-human bastard who could never hope to measure up to his full-blooded father. To think Melwar had once considered the man vital to his plan to restore the Maantecs. To think he had once considered Rondel beyond his abilities. Now the pair were nothing more than a distraction.

Melwar lowered his spyglass. There was no point in watching any longer. Those two had cost him enough. Today's losses were his fault. He had let them divert his attention. The only thing worthy of his focus now was the war.

And it had begun.

CHAPTER TWENTY-SEVEN
Flash of Light

The second junk sank. Minawë's breath came in heaves. It was all she could do to keep conscious. She could manage one or two more, if she was lucky. She hoped that would be enough.

She was about to send kelp to attack the next junk when the ships changed shape. Oars appeared from both sides of all of them. The Maantecs were rowing out to sea.

Minawë tightened her grip on the Chloryoblaka. It was hard enough dealing with the ships when they were stationary. Worse, the farther from shore they went, the harder it would be to control the kelp that attacked them. She had to hurry.

She started on the third ship. To stall it, she had the kelp break its oars.

Above Minawë the sky brightened. She shouldn't let it distract her, but the light was wrong. It came from a different direction than the morning sun. Minawë's shadow drifted from her right to against the driftwood log in front of her. She turned around, curious as to what could cause such a change. Then she gasped.

The glow came from the hill Rondel had set on fire, but the flames weren't responsible for it. The light came instead from a shining white dome halfway up the rise.

Minawë cursed. Rondel's diversion had been double-pronged. The fire drew Melwar's attention, and the ships drew Minawë's attention. They were both distractions to give Rondel a shot at her true goal: killing Iren Saitosan.

He must have been on that hill when they'd arrived. Minawë hadn't noticed him through all the brush, but Rondel's Lightning Sight would have spotted him easily.

Minawë's gaze swiveled back to the ocean. The third junk had stopped, its hull trapped by the kelp. Its crew had already abandoned it. A minute longer, and she could sink it. The rest of the fleet was escaping, but they were still in range. If she concentrated, she could probably bring down a fourth.

It was the right thing to do. If she didn't stop those ships now, they would deliver hundreds more Maantecs to Lodia's unsuspecting shores.

But Minawë couldn't help herself. She changed into a seagull and took wing, screaming all the way.

⋈

Rondel had to shield her eyes from Iren's light. Horror took her. It wasn't possible. He couldn't be doing what he was doing.

Yet the light grew in intensity. Rondel could see it coalescing around Iren's upward-facing left palm.

At last it grew dense enough that it ignited. White flame shot six feet in the air from Iren's hand. It licked at the top of his shield.

There was no stopping it now. One way or the other, Iren Saitosan had committed to casting Muryoka.

Rondel knew she should withdraw. She couldn't block that spell. She couldn't dodge it either, since Iren could both track her and move as fast as she could. Her only hope was to get far enough away that Iren had to release the spell before he could get close to her.

Unfortunately, retreating wasn't an option. That spell would be cast no matter what. If Rondel didn't do something, Muryoka's explosion would destroy Hiabi. As much as Rondel hated the Maantecs, she couldn't let a whole city of civilians be wiped out.

There was also the issue of Minawë. Iren didn't know she was down on the beach. If he destroyed Hiabi, he would unknowingly take Minawë with it.

There was only one option: Rondel had to strike before Iren did. She poured magic into her dagger. As soon as Iren lowered his shield, Rondel would thrust the blade into his chest. The attack would send lightning magic searing through him and overload his brain. As the fool died, Rondel could force his arm up so Muryoka shot into the air.

It would take split-second timing, and the odds of it working were almost nonexistent. But it was the best she could do.

The flames had condensed to a foot high. It was better than Iren Saito had managed, but it was still out of control.

Rondel counted the seconds. Iren was trying to make the technique perfect, but Rondel knew the truth. Muryoka wasn't meant to be controlled. No matter how much a Holy Dragon Knight trained, it wouldn't be enough. Only Divinion could cast its perfect form.

It was too late to tell Iren that. It was too late to do anything except end it all.

Iren's shield dropped. His palm thrust forward. "Rondel!" he cried.

Rondel stabbed. "Iren!"

The attacks passed one another. Rondel felt her Liryometa pierce Iren's flesh, but she had been a hair too slow. Iren's hand landed on her gut.

Time seemed to stop. Then, with a roar that shook the land, Muryoka erupted.

Rondel's world disappeared in white.

ରଞ୍ଜ

Minawë flew toward Iren and Rondel, crying in her gull voice. She had to reach them. She had to stop them!

She was halfway there when the blast released. A great explosion enveloped the hill, and the shockwave threw Minawë from the sky.

She collapsed on the dirt. Her last sights before blacking out were a gaping crater where a hill had been and empty air where her mother and best friend had stood.

CHAPTER TWENTY-EIGHT
Western Alliance

Thap! Thap-thap!

All around Kataile's square, soldiers loosed arrows into straw targets. Balear had positioned them so the targets aligned with the broken fountain. None of the soldiers could miss seeing it, nor forget what it represented.

Thap-thap-thap!

The groupings were good, but Balear knew they could be better. Riac was a veteran, but he was no archer. Now that the catapults were finished, Balear had sent his second-in-command to oversee the siege weapons while the general himself took over archery practice.

Balear walked down the line and corrected the soldiers' forms. Before he'd lost his arm, he'd been one of the Castle Guard's finest bowmen.

Another round flew, and this time the arrows packed tighter on the targets. Balear smiled. They were close. In a few more days, all his efforts would pay off. Kataile would become impregnable.

A boy, not yet thirteen, ran down the steps into the square. Balear thought the boy would have the sense not to charge into a hail of arrows, but the child showed no sign of slowing as he neared the fountain. Rolling his eyes, Balear called a halt to his men.

The boy ran up to him. "General Platarch! General Platarch! Come quickly!"

Balear put a gentle hand on the boy's head. "We're in the middle of something important right now. Maybe later."

"But the mayor said you had to get to the plateau right away!"

Balear frowned. What did Elyssa want now? The last thing he wanted today was to be distracted by her and that scroll she kept dangling in front of him. He was starting to doubt whether the supposed note from his father even existed.

"I'm sure whatever the issue is, Captain Riac and Mayor Cyneric can handle it," he said. "They're up there with her."

The boy adopted the exasperated expression only possible by an adolescent. "It was Mayor Cyneric who sent me!"

Balear looked at the boy closer. He wasn't from Kataile; he was Veliafan.

That changed Balear's mind. "Lead the way."

The boy took off. As Balear left the square, he shouted over his shoulder, "Get back to it! Any man who slacks off scrubs the latrines of every tavern in the port district!"

Thap-thap-thap-thap-thap-thap!

Balear had to run to catch up with the Veliafan child. When they reached the plateau, the boy pointed Balear in the direction of the northern catapults and then excused himself. Balear walked over to the siege weapons, and he saw Elyssa, Dirio, and Riac. Their expressions were grim.

"What's going on?" Balear asked. "Why the panic?"

Dirio pointed across the cliff. In the distance three columns of men marched across Lodia's fields. They were headed straight for Kataile.

"It looks like you were right," Riac said. "The three western cities have formed an alliance. Each one's flag leads up one of those columns. But how did you know they would do that?"

"Because it was the best way for them to get what they wanted," Balear replied. "Neither Orcsthia nor Caardit could win the war alone, but each would prefer a western Lodian king to an eastern one. If they allied, they could press on to Terkou without fear of another city attacking them. Terkou would have more soldiers than either Orcsthia or Caardit, but it wouldn't be able to match them both. Terkou joined up with them because it had no choice. Now they're coming here, the only remaining city that can resist."

"How many do you think there are?" Dirio asked.

Balear did some quick estimates based on the length and width of the columns. "Four thousand," he said. "They aren't as large as what Amroth threw against the Kodamas, but they're close."

Elyssa poked Balear in the chest. "Time to pay back the hospitality we've shown you and the Veliafans," she said. "You said you could handle this invasion. Get to it."

Balear shook his head. "We aren't in position. They'd breach our defenses too quickly. But we aren't beaten."

Elyssa glowered at him. She opened her mouth to speak, but at that moment a dozen horsemen including the three flag-bearers broke off from the army and galloped toward the city.

Riac folded his arms. "They're coming to convince us to surrender."

"I'd best meet them, then," Balear replied, ignoring Elyssa's still smoldering expression. "Riac, bring the archers up here. They'll be tired from practice, but we have no choice. Dirio, I'd like you to lead the catapult teams. I hope we won't need them, but be ready if the worst happens."

Dirio nodded. "Good luck."

Balear smiled briefly, but then he turned serious again. He faced Elyssa. "Lady Orianna, please come with me to the beach. We need to meet those horsemen."

Elyssa's fists vibrated at her sides. "If you think I'm going to surrender after all this work to improve my army—"

"We have little time," Balear interrupted. "We must be on the beach when they arrive. We can't appear rushed."

The Katailan mayor didn't move. "I will not give in to these western bullies. If you insist on going down there, I'll remove you from your post and put someone else in charge."

Balear flared. "Do you care so little for your people? If you fight now your cause is hopeless. I've led this city's men and made them the best fighters they can be, but the one who will decide whether they live or die today is you."

Elyssa said nothing. She refused to meet his gaze.

The strong-arm approach wasn't going to work. Balear softened his expression. "Do you remember what I told you that day by the fountain when you came to observe our practice?" he asked. "About how you would need to seek a peaceful solution to this conflict?"

Elyssa scoffed. "Idealistic nonsense."

"On the contrary. It's our only chance. I'm not going down there to surrender. I have a plan. You need to trust me."

The mayor was silent for a long moment. Finally she sighed, threw up her hands, and said, "What would you have me do?"

Balear grinned. "I'll explain on the way."

The pair of them left the plateau and headed down the steps to Kataile's lower levels. Riac had gone ahead of them, and the archers were vacating the square as Balear and Elyssa reached it.

As they walked, Balear explained his strategy. Elyssa said nothing, but Balear could tell the mayor was worried. His plan relied on her more than anyone else. If she failed, everyone in Kataile would die.

The mayor and Balear came to the beach just as the incoming cavalry slowed to a walk. "Welcome to Kataile!" Elyssa shouted. "I'm Elyssa Orianna, mayor of this city. I'm afraid you will have to turn around. Our beach will be too crowded if all your men want to swim at the same time."

Balear suppressed a smile. Elyssa hadn't led Kataile for twenty years for no reason. Despite the stakes, she showed no sign of her nervousness. Balear had been counting on that resolve. It was their only hope of pulling off this crazy bluff.

"We aren't here to sightsee," one of the horsemen said.

"Then why have you come to my fine city?" Elyssa asked.

The horseman approached. He carried a spear, and its point was now only a few feet from Elyssa's chest. "You see our numbers," he replied. "Your city can't withstand an assault from us. Renounce your claim to the throne, and your lives will be spared."

"That's a tempting offer," Elyssa said, "but I'm afraid I must refuse. I've seen your numbers, and you would break upon these walls. Surely you have noticed our siege equipment." She pointed up the cliff face beside them. "And if you think to starve us, you're in for a long wait. We have access to food and water. You can block off neither."

"We'll storm your beach."

"That might work," Elyssa admitted, "except for one problem. You'd have to get past him." She gestured at Balear.

Reacting to the cue, Balear pulled out the Auryozaki. He twirled the enormous weapon above his head so quickly the sand whipped around them. The horsemen shifted in their saddles, riveted by the display.

The one in front though, the one with the spear pointed at Elyssa, looked unimpressed. "I know this man," he said. He turned to his compatriots. "This is the traitor, Balear Platarch! He came to my city last year. I arrested him and sentenced him to death, but he broke free thanks to an accomplice. He's a demon!"

Balear cursed silently. The spearman must be Orcsthia's mayor.

Though Balear hated being called out so quickly, he wasn't surprised to see the man here. The armies of each city needed their mayors with them to maintain discipline. There were no other leaders who could keep them from attacking each other.

Through the tirade, Elyssa maintained her composed expression. "A demon he might be," she said, "but he's our demon."

Balear suppressed a wince. Considering all the times he'd called Iren a demon, he supposed he deserved to have the name thrown back at him. Still, it was hard to hear.

"Fight him if you wish," Elyssa continued, "but do so at your peril. He's not the same man you tried to execute. He's the Sky Dragon Knight now, wielder of magic that would have rivaled King Angustion's."

That set the group on their heels. Balear smirked and cradled the Auryozaki over his shoulder.

"So if you think you can overcome a mage, our walls, and our catapults, go right ahead," Elyssa pressed. "Otherwise, I have a better suggestion."

Another of the horsemen stepped forward. Balear recognized him as Terkou's mayor. The man had a thin face and a long nose that gave him a wolflike appearance. "What would that suggestion be?" he asked.

"Simple," Elyssa answered. "Since you two are here, I'm certain Caardit's mayor has come as well. That means we've gathered here the mayors of Lodia's four largest cities. No one would dispute that one of us would become ruler of this land should this war drag on to its bitter end. So let us dispense with violence and instead do our jobs. Let's hold the Succession Council right here, right now. I'll make a space in my city hall for us to meet."

A third horseman rode forward. He had a pudgy face and dark brown hair. His doughy appearance looked out of place compared with the other soldiers. Balear figured he must be Caardit's mayor.

The three invading mayors bent their heads and conversed in hushed tones. After a brief discussion, they returned to face Elyssa. "We agree," the Orcsthian mayor said.

Balear forced himself not to sigh in relief. In truth though, he wasn't that surprised. As he'd explained to Elyssa on their way here, the Succession Council was really the newcomers' only option. For all its size, their army was in no shape to fight. The western cities might have formed an alliance, but they hadn't united. Their army's three distinct city banners proved that. If the balance of power shifted, say by one mayor losing more troops relative to the others, their distrusting alliance would fracture. Elyssa and Balear hadn't needed to convince the mayors that Kataile was invincible, just that it was strong enough to inflict significant casualties. Presented with that risk, the mayors had no choice but to accept politics.

"We do have one condition," the Terkouan mayor interjected on Balear's thoughts. "We will hold the council, but not in Kataile. It would be too easy for you to kill us and then claim the throne for yourself. We'll use our command tent instead. We'll set it up in neutral territory between your city and our forces. That way both sides can watch the other for treachery."

Elyssa looked sideways at Balear. He nodded. Their terms made sense.

"I accept your recommendation," Elyssa said. "As it's already past midday, let us retire and meet tomorrow an hour past sunrise."

The other mayors turned their horses around and rode away from the beach with their escorts. Balear grinned as they left. "We did it," he said.

Elyssa's formerly confident expression darkened to reveal her true feelings. "We have done nothing. You have your council, Balear, but it holds no meaning. Whoever emerges triumphant, bloodshed will follow from the defeated. Trust me."

Balear's smile faded. He said nothing. He didn't have to. Elyssa was right.

CHAPTER TWENTY-NINE
Afterlife

Iren Saitosan was in a world of white. As far as he could see in every direction, infinite blank space immersed him. He had his clothes and the Muryozai's sheath, but the sword itself had disappeared.

He thought back on the past few minutes. He remembered drawing magic for Muryoka. He had lowered his shield and attacked Rondel. They'd struck each other at the same time. A flash of light had followed, and then, this place.

If he'd died, it was a more peaceful experience than he'd ever imagined. There had been no pain, even though he knew the tip of Rondel's dagger had reached his flesh.

But what else could this be? It was different from the mental seasides where he met with Divinion.

A miniscule dot appeared in the distance, a lone speck of color against the unending white. With nothing better to do, Iren walked toward it.

Although he could see nothing but white below him, the place appeared to have an invisible floor. He approached the dot, and as he did, its shape changed. It was a person. A little farther on, Iren realized who it was. He scowled.

It was Rondel.

She must have noticed him too, because she moved toward him. The pair closed and glared at one another.

"What did you do?" Rondel demanded. The burns she'd received from the fire on the hill were gone. Unlike Iren she had her Ryokaiten, though she had put it away.

"Don't look at me," Iren shot back. "I didn't do this."

"It's your damn fault for using Muryoka. What were you thinking, casting a spell like that? You probably leveled Hiabi, and Minawë along with it."

Iren turned ashen. "Minawë was there?"

"She was destroying those ships."

"You used me as a diversion!" Iren swung a fist at Rondel.

The space glowed, and Rondel disappeared. Iren looked around. He was alone again.

Wait, no, he wasn't. There was a dot in the distance. He headed toward it.

Rondel met him. This time she didn't wait to have a conversation. She drew her Liryometa and stabbed Iren in the chest.

Before the blade could pierce him though, the space glowed again. When it returned to normal, Rondel was a dot in the distance once more.

They stalked back to each other. Iren put a hand on his forehead. "Wonderful. I have to spend eternity stuck with you, and I can't even beat you up. Forget this. Don't follow me. I'd rather be alone forever than deal with you." He took off at a run away from her.

He ran for several minutes. When he looked back, Rondel was a dot again. Iren kept on going. If this space was infinite, then he would get as far away from her as possible.

A dot appeared in front of him. He smiled; it was another person! Stupid Rondel could spend eternity alone, but Iren had found someone. He hoped they were friendly.

As the dot grew, Iren's smile vanished. The dot took the form of an old crone standing by herself in the void.

Rondel walked up to him. "Couldn't get away from me?" she asked with her sarcastic grin. "I do have that kind of personality."

"Shut up!" Iren punched her, and they separated again.

Iren sighed. So that was the game. They couldn't attack each other, and they couldn't get out of sight from one another. If this was death, then death had an annoying sense of humor.

"Guess we're stuck with each other," Rondel said when they reconvened.

"Grand," Iren spat. "What are we supposed to do now?"

"Listen," a male voice boomed.

Iren and Rondel faced the voice. "Who's there?" Iren called.

A new dot appeared in the distance and approached them. "You figured out the rules of this place quickly," the voice said. "I'm impressed. I expected you to fight for at least a day before you gave up."

The dot became a man. In age he looked a little older than Iren's outward appearance, perhaps forty. He wore his tan hair short in the Lodian style, and he had sky blue eyes that reminded Iren of Divinion's.

Rondel trembled as the man reached them. "You," she said. Her voice vibrated in sync with her body. "You can't be here."

Iren looked from the newcomer to Rondel and back again. He couldn't figure out what made her react so strongly.

"Welcome, Rondel," the man said with a smile. "It's good to see you again." He faced Iren. "And you, Akio, I've waited almost twenty years to see how you would turn out. I'm glad I managed to meet you as an adult. The last time I saw you, I could hold you in my arms."

Iren's heart thudded. Tan hair and blue eyes . . .

Rondel gritted her teeth. "What on Raa is going on, Saito?"

Iren Saito smirked. "Welcome to my afterlife," he said. His expression turned serious. "Settle in. We have a lot to talk about."

CHAPTER THIRTY
Saito's Last Spell

Rondel seethed. Before her was the man she'd loved, the man she'd killed. Iren Saito stood there as though nothing had happened, like they were all good friends gathered to discuss how their days went.

She lunged at him. Her rondel flew for his stomach. The dagger passed through him, and the rest of her body with it.

Saito turned and regarded her. "That won't work," he said. "You can't hurt someone who's already dead."

Rondel's fists and teeth clenched so hard she thought she might break them.

"You might as well listen to what I have to say," Saito continued. "You aren't going anywhere until you do."

Next to his father, Iren folded his arms. "So we're not dead."

Saito nodded. "That's right. This is *my* afterlife, not *the* afterlife. You're just guests here. Of course, depending on your actions, you could be guests for a long time."

Rondel's hammering pulse slowed a fraction as she forced herself to calm down. Whatever game Saito was playing, she wouldn't fall for it.

Still, he seemed in control at the moment. The best answer was to follow along and look for an opening. That was how she fought. It could work here too.

Getting information was the first step. She sheathed her rondel. "What is this place?" she asked. "How did we get here?"

Saito stroked his chin a moment. Then he called, "Divinion! If you're around, why not join us?"

A roar issued from the blank space. Rondel faced it, and she beheld a serpentine dragon flying toward them. White scales flecked with blue covered his body, and blue hairs ran down his spine. As the creature neared, Rondel saw that it had blue eyes that matched those of both Saito and Iren.

Rondel had never seen Divinion before, but she knew the stories. With one look at the beast before her, she knew he must be the Holy Dragon.

"Divinion!" Iren shouted, removing any doubt Rondel might have had about the dragon's identity. "You're here too?"

"This is where I've been for five thousand years," the dragon growled.

Realization dawned on Rondel. "This space . . . we're inside the Muryozaki, aren't we?"

Saito grinned. "You haven't lost your edge," he said. "When you two delivered what would have been fatal blows to each other, you triggered the spell I placed on the Muryozaki the night I died."

"The spell?" Iren asked.

"During my fight with Rondel, I put magic into the Muryozaki," Saito explained. "I knew I would die, but I wanted the chance to spare your mother."

"What did your spell do?"

"It was a dormant shield designed to protect both the Holy Dragon Knight and my murderer—you, Rondel. If either dealt a fatal blow to the other, the shield would pull both murderer and victim into the Muryozaki and away from the attack."

"That's a convoluted spell," Rondel said. "Why do something so drastic? If you could set up the Muryozaki with a spell that triggered at a certain time, why not use something straightforward? A beam of light to take me by surprise would have made more sense."

"You already know the reason," Saito replied. "I never wanted any of you to die. You, Akio, and Carita are the most important people on Raa to me. I hoped Carita would pick up the sword. If she had, then you, her, and I could have met. There were so many things I never told her, things she deserved to know."

Through her anger at Saito's meddling from the grave, Rondel couldn't help but notice that Iren had become pensive. The names must have sunk in with him. Carita was his mother's, and Akio was his.

"But Carita didn't pick up the sword," Saito went on. "Instead, Akio became the Holy Dragon Knight. When I found out, I grieved for Carita, but at least now I get to see my son grown up."

Rondel glared at him. "Let me get this straight. You were willing to trap both me and Carita in the Muryozaki just so you could see us? How selfish can you be?"

Saito shook his head. "I haven't trapped you here. You're free to leave, if you can figure out how."

Rondel kept her face blank, but inside she grinned. There was a way out. Now she just had to find it.

"I didn't want you to hate each other," Saito continued. "Whether it was you and Carita, or you and Akio. I bear no grudge against you, Rondel. I never have. In truth, I would have let you kill me centuries ago. But on the last day of the Kodama-Maantec War, Divinion ordered my punishment." Saito gestured to the dragon. "He commanded me to live. I ran from you each time we fought because I wanted to honor his decree."

Rondel stared up at the Holy Dragon. "How could that be your decision?" she demanded. "How could you let this mass murderer run free?"

Iren looked at Rondel like she was crazy. Rondel had to admit the expression was justified; who of sound mind would argue with a dragon?

Yet Divinion took Rondel's challenge in stride. "It was justice," he said.

"Okthora's Law is justice," Rondel retorted. "Evil must be annihilated."

"That's what happened. Saito so regretted his actions that he could never contemplate doing them again."

"He would corrupt you," Rondel said. "That's why the Storm Dragon Knight has to slay the Holy Dragon Knight when he becomes evil."

"I had no cause for worry. The evil in Saito was gone after that day, so there was nothing to corrupt me."

"How can you say that?" Rondel screamed. She didn't care that Divinion had teeth and claws longer than her body was tall. She didn't care that he was the most powerful creature ever to walk Raa. She shouted at him like the fool he was being. "Saito killed thousands that day! He butchered the Kodamas, and he sentenced the few survivors to an eternity imprisoned in their forests."

Saito raised a hand. "Actually, that's the other reason I set up my last spell to bring you here. I've had a thousand years to think about it, and I don't think I cast the curse on the Kodamas."

Rondel punched him. She knew it made no difference, that she would pass through his body as she had before, but that didn't stop her. She punched him again and again, swishing through his incorporeal form. "Liar!" she yelled. "I was there! Don't you dare deny it!"

"I won't deny that I caused the Kodama-Maantec War," Saito said. "I won't deny that the blood of Kodamas and Maantecs alike is on my hands. But of that final curse I am innocent, and in this place, I intend to prove it."

Iren spoke for the first time in a while. "How? Those events happened a thousand years ago."

"True, and that's why we needed to be inside the Muryozaki together. Here we have access to the perfect memory not only of Divinion, but of Okthora too." He gestured at Rondel's dagger. "If we combine the two, I believe we'll see a true picture of what happened that day. Will you help us, Rondel?"

There was no reason for her to. Saito just wanted to cover up his crimes. She wouldn't be taken in by this nonsense.

Then again, Saito had said there was a way out. He and Divinion were in charge of this space. If she wanted to escape, she had to play by Saito's rules.

"Fine," she spat. "Show anything you want, but don't expect me to believe it."

Saito shrugged. "Believe what you will. I intend to do the same." He turned to the Holy Dragon. "All right, Divinion? Let's go."

CHAPTER THIRTY-ONE
War's End

The white space around Rondel filled in. As it did, her breath caught. She knew this place all too well.

She, Saito, Iren, and Divinion were on a vast, scorched plain. Smoke covered the landscape, and jets of white flame lanced from fissures in the ground. A mighty storm raged overhead, but not a drop of water reached the baked soil. This was Serona.

It wasn't the lifeless Serona of today. Instead, mobs of Maantecs and Kodamas filled it. They smashed against one another. Swords cut, arrows shot, and spells launched from both sides. Cries from the fighting and screams from the dying made the landscape so loud Rondel wanted to cover her ears.

Then, amid the chaos, Rondel saw something that made all other thoughts flee. Two people fought back-to-back with one another. One was a Kodaman man with wooden armor and a bow covered in living vines. The other was a short old woman wearing Maantec lamellar armor who fought other Maantecs. Rondel gulped. The man was King Otunë. The woman was her.

"What is this?" she yelled over the din. "What have you done?"

"Better halt it, Divinion!" Saito called. "No use explaining everything with shouting."

The dragon nodded. At once all sound and motion on the plain ceased. Fighters paused in mid-stroke. Dust hung in the air. Even the flames paused in their dancing.

Iren picked his way through the battlefield. He tried to touch one of the frozen combatants, but he passed through him. "Is this a memory?" he asked.

"Memories, to be precise," Saito replied. "This space blends my memory with Rondel's. Thanks to Divinion and Okthora, who have perfect memories, we can observe every detail of what happened during the final battle in Serona."

Iren whistled. "When I've looked at memories in the past, they were always through the eyes of the person experiencing the moment. This offers a much better perspective. But even if the dragons have perfect memories, there's no way they could be this detailed. How is it possible to know how all these people were fighting when neither you nor Rondel was paying close attention to them?"

Before Saito could show off any more than he already had, Rondel jumped in. "Because of Lightning Sight," she said. "It sees every detail, even over extreme distance. There's a limit to what I can process though, so I only focus on a few elements at a time. But with Okthora's perfect memory, he can recall everything about what happened even if I wasn't focused on it."

Saito nodded. "Well done."

"Don't patronize me," Rondel spat. "Even if we can see all this detail, what difference does it make? I know what happened. I've seen these memories in my nightmares for a millennium. You aren't going to show me something I haven't seen thousands of times before."

"It's possible," Saito admitted. "Divinion, should we change our vantage point?"

The dragon growled an affirmative, and the frozen battle shifted beneath them. They rose in the air and shot toward the thousand-foot tower that loomed over the battlefield. Rondel grimaced at the sight of it: Edasuko Tower, palace of the Maantec emperor.

They stopped when they reached the tower's roof, and now they overlooked the plains of Serona. A young-looking Maantec, all but identical to Iren Saitosan when he and Rondel had first left Haldessa Castle together, stood frozen at the roof's edge.

"I've seen this memory," Iren said. "It came to me when I was unconscious in Ziorsecth Forest after rescuing Minawë. At the time I thought it was a bad dream."

"I knew the battle was lost," Saito said. "Rondel, you were the strongest of the Maantecs. When I saw you fighting alongside Otunë, I decided to surrender."

"Liar," Rondel sneered. "You wouldn't surrender. You cursed the Kodamas rather than face the shame of defeat."

"Shall I show you my memory?"

"If it gets me out of here."

The scene moved again. A blur flashed down onto the stone. It belonged to a man with flowing blonde hair and a massive seven-foot sword. He bowed to the floor before the younger Saito. "Exalted Emperor!"

Iren blinked twice. "Balear?"

It wasn't his friend. The Saito in the memory said, "Rise and report, Belias. What's going on down there?"

"More Kodamas pour forth from Ziorsecth," the Sky Dragon Knight said. "Our forces are clashing with them all over the country. The Kodamas' Ice and Stone Dragon Knights were overwhelming Nadav's men, so he unleashed the fires beneath Serona. All three are dead now. The Water Dragon Knight also perished when she and the traitor tried to calm the storm."

"What of Rondel? Did she die too?" The young Saito sounded panicked.

"No," Belias said, "the traitor lives, but she used most of her biological magic to help the Water Dragon Knight. She's become an old woman. She would have lost consciousness, but Otunë gave her some of his magic."

The young Saito loosed a visible sigh of relief. Belias seemed to take it as a sign that his leader had a plan for victory. "Exalted Emperor, come down with me. You and I will fight Otunë and the traitor. We will avenge our fallen brothers!"

Saito looked across the battlefield. He said nothing for a long time. At last he spoke, "Belias, you have always served me faithfully. I must ask you to continue in that tradition and obey my final command."

"Anything you ask."

"Leave this battle," Saito said. "Fly to Lodia and live with your daughter in peace."

Belias dropped his mouth open. "I don't know what you—"

"Yes you do. You kept it secret, but it's my business to know what my lieutenants are doing. My respect for you is no lower because you fell in love with a human. Actually, it's greater. I wish I'd learned the same lesson you did. This war is pointless. It's always been pointless. Katashi believes Maantecs must rule the other races to bring about peace. I believed him. Too late, I see the truth. Katashi is wrong. I am wrong. The way to peace isn't conquest, but to end this war. Go to Lodia. Love your wife and daughter as faithfully as you have loved me. That is my command."

Belias hesitated only a moment before he said, "I would have fought to the death for you. But if this is how I may best serve you, then I will see it done. Still, I must ask. What will you do now?"

"End the war," Saito said. "I'll negotiate a Maantec surrender with Rondel and Otunë."

"They'll attack you as soon as you go down there. I saw the traitor fighting earlier. Even weakened she's a whirlwind. No one can stand against her."

"She won't be able to hurt me, nor I her. I'll use my biological magic and create shields around everyone in Serona, both Maantec and Kodama. That should stop the fighting long enough for Otunë and I to arrange a truce before real negotiations start."

Belias bowed to his emperor once more, then leapt into the sky. Supported on a wind current, he flew southeast toward the Eregos Mountains.

"I never did find out if Belias survived," the older Saito said as the Sky Dragon Knight disappeared into Serona's smoky haze. "I like to think that he did."

Rondel recalled the man's blonde hair, and the way he'd fallen in love with a human. Something told her he had made it to Lodia.

She focused her attention back on the younger Saito. So his older self had spoken the truth; he hadn't intended to curse the Kodamas.

But that was irrelevant. Intentions didn't matter. Actions did.

The younger Saito returned to the tower's edge. He focused, and white light swirled around him.

This was it. Saito was readying his final spell. Even though nothing that happened would change her mind, Rondel had to admit her ex-husband had peaked her interest. As twisted as Saito had become, he was never the type to lie to people, especially not a faithful servant like Belias. Saito had come to regret the war and his belief in Maantec superiority.

With that mindset, there was no way his spell should have become a curse on the Kodamas. What had gone wrong?

"When I first awoke, I believed my spell had gone awry," Saito said as he watched his younger self summon more magic. "Over time though, I rejected that possibility. I intended to create shields for both Kodamas and Maantecs, yet the final spell only affected Kodamas. Had I made a mistake and turned the shield magic into attack magic, I would have cursed the Maantecs too."

Rondel scowled, but it wasn't because she was angry. It was because, despite her hatred of Saito, she had to agree with him. She had made the same observation.

"If your spell didn't go wrong, what happened, Father?" Iren asked.

"I've had a thousand years to think on it. I've watched this memory over and over, searching for a clue. It took me hundreds of repetitions, but I finally saw it."

"Saw what?"

"Wait a few more seconds. My younger self is almost finished drawing his power. It will happen right before he releases it."

They all watched the younger Saito. The light around him stopped spinning and formed a glowing white ball in front of him. Rondel triggered Lightning Sight. Whatever was about to happen, whatever signal Saito claimed existed, she wanted to see it.

Just before the younger Saito cast his spell, he dropped to the floor, unconscious. The memory went black. As it did, Rondel gasped.

"Well?" Saito asked.

"Well, what?" Iren replied. "You lost consciousness. What are we supposed to be seeing?"

"A shadow," Rondel whispered.

Iren regarded her. "A shadow?"

Rondel looked at Saito. However much he had changed, he still had those same beautiful sky blue eyes, the ones that had rescued her from her loneliness so long ago. "The ball of light was in front of you, and it cast a shadow behind you," she said. "But right before you released the spell, that shadow grew and expanded partially in front of you."

"I should have known Lightning Sight would notice it," Saito said. "I wish I could have seen it that quickly. You're right."

"What does a shadow have to do with anything?" Iren asked.

"There's only one light source on top of this tower: Saito's spell," Rondel said. "The sun is obscured thanks to the storm the Water Dragon Knight and I created. Any shadows should be behind Saito, because his spell is in front of him. How could there be a shadow on the ground that extends a few inches in front of his feet?"

"I can come up with only one explanation," Saito said. "Someone else was up here with me. That person used shadow magic to come up through the tower roof. That's why the shadow is an unnatural shape."

Rondel folded her arms. She didn't want to believe it, but the facts staring her in the face wouldn't let her do otherwise. Saito hadn't cursed the Kodamas. Someone else had taken his magic and manipulated it.

"I suspect I know who that person was," Saito said, "but I've never been able to prove it until today. Rondel, let's return to your memory."

The scene switched back to the ground. Rondel and Otunë fought alongside each other, carving through the Maantec forces on their way to Edasuko Tower.

"You focused on your opponents," Saito said, "but I'm sure you also kept looking at me. You knew I was up there, and that I was planning something. You wanted to reach me and kill me."

Rondel nodded. She saw where he was going. "We can use Lightning Sight to see who was behind you," she said, "and what they did after you lost consciousness."

At the top of Edasuko Tower, the ball of light the younger Saito was creating grew larger and brighter. Rondel activated Lightning Sight, knowing Okthora's memory would have recorded every detail. Whatever had happened up there, now they would see the truth of it.

The ball reached its apex. Rondel couldn't see the shadow on the floor, but she knew it would appear soon.

Then she saw a man appear behind Saito. Rondel gritted her teeth. She knew the face the instant she gazed upon it.

Katashi Melwar swung a metal pipe and struck his emperor in the back of the head. Saito collapsed, but his magic floated in midair. Melwar fed his own energy into it. The ball twisted and darkened. Melwar must have used some biological magic too, because he aged ten years as he cast his spell.

Then he released it. The black energy leapt across the battlefield and struck the Kodamas. It shot past Serona and into Ziorsecth Forest. Some even went south, heading for the Kodamas in Aokigahara.

A bolt landed next to where all of them stood. It blanketed Rondel's former self and Otunë in shadow. When the darkness faded, Otunë's hair changed from green to white. He aged and died in Rondel's arms.

The Rondel watching the memory turned away. "End it," she said. "I don't need to see any more."

CHAPTER THIRTY-TWO
Parting Words

The vision of Serona vanished. Rondel, Saito, Iren, and Divinion were back in the white space inside the Muryozaki.

"What did you see?" Iren asked.

"Melwar," Rondel replied. "Katashi Melwar cast the Kodamas' curse. He knocked out Saito and took over his magic."

Saito dropped his gaze. "I didn't want to believe my friend would betray me, but it makes sense. Katashi believes in Maantec dominance. He knew I was having doubts about the war, and that if the Kodamas took the advantage, I would surrender rather than do whatever necessary to wipe them out."

Rondel knew Saito was right. She knew it, but it didn't change anything. She glared at her former husband. Lightning Sight burned in her eyes. "So Melwar cursed the Kodamas. Who cares? You led the war effort. You're still responsible for all the dead out there."

"I know," Saito said. "Akio, that's why I wanted you to see all this. It wasn't just so I could show Rondel that I didn't curse the Kodamas. It was also so I could convince you that she was right to kill me. I need no one to avenge me, least of all you."

Iren frowned. "Even if I can forgive Rondel for killing you, what about Mother? She had no part in the Kodama-Maantec War."

Saito blinked back tears. "I never wanted Carita to become involved in my struggle with Rondel, but your mother had the strongest will and the most giving heart of any person I've ever met. I should have known she would never abandon me, that she would never stay in the house and away from danger while I faced an enemy outside."

The emperor paused and cleared his eyes. "Let me tell you a story, Akio. A year after I settled outside Tropos, the villagers came to attack me in a mob. They didn't want a Left living near them. I stood alone against them, and I would have left Tropos had a young woman not stepped forward and shielded me with her own body. She said I had done nothing wrong, and if the townsfolk wanted to kill me, they would have to kill her too. The people backed down, but they told the woman that since she had defended a Left, she was no longer welcome in their village. Her decision to help me made her homeless. I couldn't let her be cast aside like that, so I took her in. We were never officially married, but I like to think Divinion would have consecrated it had he been able."

The Holy Dragon smiled. He hadn't spoken in so long that Rondel had almost forgotten he was there. But then, this was a Maantec matter. It wasn't the dragon's place to force any of them into a decision, and he knew it.

"You two loved each other as much as any pair I've seen," Divinion said. "You were bound together."

"So, Akio, if you need someone to blame for Carita's death, then let your anger be with me," Saito said. "I knew Rondel stalked me, and I knew that living with me would put Carita in danger. I avoided personal ties for a thousand years for that very reason. Every time Rondel caught up to me, I ran from her. But I couldn't do that with you and Carita, because for the first time I had people who cared for me, and whom I cared for in return."

"But I can't just let it go," Iren said. " How can I turn my back on what Rondel did?"

"If you won't accept my reason, then know this: Carita would not have wanted you to burn your life away seeking revenge. What she would wish for is your happiness. If you want to honor her, don't do it through vengeance. Do it through joy. Do it by living the happiest, most fulfilling life you can."

Iren exhaled. He looked at Rondel a second. Then his gaze turned away.

Saito faced Rondel. "You've both heard what I had to say. That was the secret to escaping this prison, to listen."

Rondel's mouth fell open. "What?" she exclaimed. "I thought there was some deep meaning behind all this, like Iren and I had to reconcile and sing songs of praise to one another."

Saito laughed. "That's like you. I haven't laughed in so many years; I miss it. No, Rondel, I'm through being emperor. I'm through forcing people to do what I want. I've given you two my side of the story. You decide what to do with that information. If you still want to kill each other, then I can't stop you. The shield spell only works once."

Rondel looked at Iren. She wondered what passed through his head. What would happen when they returned to the real world?

She would find out soon enough.

⚃

Iren Saitosan stared across the white expanse at his father. He didn't know what to make of all this. He had seen the truth of the past. His father was innocent of the crime Rondel had slain him for, yet the man himself didn't hold his murder against Rondel.

It didn't matter. His father could forgive Rondel, but Iren never would.

Saito spread his arms. "Before you leave, I have a few final words I'd like to share with each of you individually. Once I finish, you'll disappear from this place and return to the spot where you were fighting."

Rondel stepped forward. "Let's get this over with."

Saito walked over to her, and their mouths started moving. No sound came from them. Iren frowned. They were at most ten feet away, yet he couldn't hear a word of what they said.

They'd spoken about five minutes when Rondel reached up a hand and slapped Saito across the face. Iren expected her hand to pass through Saito the way it had earlier, but this time the impact rang out.

Saito didn't get upset. On the contrary, he smiled at her. In that instant, Rondel disappeared.

As though nothing had happened, Saito walked over to Iren. "Your turn, Akio," he said.

"What did you tell her?" Iren asked.

"If it was meant for you to hear, I would have let you hear it."

Iren scowled, then grinned despite himself. "Fine. In that case, what would you like me to hear?"

"Exactly what I said to you earlier. Don't judge Rondel. I don't want vengeance, and your mother doesn't either."

"How do you know that?" Iren asked. "How do you know she wouldn't want me to avenge her?"

"That's the first thing I wanted to share with you. There's a memory you should see. Not here, but later, when you're in the real world. I can't watch it again. Tell Divinion you want to see the memory from sunset on the summer solstice the year you were born. He'll know what you mean. He always does."

Iren cocked an eyebrow. "What happens in that memory? Some kind of fight?"

Saito shook his head. "Just watch it. If afterward you still want to kill Rondel, then I'll have done everything I can to dissuade you."

Iren didn't see how watching a sunset would change his mind, but his father had said stranger things during this time inside the Muryozaki. "All right," Iren replied. "I'll ask Divinion to let me view the memory."

Saito nodded. "Good. Then before you go, there's one last thing I want to tell you." He loosed a deep breath as though steeling himself. "It's the secret to perfecting Muryoka."

CHAPTER THIRTY-THREE
Greater Evil

The last Iren saw of that white space was his father's smile. In a blink, his landscape changed. He was at the bottom of a crater a thousand feet across and nearly three hundred feet deep. It surpassed even the devastation where the Heart of Ziorsecth had uprooted itself. Iren gulped as he realized what the place was: the aftermath of his failed Muryoka.

He glanced around and started. Rondel was behind him. Iren ducked, grabbed the Muryozaki at his feet, and came up in a defensive stance. Rondel raised her dagger. Lightning Sight flashed in her eyes.

Iren cursed silently. He couldn't sense his magic. The time spent inside the Muryozaki hadn't restored it. Rondel, though, had some energy left. If they fought, she would win.

She would win . . . unless Iren used the new knowledge his father had given him. He could defeat her with Muryoka's perfect form.

He switched the Muryozaki to his right hand.

Rondel saw the shift and must have known what Iren intended. She stepped forward to counter.

Then she stopped. The ground shook beneath them. Iren frowned. Hana should be miles away with Melwar. She couldn't be causing this.

The rocks beneath Iren and Rondel split open. A tangle of vines ripped from the earth and snarled around both their bodies up to their shoulders. The plants tugged on Iren's wrist, and in pain he dropped the Muryozaki. The same happened to Rondel, and her Liryometa fell to the ground as well.

"What the—" Iren began, but then a spike grew from the vine

closest to his neck. It stopped less than an inch from his windpipe. A similar thorn sprouted in front of Rondel's throat.

Minawë stepped between them. Her emerald eyes bored first into Rondel, then Iren.

Iren gulped again. He'd never seen Minawë like this. She looked crazed. Her fists worked. Her right hand clenched the Forest Dragon Bow with such fervor that Iren wondered if she would crack the weapon in half.

"What . . ." Minawë seethed, "on Raa . . . do you think . . . you're . . . doing!?"

Her last word screamed across the crater. It echoed again and again as it bounced off the steep walls.

Minawë's baleful stare gave equal time to Iren and Rondel. "Which of you is going to Lodia with thousands of soldiers?" she demanded. "Which of you intends to conquer Raa and commit genocide?"

"Minawë . . ." Rondel's tone was placating.

"Shut up!" Minawë roared. The thorn pointing at Rondel's throat edged a hair closer. "I swear I'll kill you if I have to."

Minawë stormed up to her mother and slapped her across the face. Then she marched over to Iren and did the same to him. The blow sent shocks through his jaw; Minawë hadn't held back at all.

"Can't you see we have bigger problems than your stupid feud?" Minawë asked. "This was our one chance to stop Melwar before he launched his war. But no, you two decided the time was better spent blowing each other up."

Iren's eyes dropped to the ground. He'd left Goro and Chiyo's farm to stop Melwar. Instead he'd let the fleet escape.

They were beyond reach now. Even if he left right away, he would need months to get to Lodia over land, and that assumed he could survive the wilds of Aokigahara Rainforest. Melwar had won.

"What would you have us do?" Rondel dared to ask.

Minawë whipped to face her mother, and as she did Iren saw a few tears fly from her face. Minawë was furious, but she was also on the edge of breaking down.

Rondel's direct question, though, seemed to force Minawë back to reality. "We need to go after Melwar," the Kodama said. Her voice still hummed with anger, but its manic pitch was gone. "Put your fight aside until we stop him. After that, you can do what you want. I won't stop you."

Iren met Rondel's eyes across the crater's expanse. "Melwar framed my father and set you on the path to killing him and my mother," he said. "He's at least as much to blame for their deaths as you are. I'll still take my revenge on you, but I'll agree to Minawë's terms."

Rondel glanced from Iren to her daughter and then back to Iren again. Iren wondered what the old hag was thinking. She'd seen first-hand that she'd been wrong about Saito, but she hadn't changed. She would hold true to Okthora's Law for all her days. If she saw Iren as evil, she would slay him. That was her duty.

"Evil must be annihilated," Rondel said at length, "but some evils are worse than others. If I have to work with a lesser evil to defeat a greater one, then so be it. I won't kill Iren until we defeat Melwar."

"Just to be clear," Minawë said, "if either of you breaks your word on this, I'll kill you myself. I don't want to, but two of us against Melwar is better than one. We can't risk another battle like you had today."

"Blame Iren for that," Rondel growled, "him and his stupid for-bidden technique."

Minawë's eyes regained their brutal look, and even the implacable Rondel wilted under them. "Fine, fine, forget what I said," the old Maantec grumbled. "I'm as much to blame."

"That's better," Minawë spat. Iren gulped for the third time since leaving the Muryozaki. Minawë had always possessed a strong will, but this Minawë scared him.

Still, he had to concede that her sense of authority impressed him. She was starting to sound like the Kodaman queen.

Minawë stretched out her hands, and the vines ensnaring Iren and Rondel slithered back into the rocks. The two Maantecs knelt and re-trieved their weapons. Under Minawë's harsh glare, they put them away.

"So what's your plan for getting us to Lodia?" Iren asked Minawë. "Going over land will take too long. Melwar will have finished his invasion by the time we reach him."

"I had a thought about that," Minawë replied. "Come with me."

Iren and Rondel followed her up the crater wall. Though Minawë couldn't see them, they both kept their weapons sheathed.

When Iren reached the crater's lip, he paused a moment in shock. The crater stopped less than a hundred feet from Hiabi's northern wall. They had fought away from the city, yet his failed Muryoka had still almost taken out a portion of it.

Considering how close the explosion had been to Hiabi, Iren expected to see Maantecs swarming around the crater. But no one was around. It was as though they knew what had caused it and feared to venture too close.

"That's my plan," Minawë said, pulling Iren from his thoughts. She pointed across the city to the sea.

Iren half-smiled. It was a good plan.

A single junk sat in the water. Kelp swarmed over its sides, but its hull was intact.

"I was in the middle of attacking it when I noticed your fight," Minawë explained. "The crew abandoned it, but all I did was break the oars. Once I remove the kelp, it should be seaworthy."

She turned to Rondel. "You said you're familiar with these ships. Can three of us control that thing?"

Rondel put a hand to her chin a moment. "Junks house a thousand people and take a hundred crewmen," she said. "Then again, Iren and I can move faster than regular Maantecs. It might be possible. She won't be as responsive as a fully crewed ship, but I think we can get her moving."

"Good," Minawë said. "Let's swim out to her. I'll be the captain."

Neither Iren nor Rondel argued with her.

CHAPTER THIRTY-FOUR
Deadlock

Balear tugged on the straps of his sword harness. They clung to his body, and no matter how he shifted, he couldn't relieve the pressure.

In the open air it wouldn't be a problem, but here in the confines of the western mayors' command tent, the harness and his borrowed Katailan uniform stifled him. Sweat beaded on his forehead, and he could feel it on the back of his neck too. That was a bad sign. If this meeting went on too long, he was likely to pass out.

Then again, as bad as he had it, Elyssa had to have it worse. Her servants had done her up in her most formal dress. She must be dying beneath all those petticoats.

Yet she sat, poised and confident, seemingly oblivious to the unusually hot spring day. The sheen on her face only made her look more elegant, in contrast to the sweat-soaked Balear.

At least Balear and Elyssa weren't alone in their suffering. Each of the mayors had two accompanying soldiers to serve as honor guards, and all the men looked ready to collapse in the windless tent.

Balear stared sideways at the man beside him, the one he'd chosen as Elyssa's second guard. The man eyed the ground as though he wanted to fall into it.

"Let's start by identifying ourselves," Terkou's mayor said.

Balear marked that one. The Terkouan looked even more wolf-like without the helm he'd worn yesterday. His ears pointed at the tops, and he kept his gray hair trimmed and sharp. His narrow eyes took in the whole tent, daring someone to question him. Speaking first had been his less-than-subtle way of putting himself in charge of the meeting.

No one seemed keen to dispute his tactic. Instead they went around the table and announced themselves.

"Kras Menage, Mayor of Orcsthia."

"Otto Dunbar, Mayor of Caardit."

"Elyssa Orianna, Mayor of Kataile."

"And of course, I am Horace Attan, Mayor of Terkou. Very well, let us commence. As there are only four of us, this meeting should go quickly. According to the Succession Law, any of us may become the next leader of Lodia. We will work on a simple majority vote. Agreed?"

Kras and Otto nodded, and Balear suppressed a frown. He had expected a call for consensus, that everyone should discuss and agree on the new ruler. Now that he saw the expressions on the western mayors' faces, though, he understood their plan. They had already worked out how this meeting would go. Likely they'd chosen who among them would be king in exchange for certain privileges, and with majority rule, they could cut Elyssa out of the proceedings.

There was no other choice. It was time for Balear to put forth his secret weapon.

"Excuse me, my lords and lady," he said, "but before you begin, I'm afraid the introductions aren't complete."

All the mayors, even Elyssa, glared at him. It wasn't the place for honor guards to speak. Their purpose was to silently keep the peace . . . and to butcher all their enemies if peace couldn't be maintained.

"What are you talking about, traitor?" Kras snapped.

Balear forced himself not to wince. "There's another mayor in this tent," he said. "He's standing right next to me."

Elyssa's second guard snapped up his head. His glare joined the others. "Balear . . ."

"Sorry, Dirio, but I have to. My lords and lady, let me present Dirio Cyneric, mayor of Veliaf."

"You told me I wouldn't have to do anything," Dirio said. "I don't want to be king."

"That doesn't mean you can't or shouldn't participate in the discussion of who will be," Balear replied. "You have as much right to sit on this council as any of them."

"Nonsense," Otto interjected. "Lord Attan's agents informed us that

Veliaf was destroyed. He isn't eligible."

The edges of Elyssa's lips tightened. "Ah, but he is," she said. "He was mayor at the time King Angustion perished. His town had enough people to qualify for the Succession Law. As to Veliaf's destruction, that's irrelevant. A town can be rebuilt. His people survived. They're what matter. We've sheltered them in Kataile, but they remain Veliafans. Throughout their stay Dirio has remained responsible for them."

"I won't allow it!" Kras roared. He jabbed a finger at Balear. "Why should I believe the word of a traitor? This man could be anyone!"

"I agree," Otto put in. "It's highly suspect."

Balear looked at Horace. He expected the Terkouan mayor to put up the same resistance as his allies. Instead, the wolf-faced man's narrow eyes glittered. "Hold a moment, sirs," he said. "It is not the traitor's words we must consider, but those of Lady Orianna and this man Dirio. My spies indeed told me of Veliaf's destruction, but they also told me of its new mayor. Apparently he saved his village from a Quodivar invasion. He's a fine man. I say he may participate."

The two western mayors gaped at their ally. Balear kept his expression neutral, but inside he smiled. Now he understood. Horace was the same as Elyssa. He weighed the costs and benefits of every action. He'd sided with the western mayors because they had a larger army, but he hadn't truly joined them.

He also hadn't given up his desire to become king, and for that, Dirio was the wrinkle the Terkouan needed. With four mayors, Kras and Otto didn't need him for a majority. With five, the throne was in play again.

"Well then," Elyssa said, "it seems Mayor Cyneric is welcome at our table. Come and join us, sir."

Still glaring at Balear, Dirio sidled up to the table where the other mayors already sat. There were only four chairs, so Dirio had to stand. That only made his expression even darker.

"Are there any other mayors anyone would like to spring on us?" Kras growled. "Or can we move on?"

No one replied, so Kras continued, "In that case, let's get this over with. I nominate myself."

Otto, Caardit's mayor, went next. He nodded at Kras. "I put in a second vote for my esteemed western comrade, Lord Menage."

Dirio was next to Otto, so it was his turn. He mumbled, "I'll nominate Lady Orianna."

Elyssa gave herself a second vote, which left only Horace.

The wolfish man sat in silence for a long time. Balear felt the stifling atmosphere getting to him again. His head spun. His vision tunneled. Who would the man choose? The vote was tied, two to two. If he voted for Kras, Elyssa would surely mobilize her city's army. And if he picked Elyssa, Kras and Otto's guards would just as surely try to strike down the female mayor before she left the tent.

Balear worked his hand. There wasn't enough room to swing the Auryozaki in here. No matter what happened, though, he would defend Elyssa and Dirio.

At last Horace leaned back in his chair. He folded his arms across his chest. A thin smile sprouted on his lips. "I nominate myself."

Everyone in the tent groaned. The vote was deadlocked. Horace had been wrong. This meeting wouldn't be short after all.

CHAPTER THIRTY-FIVE
At Sea

From the junk's bow, Rondel scanned the whitecaps ahead of them. They were sailing far enough from shore that they shouldn't have to worry about sandbars, but there was still a chance. None of them had experience navigating on the water. The only way to mark their progress—and confirm they were actually headed north—was to keep Raa's east coast in view at all times.

"See anything?" Minawë called from behind her.

Rondel ended Lightning Sight and faced her daughter. "The way looks clear as far as I can tell," she said.

The two of them stood on the highest deck at the front of the ship. Rondel served as lookout, while Minawë handled steering. Six weeks had passed since they'd left Hiabi, and the Eregos Mountains had just appeared on the horizon. By Rondel's best guess, they still had another two weeks before they reached Lodia.

Rondel looked past her daughter to the brown kimono-clad figure zipping across the lower decks. Iren Saitosan dashed from mast to mast, using the ropes hanging from the sail battens to catch the shifting wind.

Minawë noticed Rondel staring and craned her neck around. "Think we should give him a break?" she asked.

"Nah," Rondel replied, "it's good for the slacker to get some exercise."

"You said manning those sails usually takes dozens of Maantecs. Iren can't be having an easy time of it. He has the toughest job of all of us."

"Do you feel bad for him?"

"Of course. Don't you?"

Rondel didn't reply to that. Six weeks at sea left too much time to think. She didn't know how she felt about Iren Saitosan. She didn't know how she felt about anything. Damn Saito.

"I'm going to tell him we're all right for the moment," Minawë said. "You can come if you want." She jogged down the steps to the lower deck.

Rondel stayed where she was. She might not know how she felt about Iren, but she knew how he felt about her. Going down there would just lead to anger, and anger was one thing they couldn't afford on this trip. They were barely keeping the ponderous junk afloat. No one was getting enough sleep, and if it hadn't been for the unseasonably good weather, they would long ago have capsized and drowned.

Below Rondel, Iren had stopped running and was talking to Minawë. Neither looked comfortable with the conversation. Iren was eyeing the floor more than the woman in front of him, and Minawë dug her toe into the deck so hard Rondel wondered if the wood could handle it.

Rondel went back to the bow and cast Lightning Sight. The water must be deeper in this area; she couldn't spot any sign of sandbars or other obstructions. They should be good for a while.

As she was about to turn away, though, a shadow appeared ahead of the junk, just below the water's surface. The form grew from nothing into a huge, dark oval. It moved toward them too quickly to be a sandbar. Rondel ran to the stairs.

"Minawë, look off to starboard!"

Her daughter frowned. "Why? Is something the matter?"

"Just go!"

Minawë shrugged and walked to the railing. Iren followed her. He'd just reached her side when a black hump emerged from the water.

Rondel descended the steps and approached them. "What do you think?"

"What was that?" Iren asked.

"A whale," Rondel replied. "I told you they were big, Minawë."

"It must be the size of this ship," Minawë said. "Is it dangerous?"

"Only if it surfaces underneath us, which isn't likely."

The whale flicked its tail into the air as it dove back down. Minawë and Iren stood spellbound next to each other.

Rondel turned to head back to the bow. She was halfway there when she heard the screams. She whipped around to see what had attacked her daughter, and then she laughed. She was just in time to see the whale peak in its rise as it breached the surface. Its broad snout lifted as high as the ship's deck, its eye level with Rondel's.

The whale gave a long, low cry that sounded both jubilant and sad. Then it rotated and splashed into the water back first. Spray shot over the junk's side and soaked all three onlookers.

Minawë slapped both hands on the railing. "That was incredible!" she said. "I hope we see more of them."

Rondel smiled and started to reply, but then she stopped. She happened to glance at Minawë's hand. When Minawë had grabbed the railing, she hadn't realized that Iren had already done the same. Her hand had landed on top of his.

Minawë realized the situation a moment after Rondel did. The girl's cheeks flushed, and she put her back to Iren.

Iren was just as red. He swallowed hard. He seemed like he might say something, but then he noticed Rondel looking at him. "The wind's shifting," he said. "I'd better check the sails." He dashed off.

Rondel returned to the bow. A moment later, she heard Minawë's steps as the Kodama took her place at the helm.

The old Maantec sighed. Iren was right; the wind was shifting. But which way it would blow, and where it would take them, were things even Lightning Sight couldn't tell her.

CHAPTER THIRTY-SIX
Safely through the Storm

Hundred-mile-per-hour gusts lashed at the sails, lightning arced across the sky, and thunder threatened to deafen everyone on board the *Torment*, but even seasick-prone Hana was calm and relaxed. Despite the storm around them, the junk sailed on as easily as it had during the clearest weather.

Hana turned the junk's wheel to stay on an even course with the ships ahead of her. *Torment* was the fleet's rearguard, while Shogun Melwar's *Shadeen* took point.

Hana could just make out her master's ship through the torrential rain. As the fleet traveled, the shogun used Mizuchi's magic to flatten the sea around them. Fifty feet on either side of the column of ships, waves rose level with the uppermost deck. Within Shogun Melwar's protective zone, though, the ocean was flat as glass.

The message to the conscripted army was clear. Follow the shogun, and he would keep you safe. Wander outside his service, and you would drown.

Hana's lips pursed. The storm had hit farther north than she'd expected. They were almost to Lodia. Another day or so, and they would land in Ceere. From there, she already had her orders. While Shogun Melwar secured Haldessa Castle, Hana would take half the army to Kataile and attack it.

Kataile. Hana wondered if Balear was still there.

It didn't matter if he was. He couldn't save her from this storm. Her only hope was Shogun Melwar.

CHAPTER THIRTY-SEVEN
Sideways

Iren had grown up loving the ocean. The sound of the waves, the glittering light on the water, and the sweet and salty seafood all made him feel at peace.

As the junk turned sideways, he reconsidered that assessment.

They had sailed into the storm an hour past sunset two months into their journey. Rondel's Lightning Sight had picked up on the black cloud with plenty of notice, but it was so massive there was no avoiding it.

"Any time, Iren!" the hag roared. Iren could barely hear her over the wind and rain.

Not that he needed to. He knew what to do. Wrapping his right arm around the junk's center mast, he shot a white beam from his left hand into the water below them. The recoil pushed back against the mast, and the ship stopped its tilt. As the wave beneath them crested and passed, the ship righted itself.

The sudden change in orientation slammed Iren onto the deck. Through the pain, he forced himself to crawl to where Rondel held tight to another mast.

"It's too top-heavy!" Iren shouted. "We need to do something about the sails."

Rondel nodded and looked up, but she didn't offer any suggestions. There were none to be had. They'd been over it before the ship had entered the storm. With only three of them, they couldn't handle all the ropes needed to furl the junk's massive sails. Now, every time the storm winds shifted, they yanked the junk off center and threatened to capsize it.

"I'll cut through the masts with the Muryozaki," Iren offered. "We'll let them fall overboard."

"Not going to work," Rondel said. "If we lose the masts, we're stranded. We don't have any oars."

Yet another swell lifted the ship fifty feet in the air and dropped it a second later. The impact knocked both Iren and Rondel to the floor.

The Muryozaki healed Iren's bruises, but Rondel looked battered after half an hour in the storm. Minawë was still at the helm, doing her best to keep the ship on track.

At least, that's where Iren hoped she was. He couldn't see up there at the moment.

"You're the Storm Dragon Knight," Iren said. "Can't you do something about this?"

"Maybe a thousand years ago," Rondel replied. "This beast is beyond me."

"Grand. So we just hang on and hope for the best?"

"Unless you have a better plan, slacker."

"What did you call me, you grumpy old hag?"

A wave washed over them and sent them skidding across the deck. Iren crashed into the railing. Rondel hit a moment later.

But Iren's impact must have weakened the wood. As Rondel struck the rail, it cracked and shattered. With a curse, Rondel went overboard.

Iren didn't think. He rolled onto his belly and whipped out his hand. Flesh touched flesh. Fingers gripped fingers. Rondel hung from the side of the ship, kept from the water only by Iren's grasp on her right hand.

Time slowed. Rondel was helpless. Iren could get his revenge right now. He wouldn't have to fight her. He wouldn't have to use Muryoka. All he had to do was relax his grip. Minawë would never know. It was a storm; anything could happen.

Their eyes locked, and Iren nearly dropped Rondel out of pure shock. In times past he had seen the old woman nervous, like before she'd fought that Oni in Akaku Forest. But he'd never seen her like this, with eyes wide in genuine terror. She knew her life was about to end, and that there was nothing she could do about it.

Iren reached out with his other hand. He grabbed Rondel's wrinkled arm and tugged. They flew back onto the deck together, panting as they lay on the slick wood.

"Why?" Rondel asked.

Iren shook his head. "I don't know."

He forced himself to rise. Now wasn't the time to think about it. "Get up," he spat. "Let's figure out how to survive this thing."

The old woman stood and brushed herself off. "You're right; the masts have to go," she said. It sure hadn't taken her long to recover from her near-death experience. "At least the tallest ones. We can still sail with two."

Iren was already running to the first. The Muryozaki flashed from its sheath and cut through the three-foot-wide mast in a single slice. He pushed with his shoulder, and the mighty timber and its jointed sail crashed overboard. Three more fell in quick succession.

With the weight removed, the ship floated steadier. The rushing winds yanked on the remaining sails, but the force wasn't enough to throw the junk off balance.

Iren took his first steady breath in what felt like years. "Let's check on Minawë," he said. "She'll have noticed the masts dropping. She'll be worried about us."

Rondel threw out her sarcastic grin. "Or perhaps you're worried about her?"

Iren rolled his eyes. "Give it up. I know you are too. Come on."

The two of them rushed up the steps to the top deck. Minawë stood at the helm. Her white-knuckled hands gripped the wheel. She held firm to the deck by tree roots that grew out of the wood and wrapped around her legs.

"What on Raa were you two doing down there?" she asked when Iren and Rondel arrived.

Iren cocked an eyebrow. "Nice to see you too. We were keeping this bucket afloat."

"We aren't safe yet," Rondel said. "The waves are getting bigger. A large enough one could still topple us."

"I take it you have a plan to deal with that," Minawë replied.

"I do." The hag activated Lightning Sight. "From this vantage point I should be able to give us at least a few seconds' warning."

"And do what?" Iren asked. "Warning or not, we're going overboard."

"Not if you can still make a shield like you used to protect me from Feng."

Iren squeezed the rail between this deck and the one below it. Could he create a shield that large and strong again? He hadn't tried to make one back then; he'd cast it instinctively out of his desire to keep Rondel safe. He didn't have that desire now.

Didn't he?

"One's coming in!" Rondel cried. "Portside!"

Iren couldn't create a shield to protect Rondel, but that was all right. There was someone else on this ship, someone he did want to keep safe.

White light shot from his outstretched palm and wrapped around the junk's side. The wave smashed into it, as powerful a blow as Feng had managed. The shield held, but it sapped Iren's strength more than he'd expected.

"Another one! This one aft!"

"Can't you just say back like a normal person?" Iren shouted, but he pushed the magic out all the same. The wave split and ran along both sides of the ship, the water as tall as the remaining masts.

Iren kept up the dance another half hour. Between waves he dropped the shield to save magic.

Even so, the duration wore him out. Against the Fire Dragon he had maintained a shield for just a few minutes, and it had been small compared with what he needed to protect the junk. His control over magic had improved since Feng, but it wasn't enough.

He went down on one knee. As he did, Divinion's mind brushed against his. "You're at your limit," the dragon said. "You can't afford to go over the edge here."

"If I became a dragon, you would protect the ship."

"Not necessarily," Divinion replied. "I can't fly in these conditions, and my weight would make the ship too top-heavy. We'd capsize."

"Then let me become the Dragoon," Iren said. "We have to survive.

We're only a day or two from Lodia. We've come so far; we can't die now."

"I know that, but you can't become the Dragoon. If you do, you'll lose the ability to use magic again. I wouldn't count on Melwar helping you regain it a second time."

"Ok then, I'll use biological magic like Father."

"Iren, wait!" Minawë cried.

Iren had forgotten that Minawë and Rondel could hear his half of the conversation. Minawë knelt and took his hand in hers. She pulled him to his feet.

"Use my magic," she said. "I'm a Kodama. I can draw magic from other living things, and I can give it to them too."

"Minawë, there's a fine line between giving Iren magic and killing yourself," Rondel warned.

"It doesn't matter," Minawë replied. "If this ship sinks, we're dead anyway."

Iren knew better than to argue with her. He relaxed, and he felt a slow current through his body as Minawë transferred her magic to him.

The energy was foreign, yet it was comforting too. It knew he could handle this. It knew he could save them.

Lightning Sight danced as Rondel spun in a circle on the lookout for waves. Each time she called one out, Iren beat it back. And every time he was about to fall, Minawë gave him a little more magic.

At last Rondel cried, "I see the end of the storm. We're almost through!"

Iren loosed a long sigh of relief. Even with Minawë's help, he was exhausted.

After what seemed an eternity, the rain slowed. The wind slackened. The sea calmed. Iren released Minawë's hand, and unlike that time with the whale, tonight she seemed reluctant to let him go.

"We made it," Rondel breathed.

Iren dropped to the deck. "Awesome," he said. "I think I'll take a little nap now."

He was out before Rondel replied.

CHAPTER THIRTY-EIGHT
The Overlook

Balear sat on the bluff above Kataile, his gaze falling north across the morning fields. Two months. He couldn't believe it. There were only five of them. Politicians sure could talk. A group of five soldiers would have sorted out their differences and chosen a leader in half an hour.

Instead, discussions among the mayors had degenerated into minutia over trade agreements, taxation, and positions of favor in the new government. New feuds and rivalries cropped up almost daily. Kras continued to insist that Dirio had no place at the talks, and he used Balear's traitor status to weaken Elyssa whenever possible.

Fortunately, that strategy was working against him. The other mayors had stopped listening to Kras's outbursts. Even Otto of Caardit no longer unconditionally defended his hotheaded western ally.

But what Kras had lost in favor, Horace of Terkou had gained. Signs now indicated that Otto might switch sides and support Horace, although that wouldn't end the stalemate.

Balear shook his head to clear away yesterday's meeting. Today's talks started in an hour. He had to think about politics enough without it intruding on his down time.

In reality, he was less concerned about the talks than the effect so many new entrants to the region might have. The western cities' army had the makings of famine, disease, and revolution. In two months the force had split into different camps by city, each claiming territory for itself. Many of the soldiers were farmers, so they'd taken advantage of the surrounding fields to grow crops for their compatriots. Others had taken up positions near the sea to collect food from it.

It wasn't enough though. These lands weren't used to supporting so many people. Balear hadn't entered the camps to be certain, but like Elyssa, he had done the math. Time was running out. If the mayors didn't reach a deal soon and disperse their armies, hunger would prompt a battle.

"May I join you?" a voice from behind Balear said. Balear looked over his shoulder. Dirio was walking toward him.

Balear smiled and gestured for the Veliafan to take a seat on the rock beside him. Dirio was the one bright point in all the political nonsense. While the other mayors bickered, he kept focused on solving the crisis. Alone among them, Dirio seemed to recognize that the best thing for Veliaf—and all of Lodia—was to end these talks and choose a new king as quickly as possible.

Dirio sat. "What brings you up here?" he asked.

"I come up here every day before going to the talks," Balear replied. "From here you can see most of southern Lodia. It reminds me what's at stake."

"You don't even get a say in the negotiations. Why beat yourself up over them?"

Balear shrugged. "Because I'm a defender of Lodia. I'm present during the meetings. That's reason enough to pay attention. Besides, who says I don't get a say? I'm the reason you're involved, after all."

Dirio frowned in such a way that Balear couldn't tell whether the man was angry or just sarcastic. "Don't remind me," the mayor said. "I'm not like those other four. I'm a miner. I don't get into all this politicking."

"Maybe that's what Lodia needs."

"Don't even start. It's bad enough that I'm part of these talks. Lodia doesn't need a past-his-prime miner for a king. Even if it did, none of the other mayors would support me. I have the least clout of any of them."

"Best personality though."

Dirio laughed at that. "You say that now, but remember the time I knocked you on your ass? You didn't feel that way back then."

Balear reddened. "Well, I suppose there was that. I see now why you did it, though. You wanted to help me." He paused to clear his throat. "You know something, Dirio? You could lead this country. You'd certainly be better at it than those four, even Elyssa. She's all numbers. One thing I learned from Amroth—the real Amroth, before Feng took him over—is that leaders need heart. You can't force people to do what you want them to do. The best you can do is guide them along the path."

The Veliafan cocked an eyebrow. "Maybe you should be king."

Balear blinked twice. "What do you mean? I'm ineligible."

Dirio shrugged. "A pity."

They sat in silence after that, watching the fields together. The sun had come up just an hour ago, but already the men below were hard at work tending crops and fishing.

At length Dirio stood. "I should get going. The negotiations will end today, and I need to be ready."

"I'm impressed you can be that optimistic," Balear said. "Do you tell yourself that every day to keep going?"

Dirio shook his head. "No. I'm switching my vote. I'm supporting Horace."

Balear was stunned. "You're what? Elyssa's sheltered your people all this time! It's a betrayal of her!"

"Maybe, but it's for the good of Lodia. Otto's ready to switch too. He knows Kras hasn't a chance of winning, not the way he's alienated me and Elyssa. When I switch to support Horace, Otto will too. That'll give Horace a majority, and that will be that. There won't even be a chance for fighting afterward, because the two defeated forces—Orcsthia and Kataile—will be separated by city walls and the length of a country."

Balear couldn't believe what he was hearing. Horace had the same calculating mind as Elyssa, but while Elyssa put that nature to work for Kataile, Horace used his for personal gain. He would be a miserable king.

Then again, even a miserable king was better than a civil war. "I believe in you," Balear said. "Do what you have to do. I'll support you."

Dirio grinned. "That's why I came up here to see you. Officially, you don't have a place in these negotiations, but you were right before. You do have a say. A big one."

The mayor rose and started toward the cliff stairs. Balear put his attention back to the north. At last, Lodia would have peace. Balear could return to Haldessa and help them rebuild. Horace would owe

Dirio a huge favor for switching his vote; maybe Dirio could convince the Terkouan to pardon Balear.

And what then? Horace would need to reform the Castle Guard to serve as peacekeepers, and Balear was the obvious choice to lead them. The young general smiled. He would make the guard better and stronger than it had ever been. It all started today.

Balear stood and stretched. For the first time in two months, he looked forward to entering that stuffy tent.

He was about to head across the plateau and out to the fields when he saw a cloud of dust above the northern horizon. He frowned. He called for Dirio, but the mayor wasn't in earshot anymore.

Balear watched the cloud grow. It was huge, stretching for miles. The sky was clear, and it hadn't been dry enough for a dust storm. It didn't seem natural. In fact, it looked like . . .

Balear tore across the plateau. He yelled out for Dirio. When he reached the steps, the Veliafan was puffing his way back up them.

"What's the matter?" Dirio asked, his hands on his knees.

"We need to find Elyssa," Balear said. "Now."

"Why?"

"Because another army is on its way."

CHAPTER THIRTY-NINE
Moving Forward

Iren awoke to bright sun and a seagull on his face.

"Bah!" he shouted as he leapt into a seated position. The bird flew away with an indignant squawk.

A high-pitched cackle came from the helm. "Did you have a peaceful sleep?" Rondel asked. "That gull sure seemed to think so."

"At least he didn't leave me any nasty surprises," Iren replied. He climbed to his feet and checked himself anyway. "What's our situation?"

"The storm's moved off to the northeast, and I don't see any others. I wouldn't expect to either. The storms are so powerful they blow everything else out of the way. There usually aren't two close together."

"So we're safe."

Rondel shrugged. "More or less. We survived; how's that?"

"Good enough for now," Iren said. "We're still moving. That's better than I expected with just two sails."

Rondel's fake grin sprouted. "Oh, it's not the sails. I thought I could get the remaining ones working while you slept, but this ship's just too heavy."

Iren's brow furrowed. "Then how are we moving?"

"Look off the bow."

Iren walked to the front of the ship. He whistled.

Rondel had released all the ropes from the surviving battens and tied them together into multiple strands. Those in turn tied off at different points near the ship's bow and led down into the water.

And there, tugging the ship along with the ropes gripped in its mouth, was a whale.

Iren faced Rondel. He pointed his thumb over his shoulder. "I take it that's no random whale."

Rondel raised a mischievous eyebrow. "Well, I was planning some joke about how we roped it into helping us."

Ouch. It was better not to even entertain that bad of a pun. "Minawë sure has come a long way since Ziorsecth," Iren said instead. "She gave me magic last night, and she still had enough to transform into a whale this morning?"

"That girl is stronger than us both," Rondel replied. Her eyes looked past Iren to the horizon. A softness Iren wasn't used to seeing in the fierce old woman appeared on her face.

Then Rondel seemed to realize she'd spoken aloud. She flushed. "Don't tell Minawë I said that."

Iren couldn't help himself. He laughed.

CHAPTER FORTY
Reunion on the Beach

Elyssa Orianna lowered her spyglass. "Who could they be?" she asked. "No city uses purple banners."

"Maybe it's Ceere," Dirio replied. "Perhaps they heard about the negotiations and have come to join."

"Who would have told them?" Balear put in. "Besides, hardly anyone's left in Ceere. There's no way they could gather an army that large."

"What about Tacumsah?" Elyssa asked. "We've continued to trade with them. Word of the civil war will have spread across the islands by now. They might have decided to take advantage of our weakness and invade. They could land easily at the Bay of Ceere."

Balear didn't look convinced. "Lady Orianna, hand me the spyglass."

Elyssa gave it to him without hesitation. Balear had that scary, determined expression on his face. The man knew who these invaders were; he just wanted to be certain before he said it aloud.

The general raised the spyglass and scanned the approaching army. "They aren't Tacumsahens," he said. "The islanders have dark skin. These newcomers are as fair as Lodians."

"So who are they?" Elyssa asked.

Balear's scowl deepened. "Those banners carry a symbol of a mountain. I've never seen such a mark. Whoever they are, they must think themselves royalty to fly purple."

The general surveyed the approaching force a moment longer. Then, without warning, he released the spyglass. It fell to the stone, and the lenses shattered.

Elyssa glared at Balear. "That was my finest spyglass!" she shouted. "What did you drop it for?"

The man didn't answer. He stood transfixed, as though someone in that distant army had reached out and removed his heart. His lone hand quivered at his face. He seemed not to realize he'd let go of the spyglass.

"No . . ." he murmured, "no, it can't be . . ."

"Balear?" Dirio asked. He gripped the general's shoulder. "What is it? Did you figure out where that army comes from?"

Balear was ashen. "I don't know where they're from," he said, "but I know who they are. They're Maantecs. I also know who leads them. I saw her face clearly. It was Hana."

Dirio's brow furrowed a moment. Then he said, "Isn't that the girl who came with you and Iren to Veliaf last year?"

"Yeah," Balear said. "She's also the Stone Dragon Knight."

Elyssa jumped in front of him. "Wait a second! You're saying they have another like you leading them?"

Balear didn't even look at her. His gaze remained on the approaching force. "I'm nothing like Hana," he said. "She can kill me and everyone in this city without breathing hard."

"What do we do?" Elyssa demanded.

Balear said nothing. He seemed to have lost his wits.

Dirio took charge. "Get a messenger to the other mayors," he told Elyssa. "Have them bring their forces inside the city. That army's at least as large as the one the three cities brought with them. But if the enemy is made up of Maantecs—of Lefts—then the men outside will stand no chance against them. Our best hope is to attack from the safety of the city walls and this plateau with archers and catapults."

Elyssa didn't like taking orders from some provincial miner, but the man was right. "What about you and Balear?" she asked.

"We'll rally Kataile's soldiers. You convince the other mayors to find sanctuary here. Tell them not to dawdle! That army will be on us in a matter of hours!"

Elyssa didn't waste time. She ran.

 C

As the sun reached its peak, General Balear Platarch watched the Maantecs approach from beside one of his new catapults. The siege weapon's team had loaded their first stone and readied the machine to launch it. Balear hoped they wouldn't have to.

He was still in disbelief. Hana was here. He knew he'd seen her in Kataile earlier this year.

But where had this army of Maantecs come from? Why was she leading them?

And were they friend or foe?

Balear would find out soon enough. Most of the western Lodian soldiers had heeded Elyssa's warning and retreated to the city. Two thousand archers from Kataile, Terkou, and Caardit now lined the plateau alongside the catapults.

One city, though, had chosen not to withdraw. Kras and the men of Orcsthia remained outside.

"Fool," Balear spat as he shifted his gaze to the Orcsthian force. If the Maantecs had come for a fight, it was now too late for Kras to escape.

The Orcsthian army looked puny compared with the Maantecs'. Hana had easily brought five thousand men with her, and while they had only foot soldiers, that meant little. They were Maantecs. Balear knew what they could do.

A group on horseback galloped from Orcsthia's position toward the new army. Balear focused on them, and he spotted Kras's armor and horse. The cavalryman next to him carried a white truce banner, not that the Maantecs would know or care what it meant.

"Fool," Balear repeated. Now he saw Kras's strategy. The man intended to betray them. He knew he couldn't win the throne through the Succession Council. If he could persuade this new force to join him and attack Kataile together, though, he might still become king.

That was Kras's plan, but it didn't go the way he wanted. As the horses neared, Hana stepped forward. She swept her hand across her, and stone spikes shot from the ground. Balear gripped his chest. Kras and his cavalry never saw what impaled them.

So that was it then. Hana had shown her army's intention. They weren't here to talk. They were here to kill.

Balear made up his mind. "We have to support the Orcsthians," he told the catapult team. "We need to give them time to reach the city. At this range the catapults should make it over the Orcsthians and into the invaders. Fire at will."

The men blanched, but they nodded. The first shot launched.

It didn't get far. Halfway through its arc, the boulder halted in midair. A second later, it dropped straight to the ground without even reaching the Orcsthian line.

Balear was already dashing to the next catapult to spread the attack command, but he stopped in midstride. He should have known. Hana was the Stone Dragon Knight. These rocks were her toys.

It didn't matter. He ran on and yelled to the catapult teams to attack. More shots launched, but Hana made each fall short.

In a lucky burst, three stones lifted at once. It still wasn't enough. One almost reached the Maantecs, but at the last second, it halted a few dozen feet off the ground. It then hurtled sideways and into the ocean.

Balear swore. He'd planned Kataile's defense around human foes. They weren't prepared to handle magic.

The Maantecs closed on the Orcsthians. The westerners had broken and fled after watching their leader impaled, but their efforts were useless. Humans couldn't outrun Maantecs.

As the slaughter commenced, Balear left the catapults behind. He found Riac and told him to take command of the siege weapons. Balear's place was at the front, on the beach. That was where the enemy would come.

"Archers!" Balear shouted as he ran along the plateau. "Those from other cities, stay up here and shoot the Lefts as soon as they come in range. Katailans, you're with me. This is what we trained for. Take up your assigned defensive positions inside the city. Shoot any who come past the beach!"

He didn't bother waiting for a reply. He heard Riac bellowing orders behind him, and he heard the rushing feet. That was enough. What the other cities' men would do was unknown, but for the Katailans at least,

Balear knew they would follow his commands. They would fight to the death for their city.

Balear raced down Kataile's steep stairs as quickly as he dared. The Orcsthians were likely all but wiped out by now. If he didn't get to the city entrance soon, it would be too late to set up any kind of blockade.

He arrived on the beach and came around the side of the plateau just in time to witness the last Orcsthians fall. Balear had to struggle to keep his feet. Hana wasn't like this. She wouldn't bring such butchery even to people she hated.

"Stay strong, General!" a voice beside Balear called. "We're with you!"

Balear looked over at the man who'd spoken and almost laughed aloud. It was Pito, the teenager he'd attacked with the Auryozaki. The boy had come with his squad to stand at the vanguard with their general.

The young man looked transformed from the snot-nosed kid of a few months ago. He carried a long spear and boiled leather armor. His eyes glittered with the blend of excitement and fear of someone who had never been in battle before. Pito had to know this position was suicide, but if Balear was willing to face it, then he and his squad would do the same.

The Maantec army shifted and headed toward the plateau. More catapult stones launched, but they were as useless as they'd ever been.

The archers might have a better chance. As the Maantecs came within range, the bowmen atop the plateau unleashed a volley. Balear smiled. Riac had gotten the men working together quickly. Hana might be able to stop stones, but this many arrows were beyond her.

They weren't beyond her army though. As the volley approached the Maantecs, the men in the front line raised their hands. Flames shot from each soldier in a column fifty feet high. As the arrows passed through the inferno, the shafts burned away. The arrowheads fell harmlessly against the Maantecs' armor.

Balear gaped. What could they do against that? It was bad enough that Hana had a dragon at her command, but even her soldiers had some magical abilities.

He forced himself to calm down. That magic had to have limits. Those Maantecs weren't Dragon Knights, so using a spell that large would drain their energy in a few minutes. The men on the plateau had plenty of arrows, and they were all but untouchable up there. If Balear, Pito, and the archers here on ground level could keep the Maantecs out of the city, the men on the plateau might still win the day.

Unfortunately, Balear wasn't up there to tell them that. A few more arrows shot, but the barrage was nothing like the first volley. Riac must be having trouble keeping the men disciplined.

Assuming, of course, that Riac himself hadn't fled at the sight of those flames.

Balear needed to do something. His men needed confidence. They needed to know they could keep fighting, that they had a chance of winning even against this vastly superior foe.

But what could he do? He couldn't abandon his post here. If he sent Pito or any of his squad, no one would listen to them. They were kids.

As Balear struggled to decide, Hana stepped in front of her fire mages. She raised her hands. From up on the plateau came a horrendous cracking sound.

Then came the screams. Massive chunks of the plateau, dozens of feet across, ripped free. They crashed to the ground, carrying catapults and archers alike with them. Pito and his boys wailed in horror. Even Balear felt like he might be sick.

New cracks like thunder issued above Balear. He looked up and saw a section of plateau break off above him. He leapt back and shielded his eyes.

A second later the enormous rock smashed into the beach. It missed him by less than ten feet. Sand erupted from the impact.

Balear wiped his eyes clear and gaped at the boulder. It was taller and wider than he was. Had he been standing beneath it, there would have been nothing left of him.

There was something weird about it though. The rock was terrifying for sure, and even though it hadn't hurt anyone, it had still devastated Balear's front line. Pito and all his boys were on the ground crying.

And yet, something wasn't right about it. Hana had perfect control of her magic. She had grabbed catapult stones from midair and flung them wherever she chose. There was no way she should have missed Balear and his men.

Then he understood. He knew what he had to do.

"Pito," he said, his voice carefully controlled, "I need you to do something for me. Go up to the plateau and tell them they can still win. Magic has a limit. Those fires won't last. When the Maantecs come again, the archers need to fight with everything they have. Understand?"

"Sir, do you really think they'll listen to me?"

"No," Balear replied. "Find Riac. Tell him I sent you. He'll listen and spread the word."

"And what are you going to do? Hold them here by yourself?"

The corner of Balear's mouth curled up. "Something like that. I'm going out there. I'm going to stop their leader, the one making the rocks fall. That way the archers will be able to attack from the plateau without risk."

Pito's eyes were huge. "You can't! You saw what she did! You'll die!"

Balear put his back to the boy. Pito had a long way to go, but he had the makings of a good man. Balear hoped the young officer lived through today.

Balear stepped around the boulder Hana had dropped. Hana threw her arm to the side, and her advancing soldiers halted. Everyone on both sides seemed to hold their breath as Balear stepped into no-man's land.

Hana left her army. She walked onto the sand and headed down the beach toward Balear.

As they approached each other, Balear couldn't help but feel a touch of nostalgia. How long had it been since they'd spoken? A year, at least. Hana led an army that wanted to kill them all, yet Balear couldn't bring himself to hate her. He could still feel her finger on his nose, her tears on his hand as she mourned the loss of his arm.

A hundred yards from Kataile, the pair reunited. Balear opened his mouth. "Hana, I—"

She held up a palm. "Don't even try," she said. She reached down, and her Enryokiri, her Stone Dragon Hammer, emerged from the ground. She clutched it in both hands. "I didn't kill you back there because no one would have seen it. I want them all to know how hopeless their situation is. Now everyone in Kataile can watch their champion die."

CHAPTER FORTY-ONE
Duel

Her pulse hadn't risen. Her breathing hadn't tightened. It was an illusion.

Hana kept telling herself all that as she stared at the face of Balear Platarch. They were enemies, and that was all there was to it. She had her orders.

"Lead half of the army south to Kataile," Lord Melwar had told her. "Attack the city."

She had known Balear would be waiting for her. She couldn't let him die from some random soldier's arrow, spear, or burst of flame. She had to do this herself.

"I'm going to kill you, Balear," she said through gritted teeth.

Balear looked at her with sad, world-weary eyes. They seemed out of place on so young a man. "If at all possible," he said, "I would prefer not to fight you."

He wasn't angry. He didn't shout or scream or cry. Hana wanted him to. She wanted him to rage at her, to swear vengeance upon her for murdering the men on the fields and the plateau.

But he didn't. Stupid, stupid, beautiful man.

"Shogun Melwar's orders cannot be defied," she told him.

"Melwar . . ." Balear said. He paused a moment. "He's the one you and Iren went to see last year. He's your teacher."

"My master," Hana corrected. "He's in Ceere with the rest of the army. Your nation, your people, will die. The Maantecs will be free at last."

Why was she explaining this to him? She could call up two walls of stone, crush him, and be done with this nonsense in a second. He was nothing compared with Shogun Melwar, or Faro, or even that insufferable Forest Dragon Knight. He was a worthless, stinking, rotting human.

Balear loosed a long sigh. "The people of this country have a lot to answer for when it comes to Maantecs," he said. "We've treated Lefts like demons. We've ostracized them, even murdered them. I'm as guilty of it as anyone else. I can understand why Maantecs would hate us. What I can't understand, though, is why you would enslave yourself to a genocidal madman."

"You don't know Shogun Melwar," Hana replied. "I can't defy him. He'll kill me."

"So you know what he is," Balear said. "You didn't even try to argue. You aren't loyal to him. It's written all over your face. Join with me. We'll find Iren, Rondel, and Minawë, and we'll stop Melwar together." He stretched out his hand to her.

She slapped it away. "Don't you get it?" she yelled. "Lord Melwar could kill us all in a second. He's become more powerful than any Dragon Knight. This is the only hope we have for survival!"

Balear's eyes narrowed. "What kind of survival is that, to be the dog of a deranged master?"

"You're a fine one to talk," Hana scoffed. "You served Amroth."

"And abandoned him. You can do it too."

Hana stormed up and down the beach. "You just don't get it, do you? Amroth was a low-class who up-jumped his status by getting his unworthy hands on the Karyozaki." She jabbed a finger at Balear. "Did you know he didn't even have a clan name? That's why he adopted the human name 'Angustion.' Shogun Melwar's different. He's the highest of the high. I don't want him to kill me."

"You're afraid of death," Balear murmured.

"Shut up! What do you know?"

Balear met her eyes. She looked away.

"I know you wear that armor for more than fighting," Balear said. "I know you hide from the world because it's too painful for you to face. I know you're stronger than you believe yourself to be. I know I love you, and I know you love me too."

Her gaze flashed up to his. "You . . . I . . ."

There was no point in denying it. Her heart raced. Her breath came in spurts. She wanted nothing more than to run to him, wrap her arms around him, and kiss him in front of both armies.

No. She couldn't. This had to stop.

And there was only one way to do it.

"I will kill you, Balear," she said, "and then I will raze this city to the ground. That way I won't die."

Balear shook his head. "If what you fear most is death, than coming here was a mistake. You've trapped yourself into death. If you leave, Melwar will kill you. If you stay, I will kill you."

Hana laughed. It sounded strained even to her. "You'll kill me? You're a human. You're hopeless."

She forced herself under control. "Fine, I'll make you a deal." She looked over her shoulder and shouted, "Commander Daichi!"

A man in heavy lamellar armor jogged forward. He bowed as he approached. "How may I serve, my lady?"

"Balear, this is the deal I make to you," Hana said. "Let's settle this battle in the ancient custom of the Maantecs, with a duel of champions."

"Duel of champions?"

"Maantecs reproduce slowly. In ancient times, to keep from wiping ourselves out in wars, we didn't fight open battles. Instead, we settled conflicts by each side electing a single champion to represent them. The pair would fight to the death, and the winner's side won the war."

"That's what you propose for us, then," Balear said.

Hana nodded. "If you win, this army will withdraw to Ceere and leave Kataile. But if I win, they'll slay every man, woman, and child in the city."

Daichi bolted upright. "My lady! What would Shogun Melwar think of this?"

"He gave me two commands," Hana said. "Lead the army to Kataile, and attack it. I've done both. He gave this army no orders, only me. So, Commander, I give you this order. If this man defeats me, then take the army and return to Ceere. Leave Kataile intact."

"But my lady!"

"If you cannot follow such a simple request, then I will order you to commit seppuku, and I will find a replacement who obeys his superiors!"

The commander bowed as low as he could in his bulky armor. "Of course, my lady. I will do as you say."

"Besides," Hana said, "my order makes no difference. Balear can't defeat me, so you'll never have to follow it. Now get out of my way."

Daichi scrambled back to the rest of the army. Hana watched him go, then put her eyes on Balear. She raised her Stone Dragon Hammer. "Now, let's begin."

Balear freed his Sky Dragon Sword. "Yes, let's."

CHAPTER FORTY-TWO
Lodia's Champion

There was no more need for words. Balear struck.

The Auryozaki rang against Hana's hardened skin armor. The female Maantec didn't even flinch.

Balear swung a second time, this time an overhead blow. Again Hana's armor stopped the attack.

The Lodian grimaced. His Auryozaki was immensely heavy to everyone but him. No one he had fought before could withstand a direct strike from it. Even a blocked attack sent the defender sprawling.

Yet Hana just stood there, immune.

She didn't smile or gloat, despite her obvious advantage. When Balear looked at her, he could tell. She didn't want this any more than he did.

Hana raised an arm. Balear braced for an attack that could come from anywhere.

A cracking sound behind him signaled that Hana had freed another section of rock from the plateau. Balear looked over his shoulder in time to see a boulder the size of his torso flying toward him.

It was an impressive sight, but the rock's size made it slow. Balear jumped out of the way, and the boulder sailed past him harmlessly.

But instead of continuing straight, the rock careened in an arc. It was coming back.

Dodging it wouldn't do Balear any good. He faced the stone. As it approached, he swung the Auryozaki down and split the rock in two. Both sections smashed into the beach.

"I won't die that easily," Balear said.

Hana looked at him, then at the boulder's halves, then back at Balear. She raised her arm again. This time, rather than a rock, a curtain of sand lifted into the air.

"It's as heavy as that boulder," she said, "but just try knocking it out of the way."

Balear scowled. Hana was right. Swinging the Auryozaki wouldn't do anything against sand. The sand would curl around it and hit him anyway.

There was only one way he could stop it. He'd promised not to, though. He'd sworn an oath.

For a moment he was back in Veliaf, floating above the frozen town. Wind whipped in a sphere at its center. The ball's pressure released, and tiny, glittering shards that had once been homes rained from the sky.

It had been his fault. He'd sworn he would never let it happen again.

The sand charged toward him. Balear swung at it on instinct, but the attack was useless. The sand flowed around his sword and struck him in the chest. He landed on his back on the beach.

Balear stumbled to his feet. When he did, gray rings formed around his vision. That blow had almost knocked him out. He couldn't take another hit like that.

Hana was already raising a second sand curtain. Balear had no choice. He'd known it from the moment he'd stepped beyond the city. Yes, he'd made an oath not to use magic. But he'd made a second oath, one even more important.

He'd sworn to protect Lodia.

The sand rushed for him. But this time, when Balear swung, he let magic into the blow. Wind danced around the sword's edges, and it scattered the sand in all directions.

Hana stepped back in surprise, and that gave Balear an opening. He charged and thrust. Unlike his previous attacks, wind magic gave this one added speed and strength. Hana's armor wouldn't stop it.

Hana must have realized that too, because at the last second, she raised a wall of sand to protect herself. The Auryozaki's wind pressure blew aside the defense, but the effort cost it momentum. The sword knocked Hana off her feet, but it didn't pierce her armor.

The Stone Dragon Knight rose, unharmed. Balear looked at her with pity. "I saw what you did to that Fubuki in Akaku Forest last year," he said. "You could have killed me a dozen times over by now. Your heart isn't in this fight."

"I'll show you what my heart's in," Hana spat. She raised a hand. The sand around Balear's ankles rose up and trapped him. It covered his legs, chest, and arm until only his head remained exposed.

Balear couldn't help but appreciate the irony of the situation. The Ice Dragon Knight had defeated him in Veliaf last year using a similar trap.

Hana approached Balear's helpless form. "So," she said, "how would you like me to kill you? I could compress the sand against your chest and cave it in. I could sink you a half mile underground like I did to the Water Dragon Knight. Or maybe you'd prefer burial at sea like your father. I could send you out over the ocean and let you drown."

Balear wasn't listening. Hana's words were for herself, not for him. Besides, he needed to concentrate. It was time.

He pulled in air from outside the sand surrounding him. The trap looked solid, but there was a lot of space between each sand grain. Air rushed in and forced them apart. Balear shouted in defiance as a small tornado whipped around him. It scattered the sand and sent Hana launching fifty feet up the beach. Balear landed on his feet, free.

Not for long though. He knew from Veliaf that tornado spells demanded a lot of magic.

A presence brushed against his mind, one he knew all too well. "Hello, Ariok," he said.

"Balear," the dragon sneered the name, "what happened to your oath? What happened to your honor?"

"Shut up," Balear snarled. "I have more important issues here."

"I would say so. How are you going to kill her when you've used up all your magic?"

Balear knew the answer, but he couldn't bring himself to say it.

"I know a way," Ariok said. He pushed against Balear's mind.

"No!" Balear shouted. "Stay out of my head!"

But the transformation had already begun. Balear's legs bulged. They grew blue and scaly.

Hana had recovered and come back to Balear. Now she stepped away in fear. "Balear," she gasped, "you're becoming a dragon!"

"You . . . didn't know," Balear managed. "That Fubuki returned to Veliaf. I fought him, but I couldn't win. I transformed into Ariok, and he slew the beast. Afterward, though, he destroyed the town."

Hana's arms fell to her sides. "No . . ."

"How many more times?" Balear asked. He was growing taller as his body elongated into a serpentine shape. "How many more times will you make us murderers? You gave the Fubuki the Ice Dragon Hammer. He told me so."

"It was Shogun Melwar's order. Balear, I—"

"Enough!" Balear's mouth filled with needle-sharp teeth. "I obliterated a town. Wasn't that enough? Now you'll make me wipe out a city?"

"You have no choice," Ariok said inside his mind. "You know this is the only way to kill her. You've known that ever since you stepped out here. Don't worry. Once I finish with her, I'll slaughter the Maantec army for you too. So what if Kataile shatters in the process? If Hana defeats you, the Maantecs will destroy it. At least this way your enemies die too."

"I won't let you," Balear replied. "I swore to protect Lodia. How is it protecting them if I kill them in the process?"

"Sometimes we must sacrifice a city to save a nation. It is the only way."

"Not . . . this time," Balear struggled to say. "There is another way. I'm taking your power, Ariok. I won't become a dragon. I'll become a Dragoon."

Ariok laughed. He threw his will at Balear. "You'll what? You're a weakling!"

Balear met the dragon's mind head-on. "You heard Hana. I'm Lodia's champion. I swore to protect its people. I would fight any battle, any foe, to keep them safe. Even you!"

Ariok cowered against the force of Balear's will. In his mind's eye, Balear saw the dragon give in. The mighty creature, a god, bowed to him.

Balear's body shrank. The needle-teeth retracted, and the serpentine shape collapsed. His legs regained their human form.

Then blue scales formed around them. They rose up and coated his body in gleaming armor. Balear cried out, and a pair of white, bat-like wings twenty feet long erupted from his back. Wind spiraled around him. It floated him six inches off the ground. The sand shot from beneath him in a tempest.

Hana shielded her eyes. "Impossible!"

Balear looked down at her. Ariok touched his mind, but the dragon was no longer a threat. "Do you mind if I speak to her?" Ariok asked. His tone was one of subdued respect.

"Very well," Balear replied.

"Stone Dragon Knight," Ariok said through Balear's mouth. "You believe Maantecs are superior because of your magic, but I have seen the truth. Humans are stronger than all of you. What they lack in magic, they make up for in willpower. That's why ever since my first human Dragon Knight, I have only accepted those with human blood. I knew that someday, one of them would have a will that could challenge me, that could best me, that could do what no Maantec could: become the Dragoon."

Hana raised a wall of sand forty feet high. It encircled Balear and then, all at once, slammed toward him.

Balear didn't move. As the sand approached, bursts of wind shot from every direction and blasted it away.

Hana next reached out over the ocean. A dozen massive boulders erupted from the water. They launched at Balear, but the wind flashed out again and halted them in midair. Hana struggled, but she couldn't make them move. They dropped to the ground.

"The air is my weapon," Balear said. "Anything you use must travel through it to reach me. Now that I'm a Dragoon, you can't even touch me."

The Stone Dragon Knight's fists clenched around her hammer. Balear's eyes narrowed. That hammer was the key. That was how he would save everyone, including Hana.

He pointed the Auryozaki at her. Wind lashed about Hana, and then her left arm snapped back. Much as Ariok had done against the Fubuki, Balear had created an airless void that gripped Hana's limb in place. He summoned three more, one around her right wrist and two around her ankles. They lifted her off the ground. As they did, a fifth void wrenched the Stone Dragon Hammer from her hand.

"What are you going to do?" Hana asked. Her eyes were wild. She knew she was at his mercy. He could split her into shreds of flesh on a whim.

Balear didn't bother responding. Instead, he concentrated on the void holding the Stone Dragon Hammer. He poured magic into it, letting the void grow in size and strength.

Iren Saitosan had needed an explosion a mile across to destroy the Karyozaki. He had barely managed it even as a Dragoon. Balear didn't know if his plan could work, but he had to try it.

The wind pressure intensified. A great renting sound filled the beach. It screamed and tore at Balear's hearing, but he pressed on.

At last the Enryokiri, the Stone Dragon Hammer, shattered into a thousand splinters.

The remnants of Hana's weapon plopped onto the sand, all but one. A gleaming yellow gem still floated in midair.

"The Rock Topaz," Ariok explained. "The gems that imprison us can't be destroyed."

"I know," Balear said. "I remember what happened to Feng's Burning Ruby. As long as these gems are in the hands of people—of whatever race—there will always be a chance that they could be turned into Ryokaiten again. That's why there's only one option for what to do with that stone."

Balear flicked his wrist, and a wind current flung the Rock Topaz out to sea. It disappeared over the horizon.

"Even I don't know where it landed," Balear told Hana as he released the wind currents holding her and returned her to the beach. "Wherever it did, it will sink to the bottom. The Rock Topaz is beyond anyone's reach now."

Hana knelt in the sand. She looked like she wanted to cry and scream and hit him all at the same time. Her mouth moved in an attempt to form words, but she said nothing.

"You did well, Balear," Ariok said.

"I never expected to hear praise from you," Balear replied. "You told me you hated people for imprisoning you. I thought you wanted to destroy us all."

Ariok chuckled inside Balear's mind. "I did say that, didn't I? But I also said that some dragons have more honor than others."

"Yes, and then you lied to me. You said you wouldn't rage like Feng, and then you blew up Veliaf."

"How was that a lie? I didn't rage like Feng. He almost exterminated the Kodamas. How many humans did I kill that day?"

Balear frowned. "Well, none, but—"

"Exactly. The point of destroying Veliaf wasn't to rage. It was to push you. I knew you had the potential to become the Dragoon. I wanted to see if you were capable."

"You're saying you did it to help me?"

"To motivate you. You kept on saying you wanted to protect Lodia. I wanted to show you the consequence of failure. After seeing that, I knew you would succeed the next time."

Balear shook his head. "You're a crazy bastard, you know that?"

"I suppose, but if I am, then so are you. After all, you used the same approach on that fountain in Kataile to motivate your soldiers. Do you see? Dragons choose their knights based on people who reflect their personalities and the traits they value most."

"Hana told me last year that you test knights on their bravery."

"Bravery, honor, and willpower. You passed all three."

Inside his mind, Balear offered a hand to the dragon. "Ariok, I'm glad I got to meet you."

The dragon touched Balear's hand with a clawed finger. "Likewise," he said, "but your time as a Dragoon is nearly up. And Balear, your transformation won't be like Iren's."

Balear smiled sadly. "I know. I've known all this time. We may have more willpower than Maantecs, but human bodies still aren't designed to handle this kind of magic. I can already feel it. The energy's done something to me inside. I'm not walking away from this one."

"You knew?" Ariok asked. "Yet you still . . ."

"It's what I had to do, as Lodia's champion."

The edges of Ariok's scaly mouth crinkled. "And you called me a crazy bastard."

The dragon faded. The armor around Balear disappeared. His wings pulled back into his skin, and he dropped to the sand. He lay on his back, unable to stand, unable to move. He coughed, and the red spurt told him the truth.

Hana rushed over to him. "Balear!" She cradled him in her arms. "Why, Balear?"

He smiled. "Because I couldn't choose. You and Kataile were both worth saving."

"Balear . . ."

"Enough. Listen to me, Hana. Don't be a slave. You're better than that. Don't go back to Melwar. Help us stop him."

"You don't understand—"

"You're right. I don't. I've never met him. Maybe he is every bit as powerful as you say. But still, I'm fighting him. I'm sure Iren and Rondel and Minawë will too. Even if we're outmatched, we'll still fight, because that's what's best for this world."

Hana gripped him tighter. "Why would you fight for this world?" she cried. "You know what it produces. You saw what Amroth did to Ziorsecth. You saw what your own people did to each other in the civil war. What kind of world is that, that you would die for it?"

"A world that has people like you," Balear said. "You're reason enough to fight for it. Hana, I never gave up on you. I've loved you ever since we first crossed Lodia together. I never told you, but I promised myself I would give you something for journeying with me and Iren last year. I promised I would give you faith. Did I?"

Hana cried. Not a few tears like when Balear had lost his arm, but long, wet, wracking sobs. She clutched Balear and pressed her head into his chest. "I love you," she said. "I love you. I'm sorry, Balear."

They were the last words he heard as darkness took him.

CHAPTER FORTY-THREE
Late Arrivals

Dirio Cyneric paced the audience room in Kataile's city hall. He avoided looking at Feidl's mural of the city at dawn. That was Kataile as it should be. It wouldn't look like that much longer, not with five thousand Maantecs bearing down on it.

Damn! He could shoot a bow. He could thrust a spear. He could do something besides sit here while everyone else got butchered.

The other mayors waited in the room with him, but none of them walked around. They all sat against the far wall. They didn't speak. They didn't move. They had given up. They were all just waiting for the end.

Forget them. Dirio stalked to the door. "I'm going," he said. He grasped the handle and pulled.

The door almost smacked him in the face. Riac burst through, and Dirio barely had time to scramble aside.

"Lady Orianna!" Riac shouted. "Lady Orianna!"

Everyone in the room stood. "What news?" Elyssa demanded.

"It's the Left army! They're withdrawing!"

Dirio grabbed the man by both shoulders. "What did you say? Did the combined armies push them back?"

"No! General Platarch did it. He fought the Left's leader all by himself. He was amazing! He flew in the air!"

Dirio grinned. That Balear . . . Dirio had always known the man was something special.

"Let's go congratulate him," Dirio said.

Riac's face fell. "About that . . ."

"Out with it," Elyssa barked. "Where's Balear?"

Before Riac could say anything, another man burst through the doors. He was young; "man" might not be the right term for him. It took a moment for Dirio to recognize him as Pito, the teenaged squad leader.

The boy looked on the verge of passing out. Sweat poured from him, and his chest heaved. "Captain!" he panted. "I'm glad I caught up to you. I saw it on my way up the steps. There's something coming!"

Riac frowned. "What did you see? What's coming?"

"A ship! It just entered the bay."

"Ships come and go all the time," Elyssa spat. "We have bigger issues right now, child."

Pito quailed beneath the mayor's gaze, but he somehow found the courage to say, "Not like this one, ma'am. It doesn't look like any Lodian or Tacumsahen ship I've ever seen. And there's something weird about it. I think it's a Left ship."

Dirio cursed. So the army had been a diversion. It would draw their attention, and meanwhile a special Maantec unit would land inside Kataile's defenses at the harbor. A ship couldn't hold that many soldiers, but even a few hundred would prove devastating. With Balear outside fighting Hana, they had no mage to counter them.

That was where Dirio belonged then. "Show me to the docks," he commanded Pito. "Riac, you're coming too."

Even though Dirio wasn't their mayor, neither soldier questioned him. The trio launched from the room without another word.

They charged through the city. As they ran, Dirio snagged a bow and quiver from the training square by the fountain. He also called to any archers he saw to join him at the docks. Their only hope was to sink that ship before it arrived.

Even before he reached the pier, Dirio could tell Pito had been right about the ship. It wasn't at all like the human vessels Dirio had seen in Kataile. It was much too large, and its two sails were a different design. They must be magical, because there was no way such an enormous ship could move with just them.

Dirio ran to the pier's end and drew an arrow. Barrels of pitch lined the dock, and he dipped his arrow into one of them. Riac grabbed a torch and lit it. Dirio in turn ignited his arrow. The other archers who had joined him did the same.

The incoming ship stood no chance. One good shot would catch the vessel alight. With the training Kataile's men had received from Riac and Balear, they would sink it long before it could reach them.

The ship's condition would make the job even easier. Now that it was closer, Dirio saw that it was barely holding together. Sections of hull were loose, and a chunk of railing had broken off.

Dirio pulled back his arrow, but something stayed his hand. The way the vessel moved made no sense. Its sails were slack, yet it slid through the water. Ropes from the ship's bow came forward and down into the bay. It was as though something else tugged the ship along.

A great burst of water shot up from the sea. Dirio fell back on his rump; he'd never seen a geyser like that before. His arrow shot by accident, and it spluttered as it fell into the bay not ten feet from the dock.

Riac laughed despite the tense situation. "Never seen a whale before, miner?"

"A whale?"

"Giant creature of the deep. It's what's pulling that thing."

Dirio stood. What on Raa was this ship? Shredded to pieces and towed by an animal? No one would use such a vessel for an assault.

"Hold!" Dirio shouted. If he was wrong about this, everyone in Kataile was going to die. Yet he couldn't bring himself to sink the ship. Whatever had put it in such a dire state, the people aboard it must be even worse off.

"Bows away," he ordered. "Swords and spears out. We'll see what they want first. If they show any sign of hostility, cut them down before they can get into the city."

The crippled vessel inched its way deeper into the harbor. The whale guided it with precision. Dirio had no idea how intelligent whales were, but he doubted one could direct a ship like that on its own.

When the vessel came within what Dirio hoped was shouting range, he called out, "Hail! Who docks at the Port of Kataile?"

A man's face popped up over the bow. Dirio recognized the tan hair and blue eyes at once. He would never forget the person who'd saved his life twice.

"Ahoy!" Iren Saitosan shouted. He waved his arm in a wide arc, but then he reached back and grabbed his head. "Ow! What was that for?"

An old woman's face joined Iren's. "All this time away, and the best you can think of to say when we arrive is 'ahoy?'"

Dirio laughed. "It's all right, Rondel. I wouldn't expect anything more."

"Hey, what's that supposed to mean?" Iren asked.

"Knock it off, both of you," a female voice said from the water. Dirio had no idea where it had come from. He looked down and noticed the whale was gone. In its place was a young-looking woman with long green hair bobbing in the surf.

The Kodama swam over to the dock and climbed up. With a vigorous shaking, she flung water off her body. "Thanks for not shooting us," she said. "I hoped that water spout would convince you we meant no harm."

Only one Kodama had escaped her race's curse. "That was you, Minawë?" Dirio asked. "You were the whale?"

"I'm not in a hurry to be one again, either," Minawë said. "My days hauling ships around had better be over."

Dirio didn't know if she was joking or not. He suspected not.

Iren and Rondel leapt over the side of the ship and landed on the dock. Despite the forty foot drop, both made it without injury or even apparent effort. They joined Dirio and Minawë. Dirio motioned for the soldiers to put away their weapons.

"It's great to see you!" Iren said. "How have you been? Why are you in Kataile? Ow! Will you stop that?"

Rondel had smacked him upside the head again. "Save the greetings for later," she spat. She faced Dirio. Lightning Sight filled her eyes. "The Maantecs are invading Lodia. They're landing at Ceere. You need to be ready."

"You're a little late," Dirio said. "They've already come."

Rondel cocked an eyebrow. "This city looks in surprisingly good condition for a Maantec attack."

Dirio smirked. "That's the best part. I just heard the news. Five thousand Maantecs descended on us with Hana at their head. They would have torn this city apart were it not for Balear."

Iren grasped Dirio by the lapel. A few soldiers near him reached for their weapons, but Dirio waved them off.

"Balear did?" Iren demanded. "How? Where is he? What happened?"

Dirio gestured at Riac. "Actually, Riac here was just delivering the message when we heard about your ship. Captain, what's the situation?"

Riac gulped. "General Platarch fought the Lefts' leader on the beach past the plateau. When I came to City Hall, the Left army was pulling back north. But General Platarch hasn't returned. He and the Lefts' leader are still on the beach, or at least they were when I came to tell you."

Dirio blanched. He wouldn't believe it.

Iren looked equally pale. "Your name's Riac, right? You have to take me there."

Riac had no reason to trust the man in front of him. They'd never met. But something in Iren's expression must have convinced him.

"Come," he said. "I'll show you."

∞

Of all the people Iren had expected to meet at Kataile's docks, Dirio had been last on his list. The miner was supposed to be in charge of Veliaf far to the north. What was he doing here?

There was no time to question it now. As they ran through Kataile's streets, all Iren could think of was Balear.

Last year the pair of them had sparred in Akaku Forest. Iren knew what the man could do, and he had the utmost respect for him.

Unfortunately, Iren had dueled Hana too. As skilled as Balear was, Hana far surpassed him. There wasn't a chance the Lodian could have defeated her.

They dashed up the beach. Ahead, Iren saw a mound rising from the sand. As they approached, he saw that the mound was made by two people.

Hana stood as Iren, Rondel, Minawë, Dirio, and Riac arrived. Balear lay on his back, unmoving.

"Balear!" Iren shouted. The man made no response.

Hana stared blankly at Iren. Her face looked haunted, with puffy red eyes and deep tear lines down her cheeks. She didn't seem at all surprised that Iren and the others had somehow found a way to Lodia. "That won't work," she murmured. "He's dead."

Iren drew the Muryozaki. "How could you?" he demanded.

The female Maantec shook her head. "I didn't," she said. "He did it to himself. He became the Dragoon."

Iren had nothing to say to that. He was too shocked. He had become the Dragoon almost two years ago, so he knew what the transformation was like, how near-to-impossible it was. The idea that Balear could do it boggled the mind.

"We were fighting," Hana continued. "I cornered him, trapped him in sand. He broke free, but he used too much magic. I thought he'd lost control. He almost turned into Ariok, but at the last second he overcame the Sky Dragon. He was amazing. He could have killed me in an instant, but instead he spared my life."

Rondel's hand was on her dagger, but she kept it in its sheath. "And what will you do now?" she asked.

Hana gazed down at the fallen Balear. She sniffled, but she didn't cry. She had no more tears to give. "I don't know yet," she said. "I've sent Shogun Melwar's army back to him, but I can't return with them. Balear shattered the Enryokiri and sank the Rock Topaz far out at sea."

Iren's eyes narrowed. "You can conceal the Enryokiri underground. This is some ploy, isn't it?"

When Hana's eyes met his, Iren regretted speaking. Hana could lie and manipulate without difficulty, but this time she'd spoken the truth. "If you want to kill me, Iren Saitosan, then go ahead and do it," she said. "I've failed the shogun. My life is forfeit."

Iren glanced from Hana to Balear and back again. He gripped the Muryozaki's hilt. Hana had killed Balear. Even if she hadn't struck the lethal blow, her presence had forced Balear to use the Dragoon. Iren himself had barely survived that transformation. Balear must have known it would be fatal.

Rondel let go of her weapon. Iren rocked back in surprise. Of all people, Rondel should have struck first. She lived by Okthora's Law. Hana had led an army to this place, slain hundreds of innocent people, and murdered Balear. How could Rondel let all that go?

"Twenty-five years ago," Rondel said, "I made a mistake, one of many. I tossed you aside. If I could have that moment again, I would make a different choice." Without waiting for a response, she turned and headed for Kataile.

Iren couldn't help but watch the old woman. What was going on with her? She seemed like a different person even from their time on the ship.

"Why don't you come with us?" Minawë offered. "We can stop Melwar together."

"Is that sentiment, Kodama?" Hana asked. A hint of a sneer found its way into her voice.

Minawë didn't rise to the challenge. "It's recognition," she said. "You're strong, even without the Enryokiri. We could use your help."

Hana shook her head. "Even now, I can't betray the shogun. I've lived too long in his shadow. Maybe someday I'll find another path, but for now, I need some time alone."

She put her back to them and started to walk away. Iren's hand tightened and loosened around the Muryozaki's hilt. This was his last chance to avenge his friend.

Hana glanced over her shoulder. "Shogun Melwar is in Ceere. He intends to rebuild Haldessa Castle and use it as his base. If you want to stop him, that's where you should look."

Minawë smiled. "Thank you, Hana."

Hana laughed. "Don't thank me; I haven't helped you. The shogun is invincible now. All I've done is point the way to your deaths. Farewell."

She stepped over the dunes and was gone.

CHAPTER FORTY-FOUR
A Mother's Advice

Dirio Cyneric was no stranger to death. He'd worked in a mine. He'd seen his village ransacked by Quodivar, Yokai, and Fubuki. He remembered every Veliafan whose funeral he'd ever attended: every name, every face.

But tonight's was the most difficult by far. Dirio stood in the torchlit fields outside Tropos Vilage. Everyone in the tiny community had come out to see their son committed to the flames.

Had it just been them, Dirio might have made it through the funeral as he had all the others. Instead, he could hardly move for the press of people around him. In fact, he couldn't spot the locals anymore. They were swallowed up by the thousands of others who had come to pay their respects.

Kataile had emptied. The armies of Terkou and Caardit had come as well. The Katailan soldiers had given Balear an honor guard the whole way to Tropos. Even now they crowded around the pyre that held their general, a man they'd once called traitor.

The village priest recited from Lodia's holy texts, but Dirio couldn't listen any more. He left the throng and headed back toward Tropos.

He'd just cleared the crowd when a female voice said from behind him, "Dirio, wait."

Dirio turned and saw Elyssa, Horace, and Otto approaching. He resisted the urge to groan. Of all those gathered here, he wanted to interact with politicians least of all.

"What do you want?" he asked, not caring whether his displeasure showed.

Elyssa carried a bag over her shoulder. She reached in and pulled out a scroll sealed with red wax. She offered it to Dirio. "I wanted to give you this," she said.

Dirio took it. He pressed his thumb under the seal to break it, but Elyssa grabbed his wrist.

"Not here," she said. "Read it later, in private."

"Why?" he asked. "What is it?"

"Something I should have given to Balear."

"So why are you giving it to me?"

"Because you were closest to him," she said, "and because he believed in you."

"Some belief," Dirio said. He looked past Elyssa to the gathered multitude. "He's dead now."

"And he saved us all doing it," Horace said. He and Otto stepped forward so they stood beside Elyssa. "Our men all see him as a hero, even though he fought against Lodia during King Angustion's reign. That's what convinced us."

"Convinced you of what?"

Elyssa smiled. "That you should be Lodia's king."

Dirio stepped back like she had punched him. "That's ridiculous," he said. He raised his palms in front of him. "I can't do that."

"We've already voted," Elyssa said. "All three of us picked you. That's a majority, so it doesn't matter what your vote is."

"I'm a mayor of three hundred people from a destroyed village," Dirio protested. "I have no leadership experience."

"Your people followed you all the way to Kataile through snow and bitter cold," Elyssa said. "You even convinced Balear to come. If it hadn't been for you, he never would have agreed to support us."

Otto nodded his agreement. "When the rest of us would have denied you a seat at the table, Balear was the one who insisted you participate. He never came out and said it, but he knew you were the best choice."

"More practically," Horace cut in, "our forces all recognize Balear. If we went against his wishes, they'd never support us."

Dirio looked from one mayor to the next. So it wasn't about honoring Balear. It was politics. He should have figured. What these mayors thought of him didn't matter. Their people supported him, and they led at the will of the people.

Even so, it was absurd. He couldn't do it.

If nothing else, though, it would end the civil war. These mayors were in agreement, and Kras was dead. There was no one else. With a Maantec army in Ceere, they couldn't fight among themselves any more.

He looked down at the scroll Elyssa had given him. If Balear were standing here, Dirio knew what the general's opinion would be.

Dirio sighed. He was almost fifty. He'd hoped that when all this was settled, he might enjoy a leisurely retirement. No such luck.

03

Iren did his best to blend in with the crowd, not an easy task with a white katana on his right hip. He accomplished it by hiding in the back where few people would look at him. Only Minawë stood beside him, and they hadn't spoken since reaching Tropos.

The village priest lit the pyre, and Balear's corpse caught alight. Iren turned away and started walking.

"Where are you going?" Minawë asked.

Iren didn't look back. "To put a question to rest."

"Wait, I'll come with you."

"No," he said, and he meant it. Minawë didn't question him.

Iren left the gathering in the fields. He didn't have to travel far; his parents' farm lay just a mile outside the village.

The place looked as dismal as it had when he'd visited last year. The barn had collapsed, and vines overwhelmed the house. An opening remained where Iren had crashed through the door.

He stepped up on the porch, but he didn't enter. He sat gingerly on the decaying wood and closed his eyes. Drawing the Muryozaki, he concentrated until he entered the beach in his mind.

Divinion appeared. He settled down on the sand in a loose coil. "He was a true Dragon Knight," he said.

Iren didn't need to ask who Divinion referred to. "Balear was better than all of us," he said. "He fought to protect Lodia even though everyone here hated him. Why did he have to die?"

Divinion looked across the ocean. "Some questions even gods can't answer."

The dragon and Iren sat together on the beach for a long time. At last Iren sighed. "Divinion," he said, "when we were inside the Muryozaki, my father said there was a memory I should see. Would you show it to me?"

Divinion was silent a moment. The dragon couldn't make facial expressions to the degree people could, so Iren didn't know what his partner was thinking or feeling. Still, something about the glint in Divinion's eye made Iren think the dragon was dealing with some strong emotion.

"I will show you," Divinion said. "The person you are now should be ready to handle it."

The ocean faded into darkness, and Divinion disappeared. Iren stood alone in a farm field, his home in the distance. The barn was in good repair, and so was the house. He was in Saito's memory.

He had worked a long day in the field. Even for the former Maantec emperor, it had proven difficult work. But the spring planting was done, and the crops were growing well. With good weather and diligent effort, they would have a large harvest this year.

They would need it. Carita was now eating for two.

Saito still couldn't believe he was a father. When Carita had told him she was pregnant last year, he hadn't thought it possible. Now that Akio was born, it seemed even more ludicrous. Someone like Saito, with all the sins he'd committed, didn't deserve a child.

He reached the back of the house and walked around it toward the porch. He was nearly there when he stopped. Carita's voice reached his ears, low and soft. Who was she talking to? They never had visitors.

Saito pressed himself against the side of the house. The Muryozaki rested inside on the mantle, but that didn't matter. If it came to a fight, he'd go bare-handed. He wouldn't let anyone harm his new family.

He crept around to the porch, then stepped back in surprise. Carita was by herself. She had dragged one of the rocking chairs onto the porch and sat with Akio in her arms. Saito was behind her, so she hadn't noticed him. She looked west past the house to face the setting sun.

"People will hate you," Carita said. "I know they hate me. Even the people I grew up with won't talk to me anymore. If they act that way to someone who loves a Left, I can't imagine how they'll treat her son."

Saito's eyes dropped to the ground. Carita was right. Akio would have a difficult life no matter what happened. Even if Rondel never found them here, it would only be a matter of time before the villagers decided they could no longer tolerate a Left nearby. The family would have to pack up and move on. That would be Akio's whole life: hiding and running.

"But even though they'll hate you," Carita continued, "don't hate them back. They don't understand you. If you turn into some devil to spite them, you'll only justify their feelings. Don't let that happen. Love them instead. Love them with all your heart, the way I fell in love with your father. Live like that, and you will be loved in return. You might never be accepted, but you'll find friends who care about you, and people who will stay with you even when we're gone. If you can do that, I know you'll live a happy life, Akio."

She smiled at the baby burbling in her arms. "You will be loved."

Saito fell against the side of the house and wept.

CHAPTER FORTY-FIVE
On a Moonless Night

Rondel heard the crunching of boots on dirt behind her. She didn't open her eyes. She didn't rise from her kneeling posture. She didn't have to. She knew who it was.

"I wondered if you might come here," Iren said, "but I didn't expect us to arrive at the same time."

The old Maantec opened her eyes. It was a new moon, and stars filled the sky. The bundle of lilies she'd brought lay amid the weeds before her. She shook her head. "It's less of a coincidence than you think," she said. "I've been here since dawn."

Iren stepped into view. He wore the new Katailan tunic Dirio had given him to replace his torn, salt-encrusted kimono. He knelt alongside Rondel, bowed his head, and put his hands together. "The last time I visited this farm, I didn't know where Amroth had buried my parents," he said. "Thanks to Father's memories, now I can come here and pay my respects."

Rondel faced the man next to her. If he noticed her eyes on him, he paid her no mind.

It was hard to imagine that only two years had passed since they'd first spoken. Back then Iren had been an immature fool, brought up alone without anyone to guide him. At eighteen, he'd acted like a twelve-year-old. But now . . .

"You've grown up," Rondel murmured.

Iren raised his head. "If I did, it's because of you."

Rondel's mouth fell open.

Iren went back to looking at his parents' unmarked graves. "You hated me," he said. "You killed my parents. Yet despite all that, you taught me. You made me better, stronger, smarter."

Rondel lifted an eyebrow. "Smarter?"

Iren half-smiled. "Well, you were more successful in some areas than others."

"It wasn't out of loyalty to you," Rondel said. "It was the only way I could make the dreams stop."

"The dreams . . . you told me about them before. You said you saw my eyes, and that you saw me in pain or dying. Why do you suppose that was?"

Rondel shrugged. "It was guilt. I left you to die."

"You've followed Okthora's Law for more than a thousand years. Did you ever feel guilt about any other deaths?"

Rondel frowned. She wasn't used to people needling her like this. "What does that have to do with anything?" she snapped.

Iren still didn't look at her. He kept his face directed at the weeds in front of him. His hands remained pressed together. "How many people have you killed in Okthora's service?" he asked. "How many of their family members gave you nightmares? How many of them did you teach? What made me different?"

For a long time Rondel couldn't answer. She looked up at the stars. They were cold and distant.

That was what she wanted to be. That was what she was supposed to be. That was the Storm Dragon Knight.

That wasn't her.

"I don't know how many people I've slain in the name of Okthora's Law," she said at last. "I never questioned it, at least not outright. 'Evil must be annihilated.' That's the code the Storm Dragon Knight lives by. But what is evil? Who gets to decide? What if I, the judge, am evil? Were all the people I killed evil? I thought they were, but that night, your mother changed everything. She wasn't evil. I wasn't exacting justice on her. I murdered her."

She sighed. "That's what made you different. You made me realize my path was wrong. I couldn't admit it to myself back then, but now it's obvious. Without thinking I deprived you of the most important person in your life. I could never undo that, and I could never replace her. But I had to try. I looked after you because I wanted to be the mother I never let you have."

A wetness slid down Rondel's cheek. "Damn you," she said. "You and all the Saito's. I wanted so badly to forget, to run away, but you all kept dragging me back into this life."

"No one's dragging you back," Iren said. His voice was level. How could he speak so calmly when Rondel herself was on the verge of breaking down? "You killed my parents. Whether we're friends or enemies, the one thing we'll never be to each other is nothing."

This man was incredible. What had changed in him? Back in Shikari, Iren had been obsessed with vengeance. How could he kneel here and talk to her this way?

Rondel decided. "Iren," she said, "kill me."

For the first time since he'd arrived on the field, Iren lost his composure. His head snapped up. His hands dropped to his sides. He stared into Rondel's tear-stained eyes. "What did you say?"

"Evil must be annihilated. Even if I followed Okthora's Law in killing Saito, I didn't when I murdered Carita. I'm as evil as Saito was. I deserve death."

Iren stared at her for a more than a minute. She didn't flinch from his gaze.

"Melwar's still out there," he finally said. "Minawë would not approve."

"Minawë's not here. As for Melwar, you can stop him. I know you can. You don't need my help."

Iren's breathing increased. His hands worked. His left one inched its way to the Muryozaki's hilt.

He stood. The Muryozaki left its sheath.

Rondel smiled and closed her eyes. Death this way would be a mercy. In the old world of Maantecs, she would have committed seppuku for her crime. Now she could die quickly at the hands of a fine young man.

The katana whistled. Rondel heard it plunge into the ground in front of her. She felt nothing. It truly was a mercy. The Muryozaki inflicted no pain even as it stabbed its victims. She smiled again as she waited for her heart to stop.

"Open your eyes, Rondel," Iren said.

She obeyed. When she did, her head reared back. The Muryozaki stood up in front of her, pierced into the ground. Iren hadn't struck her at all.

Rondel looked at him. The man was shaking. Tears rolled down his cheeks.

"Why?" Rondel asked.

Iren wiped his face. "You asked me that same question when I saved your life on the junk. Back then I didn't have an answer. Now I do. Killing you isn't what Mom would have wanted."

Rondel shifted her gaze to the Muryozaki before her. "Are you saying you forgive me?"

"No," Iren replied, and the sudden coldness in his voice surprised her. "I have a more difficult punishment for you than death. Live, Rondel. Live with the sins you've committed. That's the judgment Divinion gave to Father a thousand years ago. Because you cut his sentence short, it's only fair that it should pass to you."

Rondel pressed her hands into the dirt. She cried, but she smiled too. "You're a harsh judge, Iren Saitosan, much harsher than Okthora. I will bear this punishment."

Iren retrieved the Muryozaki and sheathed it. "Let's find Minawë and get some rest," he said. "Tomorrow we should head to Haldessa Castle. Melwar's waiting for us."

Rondel activated Lightning Sight. With it she took in every detail of the grasses, weeds, and soil that surrounded Saito's and Carita's unmarked graves. They deserved better. At least they had a son they could be proud of.

Rondel stood. "For twenty years I avoided coming here. The emotions of that night wouldn't let me approach. Now, though, I was finally able to visit." She paused and looked at the graves one last time. "I promise to come again."

She found Iren's gaze. "Do me a favor," she said. "Wait two days before going to Haldessa. There's something I need to do first."

Iren's brow furrowed. "What could be more important than stopping Melwar?"

Rondel smirked. "I said I was confident you could handle him. That's still true. All the same, there's one more advantage I think I can gain us."

"And that is?"

Her smirk blossomed into her full-blown sarcastic grin. "I guess you'll have to wait and see."

CHAPTER FORTY-SIX
A Risk Worth Taking

Shogun Katashi Melwar paced the ghostly corridors of Haldessa Castle. No one had lived here for more than a year, yet it still stank of humans. Its harsh lines and heavy stone anchored it to the ground. It lacked all the subtlety, grace, and refinement of Hiabi.

But it would have to do. It was the closest thing to a military center in this uncivilized land. Commanding it would make wiping out the Lodians that much easier.

Of course the need for it would have been less had Hana done her job. When Commander Daichi had returned in defeat, Melwar had almost ordered him to commit seppuku. The man should never have followed the words of a clear traitor like Hana.

Melwar calmed himself. It was not Daichi's fault. The fault lay with Hana for letting her emotions take control, and with Melwar himself for trusting her to complete so important a task.

No matter. Though Hana had not returned, she was powerless on her own.

More distressing was the loss of the Rock Topaz. Once Melwar finished restoring the Maantecs, he would use the Water Dragon's magic to locate and retrieve it. It would be a near-impossible task, but he had the time. No matter how long it took, it would be worth the effort.

The tapping of metal on stone caught Melwar's attention. He turned to find Commander Daichi approaching.

At the sight of the shogun's face, Daichi knelt and put his head to the floor. Melwar strode up to him.

"Do you have a report for me?" Melwar asked.

Daichi did not rise. "I do, Shogun."

"Stand then, and deliver it."

Daichi got up. "A group of scouts has returned from the south," he said. "They report that the Lodian forces have left Kataile en masse. They've gathered in a wilderness area twenty-five miles southwest of here."

Melwar frowned. "A wilderness area?"

"The scouts indicate that there are a few houses, but otherwise it's just thickets and farm fields."

"Tropos," Melwar murmured, "how appropriate."

"Shogun?" Daichi asked. "Excuse my stupidity, but I don't understand what you mean."

Melwar saw no reason to explain it. "Prepare the army to head out," he ordered instead. "I want every soldier available. We will crush the Lodians with a single battle."

The shogun's pulse rose in anticipation. Why the Lodians had chosen Tropos as their rallying point he could not say, but their mistake was made. It was an indefensible open field. Nine thousand Maantecs would descend on the humans, and that would be the end of Lodia. Tacumsah, Ziorsecth, and even Aokigahara would follow.

Melwar smiled. It was about time.

CHAPTER FORTY-SEVEN
Reminiscence

"Hey, little girl, are you all right?"

The five-year-old fluttered her eyes. She lay on hard ground, and standing over her was a grownup Maantec woman wearing a tan kimono. On the adult's hip sat a katana with a plain wooden hilt and sheathed in a plain wooden sheath.

"I think so," the girl answered in a monotone.

The grownup looked pleased. Her pinned-up black hair held firm against the light breeze. "You're probably in shock," she said. "Do you have any idea what happened?"

The girl struggled to sit up. She shook her head. "Who are you?" she asked.

"I'm Caly Thara."

Caly Thara . . . the name wasn't familiar. She wasn't one of the local farmers, at any rate.

"What's your name?" Caly asked.

The girl frowned. "I don't know."

"You don't know your own name?"

"I can't remember."

Caly folded her arms. "It doesn't surprise me. You took a hard blow."

"What happened?"

"Look around."

The girl craned her neck and gasped in horror. The charred remains of more than a dozen bodies lay strewn across her family's garden. The ground was scorched, and the house that she had lived in her entire life was a pile of ashes.

Flashes of memory came to her. She and her brother had been playing in the fields. They'd heard their mother call them, but the girl had tripped and fallen.

By the time she'd climbed to her feet and reached the house, everything had been in flames. Her father had stood over the burned corpses of her brother and mother while a dozen masked men in black descended upon him with steel and magic. They'd killed him and then come for her. She'd run to her father's corpse, clutching his dagger as though it would keep her safe against the murderers.

Then she'd felt a great power surge inside her. It had rumbled in her body like thunder. She'd blacked out.

"What happened?" she asked again.

"They're called the Akushi—servants of the Dark God, Plutanis. I'm impressed you survived when so many attacked."

The girl looked numbly at the scene before her. "I don't know how."

Caly's face filled with sympathy. "Nor do I," she said, but the girl noticed that Caly didn't look her in the eye when she spoke those words.

"Well," Caly continued after a brief pause, "why don't you come with me?"

The girl folded her brow, confused.

"You can't stay here by yourself," Caly said. "I'll take care of you."

The grownup offered her hand. With more than a little hesitation, the girl took it.

"There you go," Caly said. "Now I suppose you need a name seeing as you don't remember your old one. And in any case it's appropriate because that part of your life is over now. Say, I have an idea. Instead of me giving you a name, what would you like to be called?"

The girl rubbed her eyes. "I don't know," she said. Nervous at being put on the spot, she picked up her father's dagger and held it to her chest, seeking security in its familiar shape.

An idea came to her. "What's this thing called?" she asked. She held out the dagger for Caly's inspection.

"This?" Caly took it and looked it over. "It's called a dagger," she said, "but I don't think you should name yourself that. It would sound too weird."

Caly started to return the weapon, but then she stopped short. "Well, now, there is something," she murmured. "This dagger, when I look closer, it really is something special. You see this round hilt? The pommel and crossguard are round too." She pointed to each part of the weapon in turn. "This isn't a Maantec weapon. It's human, from a faraway place called Lodia. A long time ago I visited there, and I saw a dagger like this one. They had a special name for it. They called it a rondel."

Caly handed back the blade. After a few seconds, the girl grinned. "That will be my name: Rondel."

CHAPTER FORTY-EIGHT
Serona's Storm

The twelve-hundred-year-old memories filled Rondel's mind as she raced through the open understory of Ziorsecth Forest. She tried to think about those days as little as possible. Caly had told her that that part of her life was over. In the ensuing years of training to become the Storm Dragon Knight, Rondel had forgotten her birth home. Even now she could barely picture her family's faces, and she had no memories of the days before they'd died.

Iren Saito's private words inside the Muryozaki came to her. What if he'd been right? Was it really possible? She'd always assumed her family's murders were a random act. The Akushi were marauders who lived outside the bounds of Maantec society. Surely their attack had been another arbitrary slaying by a group of madmen.

But if Saito was correct, then the murders hadn't been random at all. Despite living outside the Maantec order, the Akushi had a fierce streak of pride for their species. They hated other races and believed them inferior.

The mere mention of the possibility had been enough for Rondel to slap Saito in the face. Now, though, she had her doubts. Whatever else Saito might be, he was no fool. Those final moments inside the Muryozaki were his last chance to speak to her. He wouldn't waste words on nonsense.

Rondel stopped as she reached her destination. Ahead of her Ziorsecth's trees thinned and shortened into scrubby brush. Dry air sucked the moisture from her body, and a great heat welled in front of her.

The old Maantec steeled herself, then took a few final steps. As happened every time she came here, her breath caught when she laid eyes on it.

Serona.

The broken land shot jets of white flame hundreds of feet into the air. In the sky a great storm raged, a thousand-year tempest Rondel herself had created almost at the cost of her life. Its rain poured down, but the water evaporated before it reached the ground.

Rondel hesitated. Why had she come all the way here? She could have tested Saito's theory on any tree between here and Tropos. Every second mattered if they wanted to defeat Melwar.

Yet she could go nowhere else. Serona was her fault. Two years ago she'd told Iren that such disasters needed to linger. They served as a reminder of the damage wrought by evil. At the time she'd believed that with all her heart.

Not anymore. She had killed an innocent woman, yet that woman's own son had found a way to move past that tragedy.

It was all so obvious to Rondel now. Okthora's Law was wrong, or at least, it had been misinterpreted. Evil must be annihilated. For millennia Storm Dragon Knights had taken that to mean the person who committed the evil had to die. Iren, though, had found another way. So had Saito and Divinion. Evil could also be annihilated through redemption.

That's why she'd needed to come here. It was time to redeem this land.

Rondel drew her Liryometa with her left hand. At the same time, she placed her right hand on the stubby trunk of a short tree, one of the last before Serona's blistering heat. It would have little magic on its own, but thanks to Ziorsecth's shared root system, it had the strength of the whole forest coursing through it.

Rondel closed her eyes. Without intending to she lapsed into a memory. It felt more like a dream, but she knew it had happened.

She was five years old again, splashing about in the rice paddies on her parents' farm. Yet even as she played, worry touched her heart. She'd heard her parents talking. The rice was growing poorly this year. Unless something changed soon, they wouldn't have enough to cover the tribute due to the local lord. If that happened, their family would starve.

Rondel wanted to help. She touched her tiny hands to the wilted rice plants and prayed for them to grow.

When the plant she was fingering doubled in size, she fell back on her rump in shock.

She reached out and grabbed another plant. It grew too. She tried with three more until she was convinced. She ran back to the house.

"Mommy! Mommy!" she cried. "Come see what I can do!"

Her mother followed her to the paddies, and Rondel touched a plant. It grew full and vibrant. Rondel spun around and smiled her biggest smile. "Now we'll have lots of food!" she proclaimed.

Her mother slapped her so hard Rondel's ears rang and she saw stars in the daytime.

"No!" her mother shouted. "You must never do that! Get inside at once!"

Rondel didn't understand. She'd saved her family. Why was her mother mad at her?

That night she pretended to sleep. She knew her parents had their private conversations after the children went to bed. Her family lived in a one-room hut, so it was easy to eavesdrop.

"What if someone saw?" her mother asked in a hushed tone.

"It was just a few rice plants," her father replied. "We're all but alone out here. I doubt anyone noticed."

"But the Akushi—"

"It was always a risk. You and I both knew that. We married knowing it. We had kids knowing it."

"What will we do?"

"Say nothing. Forget it happened. And keep a closer eye on the kids, especially Kaede. If anyone finds out where I'm really from, the Akushi won't stop until they hunt us down."

Three days later, Rondel's family was murdered.

08

The adult Rondel went to her knees. For twelve hundred years her lack of childhood memories hadn't bothered her. She'd dismissed the amnesia as a side effect of trauma and her intense training with Caly Thara.

But that hadn't been the case. She'd blocked out those memories because she'd had no other choice. She couldn't let herself know that her parents and brother had died because of her.

Someone had seen her use plant magic. Among the Maantecs it was all but unheard of. The few who could use it needed decades, even centuries, to control it.

There was only one explanation for her inborn talent. She wasn't entirely Maantec.

Her father had been a Kodama.

That was what Saito had suggested to her, that the Akushi had murdered her family because a Maantec and Kodama had married and had children. To the Akushi, it was an unforgivable offense.

Rondel stared across Serona's burning expanse. Somewhere in that lattice of devastation was her family's farm, long since ruined. Somewhere amid the fires rested the dust of her brother and parents.

She stood and put her hand back on the tree. Magic flowed through it into her. It was a trickle at first. Then, with the memory of the rice plants vivid in her mind, it became a flood.

Rondel had never imagined power like this. How had Aletas managed it against Feng? It was incredible.

Her body transformed. Her wrinkles smoothed away. The hair whipping about her face changed from gray to dark brown.

Now came the ultimate test. Rondel raised her dagger to the sky and commanded the storm. Lightning shot from the Liryometa to the clouds.

Heat burned inside her. It made Serona's sweltering air seem as refreshing as the breeze off the Yuushin Sea. Ziorsecth's power threatened to tear her apart, but Rondel held firm. If Aletas could do it, she could do it.

The storm reacted to her addition of magic, and it intensified. The lightning that had struck the ground dozens of times a second now came at twice that pace, then triple. The rain fell harder and harder. The heat from Serona's flames couldn't keep up. With each second, the rain reached closer to the ground.

At last Rondel heard the sound she'd hoped for. The first drops hit the white fires and sizzled into steam. Rondel kept up her efforts. The fires lowered.

The storm broke through. Rain thrashed the ground, and the fires vanished. Their lattices still glowed with heat, but even that was fading before the liquid onslaught. Rondel had done it.

Rather, she had almost done it. One task remained. She reversed the flow of magic in the storm, drawing its power to the Liryometa. She let the magic course through her and back into Ziorsecth. It was the forest's energy, after all. It was only proper to return it.

All but a little. The magic Rondel had released a thousand years ago she kept with her.

Deprived of energy, the storm clouds dissipated. Rondel smiled as the sun pierced through to the ground of Serona. It was the first time in a millennium the two had met.

The fires were gone, never to return. Given time, Serona would heal. Life would grow there again. Perhaps someday, some other family would plant rice where her parents, Maantec and Kodama, once had. Rondel hoped they would.

Putting her back to her homeland, Rondel reentered Ziorsecth Forest. Half of her repentance was done.

The other half lay back in Lodia. It was time to correct her mistake. Evil must be annihilated, and in this case she hadn't the slightest doubt what it meant.

It was time to kill Katashi Melwar.

CHAPTER FORTY-NINE
Choice

"She what?" Minawë yelled.

Iren winced and did his best to hide behind the unkempt plants in his parents' abandoned field. He'd expected this conversation to go poorly. So far he'd underestimated just how poorly.

Minawë waved her hands at him. "How could she leave at the last minute like that? Did she say where she was going?"

"No," Iren replied, "but she said it would help us defeat Melwar."

He'd hoped Rondel would come back before Minawë learned the old hag had left. No chance. Rondel had only been gone a day, and despite the crowds, Minawë had figured out the undersized Maantec was missing.

And of course it was Iren's fault. It had taken him the better part of an hour to convince Minawë that he and Rondel hadn't fought to the death behind her back. Now he was just getting to explain what had really happened that night at his parents' graves. "You and I both know Rondel doesn't do things without a purpose," he told Minawë. "If she said it's important, it's important."

Minawë crossed both arms and said nothing.

"Besides," Iren continued, "we're taking the fight to Melwar this time. Rondel said two days. She'll be back tomorrow. Melwar can wait until then."

With a huff, Minawë left Iren and started back toward Tropos. Over her shoulder she said, "Moron."

Iren's eyes crinkled, and he half-smiled. The taunt was a word of endearment between them, one Iren hadn't heard Minawë say since he'd left Ziorsecth Forest more than a year ago. As frustrated as Minawë was with him, the word was a sign she was glad Iren and Rondel had put their fight behind them.

Still, he understood why Minawë was worried. If Melwar attacked while Rondel was away, fending him off would be next to impossible.

For his part, though, Iren wasn't concerned. He knew Melwar better than Minawë did. The self-proclaimed shogun wasn't a leader like Amroth, Balear, or Father. Those men knew they had to stand in the front and inspire their men. Melwar led from behind. He had never shown a tendency to take action himself, not when he could rely on others to fight for him. He was a noble, not a soldier. With Hana gone and the Maantec army in retreat, Melwar would take his time in responding. One more day wouldn't make a difference.

Iren walked from his parents' field back to the ruined farmhouse. The ivy that covered it glimmered in the afternoon sun.

Maybe, when all this was over, he would rebuild it. He would have to tear this one down and start over, but it would be worth it.

He sat on the porch where his mother had held him long ago. The simple home really did have a beautiful view. It was too far and faced the wrong direction to see the ocean, but the open fields were like an ocean unto themselves, a waving green and gold sea that seemed to stretch forever.

The crashing of hooves on the other side of the house pulled Iren from his thoughts. He stood, and a moment later Dirio arrived on horseback.

"Congratulations, Dirio," Iren said. "Rumor has it you're the new king of Lodia."

Dirio blushed and grimaced at the same time. "Word travels too quickly. Anyway, I might not have a chance to lead this country. The Maantec army is on the move again."

Now it was Iren's turn to grimace. So much for knowing Melwar. The shogun was done waiting.

"Where are they headed?" Iren asked. "All the cities are undefended. Melwar could take any of them."

Dirio's frown deepened. "That's why I came looking for you. According to Horace's scouts, they're coming here."

"Here?"

"They must have seen all the people gathered for Balear's funeral and assumed it was a strike force. They're coming to meet us on the open field."

At last Iren understood. "Melwar knows his army has the upper hand," he said, "but he still doesn't want to risk any more men than he has to. If we holed up in one of the cities, we would do a lot more damage before he broke us. Out in the open, though, we're exposed. We have women and children here. It will be a slaughter."

"My thoughts exactly. So how do we respond?"

Iren put his hand on his chin. "How much time do we have?"

"The scouts reported that the Maantecs are all on foot. Apparently they didn't bring cavalry on their ships. They also don't have siege equipment. They move faster than humans, but with so many of them I'd guess we have six hours until they arrive."

What should they do? Iren paced the porch as he thought. They could stay and fight, but there were at least as many civilians as soldiers gathered here. The Maantecs would overwhelm them.

They could withdraw to Kataile, but the Maantec army would likely catch them before they reached the city. Even if they made it, Melwar's upper echelons included mages. The Katailan forces had described jets of flame that reduced incoming arrows to nothing. If Melwar used his mages for attack rather than defense, they could bring down a city wall more quickly than a catapult barrage.

Iren wished Rondel were here. Considering that a few weeks ago he'd wanted to kill her, it amazed him that the desire came so readily. But they needed her now more than ever. She'd known Melwar since they were children. She understood him better than anyone else. More to the point, she was the best tactician Iren had ever met, and she had experience leading Maantec armies.

He needed to think like her. How would Rondel counter Melwar?

Iren looked across the fields toward the spot where his parents rested. Last night's memories played in his head. He and Rondel had knelt there together. The words she'd spoken returned to him: "As for Melwar, you can stop him. I know you can. You don't need my help."

Rondel was fond of frivolous and sarcastic comments, but when she was serious, she didn't spare anyone. She'd said those words to give Iren permission to kill her. She'd meant them all.

He made up his mind. "Dirio, I need to borrow your horse."

Dirio's brow lowered. "You have that look that says you're about to do something crazy."

"I'm going to stop Melwar myself," Iren said. "In the meantime, take everyone and head for Kataile. If I fail, it will be your last chance."

"Hold on," Dirio said. "Even if you defeat Melwar, what will you do about the nine thousand troops he has with him?"

"I won't have to fight them. I have an idea."

Dirio put a hand to his head. "I hate this plan."

"You asked for my suggestion. Now let me use your horse."

The new king sighed, but he dismounted. "Otto gave me his horse as a sign of friendship," Dirio said. "He'll be incredibly upset if I lose her."

Iren leapt up on the roan. He nodded. "I understand. I'll bring her back alive."

He took a few hesitant steps; it had been more than a year since his last time on a horse. When he felt confident of the animal's gait, Iren looked over his shoulder. "One more thing," he said. "Tell Minawë not to follow me."

Dirio blanched. "I passed her on my way here. Tell you what. Why don't you go talk to her, and I'll ride out and fight Melwar? Suddenly that seems like the easier task."

Iren smirked. "The king always gets the hardest job. It's part of leadership. Later!" He took off.

It was the stupidest thing he had ever done, and he had plenty of those to rank it against. All the same, he felt not the slightest doubt. Rondel believed in him. That was enough.

ഷ

Minawë grabbed Dirio by the lapels. "Are you insane?" she shouted. "You let him go?"

What was wrong with everybody lately? First Iren had let Rondel disappear to the dragons knew where, and now Dirio had handed over his horse so Iren could charge alone against Melwar's army. Since when had Minawë needed to be everyone's voice of reason?

She released Dirio. It wasn't the king's fault. It was Iren's. He had changed a lot in two years, but deep down, despite everything he'd gone through, Iren Saitosan was still the same headstrong, self-sacrificing boy he'd been when Minawë had first met him in Akaku.

That was why she loved him. That was why she changed into a horse and ran after him.

CHAPTER FIFTY
Shogun and Emperor

Iren rode across Lodia's open fields. It took him less than an hour to spot Melwar's army on the horizon. It filled the land, an endless expanse of armor and weapons. The force had a single purpose: to take the world for Maantecs.

But while that was the army's objective, it wasn't the reason nine thousand men had come here. Melwar was their shogun. He commanded them, so they obeyed. That was how Maantec society worked. The lower classes obeyed the upper classes. There was no thought among that army of dissenting with Melwar, even if many of them—probably most of them—would rather be back on their farms.

Iren was counting on that loyalty. It was Lodia's only chance for survival.

Melwar was easy to spot. Four Maantecs carried a palanquin at the head of the column. Even with the limited space his ships had allowed him, Melwar had found room for it. He wasn't about to dirty his feet on human-trod soil any more than he had to.

Iren rode up to the palanquin. A call rang out and spread across the army. The men stopped. A soldier in lamellar armor stepped forward and drew his katana.

Iren leapt off his borrowed horse and pulled out his own weapon. The advancing soldier stopped midstride. A moment ago he'd been set to cut down this peasant for daring to interrupt them. Now he was caught in dishonor. Every Maantec knew Iren's sword.

"Tell me your name," Iren said. He tried to make his voice as confident as he could. The soldiers needed to be impressed with him, and more important, Melwar needed to know who was out here.

"I am Daichi Kui, commander of this army."

"Then you are its leader?"

Daichi bowed. That was something. He still had his katana out though. "I am not," he said. "I serve Shogun Melwar."

"I see," Iren replied. "I confess myself disappointed in you, Daichi. Have you so little honor that you would follow a shogun when your emperor stands before you?"

Daichi looked up while keeping his body inclined. His eyes widened. His gaze settled on Iren's sword, then his hair, and then at last on his sky blue eyes. "Emperor Saito?" he murmured.

The palanquin's folds flew open. Melwar stepped out, dressed in a plum-colored shirt with the symbol of a mountain on its back. "Why have we stopped?" he demanded, though Iren knew the Maantec lord had heard everything.

"Hello, Katashi," Iren said. He didn't bow at all. The soldiers within earshot gasped. No one referred to Melwar by his first name. It was unforgivable to address a man of his station so loosely.

Melwar stared at Iren with wrath. "What is this pest, Daichi? Why have you not slain him?"

Daichi went to the ground. "Shogun, he has the Muryozaki. He claims to be the Maantec emperor."

"Emperor Saito is dead," Melwar said. "The traitor Rondel Thara murdered him."

"That doesn't matter," Iren cut in. "I'm the Holy Dragon Knight, and by tradition the Holy Dragon Knight is also the Maantec emperor."

Melwar's eyes were slits. "Only because the Muryozaki was passed down through the royal Saito bloodline, a bloodline that ended with the emperor's death. Whoever carries that sword now is just another Dragon Knight, not someone worthy of being the emperor."

"I don't know if I'm worthy or not, but I do know this." Iren held up the Muryozaki so as many men in Melwar's army could see it as possible. He put all his effort into making his voice carry across the fields. "Emperor Saito's bloodline has not died out! It carries on in me.

My name is Akio Saito! I am Iren Saito's son! I am the Holy Dragon Knight, and I am the rightful Maantec emperor!"

Melwar scoffed. "Anyone can make such claims. That does not make them true. Daichi! This man has sinned against all Maantecs by besmirching the name of our exalted emperor. Regain our people's honor and kill him at once!"

Daichi stood and raised his sword. He stepped toward Iren.

That was far enough. Iren loosed a torrent of magic. White light swirled around him, lifting higher and higher into the air. Iren wanted every soldier, even those in the back of the army, to see it.

"Will you kill your emperor, Daichi?" Iren asked. "Will you murder Iren Saito's son?"

Daichi looked from Iren to Melwar and back again. His head kept swapping between them. On the one hand, Melwar was a known quantity. On the other, Iren's claim, while unproven, put Iren on top. If Daichi attacked, he risked eternal dishonor by striking the emperor. If he held, he risked equal dishonor by refusing the shogun. He had no good move.

That was why Iren made one instead. He ended his spell and looked at Melwar. "Katashi, you and I know each other. I know what you want here. You also know I have no proof that I'm Iren Saito's son. That's why I propose a duel of champions. Let our fight settle this war and leadership of the Maantecs."

The faintest smile crossed Melwar's lips. "I should not sully myself on a commoner," he said, "but if it will demonstrate my authority, I will accept. Daichi, hold the men here. When I slay this fool, bring them forward. We will annihilate the humans forever."

Daichi, clearly glad to have the decision taken out of his hands, bowed to both Iren and Melwar and retreated back to the army's main line. Iren and Melwar walked together away from the army to give themselves plenty of room.

"You know, Iren," Melwar said when they had gone far enough that they couldn't see the army anymore, "there was a time when I believed you would lead the restoration of our people. To think you now stand so firmly against it. I must admit my disappointment."

"There was a time when I believed in you as well," Iren replied. "How childish that feeling seems now."

"Hate me if you want, but I am doing what you should have done. I am acting in the best interests of our people, the people you just claimed to rule. What do you suppose would result if you were to win this contest? Humans would go on hating Maantecs. We would go on having barely enough hardscrabble land to survive. I am giving our people what they deserve. You would sentence them to endless punishment."

"Never," Iren said. "I was able to find friendship among humans and Kodamas. If someone like me can do it, why can't the rest of them?"

Melwar scoffed. "Because they have pride and honor where you have none."

"If pride and honor compel you to commit genocide, then perhaps we're better off without them. Or more likely, you have no idea what those words really mean."

"You intend to debate semantics with me?"

"Not at all. There's nothing left to debate."

"Yes, I agree."

Melwar stopped walking. He reached for his hip, where no solid weapon sat. A shadow billowed around his hand, and he revealed a shifting, smoking blade.

Iren drew the Muryozaki. He'd battled Melwar before in sparring sessions in Hiabi. The noble was a master swordsman. More problematic, he excelled at No Mind, a fighting style that sacrificed conscious thought in exchange for instantaneous reactions. Rondel could have bested it by planning her moves in advance and tricking Melwar's instinctual mind, but Iren wasn't that skilled a tactician. If Melwar used No Mind, Iren wasn't sure he could overcome it.

But Melwar wouldn't use No Mind. He'd taught it to Iren, and Iren could enter the trance-like state even faster than Melwar could. In this life-or-death battle, it was too risky a strategy for the cautious shogun.

That left only the conclusion that Melwar would rely on his shadow magic. The noble had used those abilities in a practice bout with Iren the night they'd met, and that match had ended with Iren helpless before Melwar's blade. He couldn't let that happen this time.

A screeching neigh stopped the battle before it began. Melwar and Iren both faced the sound. A riderless horse galloped toward them. Iren thought for a moment that it was the one Dirio had given him, but the roan was back with Daichi. This one was different.

The animal charged straight for Iren. He groaned. He knew who it was.

The horse shrank and rose up on two legs as it transformed into Minawë. When her green hair emerged, Melwar curled his upper lip in a sneer. "Kodama," he spat. "You must be the one who hid like a coward while attacking my ships."

Minawë ignored the shogun. She jabbed a finger into Iren's chest. "What are you doing?" she asked. "I thought we were going to face him as a team."

"This is the only way, Minawë," Iren said. "Even if we worked together to defeat him, it would hold no meaning. He has nine thousand Maantecs under his command. We can't overcome them all. I'm fighting him for leadership of the Maantecs. I'll win them over as the Maantec emperor."

Minawë balled her hands into fists. "You are the most selfish moron I have ever met!"

There was a time when he would have argued with her. Today he simply looked her in the eye, smiled sadly, and said, "I know."

She stepped back. The challenge in her expression was gone. Fear—and maybe a little admiration—replaced it. "You don't have to do this," she said. "I would have fought alongside you to the end."

Iren nodded. "I love you."

Minawë's face colored. She looked at the ground a moment. Then she raised her eyes and grinned. "I love you too. Now get out there and win, moron."

The right side of Iren's mouth lifted. "Right." He faced Melwar. "Ready?"

Melwar shrugged. "You seem to be the distracted one."

"Not anymore."

The Maantecs squared off. Minawë retreated to a safe distance, but she didn't return to Tropos. Whatever the outcome, she would stay and witness it.

Melwar's sword twisted and seethed as the pair traced a large circle. The shogun had used that weapon against Iren in their practice match.

He'd combined it with shadow magic to make both sword and swords-man as insubstantial as smoke—a Shadow Form. Iren had passed right through Melwar, nearly getting decapitated in the process.

That had to be Melwar's plan. He would use Shadow Form to lure Iren in, avoid his strikes, and then counter when Iren was exposed. That's why Melwar wasn't attacking.

If Melwar wanted to fight that way, so be it. Shadow Form had to require magic to maintain, so the shogun wouldn't use it unless he felt threatened. At this distance, with the two of them not yet trading blows, he was probably solid. A fast ranged attack, launched before Melwar cast his spell, could end the fight in one blow.

Iren channeled magic into his right index finger. It was the fastest technique he had, and while it lacked the strength to kill, it could knock Melwar down. It might even knock him unconscious if it struck him in the head.

Iren's hand flashed up, and the shot lanced out. More than a hun-dred feet separated Iren and Melwar, yet the beam crossed the space in less than a second.

The shot passed cleanly through the Maantec lord. Melwar smiled.

Iren's brow furrowed. Had Melwar been keeping Shadow Form active the whole time? It seemed unlikely. Melwar wasn't the type to waste magic, especially when he knew Iren had large magical reserves. In a battle of endurance, needless spells in the early stages would guarantee defeat.

So how had Melwar done it?

The shogun didn't wait for Iren to figure it out. Melwar put his hand out in front of him, palm up, and a long, slender knife appeared in midair above it. The knife was black and without thickness; Iren could only see it because it was at a slight angle to him.

The Shadow Knife launched at Iren, spiraling end over end. Iren easily avoided it, but as he circled Melwar, he saw the knife wheel around and head back for him. Melwar created four more knives, and they all spun toward Iren.

Iren grimaced. Those blades were meant to keep him at a distance. His beam attack had been too slow after all. A second was plenty of time for a master swordsman like Melwar to react to a spell and cast one of his own. Iren would need to close with Melwar in order to attack him.

Using magic to boost his speed, Iren flashed toward the shogun. The Shadow Knives couldn't keep up with him, and he got inside Melwar's guard. The Muryozaki danced as Iren sent a dozen slashes through all parts of Melwar's body.

None of them landed. They all passed harmlessly through Shadow Form.

The knives approached. Iren dodged four of them, but the last one cut a thin line across his arm. The Muryozaki healed the wound, but the distraction was enough for Melwar to make an attack of his own. His sword stabbed out, and Iren blocked it.

The shifting blade, though, passed through Iren's guard. He ducked just in time to avoid a beheading.

This was his chance! Melwar must have become solid to make his attack. From his dropped position, Iren fired another quick beam from his index finger. It struck Melwar in the stomach, and the Maantec lord doubled over. Iren swung the Muryozaki at Melwar's left arm to end the fight.

His blade passed through without resistance. Melwar stepped back. He didn't look in pain.

While Iren was staring at Melwar, the knives spun back around. One pierced him in the shoulder. He cursed instinctively, but then he realized there was no pain.

Realization dawned. Shadow Form made Melwar immune to attack, but it worked the other way too. Melwar couldn't affect the world while the spell was active. Even for ranged attacks, he needed to end Shadow Form for them to work.

Melwar tapped his stomach with his hand, signaling that he was solid. "Not a bad shot," he admitted. "Too bad you cannot hurt me with it."

Iren frowned. Of course. Shadow Form was like smoke, and smoke could take whatever shape it desired. When Melwar became solid again, Shadow Form would remake him in an unharmed state. Even if Iren managed to hit Melwar, the man could heal as quickly as Iren could. Shadow Form was an amazing ability, on par with Rondel's Lightning Sight.

But it wasn't invincible. There was one way to defeat Melwar: a lethal, one-hit strike.

No holding back, then. Iren fired off a quick beam to put Melwar in Shadow Form, then charged forward to attack at close range. The Muryozaki stabbed, but after that, Iren switched to kicks and punches with his open hand. Melwar let the blows pass through him. All the while, Iren kept the Muryozaki in reserve.

Iren paused in his assault, and as expected, Melwar countered. His shadowy sword sliced horizontally at Iren's side.

Even as Iren pretended to block it though, he backflipped over the attack. He landed just as the blade passed through where he'd been standing. He thrust the Muryozaki at Melwar's face. It was over.

Then the ice beneath his feet exploded into shrapnel.

Iren staggered back, bleeding from both legs. Where had that come from? There'd been no ice when he'd left the ground. The weather was too warm for it anyway. Melwar used shadow magic, so he couldn't have created it. What was going on?

He was still puzzling out the ice when a wall of water appeared to his right and smashed into him like a tsunami. Though he and Melwar fought in a field, the wave from nowhere pulled Iren off the ground and sent him tumbling.

Iren broke free with a blast of light magic, but before the grasses stopped spinning, the next attack hit him. A burst of fire erupted from Melwar's hand, and it engulfed Iren's torso. He raised his arms to shield his face, and his skin peeled off as the tremendous heat burned away his shirt.

This was insane. How could Melwar use shadow, ice, water, and fire magics all at the same time? No one Iren had ever met, not even Rondel, could use more than one or two kinds of magic.

Iren retreated. He needed a moment to heal and come up with a new plan. Melwar had abilities Iren hadn't thought possible. Shadow Form was difficult to deal with by itself. Combined with all these other spells, it was beyond what Iren could handle.

Melwar must have known that, because the Maantec lord charged. A ball of flame and a spike of ice launched from his hands at the same time. Iren barely managed to dodge them. He ran for distance, but then he slipped on a patch of ice. He struggled to his feet and looked about in dismay. Similar frozen spots dotted more than a third of the field. Without careful maneuvering, Iren's high-speed runs would land him on one and send him skidding.

Iren frowned. Melwar had figured out that Iren's only advantage was his superior speed. With one spell, Melwar had neutralized that strength.

There was only one hope for victory now. Iren would have to run Melwar out of magic. Melwar wasn't a Dragon Knight. As impressive as he was with four magic types under his control, Melwar was drawing from the same well to create them. All those spells, especially the ice patches, had to require a lot of energy. By contrast, Iren had used little. If he could keep forcing Melwar to cast spells at this intensity, the Maantec lord would exhaust himself.

It was going to be a painful fight, but it was the only way. Iren took up a defensive stance and prepared for Melwar's onslaught.

Melwar raised his unarmed right hand and pointed a finger at Iren. A drop of water sprouted from the finger's tip. Iren cocked his head, confused. What could a drop of water do?

A shockwave reverberated across the field. Iren felt a fast, sharp pain, and he dropped to the ground. Blood poured out of parallel holes in both his chest and back.

Melwar approached. Water droplets formed on all his fingers. Then, one after another, they shot into Iren.

Iren opened his mouth to scream, but his lungs were full of blood. The dirt around him was soaked with it too. The Muryozaki tried to heal him, but Melwar fired the water shots faster than the sword could keep up.

Iren's vision grayed. He was going to die.

The ground around him shook. The water shots stopped, and with those extra seconds, the Muryozaki healed him.

Raising his head, Iren saw a pair of trees swinging their limbs at Melwar. They couldn't hurt the noble with Shadow Form activated, but at least they had forced him to stop attacking.

Minawë rushed forward. "I'll take it from here," she said.

Iren struggled to his feet. Even though the Muryozaki had removed his injuries, he felt exhausted. He'd never come that close to death. It had taken more magic than he'd expected to recover.

"You can't," he replied. "I have to see this through one on one. It's the only way the Maantecs will accept me."

"They won't accept you if you're dead," Minawë retorted. "Besides, do you think I'm going to stand back and let Melwar kill you?"

Bursts of flame shot from Melwar's hands and caught the trees alight. From those small fires, he turned them into a pair of infernos. They dissolved to ash.

Minawë next created a barrage of vines to attack the shogun. Brown seeds covered them, and when Melwar attacked them with flame, they didn't burn. Instead, they burst into still more vines that wrapped around him. Minawë closed her fist, and nine-inch spikes sprouted all over the green mass.

Melwar walked through the vines into the open. He smiled. "Seeds that respond to fire," he said. "That was clever. I wonder how well they handle cold."

A frozen patch of ground beneath the vine cluster erupted and covered the plants in ice. Melwar lunged with his sword and struck the vines a horizontal blow. They shattered.

Minawë grimaced, and Iren made the same expression. Melwar was beyond anything either of them could have expected.

Melwar raised his hands above his head. A great fireball formed between them, expanding until it was more than fifty feet across. Iren's eyes widened. Melwar planned to kill Iren and Minawë in one shot.

Iren grabbed Minawë by the arm to run away, but then he felt cold gripping his legs. Melwar had raised ice from the ground to trap them. Neither of them could move.

"Now die," Melwar said. He launched the fireball.

There was no time left. The inferno engulfed them.

When the flames passed, Iren and Minawë remained standing. Iren felt over his body. He was unharmed, and so was Minawë. It was impossible. How had they been saved?

Iren looked toward Melwar, and then he saw what had happened. Melwar must have entered Shadow Form, making his attack useless.

He'd entered that form because of the new arrival on the battlefield. Iren had never seen her before. Dressed in a Kodaman leather outfit similar to Minawë's, the newcomer stood with her back to Iren midway between him and Melwar. She was the same height as Rondel, but she looked no older than Minawë did. Her dark brown hair was tied in a ponytail, and her tight curves against the leather suggested a fast, powerful body.

"Who are you?" Iren asked.

"What's the matter? Don't you recognize me?" The young woman turned her head and looked at Iren with emerald eyes. Sparks danced across her irises. "I expected more from you, slacker."

CHAPTER FIFTY-ONE
Ancient Rivals

Minawë's arms hung at her sides, and her jaw had fallen equally loose. Maantecs couldn't restore their biological magic. Only Kodamas could do that.

"How, Mother?" Minawë asked.

"Iren Saito," Rondel replied. "Thanks to him I found out who I am. My father was a Kodama. It's why my family was murdered."

Rondel paused. "For twelve hundred years I tried to forget the past. Now I remember it, including the most important part: the dream my parents had for the future. They dreamed of a world where Maantecs, Kodamas, humans, and all the species of Raa could live together. I want to make that dream real. I healed Serona. The fires are gone there, and I ended the storm. Now all that's left is Melwar." She locked eyes with the Maantec shogun. "If you insist on getting in the way of my parents' dream, then I won't show you any mercy."

Iren stepped forward. The ice trap couldn't restrain him and Minawë now that Melwar was back in Shadow Form. "Stay out of this, Rondel," he said. "Melwar and I are fighting a duel of champions."

"I don't care what you're doing. I told you to wait two days, slacker. It figures you'd show initiative at the worst time. Now sit back and stay out of the grownups' way."

Melwar rolled his eyes. "I hate to interrupt the reunion, but—"

Rondel vanished. She showed no sign of movement. One instant she was standing in the field, and the next she was at Melwar's throat. Her dagger quivered an inch from his windpipe.

"You ended Shadow Form to speak," Rondel said. "Then you realized your mistake and recast it just in time. Lucky for you."

Iren whistled. "I thought she was fast before. I trained myself to move as fast as she could, to be able to respond at that speed, and I couldn't even see her just now. Could you?"

Minawë shook her head. "I always wondered about Mother. She had such strength, but she seemed insecure. I couldn't understand why, but now I do. It's because she knew how much she'd lost when she gave up her biological magic."

But more than speed gave Rondel the edge in this battle. Her aborted attack had made her other advantage clear. Lightning Sight could see Shadow Form. It could pick up on the tiny inconsistencies between Melwar's solid and non-solid appearances.

Iren smirked. "This fight's over. Melwar can't do anything against her."

Across the field, Rondel shook her head. "Underestimating Melwar isn't wise."

As if in response to her words, Melwar's Shadow Form lowered to the ground, and he disappeared. Rondel's gaze tracked across the landscape, and Minawë could tell her mother was following the Maantec lord's movements. Wherever he popped up, Rondel would have him.

A hundred yards away Melwar rose, but Rondel didn't chase after him. Minawë strained her eyes, and she saw shadows dancing in circles around Melwar's body.

"What are those?" Minawë asked.

"Shadow Knives," Iren replied, "like the ones he used against me. Since he can't attack while in Shadow Form, he's using those knives to protect himself instead. They're spinning close to his body, so even with Rondel's speed, they would cut her apart before she could land a blow."

"We should help her!" Minawë said. "Mother relies on fighting up close, but we have long-range spells. We can get through those knives."

"No," Rondel said. Her voice was low and terse. "This is my fight now. Stay out of it."

Iren gulped. "We can't help her."

"Why not?" Minawë demanded. "With all of us attacking together, Melwar won't stand a chance."

Iren shook his head. "We'd only get in her way. Besides, I get the feeling she has something personal in this."

Minawë scowled. "Yeah, well, she should get in line."

Iren smiled at that, but he didn't reply to it. Instead he called out, "Hey, Rondel! You're still an old hag to me, no matter what you look like. But if you insist on showing off, do us all a favor and end this quickly!"

Rondel half-smiled. "I intend to."

Melwar stretched out his hands. Jets of fire and ice shot toward Rondel. She flickered once, and then she vanished.

Less than a second later she reappeared behind Melwar. He whipped his right hand around, and three bangs signaled that he'd launched another round of the water projectiles he'd used to defeat Iren. Their speed was greater than anything Iren or Minawë possessed, and they put even the finest Kodaman arrows to shame.

Rondel dodged them with ease. Melwar fired dozens of shots, but Rondel avoided them all as she flashed across the battlefield.

"Amazing," Iren said. "She can see and maneuver around the ice traps even at that speed."

Minawë folded her arms. "She's only defending. She should end this fight with a bolt of lightning. I'm sure in that form she could summon one. She did it against Feng, and that was before she regained her biological magic."

Iren frowned. "You've never fought Rondel. I have. She doesn't make unnecessary moves. She's drawing this out for a reason."

Minawë wondered what that reason might be. Against Amroth, Rondel had used a similar delaying tactic to wear down the king's magic. That might be her ploy here, but Minawë wasn't convinced.

"She doesn't know what Melwar can do," she said at last. "She hasn't seen him in more than a thousand years. And while most mages can only control at best two kinds of magic, Melwar's using four. If she attacks, even when victory seems assured, it could lead her into a trap."

Iren nodded. "My thoughts exactly. But it doesn't make sense. How can Melwar control four elements at once?"

Rondel and Melwar's fight brought them closer to Iren and Minawë. The Maantec lord paused in his assault, and Rondel halted immediately afterward. She kept Lightning Sight trained on her foe.

Melwar wiped his brow. "You are as I remember you," he said. "If anything, you are stronger now than you were the last time we fought."

"Credit yourself for that," Rondel said. "You came closer than anyone else to defeating me back then. Even Saito would have lost had he not resorted to a failed Muryoka. That's why I spent thirty years developing Lightning Sight. It was because of you and Shadow Form. I needed to see through it."

"You worked for decades to find a way to defeat me. I am honored and humbled. It took me more than a millennium to figure out how to overcome you."

"Oh? What did you come up with?"

Melwar grasped his plum-colored shirt and flung it aside. It shredded to pieces in his spiraling Shadow Knives. He next removed his white undershirt, condemning it to his blades as well. Bare-chested, he smiled. "This is how."

For the first time since she'd arrived on the battlefield, Rondel looked taken aback. Minawë shared her astonishment. Attached to Melwar's skin were three gems—a ruby, a pearl, and a sapphire. Two rings of kanji symbols surrounded each of them.

"Melwar," Rondel breathed, "what madness is this?"

"The ultimate power!" Melwar roared. "With this I have surpassed any Dragon Knight. I have the magic of four dragons at my command."

Iren frowned. "Am I missing one? I only see three gems on his chest."

"Here is the fourth one," Melwar said. He held up his sword. It twisted and smoked. "This is the Yaryozaki, the Darkness Dragon Sword. Within it rests the ninth dragon, Shadeen."

Rondel reeled back. "A ninth dragon? Then all this time, you were—"

"A Dragon Knight," Melwar finished. "One of the Melwar clan is always the Darkness Dragon Knight, and whomever Shadeen chooses leads both the clan and the Akushi."

In an instant Rondel switched from astonished to furious. "You . . . then it was your bigoted allies who murdered my parents!"

Melwar shrugged. "I was an adult before I learned the truth about your disgusting origins. It was no surprise to me that you betrayed us to the Kodamas. I argued with Saito not to let you be the spy, to let me do it instead, but he insisted on you. He always favored you."

Melwar had sounded calm up until then, but he snarled those last four words. "You were always better," he continued, "even though you were a filthy half-breed from a low-class nothing. It was unthinkable. I had to get rid of you, but I could not surpass you in battle. I needed a more creative approach."

Rondel's arms quivered. "No . . . are you saying you cursed the Kodamas to get at me?"

"So you know about that," Melwar said. "You were everything to Saito. I knew that when he saw you with the enemy, his resolve would evaporate. My spell did what he lacked the courage to do: defeat the Kodamas. But yes, I had hoped it would kill you as well. Somehow you escaped it."

"It passed her over," Iren cut in. "I was able to remove your curse from Minawë because I cared about her. You say you despise Rondel, but the truth, deep down, is that you admire her. Your hate-filled curse couldn't act on a person you respected so much."

"What would a child know about it?" Melwar snapped. "You are as bad as her, a half-breed who would lead our race to extinction. I will unite us. I will—"

He grasped at his chest. "What? No, it's too soon!"

Rondel's eyes widened. "You wouldn't. You've been using magic all this time to keep those Shadow Knives whirling . . ."

Melwar was on his knees. He spoke in rushed tones, "I could not defeat you myself. It took me a thousand years, but I found an Akiyama and gave her the Enryokiri. Their clan has always been skilled in earth magic. I thought in Hana I had found a way to kill you, but she could not. I thought if I controlled four dragons I could kill you, but I could not. Now I see the truth. Only a dragon can kill you. And it is just about time. I can hear Shadeen's voice in my head. I can hear all their voices. They have taken their chance at freedom and joined forces against me. I do not mind. Shadeen and his brethren will win me the world."

The shogun screamed. His body stretched and bulged. His hands and feet morphed into long claws with wicked talons. His torso elongated into that of a great serpent, and his head became blocky and angular. Great black horns sprouted from above his eyes. His skin blackened as well, as though he had been charred. Great, batlike wings sprouted from his back. Last of all, his eyes turned a sulfurous yellow, glowing from within like a Yokai's.

Shadeen roared his triumph and took to the sky. From beyond where Minawë could see came the gasps and cries of the Maantec army as they watched the monster rise.

As the dragon flew higher, it changed yet again. Just ahead of its front legs, three new necks and heads sprouted. One was white, sharp, and glistened. Another was blue and fluid, twisting its shape as it desired. And the third . . .

The third was one Minawë had hoped she would never see again. Orange and red flames formed it, and its head narrowed into a pointy beak like an eagle's.

"Feng," Minawë murmured. "That's Feng."

"The other two are Yukionna the Ice Dragon and Mizuchi the Water Dragon," Rondel said. "To think he would go this far. I've never seen anything like it."

The four-headed dragon rolled in midair so that it pointed southeast. Shadeen opened his fang-filled mouth, and a black ball appeared before it. The ball grew to fill the space between his teeth.

Then he fired. The ball arced across the landscape and fell to the horizon. An explosion blasted into the air, a mushroom-shaped cloud miles high. Then, several seconds later, the ground shook and knocked Minawë, Iren, and Rondel off their feet.

Iren struggled to stand. "That must be the Darkness Dragon Flame," he whispered in awe, "Yaryoka."

Rondel focused Lightning Sight in the direction of the blast. "That was Kataile!" she breathed. "The plateau is completely gone. Shadeen destroyed it in one shot!"

CHAPTER FIFTY-TWO
The Flames of Dragons

Shadeen spiraled overhead, no doubt seeking his next target. "What do we do?" Iren asked.

To his shock, Rondel grinned. "We annihilate evil," she said. "Okthora, I trust you have no complaints?"

What Okthora responded was inside Rondel's mind, so Iren couldn't hear it. But he knew what the Storm Dragon must have said.

Rondel's skin glowed blue and purple. Scales grew over her body and formed a sparking suit of armor. A pair of electric wings sprouted from her back.

"I meant what I said earlier," she told Iren and Minawë when her Dragoon transformation finished. "This is my fight. Stay out of my way."

She crouched, then jumped into the air. She vanished in a flash.

Iren clenched his fists. He had worked so hard to match her. Now she'd left him far behind.

He wouldn't allow it. Even with Rondel's regained youth and a Dragoon form, that was no ordinary dragon up there. Shadeen had the energies of four dragons to draw on. If he could level Kataile in an instant, he could wipe out all of Raa if he wasn't stopped.

Magic coursed through Iren. He let it flow from his body, flaring around him in a storm of white light.

"Let's go, Divinion!" he shouted. "I won't let Rondel do this alone!"

"She told you to keep out of it," Divinion said.

"Of course she did. What did you expect? That she would admit she needed our help?"

Inside Iren's mind, he felt the dragon sigh. "Have it your way, then. Get up there."

"You won't fight me for control?"

"No. We're partners, now and forever."

Iren smiled. The white tempest condensed on his body and changed into a gleaming scale armor. Wings of light erupted from his back. For the second time in his life, Iren Saitosan had become the Dragoon.

"Minawë, find a place to hide," Iren said.

The Kodama shook her head. "Where would I go? That thing can blast apart a city. I'm staying to help you."

"Your plants can't scratch that thing."

"Not like this," Minawë said, "but there is a way I can help." Her eyes brightened. "You and Rondel can do it. I know I can too."

Minawë folded her arms across her chest, and a cocoon of vines encircled her. A moment later they fell away, and Minawë had changed. A hard, brown coating covered her body. Feathered wings grew from her back, and flowers bloomed at her feet.

"The Forest Dragoon," she said. "Dendryl and I command the powers of life and death. Tell us what you need, and we'll get it done."

Iren looked up. Rondel flashed around Shadeen, striking him with lightning bolts from her hands, but her shots had no effect. Iren wasn't surprised. Divinion had scales immune to magic. It made sense that Shadeen would too. Dragoon or not, Rondel couldn't penetrate that armor.

Not that Iren would have better luck. Even the final attack he'd used against Feng hadn't dented the dragonscale Muryozaki. That spell had taken five minutes of gathering magic, and it had exhausted the Dragoon's reserves. A blast like that would be useless against Shadeen.

There was one spell, though, that might work. The Muryozaki had been forged from one of Divinion's scales, and Divinion himself had provided the heat for the forge. His flame could overcome Shadeen's armor.

Iren turned to Minawë. "You asked what I need," he said. "I need time. You and Rondel have to distract Shadeen. I don't want him to get too far away, and I definitely don't want him to destroy any more cities."

"How much time do you need?" Minawë asked.

"Five minutes."

"You got it." She leapt into the air and was gone.

ଔ

Minawë had flown numerous times as a bird, and she never tired of it. The feeling of total freedom, of weightlessness, gripped her with a euphoria that refused to let go.

As she flew toward Rondel, Minawë tamped down that excitement. She couldn't get carried away this time, not when so much depended on her.

Above her, Rondel clashed with Shadeen. The Maantec flashed across the sky, so fast Minawë could only see her when Rondel changed direction. At each stop, Rondel shot a lightning bolt from her hands. Shadeen's armor resisted each one, and he countered by hurling dozens of Shadow Knives. The other dragons joined him, launching waves of fire, ice, and water.

Rondel vanished again, and an instant later she appeared in front of her daughter. "I should have told you this a long time ago," she said. "I'm proud of you."

Minawë beamed, but she couldn't waste words. "Iren needs five minutes."

Lightning Sight flicked down. "I see," Rondel said, "and Shadeen will too. He needs cover."

"I can handle that." Minawë gestured at the ground, and a small pine forest sprouted from the plains around Iren. Their dense needles shielded him from view.

"Impressive," Rondel said, but then she shoved Minawë. Fifty Shadow Knives cut through the space the pair had been floating in a second earlier.

Minawë channeled some magic and created a wooden shield three feet thick that she put between her and Shadeen. Rondel flashed over to it.

"This should give us a few seconds, anyway," Minawë said.

Beneath her sparking helm, Rondel's face was grim. "I trust you have a plan for keeping Shadeen occupied?"

Minawë nodded. "We should aim for whichever claw of his is holding the Darkness Dragon Sword. If we can knock it out of his grasp, he won't be able to sustain his dragon form."

"Unfortunately that option's out," Rondel replied. "Feng must have told Shadeen that we used that strategy against him. The first thing Shadeen did when he saw me coming was swallow the Yaryozaki."

"Wonderful," Minawë said, frowning. She thought a moment. "In that case our best option is to go after the other three dragon heads. Their armor doesn't look as strong as Shadeen's."

"Good idea. I can take Yukionna and Mizuchi. Can you handle Feng?"

Minawë clutched Dendryl's bow to her chest. Could she handle Feng? Her adopted mother had died fighting that beast. Aletas hadn't even managed to wound him.

No, Minawë wouldn't let herself doubt. She could do it. What's more, she knew how. It was time to see what this Dragoon form could do.

"I can," she said, "but I'll need time just like Iren. He needs five minutes; I need two. Keep those dragons off me."

Rondel agreed, and the pair separated. Minawë's wooden shield splintered as Mizuchi soaked it, Yukionna froze it, and Shadeen's Shadow Knives shattered it.

The attacks were wasted though, because neither mother nor daughter was behind the shield anymore. Minawë had dropped to the ground, while Rondel had resumed her lightning barrage.

Minawë put a hand to the grass. She felt its power. She had done something like this in her fights against Azar and Hana, but the scale she planned now was beyond reckoning. More than a hundred miles separated her from Ziorsecth Forest, but that didn't matter. That was the power she needed.

Her magic shot into the ground, and the plants near Minawë knitted their roots together. They joined to their brethren west of them, who connected with those west of them, and so on across Lodia.

Minawë felt their combined energy build. The line of joined plants reached Orcsthia, but that still wasn't enough.

Then a jolt of energy ripped through her, at least an equal to the Dragoon's magic. Her plant network had reached Ziorsecth, and its shared root system now gave her access to tens of thousands of square miles of ancient trees.

Above her, a gut-wrenching scream filled the air. Rondel had sent a ball of lightning into Mizuchi's neck. The water carried the lightning throughout it, and the beast stopped moving.

Rondel plunged into Mizuchi. A moment later she emerged, and as she did, the Water Dragon vanished into rain.

Minawë smiled. Rondel had removed the Aqua Sapphire from Shadeen's scales. Without that connection, Mizuchi couldn't hold physical form.

There was no time to celebrate. Minawë focused all the energy she had gathered on a single tree seedling at her feet. In seconds it transformed into a gigantic maple, the equal of any in Ziorsecth. Minawë rode up its boughs as it grew.

The magic of innumerable plants coursed through the tree, and it shot skyward. Higher and higher it rose, until at last it stood a mile in the air. Wind whipped around Minawë like when she flew as an eagle, but she wasn't flying. She sat atop a new, fully formed Heart of Ziorsecth.

Rondel must have been watching her, because the Maantec paused in her flight to gape at Minawë. Shadeen halted as well, no doubt surprised by the enormous tree that had just sprouted from thin air.

Impressive as it was though, the tree was only the first step. Its sole purpose was to collect energy from all the other plants. Now Minawë would put that power to use.

She retracted the Dragoon armor around her feet so they made direct contact with the Heart. Its strength coursed through her, and in concert with the Dragoon's magic, it threatened to overwhelm her. Her body grew hot, like she was standing inches from Feng himself, but she ignored the pain.

"Minawë," Dendryl warned, "you will self-combust if you continue."

Minawë didn't respond to the Forest Dragon. She didn't care what happened to her. If they didn't stop Shadeen here, she and everyone else on Raa would die anyway.

A second scream rent the air, and Minawë saw Yukionna break apart into snow. Rondel had used the same weakness against lightning to paralyze the Ice Dragon and create an opening to remove the Frozen Pearl.

That left only Shadeen and Feng, and Minawë was going to finish them both with one shot. Let Iren create his spell. Minawë loved the idea of him emerging from hiding only to find the Darkness Dragon already beaten.

The magic was ready. Minawë raised her hands toward Feng, aiming for the spot where his neck joined Shadeen's body. "I am the Forest Dragon Knight," she said through gritted teeth. "I command the powers of life and death. And here, in this place, I command you to die!"

A fifty-foot-wide beam of yellow light lanced from her hands. All the solar energy that every plant from here to Serona had gathered in the past day shot up the Heart of Ziorsecth, through Minawë's body, and out at Feng and Shadeen.

Neither dragon had time to dodge. The blast struck home.

At first Shadeen's armor resisted, but then Minawë heard the third scream of the battle. Feng dissolved into smoke as the scales holding the Burning Ruby cracked.

Minawë kept up her effort. With Shadeen's scales breached, she needed only a few more seconds to finish him.

But the beam thinned, and then it died. The plants had more energy, but not even the Dragoon could handle any more of it.

Minawë dropped to her knees. Her Dragoon armor vanished, and her wings retracted into her back. Gray tunnels formed around her vision.

The last thing she saw before she blacked out was Shadeen. He was alive, and he was aiming his Darkness Dragon Flame right at her.

CB

Rondel shielded her eyes from the glare of Minawë's attack. It was like the sun itself. In both size and power, it far surpassed the beam Iren had created in Ziorsecth Forest two years ago. In her wildest imaginings Rondel had never suspected her daughter could do something like that.

As the beam ended though, Rondel's astonishment turned to dismay. Feng had vanished, but Shadeen remained. The beam had amazing strength, but it was spread over too wide an area. That weakened its penetrating ability, and that had made the difference.

Still, Shadeen hadn't escaped unscathed. With Lightning Sight, Rondel spotted the wound just in front of the dragon's right foreleg, the spot where the Burning Ruby had sat. In addition to the ruby, Shadeen had lost three scales there.

Rondel might have used that information, but there wasn't time. Shadeen had gathered enough magic to release his flame again, and Rondel knew where he would launch it. There was nothing she could do to stop the blast.

But she wasn't helpless. Even as Shadeen fired, Rondel flashed toward the Heart of Ziorsecth.

Shadeen's attack seemed to slow. Everything seemed to slow. Rondel had never moved this fast before. It was like riding a lightning bolt.

She landed on the branch where Minawë lay. The girl had lost her Dragoon form and passed out. Rondel scooped her up, and with a crack of thunder, she dashed away. Time slowed again, and she landed on the ground five miles west of the Heart.

Rondel looked back just in time to see Yaryoka strike the tree. A mushroom cloud erupted, and a second later the shockwave struck her. Rondel was thrown to the ground, which was good considering how much wooden shrapnel flew over her. Even with her speed, she doubted she could have avoided it all.

When the debris passed, Rondel stood. Panic took her. That blast could level a city; had it taken out Iren's hiding spot as well?

Lightning Sight pierced the distance, and Rondel breathed a sigh of relief. Shadeen had aimed Yaryoka too high, shooting to take out Minawë directly. The blast had incinerated the Heart, but the smaller pines had escaped with only cracked limbs. Iren, concealed by their boughs, should be safe.

For how much longer, though, was unknown. Rondel did a mental estimate. Three minutes had passed. Iren needed two more for Muryoka, assuming the slacker could even manage it.

Rondel was his only chance. She had to keep Shadeen busy.

Leaving Minawë at a hopefully safe distance from the battle, Rondel shot back, covering the five miles to Shadeen in an instant. The needles on the pines surrounding Iren still quivered from Yaryoka, but as Rondel flew past them, they seemed to pause in their vibrations.

Rondel rose up to meet Shadeen face-to-face. The dragon roared in challenge, and Rondel responded with a lightning bolt to his eye socket.

The shot didn't faze him. The scales on the dragon's face darkened, and a barrage of Shadow Knives launched from them toward Rondel.

They were easy enough to dodge, but after experiencing them multiple times, Rondel had noticed a pattern. The number of knives Shadeen used against her increased every time he cast his spell. The monster wasn't opposed to using his power, but he also had an intense pride. He wouldn't use more magic against her than he had to.

Rondel leapt across the sky, lightning arcing from her hands. Shadeen launched wave after wave of knives, but none of them kept up with Rondel's speed.

In her head Rondel counted down the seconds. It was almost time. She risked a glance away from Shadeen and toward the trees where Iren gathered his energy. Three . . . two . . . one . . .

A white blur shot up from the pines. Rondel flashed over to Iren and appeared in front of him.

Aside from his Dragoon form, the young man looked normal. No flames curled around him; no ball of fire was in his hand.

"Where is it?" Rondel asked.

Iren opened his left palm. "Here."

Rondel looked. Even with Lightning Sight she couldn't see anything. "I hope you know what you're doing."

"Don't worry," Iren said. "We do. We just need to know where to put it. We need a point-blank shot for it to work. Is Shadeen using Shadow Form?"

"No," Rondel said. "I think he believes he's invincible, so there's no reason for him to. As for where to hit him, Minawë wounded him just in front of his right foreleg."

"I'll need cover."

"No problem."

Iren smiled. "Rondel, I'm glad we get to end this together."

Despite herself, Rondel returned his grin. "Me too," she said. "Now enough sentimental rubbish. Let's go."

The pair of them climbed together into the sky. Iren wasn't as fast as Rondel, but she was surprised how well he kept up. His control over the

Dragoon's magic was beyond compare. Maybe that was because he had done it twice.

Shadeen bellowed as they neared, and a curtain of Shadow Knives descended on them. Rondel flickered around it, while Iren let his Dragoon armor protect him. Divinion's scales were immune to magic, so the knives dissipated across them.

Rondel shot lightning bolts at Shadeen, but the dragon ignored her. He kept his gaze on Iren. Shadeen might believe himself invulnerable, but he knew not to underestimate Divinion.

He also knew about his missing scales. As Iren neared Shadeen, the dragon twisted to protect his wound. At the same time, he slashed with his claws and fired beams of shadow from his mouth. Iren dodged them all, maneuvering with a precision that impressed even Rondel.

At this rate though, Iren would have no chance of getting Muryoka into that wound. Worse, if he dropped the tiny attack, all their effort would be wasted. Rondel had to get Shadeen's attention back on her.

Time to give it everything, then. Rondel stretched the Liryometa above her head and channeled all the Dragoon's magic into it. Lightning burst from it into the sky, and clouds formed above her. The sun vanished behind the brooding storm, and seconds later a torrential rain soaked all three combatants.

Rondel fed more magic to the storm. It was like recreating the tempest over Serona, but Rondel kept this one centered on Shadeen.

The air crackled. It would come soon.

At last the lightning broke free. The bolts smashed into Shadeen, hundreds landing on him each second. Rondel screamed as she released every scrap of energy the Dragoon had left.

Her wings flickered. She was out of time. Hoping the storm would last long enough, Rondel headed for the ground. It was up to Iren now.

ॐ

Rondel continued to amaze Iren. She kept surpassing herself. Even after her retreat, the storm was doing her job for her. Shadeen roared in frustration against the lightning barrage, but the deafening thunder drowned out his cries.

Yet through all the tempest's fury, Shadeen kept up his twisting movements. He knew the storm was a diversion. Iren had spotted the wound Rondel had described three times already, but he couldn't get close enough to strike it with Muryoka. The target was just too small. If only there were a bigger one!

The dragon howled at the storm as it intensified. As he did, he turned his massive gullet toward Iren.

Iren sighed. He knew what he had to do, and he wasn't going to like it.

Then again, Shadeen would like it a whole lot less.

Iren flew toward the wound on Shadeen's belly. The dragon needed to think that spot was still Iren's target. He landed on the monster's stomach and raised the Muryozaki in his right hand as if to strike. Shadeen twisted again, and Iren made a show of losing his balance. He hovered in midair.

The dragon leveled with him, and the beast's mouth opened. Yaryoka's black sphere formed between his jaws.

Now! Before he could fire!

Iren flew forward, in control the entire time. He passed between the rows of eviscerating teeth and through the heart of the growing Yaryoka. His left hand touched the back of the dragon's throat, and he spoke a single word.

"Farewell."

Ψ

Rondel stood at the edge of the pine forest Minawë had created. Her Dragoon form had ended, and with it, she felt her magic disappear. Just like with Iren's Dragoon form against Feng, the transformation had sealed it away. She couldn't even use Lightning Sight to follow the battle. She could see the Darkness Dragon, but Iren was impossible to spot amid all the lightning.

Then she shielded her eyes. Shadeen glowed from within. White light burst from between his scales. It shot into the storm and broke it apart, letting clear sun onto the battlefield.

Rondel grinned. Iren had done it.

A second later, though, the old Maantec's smile turned to an open-mouthed cry of terror. Shadeen detonated. Muryoka's energy exploded from his body, and Rondel was left momentarily blind. When the glare cleared, Shadeen was gone.

And so was Iren.

A spot of red, like a falling star, appeared in the distance. Rondel ran toward it, frustrated at how slowly she moved now. Sweat poured off her, but she kept running.

She arrived just as Iren hit the ground. His impact threw up a cloud of debris.

"Iren?" Rondel yelled as she neared the impact site. "Iren!"

Coughing told her he was alive. Rondel stumbled her way into the crater the young man had made on impact. "Iren!" she cried again.

"Over here," came the stifled response. Rondel followed the voice. At last she found him. He was still in his Dragoon armor, but his wings had vanished.

Iren stood and shook all over. The dragonscale melted back into his skin. "It's done," he said.

Rondel slapped him on the back. "I told you you could handle him!"

"Ow!" Iren shouted. "Can we save the jumping around and celebrating for tomorrow?"

Rondel smirked. "Sure, slacker. You've earned it."

They crawled out together from the crater, Iren leaning on Rondel's shoulder for support. The dust had settled, and Iren gazed up at the clear sky. He whistled. "I can't believe I walked away from that one. I'm glad that ended it."

"As am I," a voice said from behind them.

Rondel's blood froze. She turned around. She was so shocked she dropped her dagger. It clattered against the ground.

Melwar floated ten feet in the air.

But he was more than Melwar. Dark scales wrapped around his body. Black, smoky wings smoldered behind him. His eyes burned with an inner yellow light.

Iren gaped. "That's impossible."

"I must express my gratitude," Melwar said. "I stood no chance against Shadeen in a contest of wills, let alone against four dragons. Now

I need not worry about them. Since you defeated Shadeen, I can take his magic without resistance. Thanks to you, I have become the Darkness Dragoon."

CHAPTER FIFTY-THREE
Final Shot

Iren trembled. If he and Rondel still had their Dragoon forms they might stand a chance. But like this, exhausted and without magic . . .

Rondel knelt and picked up her dagger. Her hands didn't shake. She must be as terrified as Iren, yet somehow she held firm. "It doesn't matter what you've become," she told Melwar. "I will carry out Okthora's Law."

"You cannot even reach Okthora anymore," Melwar said. "Why obey the law of an absent master?"

Rondel raised the Liryometa. "That's why you're a poor Maantec, Melwar. You claim to follow the old traditions, but you don't understand them at all. How many Maantecs never met Iren Saito, yet faithfully served him? You haven't a clue what honor or duty or love even mean."

"I will not need to when I am the Maantec emperor!" Melwar lashed out with his sword. The blade moved so fast Iren could barely track it. It was coming for his gut. There was no time to dodge.

A blow from the side knocked him down. He rolled in the dirt and gasped.

Rondel stood where Iren had been a second ago. Melwar's twisting sword speared her chest.

"Rondel!"

Melwar withdrew his blade, and Rondel dropped to the ground. Iren crawled forward and grasped her by the shoulders.

Blood trickled from Rondel's lips, but she curled them into her wide, sarcastic grin. "A mother protects her children, no matter what."

She closed her eyes. Her breathing stopped. Yet even as she died, she kept on smiling.

Tears ran down Iren's cheeks. It had happened again. During the battle with the Quodivar leader two years ago, Rondel had seemed to die. Iren had hardly known her back then. He'd idolized her as a powerful warrior, but now he knew better. There was so much more to her. A traitor. A hero. A murderer. A parent. An enemy.

A friend.

White light, ever so faint, appeared on Iren's left hand. He eyed it with disbelief. He'd lost contact with his magic. What was this glow?

Melwar seemed not to notice. "Do not cry for her," he said. "She betrayed you. She betrayed all Maantecs."

"Stop talking," Iren murmured. He had no idea what he would do against the might of the Darkness Dragoon, but he couldn't bear to listen to Melwar's ignorance. He stood. "You think you have so much power, but for all your strength, you're a failure. You couldn't manipulate me into being your puppet. You couldn't defeat Rondel. You couldn't kill the Kodamas. You couldn't stop the dragons from taking over your body. And do you know why?" He was screaming now. "It's because you don't know anything about them! You never saw any of them as people. They were only ever obstacles for you to overcome!"

Melwar's eyes narrowed. "What makes you think you can speak about it, whelp? I have succeeded where even your father failed. I united the Maantecs. I brought them here. I will conquer this world and give it to our people. I am a Melwar. I do not fail."

"Your whole life has been nothing but failure. It's because you can't accept those failures that you've become so demented."

"Show me then how I failed from your grave!" Melwar thrust at Iren.

Iren was ready for the outburst. He ducked the blow, drew the Muryozaki, and slashed up into Melwar's Dragoon armor. There was no magic behind his attack, but the Muryozaki was dragonscale. It clanged against Melwar's armor and left a dent.

Iren ran behind Melwar and struck again, but the Darkness Dragoon was expecting it this time. He dodged, and his sword arced around and cut

Iren in the right shoulder. Iren dropped to the ground beside Rondel's corpse.

"You see?" Melwar said. "This is the power that comes with ultimate success."

From his spot in the dirt, Iren's face was level with Rondel's. She looked so peaceful. She'd died to save him, but she must have known Melwar would kill him in the end. How could she die happy, knowing her sacrifice was meaningless?

"Because it wasn't meaningless," a voice rang inside Iren's head, one he'd heard before. "Rondel told you she believed you could defeat Melwar. She died still believing that."

Iren went rigid. "Dad?"

"You can win, Akio."

Iren looked at his left hand. That faint white glow was still there.

That's right. Divinion had explained it to him before. Strong emotions could make magic act unpredictably. It had happened before when Rondel had seemed to die.

Except Iren didn't have any magic. He'd exhausted it all as the Dragoon.

No, that wasn't correct. He had one more source he could draw on.

Iren rose and faced Melwar. He sheathed the Muryozaki. He didn't need it for this. He held out his left hand, palm up. The glow brightened and enveloped his hand.

Then it ignited.

"What?" Melwar asked. "You can't use magic."

"Stand there and take it, then," Iren growled.

White flames shot up from his palm. He forced his will into them, ordering them to condense.

Beneath his helmet, Melwar's sulfurous eyes went wide. "That can't be!" He swung his sword.

The flames released a tendril that formed a shield around Iren. Melwar pummeled it with slashes, but the shield held firm.

The white fire in Iren's hand shrank. In his previous attempts he could never get it shorter than his forearm. Now it was the length of his hand, then the size of a cherry.

Iren had no idea where the will to force the magic into shape came from. It had taken both him and Divinion five minutes to create this spell as the Dragoon. This one was getting smaller by the second. The spell seemed to act of its own accord.

Maybe it was because of the magic he was using. That was the secret to Muryoka's perfect form, after all. His father had shared it with him. If you were the Dragoon, you could rely on Divinion to help cast the spell. If you weren't, the only way to create a perfect Muryoka was to use all your biological magic. You had to put so much of yourself into it that it killed you.

Yet even that sacrifice wouldn't guarantee victory. Melwar could use Shadow Form to avoid the spell.

Iren's eyes burned as brightly as the flame in his hand. He would have to wait until Melwar committed to an attack. When Melwar's sword embedded in Iren's flesh, the Darkness Dragoon would have to be solid. Then, and only then, could Iren hit him.

Muryoka finished, and Iren let its shield dissolve. Melwar's final blow came. Iren waited for it to reach within inches of his head.

He lunged. His hand reached out and touched Melwar on the chest.

White flames exploded from Iren's palm. They erupted across the land, blasting through Melwar like he wasn't even there.

As the attack faded, Iren cursed. At the moment he'd released Muryoka, Melwar's sword had passed cleanly through Iren's head. Iren was still alive. He'd failed. Melwar had used Shadow Form.

Iren sank to his knees, utterly spent. His breath came in heaves. Rondel and Dad had given him one last chance of victory, and he'd blown it.

Melwar towered over him. The Yaryozaki descended.

It never landed. Melwar screamed, a wrenching, writhing cry. His Dragoon armor glowed white. Iren averted his eyes, but the explosion was still all but blinding.

When Iren at last had the courage to look again, Melwar was gone. All that remained was a smoking black sword.

In Melwar's place was a different man, dressed not in Dragoon armor but homespun linen clothes. To anyone else he would have seemed an ordinary farmer, but Iren recognized him right away.

"Dad!"

Iren Saito smiled. "You did well, son."

"But how? What happened? Why are you here?"

"To use Muryoka, you have to sacrifice your life," Saito said. "You thought you were using your biological magic to cast it, but you weren't. You used mine. I transferred it to you while you were the Dragoon. I was the sacrifice. After your spell missed Melwar, I used my will to convert it back into a physical form. When Melwar attacked, I struck him from behind with the same energy."

"So you defeated him! And you're alive again!"

Saito shook his head. "If anyone can claim credit for defeating Melwar, it's you and Rondel. As for being alive, I'm not. I'm not truly Iren Saito. I'm the bits of magic and spirit that remain from the Muryoka, and from the spell I used to trap myself inside the Muryozaki. It's not enough to stay here. I have a few more seconds, and then I'll disappear."

"No!" Iren jumped up and embraced his father. "I finally got to meet you for real. I finally got to have a parent. Please don't leave now!"

Saito smiled again, even wider. A tear slid down his cheek. "You have no idea how happy I am to hear you say that. But I died twenty years ago. Even so, I was never at peace, because I split myself to enter the Muryozaki. Now I can finally rest." He chuckled. "Besides, Carita and Rondel have already gone ahead of me. I shudder to think what stories they might tell about me if I'm not there. It's time I joined them."

Iren wiped his eyes. "I watched the memory," he said. "Thank you."

"Don't thank me. I don't deserve it. Thank your mother. She's stronger than I ever could have been. If you've grown up the way she wanted you to, it's because of her."

Saito faded, but Iren clutched his father until the last. "I love you," he said.

"And I will always love you," Saito replied. "Good-bye, Akio."

Iren stepped forward. His father was gone.

A sharp blow to the head dropped Iren to the ground. He looked up through bleary eyes, but he couldn't stand.

A woman with long black hair walked into view. She met Iren's gaze with a jaded stare.

"Hana?" Iren managed.

Hana Akiyama ignored him. She knelt and picked up the Yaryozaki.

"What are you doing?" Iren asked. "That thing's dangerous."

"I know," Hana said. "That's why I'm taking it."

"Where?"

"Where no one else can get it. Even without the Stone Dragon Hammer, I can get a good ways down. I'll travel so far underground that no one can find it and return to the surface alive."

Iren's eyes widened as he realized what Hana meant to do. "Wait!" he said. "There has to be another way!"

"I followed your battle from underground," Hana explained. "I heard Rondel. She healed Serona, so I can't throw it into those flames. If I tossed it in the ocean, some fisherman might pull it up in a net. No, this is the only way."

Iren struggled with both arms to lift himself. He fell back to the dirt.

"That's why I hit you," Hana said, pointing at him. "I figured you'd do something stupid and heroic to stop me."

"Hana, please."

"This is the way I want it. It's just like your father said. I have someone waiting for me, too."

Hana sank into the earth with the Yaryozaki in hand. Iren tried once more to reach out and restrain her, but she was too far away. She smiled, and then her head vanished beneath the surface. A moment later, Iren blacked out.

CHAPTER FIFTY-FOUR
Maantec Restoration

Iren groaned as he came to. He lay on soft grass, the blades kissing his face as they waved in the breeze.

He tried to sit up, but his head swam. He reached back and felt a lump behind his left ear. Tears welled in his eyes. He'd hoped it had all been a bad dream.

With a great effort he attempted to sit again. This time he made it, though he teetered like a drunkard. Sure enough, there was no sign of Hana or the Yaryozaki.

Rondel lay next to him, still grinning. What Iren wouldn't give to hear her speak one more time! To have her berate him or call him names or launch into some sarcastic tirade. She was probably giving his father all he could handle right now.

The thought made him smile, just a little.

"Exalted Emperor?" a voice asked from behind him. "How do you feel?"

Iren's senses went on alert. He whirled around, but the movement was too much. He had to put a hand on the ground. He was helpless against whomever had shown up.

Strong hands grabbed him. Armored in layered steel, they held him upright.

Iren looked into the face of the man who steadied him. He had brown eyes and hard features under a well-crafted helmet.

It took Iren a moment, but then he remembered who the man was. "I met you before," Iren said. "You were the samurai standing beside

Melwar's palanquin. You commanded his army. Your name was Daichi, right?"

Even though Daichi was kneeling, he bowed as best he could. The motion nearly sent both him and Iren sprawling on the grass. "I am honored you remember me, Exalted Emperor."

Iren rolled his eyes. "At ease, Daichi. I'm in no shape to handle formality. I'm no good at it anyway."

The samurai returned to his previous position but said nothing.

"What brings you here?" Iren asked when the silence became uncomfortable.

"We saw you fighting the dragon," the samurai explained. "When we saw the Holy Dragoon, it removed any doubt from our minds. We knew for certain that you were our emperor, that you were Iren Saito reborn."

Iren shook his head. "I'm not. I may be his son, but Iren Saito is someone I'll never be."

"Your humility is as honorable as your fighting prowess."

Iren resisted the urge to roll his eyes again. "Anyway, why are you by yourself? What happened to the rest of Melwar's army?"

Daichi sucked air through his teeth. "Exalted Emperor, the traitor's army no longer exists."

Iren's eyes widened. "What are you saying?" he asked. He gripped Daichi's arms. "Did Shadeen kill them?"

"Forgive my poor speech," the samurai replied. "The men are all still alive. I left them where they stood so I could scope out the situation. What I meant to say is that it is no longer proper to refer to us as the traitor's army. We follow the emperor. We are yours now."

Iren put his hand to his head to fight off yet another dizzy spell. His plan had worked.

Now it was time to put that plan to good use. He pushed into a standing position, managing it only because Daichi continued to support most of his weight. "Daichi," he said, "I have a command for you as your emperor. As of now, you and all Maantecs are no longer at war with humans. The traitor's conquest was never in our people's best interests. I'll have no more killing."

Daichi bowed his head. "I hear and obey, Exalted Emperor. I will spread the word to the men." He sucked air through his teeth again. "Exalted Emperor, may I ask you a question?"

Iren was already tired of the "Exalted Emperor" nonsense. Just ask him! He sighed. "Please, Daichi, say what you will."

"Our people cannot return to Shikari," Daichi said. "Now that the traitor is dead, we have no way to calm the ocean storms. I will go where you command, but most of these men are not samurai. They were torn from their homes and farms. What will become of them if we surrender to the Lodians?"

All this time, Iren had wondered what kind of man Daichi was. The over-the-top honor and support could be tricks, ploys to convince Iren that Daichi was loyal when in fact he still believed in Melwar.

But the samurai's question solidified Iren's opinion of him. This man was a true leader, someone who put the needs of his subordinates ahead of his own. Had Daichi led the Maantecs instead of Melwar, this war never would have happened.

Iren couldn't disappoint him. "Daichi, I wouldn't abandon these men any more than you would. I'm their emperor. I'll find a way to help them."

What he left unsaid was that he had no idea what that way might be. The Lodians would never accept thousands of Lefts settling in their country.

While Iren was still puzzling out an answer, Daichi looked off toward the west. "Exalted Emperor, someone approaches."

Iren turned to follow Daichi's gaze. The moment he did, he felt both elated and dismayed.

It was Minawë.

"Daichi," Iren said, "let me stand on my own."

The samurai obeyed, and Iren, on his full weight for the first time since the battle, almost fell. He forced himself to keep upright. This wasn't going to be pretty.

Minawë pounded toward them. When she arrived, she grabbed Iren by the shirt with both fists and roared in his face, "You crazy . . . stupid . . . lucky . . . moron!"

Daichi's hand went to the katana at his waist, but Iren stopped him with a shake of his head. He deserved every name Minawë had just hurled at him.

He was about to speak when Minawë released him. She had caught sight of Rondel lying in the grass. She fell to her knees. "Mother!"

The sobs came loud and long. Minawë clutched Rondel to her chest, the tears soaking into her clothes. Iren had held back until now, but something about Minawë's outburst cut through his shock and made it all real. He cried without restraint, caring not at all for the samurai watching him.

"How did she die?" Minawë finally asked, when the two had no more tears to give.

"Saving me," Iren said.

"She sacrificed herself for you?"

"I won't ask you to forgive me."

Minawë stood. She shook her head and wiped her eyes. There was no anger in them. "Moron," she repeated. Then she wrapped her arms around him and kissed him.

"Daichi," Iren said when he could breathe again, "would you mind giving us a few minutes alone?"

Daichi bowed and stepped away. He put his back to them.

"Rondel told me how you wounded Shadeen," Iren said. "I wish I could have seen it. You were amazing."

A hint of pride flashed on Minawë's face, but it soon disappeared. Her eyes drifted to Rondel. "I would have died after that attack if she hadn't saved me. I can't believe she's gone. I've had to lose my mother twice."

Iren loosed a long breath. "I know what you mean."

Minawë released him. She eyed him quizzically.

In response to her look, Iren told her about Saito's appearance. "I didn't defeat Melwar," he concluded. "Father did. Rondel did. They're the heroes."

"Moron, you did plenty. We both did. Besides, the most important task is still left. What are we going to do about Melwar's army?"

"I was trying to figure that out when you arrived. I have no idea. They can't stay here, and they can't return to Shikari."

Minawë thought for a moment. Then her expression brightened. "What about Serona?"

"Serona?" Iren asked. "It's torn apart."

"Don't you remember? Mother mentioned it before she fought Melwar. She said she'd been there and stopped the fires. The land will grow again. The Maantecs can move there. If they want to return to Shikari, they can use the western ocean. That's how they traveled in ancient times."

Iren put a hand to his chin. It could work.

From across the field came the sound of sniffling. Iren hadn't realized Daichi was within earshot. "Daichi, are you all right?" he asked.

The samurai turned around. He was choked up, but even at this distance Iren could see the man's wishful smile. "Serona," Daichi said. "I've dreamed about it for so long. Is it really possible we could return?"

Iren nodded. "It is," he said, "and as the Maantec emperor, I'd be happy to lead you there."

EPILOGUE

Twelve Years Later

"My liege, this is not the sort of establishment a king should enter."

King Dirio Cyneric of Lodia had to agree with his bodyguard. The building before him was a dismal heap. Even calling it a building was a compliment. It only had walls up to about four feet. Above that they changed to an open reed mesh and a straw roof.

Ostensibly the mesh's purpose was so patrons could smell the salty tang of the bay not twenty feet from the restaurant. In reality, Dirio suspected it was so the stench of sweat and alcohol inside could blow away in the sea breeze.

On any other day Dirio would have avoided the restaurant even at noontime, let alone late in the evening like it was now. Today though, he had no choice but to come here. Rumor had it this was the place where the man Dirio needed to find was most likely to be.

Dirio grasped the rusty handle and pulled open the door. He coughed the moment he did. He'd been wrong. The mesh's purpose clearly wasn't to get rid of the smell.

Suppressing the urge to gag, Dirio entered the restaurant. The place was body-to-body. Dirio's two guards took up positions in front of and behind him. Even with their armor and swords, they had a hard time pushing through the throng.

There was one exception to the press of humanity. In the back corner sat a family of three, and everyone in the building gave them a wide berth.

It wasn't the family itself that caused the other patrons to avoid them. It was the man standing, arms crossed, in front of their table. He wore armor of layered steel, and on his back he carried a seven-foot sword. Its pommel was an inch away from the ceiling; the man must have needed to duck to fit through the doorway.

Dirio's guards walked up to the man, and as they did the man's left hand reached up and rubbed his shoulder. It wasn't an aggressive move, but it was still an obvious signal. The man could draw that massive sword whenever he wanted, and nothing would get in his way if he did.

Fortunately, that wouldn't be necessary. "Good evening," Dirio said. "I'd like to speak with your lord, if you please."

From behind the armored swordsman came the sound of hammers bashing on the table. *Wham! Wham! Crack!*

The hammers stopped. A girl's head popped out around the swordsman's waist. She looked about eight. Her hair was dark brown and uncombed, and her emerald eyes were wide with curiosity. "Who is it, Mr. Daichi?"

Was it Dirio's imagination, or did the intimidating warrior smile just a hair? "Some guests, Princess," the man said. "Exalted Emperor, I'm sorry to interrupt—"

"You follow everything I say to the letter, Daichi, except that," a male voice said from behind the bodyguard. "You don't need to call me that, especially in public."

Dirio laughed. "If you wanted to travel incognito, Iren, you should have chosen a subtler guard."

"Address his—"

"It's all right," the voice behind the bodyguard interrupted. "This man's a friend and an equal. Let him by. There's plenty of room, and there are more than enough crabs."

Daichi stepped aside, and Dirio at last saw the object of his search. Emperor Iren Saitosan and Queen Minawë sat at a corner booth with a steamer bucket of crabs between them. The detritus of a dozen of the crustaceans lay strewn about. Bits of shell speckled both rulers.

Dirio slid in next to Minawë and across from Iren. "I'm glad I tracked you down," Dirio said.

Iren passed a wooden mallet across the table to Dirio. "Dig in," he said. "This is the best place in Ceere. It was legendary even before I left Haldessa."

Dirio looked from the hammer to Iren. "I'm not hungry."

"You don't eat crabs to get full," Iren replied. "You eat them for the experience. That's why you come to a place like this." He paused, and a wry smile blossomed on his lips. "More important, they keep Kaede busy. If her hands are tearing up crabs, then they aren't getting her into trouble."

The Lodian king eyed the eight-year-old girl sitting next to Iren. She didn't have a mallet, but that wasn't stopping her. She pulled apart her crab with reckless abandon, and she was even more shell-covered than her parents. Dirio spied several pieces wedged in her hair.

"She reminds me of her grandmother," Dirio laughed. "I'm surprised you didn't name her Rondel."

Iren shrugged. "I wanted to, but Minawë liked Kaede better. It suits her. In Maantec, it means 'maple.'"

"Something about it sounded right," Minawë said.

"In any case, giving her the name of the Maantecs' greatest traitor would have made for a rough life," Iren added. "We had to bury Rondel in the Kodamas' graveyard just so we wouldn't have to worry about Maantecs desecrating it."

"Something tells me she'd be happier there anyway," Dirio said.

Minawë nodded. "I like to think so."

Iren, Minawë, and Kaede started on another round of crabs, and for a while they ate in silence. Dirio watched them, a lump forming in his throat. He knew what he needed to say. These were his friends. He could tell them anything. Why was he hesitating?

Maybe he could ease his way into it. "This is the first time you've returned to Lodia since you defeated Melwar," he said. "I wish I could have seen you sooner."

Iren sucked the meat out of a claw. "Well, there's a lot to do. Serona might not be bursting with flames anymore, but nothing's grown there for a thousand years. Just getting the basics going has taken most of my time. There's also the matter of Shikari. The people there didn't see my Dragoon transformation, so they weren't as keen to accept me as Maantec emperor."

"I take it that means you still can't use magic."

"Nope. Neither can Minawë. Apart from Shikari it hasn't been an issue. Down there though, it took Daichi and three thousand soldiers to restore order."

"It came in handy that the Sky Dragon Sword accepted him," Minawë put in.

"When he helped me after the battle with Melwar, I had a feeling Ariok would take a liking to him," Iren said. "He's been a fine choice to put in charge of Shikari."

Dirio looked at the bodyguard. The back of the man's neck was red, though with pride or embarrassment Dirio couldn't be sure.

"Is he the only Dragon Knight left?" Dirio asked Iren.

"The only one who can use magic. The Liryometa's hidden for now. To be honest, I hope it can stay that way."

"That sounds like a poor choice," Dirio said. "Considering how powerful Rondel was, a Storm Dragon Knight would have been a big help in retaking Shikari."

Iren shook his head. "I've spent enough time with Divinion to change how I see the dragons. They aren't weapons. They're living, thinking creatures like us. This will sound strange, but after we quelled the unrest in Shikari, I spent some time in Melwar's archives. The ancient Maantecs had far more knowledge than I ever imagined. I thought I might discover a way to free the dragons."

Dirio rocked back in the booth. "After the destruction Feng and Shadeen caused? Are you crazy?"

"I don't want to free their magic, just them. Divinion often cast aside his power and adopted the form of an old man when I talked to him. I can still talk to him when I meditate, and Minawë can do the same with Dendryl. They think it might be possible."

"What else are you learning from Melwar's archives?" Dirio asked. "Are you seeking another way to regain your magic?"

Iren blushed. "I looked for information about that a little, but in truth I don't really care about it anymore. We have bigger challenges. Chief among them is Melwar's curse on the Kodamas. I cured Minawë of it, so I'm sure there's a way to reverse it for the rest of her people too."

"We're getting close on that one," Minawë said with a grin. "A few more years, and you'll have Kodamas as well as Maantecs visiting you on trade missions."

Dirio returned the queen's expression. "I look forward to it. So is that why you've returned to Lodia? For a trade mission?"

"That's right," Iren said. "I was thinking about how before Amroth, the previous Lodian kings maintained peace in the country through trade. The Maantecs have a lot to answer for, and we won't heal the rifts between Maantecs, Kodamas, and humans any time soon. If we're lucky, it will be the work of decades. More likely it will take centuries, and I'm sure there will be some among each race who will fight the change. Even so, I think trade between our peoples is the first step to overcoming that resistance. Minawë and I have come up with an agreement that will govern trade between Maantecs and Kodamas. Now I want to go further. It's my hope that people in Shikari will soon be able to bring their goods up Raa's west coast and trade with Serona, Ziorsecth, and Lodia without braving the eastern ocean's storms." He gestured to his bodyguard. "When I told Daichi my plan, he asked to come along when we visited Lodia. I could hardly refuse."

"You're like your father in one way at least," Dirio said. "You're ambitious. But if you wanted to set up relations with Lodia, why did you come to this dive? Why didn't you come to Haldessa to see me?"

"We were going to," Minawë said, looking askance at her husband. "Iren insisted we come here first."

"For the food," Kaede interjected as she slurped down a piece of fin meat.

Iren gave his daughter a loving smile. "All right, the food was part of it. But what really motivated me was that I wanted to see what condition Ceere was in. Amroth used it as a staging area for his army, and Melwar's forces made landfall here. Between the two, I feared it might not have recovered. Now that I'm here, I see my fear was misplaced. This place looks better than it did when I lived in Haldessa."

"You can thank Elyssa for that," Dirio said. "When Shadeen destroyed Kataile, the citizens decided to move here instead. They and the Ceere survivors kept Elyssa as mayor, and it was the best decision they could have made. She's a better administrator than I could ever be."

"It's good that so many of her people came to Tropos to attend Balear's funeral," Iren put in. "It saved them all."

"Still, for Kataile to be so destroyed they couldn't even rebuild, it's terrible," Minawë said. "Did anything escape Shadeen's blast?"

Dirio nodded. "Actually, that's part of the reason I came to find you. I have something for you, Iren." He motioned for one of his bodyguards to approach. From the guard's pack, Dirio withdrew a scroll. He put out his hand to give it to Iren, but when the emperor reached for it, Dirio pulled it back.

"Clean up first," Dirio said.

Iren's brow furrowed. "What? Oh, right." He wiped his hands on a napkin and showed them to Dirio. "Good enough?"

"I swear, emperor or not, you're still the same."

"I tell him that at every opportunity," Minawë said with a wink.

Iren reddened. He pulled the scroll from Dirio's hand and buried himself in it. "So what is this?" he asked.

"Elyssa gave me that at Balear's funeral. She'd meant to give it to him, but, well, other circumstances interfered. It's a letter Balio wrote after he left Tropos. It was for his son. Balio was illiterate, so he asked Elyssa to record what he said. When I read it, I knew I should give it to you."

Iren's eyes reached the bottom of the scroll. His head whipped up. "Is this for real?"

"Elyssa penned it herself. I have no reason to doubt it."

Minawë raised her green eyebrows. "What's it say?"

Iren handed her the scroll. "I never would have guessed," she said when she finished reading, "but now that I've seen this, it makes sense. You two were so alike."

"Are you joking?" Iren asked. "We couldn't have been more different. That guy was a troublemaker."

"Point proved," Minawë laughed.

Iren's ears reddened again. Dirio joined Minawë in her laughter.

"So Balear and I were cousins?" Iren asked when the fit subsided.

"Balio's sister was your mother, Carita. After she was murdered, Balio couldn't forgive the town that had abandoned her. Carita's death broke him, but even in despair, he never forgot his son."

Iren stared at the scroll in Minawë's hands. The crabs sat in the steamer pot, forgotten.

"There's something else," Dirio said. "If it were just that scroll, I might have waited, but there's a bigger issue that demanded I speak with you. Had you not been in Lodia, I would have risked a journey to Serona to find you."

That peaked Iren's interest. He sat back in the booth and folded his arms. "What could be that important?"

Dirio swallowed hard. "Just as Elyssa has spent the past twelve years rebuilding Ceere, I've been doing the same to Haldessa. Six months ago a team of workers found a vault in the castle. It had been buried in rubble since Amroth destroyed the place. When the men opened the vault, they found a hoard of old documents."

"How come they weren't destroyed by Amroth's flames?" Iren asked.

"The vault was protected by a long corridor of stone. Like your room in the Tower of Divinion, it avoided the fires. If King Azuluu had been in that vault when Amroth attacked, he likely would have survived."

"But what's so important for us about these documents?" Minawë asked. "Do they date back to the Kodama-Maantec War or something?"

Dirio shook his head. "Nothing like that. There are a few older pieces, but for the most part the vault was a legal repository. It stored proclamations set down by the kings. I wanted to know more about how my predecessors governed, so I've been reading them. Most are legal nonsense. A few weeks ago, though, I came across one that could change Lodia forever. If it's released to the public, it would throw us back into civil war."

Minawë's eyes widened. "What do you mean?" she asked. "How can a document do that?"

"Because it proves Amroth Angustion never should have been king of Lodia."

"No arguments there," Iren replied.

Dirio shook his head. "That isn't what I mean. I mean he had no legal right to take the throne."

"When the king dies, his first legitimate son replaces him," Iren said. "If there's no legitimate son, his chief advisor becomes king. That's how succession works. Amroth was Azuluu's chief advisor. What's the big deal?"

"The big deal is that Azuluu had a legitimate son."

Iren scoffed. "You're from Veliaf, so I understand if you aren't familiar with Azuluu's reputation. I lived in Haldessa while he was in charge. That guy had plenty of children, but none of them were legitimate. If he'd sired one, we all would have known it."

"That's the trouble," Dirio said. "He didn't sire one. He adopted one."

The color drained from Iren's face. "Wait a minute. Are you telling me . . ."

Dirio motioned to his bodyguard again. The man retrieved a folded parchment from his pack and handed it to Dirio. "Only my advisors and I have seen this," Dirio said. He held out the document to Iren. "You'll understand why when you read it."

Iren's hands trembled as he took the parchment. "This is . . ."

"Your adoption certificate," Dirio finished. "When Amroth brought you to Haldessa as an infant, he convinced King Azuluu to adopt you as his son. That way Amroth could keep an eye on you without being directly involved with you."

"Azuluu was no father to me," Iren spat. "He hated me. He made me live in the Tower of Divinion. He couldn't say my name. He even ordered my execution."

"How he treated you is irrelevant. The point is that after he discovered you were a Left, he never officially disowned you. When he died, you were technically still his legitimate son."

Iren put his hand to his head. "Which means that when Amroth took over the throne, he had no authority to do it. I was first in line."

"Moreover," Dirio added, "it means that when Amroth died, the mayors had no authority to form a council according to the Succession Law. You were alive, and therefore the one who should have become king."

Dirio fell silent to let his words sink in. He had ruled Lodia for over a decade, but that didn't mean anything. There were still parts of the country, especially Orcsthia, that resented his rise to power. They had never forgiven eastern Lodia for what had happened to their army at Kataile. If word got out that Dirio didn't have authority to rule, it would mean insurrection. The rebels wouldn't necessarily want Iren Saitosan in charge, but they would use him as a banner cry in their war efforts.

"Is this why you were so intent on finding me?" Iren whispered. "Because you wanted me to become king of Lodia?"

"It's your right as Azuluu's son," Dirio said. "More important, it's the only way to preserve peace in this country."

Iren pulled in a long breath. He held it a moment, then exhaled. He stared at the parchment in his hands.

"I know this is sudden," Dirio said, "but think of the possibilities. You're the Maantec emperor. You're married to the Kodaman queen." He inclined his head at Minawë, who had her eyes locked on her husband. "If you become king of Lodia, the pair of you will have united the northern lands. We'll have peace between humans, Kodamas, and Maantecs. Our empire will reach from one ocean to the next."

Iren folded up the adoption certificate and handed it back to Dirio. "Not interested."

Dirio gaped. "What?"

"I've had enough of empires. I've seen what they do to people like Melwar, and even to those like my father. I don't want that."

"But when word gets out—"

"Rip up the certificate. Then there will be no proof, right?"

Dirio shook his head. "Enough other people know about it that destroying the evidence would only make me look guilty. My advisors would turn on me. Whatever the result, I have to face this problem directly."

"There's no other way?"

"None that I can think of."

Iren scowled. He folded his arms and stared down at the table.

Kaede tugged on her father's sleeve. "Daddy?"

"Daddy's busy right now," Iren said.

"I have an idea, Daddy."

Iren lifted an eyebrow. "You do?"

The girl's head bobbed up and down. "Yep!"

"What is it?"

"It's a secret."

Iren's eyes crinkled. "All right, whisper it in my ear." He leaned down and let her say it to him.

When Kaede finished, Iren sat back. He looked smug. Dirio took that as a bad sign.

"I've decided to do what's right for Lodia," Iren said. "To preserve peace, I will become its king."

Dirio's jaw dropped again. How had an eight-year-old convinced Iren to change his mind in a matter of seconds?

"In the presence of these witnesses," Iren said, gesturing around the table and to the bodyguards standing watch, "I hereby accept my place as rightful king of Lodia. You are officially deposed. However, though you reigned more than a decade in violation of Lodian law, you did so in the best interest of this country. It would be wrong of me not to recognize that experience and use it to my advantage. Accordingly, as my first official act, I name you, Dirio Cyneric, as my chief advisor."

The smug expression deepened. Iren paused for a breath, then continued, "For my second official act, I abdicate the throne. As I have no legitimate son, and as Lodia's misguided laws do not permit my highly capable daughter to follow me, I'm afraid there's no choice but for my chief advisor to take over the position. Congratulations, Dirio Cyneric, you are now king of Lodia."

Dirio didn't think his jaw could fall any lower. He'd been wrong. "Iren, you can't be serious."

Iren shrugged. "Now it doesn't matter what people say. Whether they acknowledge my adoption or not, you're Lodia's rightful king."

Dirio looked at Kaede. She had a toothy grin that took up more than half her face. Combined with her green eyes, it made the resemblance that much stronger.

"She really does take after her grandmother," Dirio said. "Who other than Rondel could come up with a loophole that absurd that quickly?"

Minawë and Iren laughed. "Scary, isn't it?" Minawë asked.

Dirio sat there a moment. He ran a hand over his bald head. Then he joined in their laughter. Twelve years later, and despite where their paths had led them, Iren and Minawë were still the friends he would rather spend time with than anyone else on Raa.

"You know what?" Dirio said. "Maybe I'll have a crab or two after all."

"That's the spirit!" Iren cried. "We'll order another round. Daichi, put down that sword and join us. Dirio, your men can sit too. The booth's plenty big. We'll eat, drink, and laugh until dawn!"

And they did.

ABOUT THE AUTHOR

Josh VanBrakle is the author of the perfectly logical combination—to him anyway—of epic fantasy novels and nature non-fiction. His fantasy novels include the award-winning *Dragoon Saga* trilogy, and his debut nature book is *Your Woodland: A Hands-on Guide to Doing Right by the Land You Love*.

When he isn't writing, Josh works as an education forester at an environmental non-profit promoting rural land conservation. Originally from Hershey, Chocolatetown USA, Josh now lives in the Catskill Mountains of upstate New York with his wife Christine and two ill-behaved cats.

Writing the *Dragoon Saga* has been Josh's dream since high school. It's his first book series, so please let him and other readers know what you thought of it by reviewing this book wherever you purchased it. Josh appreciates these reviews and uses them to grow as an author and improve future books.

To stay up to date with the latest news about Josh and his upcoming titles, please visit www.joshvanbrakle.com or follow Josh on Twitter @joshvanbrakle.

www.ingramcontent.com/pod-product-compliance
Lightning Source LLC
Chambersburg PA
CBHW021953190626
46807CB00005BB/1971